BETTY N

THE ULTIMATE COLLECTION

Betty Neels's novels are loved
by millions of readers around the world,
and this very special ***12-volume collection***
offers a unique chance to recapture the pleasure
of some of her most popular stories.

Each month we're bringing you a new volume containing two timeless classics—irresistible love stories that belong together, whether they share the same colourful setting, romantic theme, or follow the same characters in their continuing lives...

As a special treat, each volume also includes an introductory letter by a different author. Some of the most popular names in romance fiction are delighted to pay tribute to Betty Neels; we hope you enjoy reading their personal thoughts and memories.

We're proud and privileged to bring you this very special collection, and hope you enjoy reading—and keeping—these twelve wonderful volumes over the coming months.

Volume Five

—with an introduction from international bestselling author

Ann Major

Betty Neels will sweep you away with this touching duet of love stories...

THE SECRET POOL
THE GIRL WITH GREEN EYES

We'd like to take this opportunity to pay tribute to **Betty Neels**, *who sadly passed away last year. Betty was one of our best-loved authors. As well as being a wonderfully warm and thoroughly charming individual, Betty led a fascinating life even before becoming a writer, and her publishing record was impressive.*

Betty spent her childhood and youth in Devonshire before training as a nurse and midwife. She was an army nursing sister during the war, married a Dutchman and subsequently lived in Holland for fourteen years. On retirement from nursing Betty started to write, inspired by a lady in a library bemoaning the lack of romantic novels.

Over her thirty-year writing career Betty wrote more than 134 novels and was published in more than one hundred international markets. She continued to write into her ninetieth year, remaining as passionate about her characters and stories then as she was with her very first book.

Betty will be greatly missed, both by her friends at Harlequin Mills & Boon® *and by her legions of loyal readers around the world. Betty was a prolific writer and has left a lasting legacy through her heartwarming novels. She will always be remembered as a truly delightful person who brought great happiness to many.*

THE ULTIMATE COLLECTION

Volume Five

THE SECRET POOL

&

THE GIRL WITH GREEN EYES

Two full-length novels

Harlequin Mills & Boon Limited,
Eton House, 18-24 Paradise Road, Richmond, Surrey TW9 1SR

ISBN 0 263 83647 9

Set in Times Roman 11½ on 13¼ pt.
141-1102-87745

Printed and bound in Spain
by Litografia Rosés, S.A., Barcelona

Dear Reader

What an honour it is to me to be able to tell you why I love Betty Neels's books. I grew up on British novels, so I really love English and European settings. Betty's books feel cosy to me, and they are so easy to read that once I start one I can't stop until I get to the end. She is a wonderful writer whose stories are so universal they take her readers to the tender heart of true romance.

Betty knows a woman's secret dreams, or at least she knows mine—to fall in love with a worthy man who will love her and cherish her in return. Betty's heroines are always sweet and admirably courageous, while her heroes are tough and handsome and yet gentle too. Her heroines are passionate, but in true ladylike fashion they contain their rages and tears far better that I or my own characters ever could. Thus, there is always so much wonderful suppressed emotion in a Neels novel that I feel almost as breathless as her heroine by the time I get to the happy ending and her characters kiss and finally realise they are truly in love and deeply loved in return.

Although I feel sad that Betty will write no more novels, I am deeply inspired by the legacy she has left behind—her wonderful novels which we can read over and over again and treasure for ever.

Thank you, Betty. What a gift you have given us.

Ann Major

THE ULTIMATE COLLECTION

Don't miss **Volume 6**, on sale next month!

Curl up this winter-time with Betty Neels—and enjoy the romance of a Christmas never to be forgotten...

BETTY NEELS

Volume 6

WINTER OF CHANGE

and

A WINTER LOVE STORY

THE SECRET POOL

by

Betty Neels

CHAPTER ONE

THE early morning sun of a midsummer's day morning shone with warm cheerfulness on to the quiet countryside, the market town tucked neatly into the Cotswold hills and its numerous windows. These included those of the Cottage Hospital, a symbol of former days, fought for and triumphantly reprieved from the remorseless hand of authority, and proving its worth tenfold by never having an empty bed.

Inside the grey stone walls of this Victorian edifice, the day's work was already well advanced. Its thirty beds were divided between surgical and medical patients, with two beds for maternity cases who couldn't make it in time to Bristol or Bath, and one private ward used for any child too ill to move or anyone too ill to nurse in the wards. There was a small out patients' department, too, and a casualty room where the local GPs could be called to attend any accident. Small it might be, but it did yeoman service, easing the burden of patients on the big Bristol hospitals.

It was staffed by the local doctors, ably supported by Miss Hawkins, who still insisted on being called Matron, two ward sisters and their staff nurses, and four pupil nurses, sent from Bristol and Bath to gain experience. There was a night sister, too, and a handful of nursing aides, local ladies, whose kindness of heart and willingness to work hard when everyone else was fast asleep more than made up for their lack of nursing skills. Miss Hawkins was nearing retirement age, an old-fashioned martinet who had no intention of changing her ways. Until six months ago she had had the willing co-operation of Sister Coffin on the medical ward but that lady had retired and her place had been taken by a young staff nurse from the Bristol Royal Infirmary, who had accepted the post of sister in preference to a more prestigious one at her own hospital. It was agreed by everyone, even the grudging Miss Hawkins, that she had proved her ability and was worth her weight in gold. She had a happy knack of getting her patients better, coping with emergencies without fuss, carrying out the various doctors' orders faithfully, and lending a sympathetic ear to the young nurses' requests for a particular day off duty.

She sat at the desk in her office now, the sun gilding the mousy hair pinned neatly under her frilled cap, warming her ordinary face, escaping plainness only by virtue of a pair of fine hazel eyes, thickly lashed, and a gentle mouth. The desk was more or less covered by charts and a variety of forms and she had a pen in her hand, although just for the moment she was doing no work at all, her thoughts far away, if rather vague. She was normally a sensible girl, prepared to accept what life had to offer her and not expecting anything very exciting to happen. Indeed, the three elderly aunts with whom she lived had imbued her with this idea from an early age. They prided themselves on their honesty and plain spokenness and had pointed out on a number of occasions her lack of good looks and amusing conversation. They had done their best to dissuade her from training as a nurse, too, but she had been surprisingly stubborn; despite their certainty that she was too quiet, too shy with strangers, and lacking in self-assurance, she had gone to Bristol, done her training, and emerged at the end of it with flying colours: Gold Medallist of her year, the prospect of a ward sister's post in the not too distant future, and a circle of firm friends. The girls liked her because she listened to the details of their complicated love lives with sympathy. The young housemen liked her because she listened to them, too, about their fleeting love affairs and their dreams of being brilliant consultants. She sympathised with them when they failed their exams and rejoiced with them when they passed and, when on night duty, she was always a willing maker of hot cocoa when one or other of them had been hauled out of bed in the small hours.

But she had declined the ward offered her and had instead applied for and been appointed to the medical ward of the Cottage Hospital in her home town. All because her youngest aunt, Janet, had had a slight—very slight—heart attack and it had been impressed upon her by Aunt Kate and Aunt Polly that it was her duty to return home.

So she had come back to the small town and lived out, going to and fro from her aunts' rambling old house not ten minutes' walk from the hospital. And because she was a good nurse and loved her work, she had taken pride in changing the medical ward, with patience and a good deal of tact, into the more modern methods Sister Coffin had ignored. It had been uphill work but she had managed it so well that Matron considered that she had been the instigator of change in the first place. If she regretted leaving her training school and the splendid opportunities it had offered her, she had never said so, but just now and again she wondered if life would have been different if she had taken the post at Bristol. She would have kept her friends for a start and used her nursing talents to their utmost; and who knew, perhaps one day she might have met someone who would want to marry her.

She stifled a sigh and looked up with a smile as her staff nurse came in. Jenny Topps was a big girl, always cheerful and amiable and with no wish to be anything but a staff nurse. She was getting married in a year's time to a rather silent and adoring young farmer and her ambitions lay in being a good wife. She said now,

'We're ready, Sister. There's time for a quick cup of tea before Dr Beecham gets here. I've sent the little nurses to coffee; Mrs Wills—the nursing auxilary—is in the ward.'

'Good. Yes, let's have tea, then I'll go over to the Women's Medical. It's quiet there and Staff can cope, but I'll just take another look at Miss Prosser. Mr Owen's not responding to his antibiotic, is he? I'll see if Dr Beecham will change it. He might be better off at the Infirmary.' She took the mug of tea Jenny had fetched from the ward kitchen and sipped it.

'You must miss the Infirmary,' observed Jenny. 'It's pretty quiet here—bad chests and diabetics and the odd heart case...'

She studied Sister Manning's quiet face on the other side of the desk; she liked her and admired her and although she wasn't pretty she had a pretty name—Francesca.

'Well, yes, I do, but I do need to be near by my aunts...' She finished her tea, got to her feet and said, 'I'll be back in five minutes. Get the nurses to start making up that empty bed, will you? There is a diabetic coming in at two o'clock.'

The ward was quiet, the men waiting for the bi-weekly round from the consultant. Most of them were on the mend. Mr Owen worried her a little, and the new patient who had come in during the night, a suspected coronary, might spring something on them. She went slowly down the old-fashioned but cheerful ward, stopping for a word here and there and casting an eye on these two, and then went through the door into the women's side.

Here she was met by her second staff nurse, a small dark girl who like herself lived out.

'All ready for Dr Beecham?' asked Francesca. 'How's Miss Prosser? She was a bit cyanosed when I did the round this morning.'

'Still a bit blue. She's had some oxygen and she's quite bright and cheerful.'

They stood together and looked along the facing row of beds. It was a small ward with pretty curtains at the windows and round each bed, and plenty of flowers. Half the patients were up, sitting by their beds, knitting or reading or gossiping. Francesca walked slowly to Miss Prosser's bed and made small talk while she studied that lady. They had had her in before and she was by no means an easy patient; she would have to talk to Dr Beecham about her. She smiled and nodded at the other patients and went back to her office, tidied the top of her desk, and with a glance at the clock went back to the men's ward. Dr Beecham would be there at any moment now.

He came through the door within moments, a short stout man with a fringe of hair on a bald head and twinkling blue eyes. She had known him ever since she had begun her training; he had been one of the first lecturers she had had and as she became more senior he had occasionally explained some unusual case to her. She liked him and the smile which lighted up her face made it almost pretty.

He had someone with him. Not just Dr Stokes, who was the RMO; a tall man with massive shoulders, fair hair with a heavy sprinkling of grey and the good looks to turn any woman's head. Francesca sighed at the sight of him. She knew him, too: Dr van Rijgen, a specialist in tropical diseases who had come to the Infirmary at regular intervals to lecture the students. He lived in Holland and worked there as far as she knew, although he seemed equally at home in England. Years ago when she had begun her training she had had the misfortune to drop off during one of his lectures; even after all these years, she remembered his cold voice, laced with sarcasm, very quietly reducing her to a state bordering on hysteria. They had encountered each other since then, of course, and she had taken care never to allow her feelings to show, and he for his part had never betrayed any recollection of that first unfortunate meeting. He eyed her now with a kind of thoughtful amusement which made her fume inwardly. But she replied suitably to Dr Stokes and Dr Beecham and then bade him a frosty good morning.

He had a deep slow voice. 'Good morning, Sister Manning. I see that I must congratulate you since we last met at the Infirmary.' He glanced round the ward, half the size of those in a Bristol hospital. 'Hiding your light under a bushel?'

She said in a voice which made his fine mouth twitch, 'If I remember aright, sir, my light was a very small one—a mere glimmer.'

He gave a crack of laughter. 'Oh, dear, you have a long memory, Sister.'

'A useful thing in a nurse,' interpolated Dr Beecham cheerfully. 'What have you got for us today, Fran?'

Dr Beecham prided himself on the good terms he enjoyed with the ward sisters and none of them minded that he addressed them by their Christian names when they were away from the patients.

'Nothing much, sir. There's Miss Prosser...' She didn't need to say more, they both knew that lady well enough. 'And Mr Owen who isn't so well. All the rest are making good progress.'

'Right, shall we see the ladies first? I want Dr van Rijgen to look at Mr Owen.'

The round wound its usual way, first through the women's ward and then the men's, to spend some time with Mr Owen; this time Dr van Rijgen did the examining. At length he straightened up. 'I agree with you, John,' he told Dr Beecham, 'he should be transferred to the Infirmary as soon as possible.'

He sat down on the side of the bed and addressed himself to Mr Owen. He explained very nicely, even Fran had to admit that, with a mixture of frankness and confidence which cheered the patient. 'And if Sister can arrange it, perhaps your wife would like to travel with you in the ambulance?'

He glanced at Dr Beecham who nodded and then turned his cold blue eyes upon Fran. 'Sister?'

'Mrs Owen lives close by, I am sure something can be arranged.'

They had coffee next, squashed in her office, discussing the round, pausing from time to time to alter drugs and give her instructions.

They had finished their coffee when Dr Beecham reached

for the phone. 'I'll warn the medical side, Litrik. What about his wife?'

Dr van Rijgen turned to Fran and found her eyes fixed on his face.

'Mrs Owen? Can you get her here so that we can have a word with her, Sister?'

He frowned impatiently when she didn't answer at once. She had never thought of him as having any name other than van Rijgen; the strange name Dr Beecham had said made him seem different, although she didn't know why. A strange name indeed, but quite nice sounding. She realised that he had spoken to her and flushed a little and the flush deepened when he repeated his question with impatience.

'Certainly, sir. I can telephone her, she lives less than five minutes' walk away.' She spoke crisply and thought how ill-tempered he was.

Dr Beecham had finished with the phone, and as she dialled a number he said, 'Right, Fran. We'll go along to X-Ray and look at those films. Litrik, will you talk to Mrs Owen?'

He patted her on the shoulder, said, 'See you later, Litrik,' and went away, taking Dr Stokes with him.

Mrs Owen was a sensible woman; she asked no unnecessary questions but said that she would be at the hospital in ten minutes. 'I'll not ask you any questions, Sister,' she finished, 'for I'm sure the Doctor will tell me all I want to know.'

Fran put down the receiver and glanced at Dr van Rijgen, sitting on the window ledge, contemplating the view. She had no intention of staying there under his unfriendly eye; she picked up the charts on the desk and got up.

'Don't go,' said Dr van Rijgen without turning round. 'However sensible Mrs Owen may be, she'll probably need a shoulder to cry on.'

He spoke coldly and she, normally a mild-tempered girl, allowed her tongue to voice her thoughts. She snapped, 'Yes, and that's something you wouldn't be prepared to offer.'

The look he gave her was like cold steel; she added, 'sir' and waited for his cold calm voice to utter something biting.

'It is a good thing that my self-esteem does not depend upon your good opinion of me,' said Dr van Rijgen softly. 'Would it be a good idea if we were to have a tray of tea? I have found that tea, to the English, soothes even the most unhappy breast. Come to that, the most savage one, too.'

Fran didn't look at him but went in a dignified way to the kitchen and asked Eddie, the ward maid, to lay up a tea tray.

''As 'is nibs taken a liking for it?' asked that elderly lady. 'Not like 'im, with 'is foreign ways.'

Fran explained, knowing that if she didn't Eddie was quite capable of finding out for herself.

'Give me 'arf a mo', Sister, and I'll bring in the tray. Three cups?'

'Well, yes, I suppose so. Mrs Owen won't want to sit and drink it by herself.'

She would rather not have gone back to the office but there was no reason why she shouldn't. Dr van Rijgen was still admiring the view and he didn't look at her when she sat down at her desk. Indeed, he didn't move until one of the nurses tapped on the door, put her head round it in response to Fran's voice and said that Mrs Owen was there.

Fran sat her down: a small plump woman, her round face so anxious. 'It's Jack, isn't it, Sister? He's not so well. I'm that worried…'

Fran poured the tea and said in a quiet way, 'Mr Owen has been seen by Dr Beecham and Dr van Rijgen this morning, Mrs Owen.' She handed the doctor a cup. 'Dr van Rijgen will explain how things are…'

He had got to his feet when Mrs Owen had been ushered in; now he sat on the edge of the desk, half turned away from Fran. He looked relaxed and unworried and Mrs Owen's troubled face cleared. His explanations were concise and offered with matter-of-fact sympathy; he neither pretended that there was much chance of Mr Owen recovering, nor did he paint too dark a picture of his future. 'We shall do what we can, Mrs Owen, that I can promise you,' he told her finally and Fran, listening, was aware that if she were in Mrs Owen's shoes she would believe him; what was more, she would trust him. Which, considering she didn't like the man, was something to be wondered at.

Dr van Rijgen went away presently, leaving Fran to give what comfort she could, and Mrs Owen, who had kept a stern hold on her feelings while he had been talking, broke down then and had a good cry, her grey head tucked comfortingly into Fran's shoulder. Presently she mopped her eyes and sat up. 'So sorry,' she said awkwardly, 'but it's a bit of a shock...'

Fran poured more tea and murmured in sympathy, and Mrs Owen went on, 'He's nice, isn't he? I'd trust him with my last breath. Funny, how you can feel he means what he says. Though I suppose he has to talk to lots of people like that.'

'Oh, yes, I'm sure he must. He's a very eminent doctor even though he's not English, but that doesn't mean that he doesn't understand your husband's case, Mrs Owen, and have every sympathy with you both.'

'And you, you're a kind girl too, Sister. My Jack thinks a lot of you.'

Fran made a comforting murmur and, since Mrs Owen was calm again, embarked on the business of ways and means. 'I still have to arrange things with the ambulance; it'll be some time tomorrow morning, quite early, if you could manage that? If you could come here? The ambulance will have to come back here, but I expect you'd like to stay for a bit and see Mr Owen settled in? Do you have friends in Bristol where you could stay?'

Mrs Owen shook her head.

'Then I'll phone the Infirmary and ask them to fix you up—they have a room where you can be comfortable and they'll see that you get a meal. There is a morning bus from Bristol, isn't there? And another one in the late afternoon. I should take an overnight bag.' She added in a gentle matter-of-fact voice, 'Are you all right for ready money, Mrs Owen?'

'Yes thank you, Sister. You don't know how long I might have to stay?'

'Well, no, but I'm sure the ward sister will tell you and you can ask to see Dr Beecham and Dr van Rijgen.'

Mrs Owen went away presently and Fran went into the ward to cast an eye on things and to reassure Mr Owen that his wife would be with him when he was transferred. Other than that there wasn't a great deal to do; she sent the nurses to their dinner and Jenny with them and, leaving the aides in the ward, filling water jugs, went back to her office, where she sat down at her desk and started on the laundry list. She felt restless; perhaps it was the sight of the quiet country she could see from her window, or perhaps it was the knowledge that, after her busy days at the Infirmary, she wasn't working here up to her full capacity. Anyway, she felt unsettled and a little impatient with her life. Was she to go on for ever, living and working in this little country town? Her aunts were dears but they still treated her as though she were a child and she would be twenty-six on her next birthday. Another five years and she would be thirty... She shook her head at her own gloom; nothing ever happened. She turned back to the laundry list and Willy, the porter, came in with the second post. A handful of letters for the patients and one for herself. She got up and went into the wards and handed them all out. Jenny had done the dinners while she had been busy with Mrs Owen and the patients were resting on their beds for an hour. She made her quiet way round the two wards, stopping here and there to have a whispered word, and then went back to the office.

The letter on her desk had a Dutch stamp. It would be from a cousin she hardly knew; the aunts had had a brother who had died and his daughter had married a Dutchman and lived in Holland. Fran remembered her vaguely as a child when her own mother had taken her to visit the family. She had gone to her wedding, too, but although they liked each other their paths didn't cross very frequently.

She opened it now—it would make a nice change from the laundry—and began to read. When she had finished it, she went back to the beginning and read it again. Here was the answer to her restlessness. And one the aunts could not but agree to. Clare wanted her to go and stay. 'You must have some holidays,' she had written, 'two weeks at least. I'm going to have a baby—I was beginning to think that I never would—and I'm so thrilled, I must have someone to talk to about it. I know the aunts make a fuss if you go off on your own, but they can't possibly mind if you stay with us. Do say you'll come—phone me and give me a date. Karel sends his love and says you must come.'

Fran put the letter down. She had two weeks leave due to her and the wards were slack enough to take them; moreover it was a good time of year to ask before autumn brought its quota of bronchitis and asthma and nasty chests. A holiday might also dispel this feeling of restlessness.

She went to the office after her dinner and asked for leave and Miss Hawkins, aware of Fran's worth, graciously allowed it: starting on the following Sunday, and Sister Manning might add her weekly days off to her fortnight.

All very easy. There were the aunts to deal with, though. Fran, off duty that evening, tackled that the moment she got home. The ladies were sitting, as they always did of an evening, in the old-fashioned drawing room, knitting or embroidering, waiting for Winnie, the housekeeper, to set supper on the table. Fran, poking her head round the door to wish them a good evening before going up to her room to tidy herself, wondered anew at the three of them. They were after all not very old—Aunt Kate was the eldest, sixty-seven, Aunt Polly next, a year or two younger, and Aunt Janet a mere fifty-eight. And yet they had no place in modern times; they lived now as they remembered how they had lived in their childhood years between the two wars. It was only Fran's mother, five years younger than Aunt Janet, who had broken away and married, and had died with Fran's father in a plane crash when Fran had been twelve. She had missed them sorely and her aunts had given her a home and loved her according to their lights, only their love was tempered with selfishness and a determination to keep her with them at all costs. She remembered the various occasions when she had expressed a wish to holiday abroad; they had never raised any objections but one or other of them had fallen ill with something they had referred to as nerves, and each time she had given up her travels and stayed at home to keep the invalid company, fetch and carry and generally pander to that lady's whims. She had been aware that she was being conned, but her kind heart and her sense of obligation wouldn't allow her to say so.

She greeted them now, and whisked herself away and presently went downstairs armed with Clare's letter. Her aunts read it in turn and agreed that, of course, she must go. Looking after a cousin wasn't the same as gallivanting around foreign parts and, as none of them had ever lost their old-fashioned ideas about childbirth—a conglomeration of baby clothes, feeling faint, putting one's feet up and not mentioning the subject because it wasn't quite nice, eating for two and needing the companionship of another woman—they saw that Fran's duty lay in joining her cousin at once. She was, after all, their dear brother's daughter and Fran, they felt sure, was aware where her duty lay.

Fran agreed, careful not to be too eager, and in answer to Aunt Janet's question said that she thought that Matron would allow her to have two weeks, starting on the following Sunday. 'I'd better phone Clare, hadn't I?' she suggested and went to do that, to come back presently to say that Karel would meet her on Sunday evening at Schiphol.

'Sunday?' asked Aunt Kate sharply.

'Well, dear, he's free then, otherwise I'd have to find my own way...'

The conversation at supper was wholly given up to her journey. She said very little, allowing the aunts to discuss and plan and tell her what clothes to take; she had no intention of taking any of their advice but to disagree would be of no use. She helped Winnie clear the supper things presently, laid her breakfast tray ready on the kitchen table, wished her aunts good night and went up to bed. It was too soon to pack, but she went through her wardrobe carefully, deciding what she would take with her. Clare was only a few years older than she was and, contrary to her aunts' supposition, the last person on earth to lie with her feet up; a few pretty dresses would be essential.

There was no time to think about her holiday the next day. Getting Mr Owen away to Bristol was a careful undertaking and necessitated sending Jenny with him. Mrs Owen had arrived, breathless with anxiety and haste, and had had to be given tea and a gentle talk, so that the morning's routine started a good hour late, and that without Jenny to share the chores. Then, of course, there was a new patient coming into Mr Owen's bed and Miss Prosser was making difficulties, something she always did when they were busier than usual. It wasn't until Fran got home at last that she allowed her thoughts to dwell on the delights ahead. She was listening to Aunt Janet's advice about her journey and thinking her own thoughts when the image of Dr van Rijgen popped into her head, and with it a vague but surprising thought that she might not see him again for a long time. Not that I want to, she admonished herself hastily, horrid man that he is, with his nasty sarcastic tongue, and then thought, I wonder where he lives?

Surprisingly he came again at the end of the week, on his way back to Holland, to examine with Dr Beecham one of her patients who, recently returned from the tropics, was showing the first likely symptoms of kala-azar, or so Dr Stokes thought. To be on the safe side, Fran had put her in the single ward and had nursed her in strict isolation, so that they were all gowned and masked before they went to see the patient. Dr van Rijgen, being tied into a gown a good deal too small for his vast person, stared at Fran over his mask. 'Let us hope your praiseworthy precautions will prove unnecessary, Sister,' he said. She caught the faint sneer in his voice and blushed behind her own mask. She had, after all, only done what Dr Stokes had ordered; he had spoken as though she had panicked into doing something unnecessary.

Which, after a lengthy examination, proved to be just that. Acute malarial infection, pronounced Dr van Rijgen. 'Which I think can be dealt with quite satisfactorily here. It is merely a question of taking a blood sample to discover which drug is the most suitable. I think we might safely give a dose of chloroquinine phosphate and sulphate...' He held out a hand for the chart Fran was holding and began to write, talking to Dr Stokes at the same time. 'You were right to take precautions, Peter, one can never be too careful.' A remark which Fran considered to be just the kind of thing he would delight in; buttering up Dr Stokes after sneering at her for doing exactly the same thing.

He had the effrontery to look at her and smile, too, as he said it. She gave him a story stare and led the way to the office where she dispensed coffee to the three of them and ignored him. It was as they were about to leave that Dr van Rijgen asked, 'Who takes over from you when you go on holiday, Sister?'

'My staff nurse, Jenny Topps.'

'I believe you start your leave on Sunday?'

'Yes,' and, after a pause, 'sir'.

He looked at her from under his lids. 'A pleasant time to go on holiday. Somewhere nice I hope?'

'Yes.'

It was vexing when Dr Beecham chimed in with, 'Well, the girl can't say anything else, can she, seeing that she is going to your country, Litrik?'

'Indeed! Let us hope the weather remains fine for you, Sister. Good morning.'

When they had gone she sat and fumed at her desk for a few minutes. He had been nastier than usual and she hoped that she would never see him again. She got up and when she'd done her desk went in search of Jenny; it was almost time for the patients' dinners and the two diabetic ladies would need their insulin. There were several patients whom Dr Beecham wanted put on four-hourly charts, too. She became absorbed in the ward's routine and, for the time at least, forgot Dr van Rijgen.

There was a day left before she was to go on holiday; it was fully taken up with handing over to Jenny and, when she went off duty that evening, packing.

Her head stuffed with sound advice from her aunts, just as though she were on her way to darkest Africa, she took the early morning bus to Bristol where she caught a train to London, got on the underground to Heathrow and presented herself at the weighing-in counter with half an hour to spare. There was time for a cup of coffee before her flight was called and she sat drinking it and looking around her. A small, neat girl, wearing a short-sleeved cotton dress, sparkling fresh, high-heeled sandals, and carrying a sensible shoulder bag. She attracted quite a few appreciative glances from passers-by, together with their opinion that she was the kind of traveller who arrived looking as band-box fresh as when she had set out.

They were right; she arrived at Schiphol without a hair out of place, to be met by Karel and driven to Bloemendaal, a charming suburb of Haarlem where he and Clare had a flat. It wasn't a lengthy trip but they had plenty to talk about: the baby, of course, his job—he was an accountant in one of the big bulb growers' offices—Clare's cleverness in learning Dutch, the pleasant life they led…

The flat was in a leafy road, quiet and pleasant, within walking distance of the dunes and woods. They lived on the third floor and Clare was waiting at their door as the lift stopped. She was a pretty girl, a little older than Fran, and she flung her arms round her now, delighted to see her. The pair of them led her into the flat, both talking at once, sitting her down between them in the comfortable living room, plying her with questions. After the aunts' staid and sober conversation, they were a delight to Fran.

Presently Clare bore her off to her room where she unpacked and tidied herself and then joined them for tea and a lively discussion as to how she might best enjoy herself.

'Swimming of course,' declared Clare, 'if the weather holds.' She poured more tea. 'I rest in the afternoons, so you can poke around Haarlem if you want to. There is heaps to see if you like churches and museums. Then there is Linnaeushof Gardens and the open air theatre here and the aviary… Two weeks won't be enough.'

'You are dears to have me,' said Fran. 'It's lovely to—to…'

'Escape?' suggested Clare.

Fran, feeling guilty, said yes.

It was a delightful change after life in the hospital; Karel went early to work and she and Clare breakfasted at their leisure, tidied the flat and then took a bus into Haarlem or did a little shopping at the local shops; and after lunch, Clare curled up with a book and Fran took herself off, walking in the dunes, going into Haarlem, exploring its streets, poking her nose into its many churches, visiting its museums, and window shopping.

It was on the fourth day of her visit when she went back to St Bavo's Cathedral. She had already paid it a brief visit with Clare on one of their morning outings but Clare hadn't much use for old churches. It was a brilliant afternoon so that the vast interior seemed bathed in twilight and she pottered happily, straining to see the model ships hanging from its lofty rafters, trying to understand the ornate memorial stones on its walls and finally standing before the organ, a vast affair with its three keyboards and its five thousand pipes. Her mind boggled at anyone attempting to play it and, as if in answer to that, music suddenly flooded from it so that she sat down to listen, enthralled. It was something grand and stirring and yet sad and solemn; she had heard it before but the composer eluded her. She closed her eyes the better to hear and became aware that someone had come to sit beside her.

'Fauré,' said Dr van Rijgen. 'Magnificent, isn't it? He is practising for the International Organists' Contest.'

Fran's eyes had flown open. 'However did you get here?' And then, absurdly, 'Good afternoon, Dr van Rijgen. I was trying to remember the composer—the organist is playing like a man inspired.'

She studied his face for a moment; somehow he seemed quite friendly. 'Do you live here?'

'Utrecht.'

'But that's the other side of Amsterdam…'

'Thirty-eight miles from here. Less than that; I don't need to go to Amsterdam, there is a road south…'

She was aware that the music had become quiet and sad. 'You have patients here?'

'What a girl you are for asking questions. I came to see if you were enjoying your holiday.'

She goggled at him. 'Whatever for? And how did you know where I was staying, anyway?'

He smiled slowly. 'Oh, ways and means. Your cousin told me you would most probably be here. She most kindly invited me back for tea. I'll drive you, but there's time enough. Shall we wait till the end? The best part, I always think.'

Fran opened her mouth and then closed it again. What was there to say in the face of such arrogance, short of telling him to go away, not easily done in church, somehow? But why had he deliberately come looking for her? She sat and pondered the question while the organ thundered and swelled into a crescendo of sound and faded away to a kind of sad triumph.

Dr van Rijgen stirred. 'Magnificent. Do you like our *Grote Kirk?*'

'It's breathtaking; I didn't know it was so old...all those years building it. I must get a book about it.'

'I have several at home; you must borrow one.'

Fran stood up and he stood up with her, which put her at an instant disadvantage for she had to look up to his face. 'You want something, don't you?' she asked. 'I mean,' she hesitated and blushed. 'You don't—you aren't interested in me as—as a person, are you?'

'That, Francesca, is where you are mistaken. I should add that I have not fallen in love with you or any such foolishness, but as a person, yes, I am interested in you.'

'Why?'

She spoke softly because there were people milling all round them now.

'At the proper time I will tell you. Now, if you are ready, shall we go back to your cousin?'

She went ahead of him, down the length of the vast church, her mind in a fine muddle. But I don't even like him, she reminded herself, and then frowned quite fiercely. Once or twice during their strange talk, she had liked him very much.

CHAPTER TWO

SHE paused outside the great entrance to the church and he touched her arm. 'Over here, Francesca,' he said and led her to a silver grey Daimler parked at the side. On the short drive to Clare's flat he made casual conversation which gave Fran no chance to ask questions and once there she saw that she was going to have even less opportunity. Apparently whatever it was he wanted of her would be made clear in his own good time and not before. And since she had no intention of seeing him again while she was in Holland, he would presently get the surprise he deserved.

Her satisfaction was short-lived. She was astounded to hear him calmly telling Clare that he felt sure that she would like to see something of Holland while she was there, and would Clare mind if he came on the following day and took her guest for a run through the more rural parts of the country?

She was still struggling for words when she heard Clare's enthusiastic, 'What a marvellous idea! She'll love it, won't she, Karel?'

Just as though I'm not here, fumed Fran silently, and got as far as, 'But I don't...'

'Oh, don't mind leaving Clare for a day,' said Karel. 'I shall be taking her to the clinic tomorrow anyway—you go off and have fun.' He gave her a kindly smile and Fran almost choked on the idea of having fun with Dr van Rijgen. Whatever it was he wanted of her would have nothing to do with fun. She amended the thought; perhaps not fun, but interesting? All the same, such high-handed behaviour wouldn't do at all. She waited until there was a pause in the conversation.

'I had planned to visit one or two places,' she said clearly and was stopped by Dr van Rijgen.

'Perhaps another day for those?' he suggested pleasantly. 'It would give me great pleasure to show you some small part of my country, Francesca.'

There was nothing to say in the face of that bland politeness. She agreed to go, the good manners the aunts had instilled into her from an early age standing her in good stead.

He left shortly after with the suggestion that he might call for her soon after nine o'clock the next morning.

'Don't you like him?' asked Clare the moment the sound of his car had died away.

'Well,' observed Fran matter-of-factly, 'I don't really know him, do I? He gave us lectures when I was training and he's given me instructions about patients on the wards... He was absolutely beastly to me when I was a student and I dozed off during one of his lectures. I think he laughs at me.'

Clare shot her a quick look, exchanged a lightning glance with Karel and said comfortably, 'Oh, well, I should think he's forgotten about that by now—or perhaps he is making amends.'

A fair girl, Fran said, 'I shouldn't have fallen asleep, you know—I expect it injured his ego.'

Clare gave a little chortle of laughter. 'You know, love, once you've got to know each other, I think you and Dr van Rijgen might have quite a lot in common. He's very well known over here; did you know that?'

'No. He comes to Bristol to lecture on tropical diseases, that's all I know about him.'

'Well, he goes to London and Edinburgh and Birmingham and Vienna and Brussels—you name it and he has been there. A very clever laddie.'

Fran had turned her head to look out of the window; Fran was a dear and Clare studied her... She was a thought old-fashioned but that was the aunts' fault, and save for her lovely eyes she had no looks to speak of. But, her hair was fine and long, and her figure was good, if a trifle plump. Clare, with all the enthusiasm of the newly wed, scented romance.

There was no romance apparent the following morning. Dr van Rijgen arrived exactly when he said he would, spent five minutes or so charming Clare—there was no other word for it, thought Fran indignantly—and then led the way to his car.

'Where are we going?' asked Fran and, when he didn't answer at once, 'where are you taking me?'

He was driving south, through the country roads criss-crossing the *duinen* so that he might avoid Haarlem, and there was very little traffic about. He pulled in to the side of the road and turned to look at her. 'Shall we clear the air, Francesca? You sound like the heroine in a romantic thriller. I'm not taking you anywhere, not in the sense that you imply. We shall drive across country, avoiding the motorways so that you may be able to see some of the more rural parts of Holland, and then we shall go to my home because I should like you to meet someone there.'

'Your wife,' said Fran instantly.

'My wife is dead.' He started up the car once more. 'On our right you can just get a glimpse of Heemstede, a suburb of Haarlem and very pleasant. And down the road is Vogelenzang, a quite charming stretch of wooded dunes; we must go there one day to hear the birds...'

Fran turned her head away and pretended to take an interest in the scenery; she had been snubbed, there were no two ways about that. If these terms were to continue all day then she began to wish most heartily that she had never come; she hadn't wanted to in the first place. She voiced her thoughts out loud.

'No, that was only too obvious, but it was rather difficult for you to refuse, wasn't it?'

'I cannot think,' said Fran crossly, 'why you are bothering to waste your time with me.'

'I dare say not, but now is not the time to explain. And now, if you could forget your dislike of me for an hour or two, I will tell you where we are going. This road takes us the long way round to Aalsmeer. We shall go through Hillegom very shortly and take a secondary road to the shores of Aalsmeer which will take us to the town itself; there we shall drive down its other shore and take country roads, some of them narrow and brick, to Nieuwkoop. We have to drive right round the northern end of the lake and pick up the road which eventually brings us to the motorway into Utrecht. My home is on the far side of the city in the woods outside Zeist. We will stop for coffee at one of the cafés along the Aalsmeer.'

'It sounds a long way,' observed Fran.

'No distance as the crow flies, and not much further by car. We shall lunch at my home.'

She gave him a sideways glance. His profile looked stern; he couldn't possibly be enjoying himself so why had he asked her out? He turned his head before she could look away. His smile took years off his face. 'I haven't had a day out for a long time—shall we forget hospital wards and night duty and lectures by disagreeable doctors and enjoy ourselves?'

His smile was so warm and friendly that she smiled back. 'Oh, I'd like that—and it's such a lovely day.'

His hand came down briefly on hers clasped in her lap. 'It's a pact. Here we are at Aalsmeer. I'll explain about the flowers...'

They stopped for coffee presently, sitting down by the water's edge while he drew a map of the surrounding countryside on the tablecloth. 'There are motorways coming into Utrecht from each point of the compass. We shall join one to the south, going round the city, and then turn off towards Leusderheide—that's heathland...'

'You live there?'

'No, but very near. It's only a short run from here.'

They got back into the car and drove on through the quiet

countryside with only the farms and small villages studded around the flat green fields. But not for long. They joined the motorway very soon and presently the outskirts of Utrecht loomed ahead and then to one side of them as they swept past the outskirts. Dr van Rijgen drove fast with an ease which was almost nonchalance, slipping past the traffic with nothing more than a gentle swish of sound, and once past Utrecht and with Zeist receding in the distance he left the motorway and slowed his speed. They were on a country road now, with Zeist still visible to one side, and on the other pleasantly wooded country, peaceful after the rush of the motorway.

'We could be miles from anywhere,' marvelled Fran.

'Yes, and I need only drive a couple of miles to join the road into Zeist and Utrecht.'

'And the other way?'

'Ede, Appeldoorn, the Veluwe; all beautiful.'

'You go there often, to the—the Veluwe?'

He didn't allow himself to smile at her pronunciation of the word.

'Most weekends when I am free.'

It was like wringing blood from a stone, she reflected, wringing bits and pieces of information from him, word by word. She gave a small soundless sigh and looked out of the window.

They were passing through a small scattered village: tiny cottages, a very large church and a number of charming villas.

'This looks nice,' she observed.

'I think so, too,' said Dr van Rijgen and swept the car with an unexpected rush through brick pillars and along a leafy drive. Fran, suddenly uneasy, sat up, the better to see around her, just in time to glimpse the house as they went round a curve.

It was flat-faced and solid with a gabled roof and large windows arranged in rows across its front; they got smaller and higher as they went up and they all had shutters. The front door was atop semi-circular steps, a solid wooden affair with ornate carving around its fanlight and a tremendous knocker.

Fran didn't look at the doctor. 'You live here?'

'Yes.' He leaned over her and undid her door and her safety belt and then got out himself and went round the bonnet so that he was standing waiting for her as she got out, too. She said quite sharply, 'I wish you would tell me why you've brought me here.'

'Why, to meet my small daughter. She's looking forward to seeing you.'

'Your daughter? I had no idea...'

He said coolly, 'Why should you have? Shall we go in?'

The door had been opened; a very thin, stooping, elderly man was standing by it. 'Tuggs,' said the doctor, 'this is Miss Manning, come to have lunch with us. Francesca, Tuggs has been with us for very many years; he runs the place with his wife, Nel. He is English, by the way.'

Fran paused at the top of the steps and offered a hand. 'How do you do, Tuggs,' and smiled her gentle smile before she was ushered indoors.

It was a square entrance hall with splendid pillars supporting a gallery above it and with a fine staircase at its end. Fran had the impression of marble underfoot, fine silky carpets, a great many portraits, and sunlight streaming through a circular window above the staircase, before she was urged to enter a room at the back of the hall. She paused in the doorway and looked up at her host. 'I'm a bit overwhelmed—it's so very grand.'

He considered this remark quite seriously. 'One's own home is never grand, and it is home. Don't be scared of it, Francesca.' He shut the door behind them. 'Nel will bring coffee in a few moments and you can go and tidy yourself—she'll show you where. But first come and see Lisa.'

They were in a quite small cosy room with chintz curtains

at the windows and a wide view out to a garden filled with flowers. The furniture was old, polished and comfortable, and sitting by the open window was a buxom young woman with a rosy face, reading to a little girl perched in a wheelchair.

The young woman, looking up, saw them, put down her book and said something to the child who turned her head and shrilled, 'Papa!' and then burst into a torrent of Dutch.

She was a beautiful child, with golden curls, enormous blue eyes and a glorious smile. Dr van Rijgen bent to kiss her and then lifted her carefully into his arms. He said something to the nurse and she smiled and went out of the room and he said,

'This is Lisa, six years old and as I frequently tell her the most beautiful girl in the world.'

Fran took a small thin hand in hers. 'Oh, she is, the darling.' She beamed at the little girl, careful not to look at the fragile little body in the doctor's arms. 'Hullo, Lisa.'

The child put up her face to be kissed and broke into a long excited speech until the doctor hushed her gently. 'Let's sit down for a moment,' he suggested and glanced up as a stout woman came in with a tray. 'Here's Nel with the coffee.' He said something to her and turned to Fran.

'This is my housekeeper; no English worth mentioning, I'm afraid, but a most sensible and kind woman; we'd be lost without her.' He spoke to her again—she was being introduced in her turn, Fran guessed—and then got up as he said, 'Nel will show you where you can tidy yourself.'

The cloakroom into which Fran was ushered, tucked away down a short passage leading from the hall, was so unlike the utilitarian cubby hole in her aunts' house that she paused to take a good look. Powder blue tiles, silver grey carpet, an enormous mirror and a shelf containing just about everything a woman might need to repair the ravages upon her make-up. Fran sniffed appreciatively at the bottles of eau-de-toilette, washed her hands with pale blue soap and felt apologetic about using one of the stack of towels. She dabbed powder on her nose in a perfunctory manner, combed her hair and went back across the hall.

Father and daughter looked at her as she went in and she had the strong impression that they had been talking about her—naturally enough, she supposed; and when asked to pour out she did so in her usual unflurried manner.

Lisa had milk in her own special mug and sugar biscuits on a matching plate but they were largely ignored. She was a happy child, chuckling a great deal at her father's soft remarks, meticulously translated for Fran's benefit.

A very sick child, too, the charming little face far too pale, the small body thin above the sticks of useless legs. But there was no hint of despair or sadness; the doctor drew her into the talk, making a great thing of translating for her and urging her to try out a few Dutch words for herself, something which sent Lisa into paroxysms of mirth. Presently she demanded to sit on Fran's lap, where she sat, Fran's firm arm holding her gently, examining her face and hair, chattering non-stop.

They were giggling comfortably together when the young woman came back and Dr van Rijgen said, 'This is Nanny. She has been with us for almost six years and is quite irreplaceable. She speaks little English. Lisa goes for a short rest now before lunch.'

Fran said, 'How do you do, Nanny,' feeling doubtful that such an old and tried member of the family might look upon her with jealousy. It was a relief to see nothing but friendliness in the other girl's face and, what was more puzzling, a kind of excited expectancy.

Alone with her host, Fran sat back and asked composedly, 'Will you tell me about Lisa? It's not spina bifida—she's paralysed isn't she, the poor darling? Is it a meningocele?'

He sounded as though he was delivering a lecture on the ward. 'Worse than that—a myelomeningocele, paralysis, club feet and a slight hydrocephalus.' His voice was expressionless as he added, 'Everything that could be done, has been done; she has at the most six more months.'

The words sounded cold; she studied his face and saw what an effort it was for him to speak calmly. She said quietly, 'She is such a happy child and you love her. She would be easy to love...'

'I would do anything in the world to keep her happy.' He got up and walked over to the french window at the end of the room and opened it and two dogs came in: a mastiff and a roly-poly of a dog, very low on the ground with a long curly coat and bushy eyebrows almost hiding liquid brown eyes.

'Meet Thor and Muff—Thor's very mild unless he's been put on guard, but Muff seems to think that he must protect everyone living here.'

He wasn't going to say any more about Lisa. Fran asked, 'Why Muff?'

'He looks like one, don't you think?' He bent to tweak the dog's ears. 'Would you like to see the gardens? Lisa spends a good deal of time out here when the weather's fine.'

There was a wide lawn beyond the house bordered by flower beds and trees. They wandered on for a few minutes in silence, with the doctor, the perfect host, pointing out this and that and the other thing which might interest her. But presently he began to ask her casual questions about her work, her home and her plans.

'I haven't any,' said Fran cheerfully. 'I would have liked to have stayed on at the Infirmary; at least I'd have had the chance to carve myself a career, but the aunts needed me at home.'

'They are invalids?'

'Heavens no, nothing like that. They—they just feel that—that...'

'You should be at their beck and call,' he finished for her smoothly.

'Oh, you mustn't say that. They gave me a home and I'm very grateful.'

'To the extent of turning your back on your own future? Have you no plans to marry?'

'None at all,' she told him steadily.

He didn't ask any more questions after that, but turned back towards the house, offering a glass of sherry while they waited for Lisa to join them for lunch.

She sat between them, eating with the appetite of a bird, talking non-stop, and Fran, because it amused the child, tried out a few Dutch words again. Presently they went into the garden once more, pushing the wheelchair, Fran naming everything in sight in English at Lisa's insistence.

They had tea under an old mulberry tree in the corner of the garden and when Nanny came to take her away, Lisa demanded with a charm not to be gainsaid, 'Fran is to come again, Papa—tomorrow?'

He was lying propped up against the tree, watching her. 'Are you doing anything tomorrow?' he asked. 'We might take Lisa to the sea—the sand's firm enough for the chair.'

'If she would like me to come, then I will—I'd like to very much.'

She was quite unprepared for the joy on the child's face as her father told her. Two thin arms were wrapped round her neck and she was kissed heartily. In between kisses she said something to her father and squealed with delight at his reply. Fran looked from one to the other of them, sensing a secret, probably about herself. She certainly wasn't going to ask, she told herself, and wished Nanny goodbye, encountering that same look of pleased anticipation. It was time she went home, she decided and was instantly and blandly talked out of it.

They dined in a leisurely fashion in a room furnished with an elegant Regency-style oval table and ribbon-backed chairs and a vast side table laden with heavy silver. Fran was surprised to find her companion easy to talk to and the conversation was light and touched only upon general topics. Lisa wasn't mentioned and although she longed to ask more about the child, she was given no opportunity to pose any questions.

She was driven back to Clare's flat, her companion maintaining a pleasant flow of small talk which gave away nothing of himself. And at the flat, although he accepted her invitation to go in with her, he stayed only a short time before bidding them all good night and reiterating that he would call for her at ten o'clock in the morning.

Clare pounced on her the moment he had gone. 'Fran—you dark horse—did you know he'd be here? Did he follow you over to Holland?'

Fran started to collect the coffee cups. 'Nothing like that, love, we don't even like each other. He has a small daughter who is very ill; I think he has decided that it might amuse her to have a visitor. We got on rather well together, so I suppose that's why he's asked me to go out with them tomorrow.'

'His wife?' breathed Clare, all agog.

'He is a widower.'

'And you don't like each other?'

'Not really. He's devoted to Lisa, though, and she liked me. I like her, too. You won't mind if I'm away tomorrow?'

Her cousin grinned. 'You have fun while you've got the chance.'

The weather was being kind; Fran awakened to a blue sky and warm sunshine. She was ready and waiting when Dr van Rijgen and Lisa arrived. She got in beside Lisa's specially padded seat in the back of the car and listened, only half understanding, to the child's happy chatter.

It was a successful day, she had to admit to herself as she got ready for bed that evening. They had gone to Noordwijk-aan-zee, parked the car and carried Lisa and her folded chair down to the water's edge where the sand was smooth and firm. They had walked miles, with the shore stretching ahead of them for more miles, and then stopped off for crusty rolls and hard-boiled eggs. They had talked and laughed a lot and little Lisa had been happy, her pale face quite rosy; and as for the doctor, Fran found herself almost liking him. It was a pity, she reflected, jumping into bed, that he would be at the hospital at Utrecht for all of the following day; it was even more of a pity that he hadn't so much as hinted at seeing her again. 'Not that I care in the least,' she told herself. 'When Lisa isn't there he is a very unpleasant man.' Upon which somewhat arbitrary thought she went to sleep.

She spent the next morning quietly with Clare and Karel, and took herself for a walk in the afternoon. Another week, and her holiday would be over. She hadn't mentioned Dr van Rijgen in her letters to the aunts and upon reflection she decided not to say anything about him. She thought a great deal about little Lisa, too; a darling child and happy; she had quite believed the doctor when he had said that he would do anything to keep her so. She went back to the flat, volunteered to cook the supper while Clare worried away at some knitting and went to bed early, declaring that she was tired.

Karel had gone to work and she was giving Clare the treat of breakfast in bed when the doctor telephoned. He would be at the hospital all the morning, he informed her in a cool voice, but he hoped that she would be kind enough to spend the afternoon with Lisa. 'I'll call for you about half past one,' he told her and rang off before she could say a word.

'Such arrogance,' said Fran crossly. 'Anyone would think I was here just for his convenience.'

All the same, she was ready, composed and a little cool in her manner when he arrived. A waste of effort on her part for he didn't seem to notice her stand-offish manner. To her polite enquiries as to his morning, he had little to say, but launched into casual questions. When was she returning home? What did she think of Holland? Did she find the language difficult to understand? And then, harshly, did she feel at her ease with Lisa?

Fran turned to look at him in astonishment. 'At ease? Why ever shouldn't I? She's a darling child and the greatest fun to be with. I like children.' She sounded so indignant that he said instantly, 'I'm sorry, I put that badly.' He turned the car into the drive. 'A picnic tea, don't you think? It's such a lovely day.' And, as she got out of the car, 'It would be nice, if you are free tomorrow, if you will come with us to the Veluwe—it's charming, rather like your New Forest, and Lisa sees fairies behind every tree. We'll fetch you about half past ten?'

'I haven't said I'll come,' observed Fran frostily, half in and half out of the car.

'Lisa wants you.'

And that's the kind of left-handed compliment a girl likes having, thought Fran, marching ahead of him up the steps, her ordinary nose in the air.

But she forgot all that when Lisa joined them; in no time at all, she was laughing as happily as the little girl, struggling with the Dutch Lisa insisted upon her trying out. They had tea on the lawn again and when Nanny came to fetch Lisa to bed, Fran went, too, invited by both Nanny and the child.

Being got ready for bed was a protracted business dealt with by Nanny with enviable competence. But it was fun, too. Fran fetched and carried and had a satisfactory conversation with Nanny even though they both spoke their own language for the most part. They sat on each side of Lisa while she ate her supper and then at last was carried to her small bed in the charming nursery. Here Fran kissed her good night and went back to the day nursery, because it was Nanny's right to tuck her little charge up in bed and give her a final hug. She had just joined Fran when the doctor came in, said something to Nanny and went through to the night nursery where there was presently a good deal of giggling and murmuring before he came back.

He talked to Nanny briefly, wished her good night and swept Fran downstairs.

They had drinks by the open windows in the drawing-room and presently dined. Fran, who was hungry, ate with a good appetite, thinking how splendid it must be to have a super cook to serve such food and someone like Tuggs to appear at your elbow whenever you wanted something. They didn't talk much, but their silences were restful; the doctor wasn't a man you needed to chat to, thank heaven.

They had their coffee outside in the still warm garden, with the sky darkening and the faint scent of the roses which crowded around the lawn mingling with the coffee. She sighed and the doctor asked, 'What are you thinking, Francesca?'

'That it's very romantic and what a pity it's quite wasted on us.'

She couldn't see his face, but his voice was casual. 'We are perhaps beyond the age of romance.'

She snapped back before she could stop herself, 'I'm twenty-five!'

'On October the third you will be twenty-six. I shall be thirty-seven in December.'

'However did you know?' began Fran.

'I made it my business to find out.' His voice was so mild that she choked back several tart remarks fighting for utterance.

'More coffee?' she asked finally.

Their day in the Veluwe was a success: the doctor might be a tiresome man but he was a splendid father and, when he chose to be, a good host. They drove through the narrow lanes criss-crossing the Veluwe and picnicked in a charming clearing with the sunshine filtering through the trees and numerous birds. The food was delicious: tiny sausage rolls, bite-size sandwiches, chicken vol-au-vents, hard-boiled eggs, crisp rolls and orange squash to wash them down. Fran, watching Lisa, saw that she ate very little and presently, tucked in her chair, she fell asleep.

When she woke up, they drove on, circling round to avoid the main roads and getting back in time for a rather late tea. This time the doctor was called away to the telephone and returned to say that he would have to go to Utrecht that evening. Fran said at once, 'Then if you'll give me a lift to the city I'll get a bus.'

'Certainly not.' He sat down beside Lisa and explained at some length and then said, 'Lisa quite understands—this often happens. We'll get Nanny and say good night and leave at once; there will be plenty of time to drive you to your cousin's flat.'

And nothing she could say would alter his plans.

It was two days before she saw him again. Pleasant enough, pottering around with Clare, going out for a quiet drive in the evenings when Karel got home, all the same she felt a tingle of pleasure when the doctor telephoned. She had only two days left and she was beginning to think that she wouldn't see him or Lisa again.

'A farewell tea party,' he explained. 'I'll pick you up on my way back from Zeist—about two o'clock.'

He hung up and her pleasure turned to peevishness. 'Arrogant man!'

All the same she greeted him pleasantly when he arrived, listened to his small talk as they drove towards his home and took care not to mention the fact that in two days time she would be gone. He knew, anyway, she reminded herself; it was to be a farewell tea party.

Lisa was waiting for them, sitting in her chair under the mulberry tree. She wound her arms round Fran's neck, chattering away excitedly. 'Is it a birthday or something?' asked Fran. 'There's such an air of excitement.'

Father and daughter exchanged glances. 'You shall know in good time,' said the doctor blandly.

They took their time over tea, talking in a muddled but satisfactory way with Fran struggling with her handful of Dutch words and the doctor patiently translating for them both. But presently Nanny arrived and Lisa went with her without a word of protest.

'I'll see her to say goodbye?' she asked, turning to wave.

Dr van Rijgen didn't answer that. He said instead, in a perfectly ordinary voice, 'I should like you to marry me, Francesca.'

She sat up with a startled yelp and he said at once, 'No, be good enough to hear me out. May I say at once that it is not for the usual reasons that I wish to marry you; since Lisa was able to talk she has begged me for a mama of her own. Needless to say I began a search for such a person but none of my women friends were suitable. Oh, they were kind and pleasant to Lisa but they shrank from contact with her. Besides, she didn't like any of them. You see, she had formed her own ideas of an ideal mama—someone small and gentle and mouselike, who would laugh with her and never call her a poor little girl. When I saw you at the prize giving at the Infirmary I realised that you were exactly her ideal. I arranged these days together so that you might get to know her—needless to say, you are perfect in her eyes...'

'The nerve, the sheer nerve!' said Fran in a strong voice. 'How can you dare...?'

'I think I told you that I would do anything for Lisa to keep her happy until she dies. I meant it. She has six months at the outside and you have fifty—sixty years ahead of you. Do you grudge a few months of happiness to her? Of course, it will be a marriage in name only and when the time comes,' his voice was suddenly harsh, 'the marriage can be annulled without fuss and you will be free to resume your career. I shall see that it doesn't suffer on our account.'

Fran gazed at him, speechless. She was more than surprised; she was flabbergasted. Presently, since the silence had become lengthy, she said, 'It's ridiculous, and even if I were to consider it, I'd need time to decide.'

'There is nothing ridiculous about it if you ignore your own feelings on the matter, and there is no time. Lisa is waiting for us to go to the nursery.'

'And supposing I refuse?'

He didn't answer that. 'You intend to refuse?' There was no reproach in his calm voice, but she knew that, in six months' time, when Lisa's short life had ended, she would never cease to reproach herself.

'No strings?' she asked.

'None. I give you my word.'

'Very well,' said Fran, 'but I'm doing it for Lisa.'

'I hardly imagined that you would do it for me. Shall we go and tell her?'

Lisa was in her dressing-gown, ready for bed, eating something nourishing from a bowl. The face she turned towards them as they went over to her was so full of eager hope that Fran reflected that even if she had refused she would have changed her mind at the sight of it. She felt her hand taken in a firm, reassuring grasp. 'Well, *lieveling,* here is your mama.'

She was aware of Nanny's delighted face as Lisa flung her arms round her neck and hugged her, talking non-stop.

When she paused for breath the doctor said, 'Lisa wants to know when and where. I think the best thing is for me to drive you back and you can discuss it with your aunts. And for reasons which I have already mentioned the wedding will have to be here.' He smiled a little. 'And you must wear a bride's dress and a veil.'

Fran looked at him over Lisa's small head. 'Anything to make her happy.'

He said gravely, 'At least we can agree upon that.'

CHAPTER THREE

THEY stayed with Lisa for some time; she was excited and happy, talking nineteen to the dozen, full of plans for a future which would never be hers, but presently she became drowsy and the doctor carried her to bed where she fell instantly asleep.

Downstairs in the drawing room, over drinks and with the dogs at their feet, Dr van Rijgen observed, 'Thank you, Francesca, you have made Lisa happy. Now as to plans for the future... For a start, you must call me Litrik and, with Lisa, we must present at the least a friendly front. I suggest that I drive you home and we can tell your aunts together. You realise why the wedding must be here, of course? Lisa expects a full-blown affair, I'm afraid, and you are free to invite anyone you wish to attend. Are your aunts likely to disapprove?'

'Disapprove. Well, I don't know. You see they have made up their minds that I shan't marry, but I think that if we just told them at once they wouldn't be able to do much about it. I don't want them to know the real reason...'

'God forbid. How soon can you be free to marry me? It will take about three weeks for the formalities here.'

'I can be ready by then. It might help if you wrote to Miss Hawkins...'

'I'll go and see her. Do you want Dr Beecham to give you away? The service isn't the same as your Church of England, but I dare say you'll feel better if it's on familiar lines.'

It was rather like discussing the future treatment for a patient and just as impersonal and efficient.

'That would be nice.' She swallowed the rest of her sherry and wished that it would warm her cold insides.

'I will arrange your return here and for any family or friends whom you would like at our wedding.' He got up and refilled her glass.

'I must reassure you that you will be free to return to England after Lisa's death.' His voice was bleak. 'The annulment may take a little time but it can be dealt with here; you will have no need to be bothered with it.'

Fran tossed off her sherry. 'You had it all worked out, didn't you? Were you so sure of me?'

He smiled faintly. 'Certainly not. But Lisa was.' He got up and took her glass as Tuggs came in to say that dinner was served. 'And may I, on behalf of Mrs Tuggs and myself, wish you both happiness, Miss Manning and you, sir.'

'Why thank you, Tuggs. I shall be driving Miss Manning back the day after tomorrow; when I return we must make all the necessary arrangements. We hope to marry within the month.'

Nothing more was said about the wedding over dinner and when Fran said that she would like to go back to Clare's, Litrik made no objection. It was a warm quiet night and they had little to say to each other. Only when he drew up before Clare's flat did Litrik say, 'I'll come in with you, if I may—it may be easier for you.'

Karel and Clare were delighted at the news. Beyond remarking that it must have been love at first sight, and the hope that they would wait until she had had the baby before they married, Clare showed little surprise. She plied them with coffee and then tactfully retired to her kitchen with Karel so that Fran could bid her new fiancé good night—something she did in her normal calm manner, thanking him for her pleasant afternoon and asking if he would be good enough to let her know when he wished her to be ready for the journey back to England.

'Well, I'll let you know tomorrow. You will have to come

and say goodbye to Lisa. Can you manage the morning? I've patients to see after lunch.'

'Very well.' She hesitated. 'I think I must be mad,' she said suddenly.

'No—compassionate, kind of heart and trusting, but never mad.' He was at the door. 'Remember that Lisa loves you.' He said quietly and closed the door softly behind him before she could answer that.

There was no chance of going to bed; Clare and Karel came back and spent the next hour talking about the momentous news. 'It's fabulous!' declared Clare. 'Fran, he's rich, and I mean rich, and well known and you'll have just about everything you can possibly want. I'm so thrilled. Whatever will the aunts say?'

'I think they will be struck speechless. I imagine Litrik will convince them; that's why he is going back with me.' Anxious to keep the talk light she added, 'Of course, you'll both come to the wedding, won't you? It won't be more than a month, so you'll be able to come; the baby's not due for about five months, is it?'

'Can't you wait till after Christmas so that I can wear something smart?'

'You'll look smashing—wear layers of chiffon like the models in *Vogue*.' She escaped to her room at last but she was too tired to think clearly by then. She got into bed and went to sleep at once.

She was fetched in the morning by Litrik whose manner towards her couldn't be faulted. He was a naturally reserved man so no one would have expected him to display his feelings in public; nevertheless he managed to convey a loving regard for Fran which more than satisfied Clare. Not that it satisfied Fran. In the car she said forthrightly, 'Are we going to—to pretend all the time? I don't think I'll be much good at it. Calling you dear, and so on.' She turned her head to look at his inscrutable profile. 'You actually sounded as though you are glad that we are going to be married...'

'But I am glad—for Lisa's sake. Is that not a sufficiently good reason? And I am sure that, if you put in some practice, you'll manage a certain warmth towards me. No need to while we are on our own, of course.'

'You are impossible!' declared Fran crossly.

They spent a happy morning nonetheless. Lisa was full of plans for the wedding: the kind of dress Fran was to wear, the food they would eat at the reception, the picnics they would enjoy for the rest of the summer. The doctor translated patiently and when they had at last said goodbye to the child and were driving back to Bloemendaal, Fran remarked, 'I shall have to learn Dutch...I can understand a word here and there but not enough.'

'I'll arrange lessons for you once the wedding is over. In the meantime I know of someone in Bristol who will start you off. Your aunts won't object to her coming each day while you are with them?'

'I don't suppose so. Do I see you again once you have left England?'

'Unlikely. I will keep you informed as to plans. You do realise that you will need to wear bride's clothes? Lisa expects that.'

'You mean a veil and bouquet and a white dress? Yes, I know.'

'Good. Have you sufficient money, Francesca?'

Even if she hadn't a penny, she wouldn't have admitted it. 'Yes, thank you. At what time do we go tomorrow?'

'I'll be at your cousin's flat about nine o'clock. We'll go over by hovercraft from Calais. We should be with your aunts by teatime or a little after.'

Clare and Karel saw them off in the morning, her cousin bubbling over with excitement. The two men shook hands like old friends and the doctor made no bones about kissing Clare.

'We shall see you both at the wedding,' were his parting words.

They appeared to be, reflected Fran wryly, the very epitome of blissful love. But once they were on their way, Litrik reverted to his usual slightly mocking calm. 'Lisa sent you a book,' he told her. 'It's in the pocket of your door. You are to look at it and wear a dress exactly like the one she has encircled with chalk.'

It was a picture book telling the story, in a series of most delightful drawings, of a family of mice. And there, on the first page, was Mrs Mouse, in a wide skirted satin dress and a veil crowned with a wreath of orange blossom, her gentle whiskered face peering out from beneath it, tiny paws clasping a Victorian bouquet.

'Oh,' said Fran, and felt a lump in her throat. 'Does she really think of me like that—a mouse...?'

'The highest honour she can bestow on you, Francesca. Please copy the dress as far as possible; I will see that the bouquet is a replica.'

Fran turned the pages; Mrs Mouse's life was busy and happy; there were mouse babies in abundance, suitably bonneted and gowned, and several pictures of the cosy cottage in which they all lived. She said rather gruffly, 'I'll do the best I can about the dress; anything to make her happy.'

His stern profile relaxed. 'Thank you, Francesca.'

It wasn't until they were on the last stage of their journey that they discussed future plans, or rather, the doctor disclosed his plans. She was to leave the hospital within the next few days, merely going there long enough to hand over to Jenny Topps until such time as a new ward sister could be appointed. This, he observed casually, he had already arranged with Miss Hawkins. He would arrange for her to return to Holland in just over three weeks' time, with her aunts or on her own. He had telephoned Dr Beecham who would be delighted to give her away.

'You will, of course stay at my home until the wedding; your aunts, too, of course, and anyone else you may wish to invite.'

He slowed the car as they approached the town, only another five minutes' drive away. 'My own family will be there, of course.'

'Oh.' She was startled out of her usual calm. 'Have you a family?'

He smiled faintly. 'A mother and father, two sisters, nephews and nieces, aunts and uncles. Is that so strange?'

'Yes,' said Fran baldly, 'you don't strike me as being the kind of man to need a family.'

'We have a good deal to learn about each other, Francesca.'

He had stopped before her aunts' house. 'Well, yes, but it'll be a waste of time, won't it?' A sudden thought struck her. 'Do your family know—I mean why you're marrying me?'

He had got out of the car and had opened her door. 'No, Francesca, no one knows. It will be our secret.'

They walked up the garden path together and at the door he thumped the brass knocker. It was opened almost immediately by Winnie who, after a surprised squawk, cast her arms around Fran. 'Well, love, there's a surprise—tomorrow we thought...' She took a good look at Dr van Rijgen. 'And who's this?'

'Dr van Rijgen, Winnie.' Fran planted a kiss on the elderly cheek. 'We are going to be married, only hush until I've told the aunts.'

Winnie hushed, only pumped the doctor's arm with warmth. 'They are having their tea, like always, in the drawing room.'

Without thinking Fran caught the doctor's hand in hers and led him down the hall and opened the drawing-room door. Her aunts were sitting as they always sat, each in her own particular chair, with Aunt Kate behind the small tea table.

She had the teapot in her hand as they went in and when she saw them lowered it carefully on to the tray.

'Francesca—home a day early? You will of course tell us your reason for that. We are pleased to see you home again, child. Polly, ring for more cups and saucers and fresh tea.' Her rather prominent blue eyes were fixed on the doctor, standing by Fran, her hand still on his.

'I don't think we have had the pleasure…' began Aunt Polly.

Fran felt him give her hand a reassuring squeeze. 'Hallo, Aunts,' she said. 'This is Dr van Rijgen—Litrik. We're going to be married and he has driven me back from Holland so that you might meet him.'

The aunts weren't ladies to show their feelings but just for a moment they were caught off balance.

'Married?' asked Aunt Kate, and, 'How romantic,' sighed Aunt Janet, but it was Aunt Polly who rose to the occasion. 'This is unexpected news, you must forgive us if we are surprised. We had no idea…' She left the suggestion of a question in the air, but, since Fran didn't answer it, went on, 'Welcome, Dr van Rijgen, we are delighted to meet you.' She got up and kissed Fran and shook his hand and Aunt Janet and Aunt Kate followed suit before Aunt Kate told them to sit down. 'You will be glad of a cup of tea, of course.' Her eyes had slid to Fran's ringless hand. 'This is very recent, of course. And when do you propose to marry? Next summer, perhaps?'

'In three weeks' time, Miss Askew. In Holland.' Litrik's pleasant voice gave no hint of doubts about that.

'Three weeks—in Holland—that's quite impossible! Francesca, you have your hospital work to consider, and of course, you must be married here.' Aunt Kate, who liked to arrange other people's lives for them, poured their tea with a careless hand, her lips drawn into a thin line.

'Francesca is leaving the hospital in two days' time,' explained Litrik with what Fran secretly decided was his best bedside manner. 'That gives her time to buy anything she wishes for the wedding and join me before the wedding. We both hope that you will all come as our guests and meet my family. And my small daughter. I am a widower.'

He sat back and drank his tea while the three ladies digested this.

'But Holland,' murmured Aunt Polly, making it sound like a remote jungle in some far-flung corner of the globe. 'The church service...'

'Very similar to your own, Miss Askew. I live just outside Utrecht and have a practice there. Francesca will have plenty of friends and her cousin is only a short drive away. And I am well able to support her in comfort.'

'Your daughter...' began Aunt Kate, fighting a losing battle.

'Lisa and Francesca took an instant liking for each other.' He turned to smile at Fran and just for a moment put a hand over hers.

'She's a darling,' said Fran. 'I'm very happy and I hope you will all be happy, too.'

It was Aunt Janet who spoke. 'Of course we are, my dear. We never expected you to marry. We hoped you would be with us always, but it's all very romantic and sudden...'

'Not sudden,' said the doctor surprisingly. 'Francesca and I first met when she was a student nurse at the Infirmary. I go there to give lectures.'

The aunts, who believed in long engagements and knowing each other for years before deciding to get married, looked at him with approval. Here was a man who had taken some years to make up his mind; no flighty youth sweeping their sensible niece off her feet. 'That is different,' pronounced Aunt Kate. 'We should, of course, have preferred to have the wedding here, but you are a man of good sense, I feel sure, and Francesca and we shall be guided by you. You will, of course, stay for the night?'

'Thank you, that is most kind.' He was at his most urbane. 'I should mention that I have to leave by eight o'clock tomorrow morning—I have an appointment for the early evening in Utrecht.'

'All that way,' uttered Aunt Jane. 'You must be tired.'

Fran, casting a quick sideways glance at him, reflected that he wasn't tired at all; that he was enjoying himself in a secret way. Probably he hadn't met anyone like the aunts before.

Winnie was summoned and told to take their guest to his room. 'The car will be quite safe if you drive on to the grass verge by the gate,' he was told. 'Fran, go with Dr van Rijgen and show him.'

It was a lovely evening and the roses smelled sweet. Fran took several happy sniffs and asked, 'Do you mind? Staying the night, I mean?'

'My dear Francesca, I am delighted to do so. When do you report for duty?'

'I wasn't expected until Monday, but I'd like to go in at eight o'clock tomorrow morning.'

He wheedled the car on to the grass verge, got out and locked the doors before he spoke. 'I'll drive you there and have a word with Miss Hawkins.'

'There is no need…'

'Just leave everything to me. I see no possibility of us talking this evening. Do you suppose you could get up earlier and do a little planning over breakfast? Seven o'clock say?'

'The aunts are not called until eight o'clock, but Winnie will be up. I can get our breakfast—we'll have it in the kitchen. It'll be toast and boiled eggs. Winnie does the dining room before she starts cooking.'

They started up the garden path. 'When I'm at home I call the aunts with tea and get my breakfast; that gives Winnie a bit more time…'

'And does no one ever get up and get your breakfast, Francesca?'

'Heavens no!'

They weren't alone again for the rest of the evening; Fran helped Winnie with the supper, unpacked and got her uniform ready for the morning. She also put water, a tin of biscuits and, after an examination of her bookshelf in her room, a copy of an anthology of English verse on his bedside table. The idea of staying up late to talk to Litrik never entered her head. At least, it entered it, but was discarded at once; with four elderly maiden ladies in the house, it would have thrown a spanner into their stern way of life and quite spoilt the sober picture Litrik had presented.

She was up at half past six the next morning, trotting round the kitchen, laying the table, making tea, cutting bread for toast, boiling eggs. By the time the doctor got down breakfast was ready and they sat down together to eat it, he presenting an impeccable appearance while Fran, mousy hair hanging in soft swathes around her shoulder, buttoned into a sensible dressing-gown Aunt Kate had given her for Christmas, sat unselfconsciously opposite him, gobbling her food as fast as she could. 'I'll not be long dressing,' she told him, 'but I thought I'd better get breakfast over first—I don't suppose you like being kept waiting.'

There was no knowing what he might have replied, for Winnie came in then. Her good morning was severe. 'Miss Fran, you've no business gallivanting around as you are. It's a good thing your aunts can't see you now, sitting there in a dressing-gown—such goings on…'

The doctor's firm mouth twitched although he said nothing. It was Fran who spoke. 'Well, Winnie dear, if you take a good look at the doctor you'll see that he is not the kind of man to tolerate goings on.'

She was biting into her toast as she spoke and didn't look up, which was a pity for the gleam of amusement in the doctor's eye was pronounced. 'Besides,' she added, 'there is nothing of me showing.'

'Miss Fran, I am surprised at you! What the doctor must think!'

He offered his cup for more tea. 'Well, Winnie, times change you know. Francesca and I are to be married very shortly and as she points out, there's nothing visible to upset my normal calm.'

He glanced at his watch. 'Can you be ready in twenty minutes, Francesca?'

Fran bolted the last morsel of toast. 'Yes. Did you say goodbye last night?'

'Yes. I'll be outside in the car.'

She was ready in fifteen minutes, very neat in her uniform, a clean frilled cap perched on to smooth mousy hair. She had been to say good morning to the aunts and goodbye all at the same time, assured them that their guest had slept well and eaten a good breakfast and now she flung an affectionate arm around Winnie's shoulders and nipped down the path to where the car was parked.

'Will it make you late, coming with me?' she asked Litrik.

'No, I have allowed time for that. You have no problems? I will telephone you as soon as I can arrange a date for the wedding—the sooner the better, so try and get your shopping done and the packing within the next ten days or so. Are your aunts likely to delay matters?'

Fran considered. 'Well, they like to do things at their own pace and arrange things to suit themselves…'

'Three of the most selfish ladies I have ever met,' declared the doctor blandly. 'If they aren't ready to travel to our wedding then I am afraid they will have to miss it.'

'Well!' observed Fran. 'Well, I never… You mean that.'

'I always mean what I say, Francesca.' He parked the car at the hospital and turned to look at her. 'If they are not ready and willing to travel with you to Holland then I shall expect you on your own.'

She thought of Lisa. 'I'll promise to do that.' She took the picture book for herself from the pocket in the door beside her. 'May I keep this? So that I can copy the dress as nearly as possible. Tell Lisa that, and give her my love.'

They spent fifteen minutes or so with Miss Hawkins and Fran watched the doctor calmly getting everything all his own way while the unsuspecting Miss Hawkins agreed with all he said. They bade her farewell presently and Fran went back to the car with him. 'Have a good journey,' she begged him and offered a hand.

He took it and held it fast. 'We shall need to put in some practice,' he observed and bent to kiss her.

She stood watching the car gather speed. She had enjoyed the kiss; perhaps he was beginning to like her and not just because she was marrying him to make Lisa happy. The thought warmed her insides, but only for a moment; when she turned round it was to see faces at most of the windows. He had been seen and had seen them, too, and had acted accordingly; it would have been odd if a newly engaged couple had parted with a hand-shake. The pleasant warmth gave way to rage so her cheeks were fiery with it. The heads at the windows nodded and nudged each other and there were vague remarks about blushing brides, before those of the nursing staff who could leave the wards for a minute or two surged around Fran to offer congratulations.

She received them in her usual calm manner, her cheeks still pink, her eyes sparkling, her thoughts anything but romantic, and presently, since the day's work had to be done, they dispersed to their various duties leaving her and Jenny to go along to her office and begin the job of handing over.

It wasn't just the patients, it was every single article on the wards themselves which had to be accounted for. After a round of the patients and a few instructions to the nurses, the pair of them shut themselves in with a tray of tea and got down to work. Jenny had agreed to take over, at least until the new sister could be appointed, which made things a little easier, for she knew the patients and their treatments and understood the ways of the visiting doctors. All the same, what with the various interruptions from Dr Stokes and the dietitian, the dispensary and the laundry, and, over and above these, the treatments needed by the patients, it was six o'clock before they had finished to their satisfaction. Of course, there was still the ward inventory, a formidable undertaking by Miss Hawkins herself. Fran let Jenny go off duty, made sure that the patients were nicely settled and went into the linen cupboard. She emerged to write the report for the night nurse, phone her aunts to say that she would be home late, and plunged back into the welter of sheets, pillow-cases and blankets. She was still hard at it when the night nurses arrived and it was ten o'clock before she had arranged everything in orderly rows to her satisfaction. In the morning, Jenny could take over the ward, and she would see to the rest. The kitchen wouldn't take long; there was plenty of room in which to lay out crockery and cutlery; the beds could have the bedclothes turned back to make the counting of them easy. The nurses could have time to assemble the contents of the sluice rooms and the bathrooms. Fran went home at last, ate a hasty supper and fell into bed. The aunts would have liked to have talked about the wedding, but there would be time enough for that once she had left the hospital.

The following day was slightly worse although it had its mitigating moments. Fran, gobbling a hasty sandwich after Miss Hawkins's eagle-eyed inspection of ward equipment, was surprised and delighted to find her office suddenly invaded by the other sisters in the hospital, bringing a bottle of sherry with them and a large cardboard box gaily wrapped. She had opened it to find table linen and a rather sentimental card wishing her and Litrik every happiness and she had almost cried at the sight of it. The givers imagined that she was in love and marrying for that reason and she felt sad and guilty all at the same time. And the other good moment of the day was when Dr Beecham came, ruthlessly disturbing Miss Hawkins's inventory, to tell her that he was delighted and more than pleased to be giving her away.

'And I must say you are a fine pair, keeping it dark until the last moment. The wife's coming, of course, and she has bought a new hat, too. Must keep our end up with Litrik's family swanning around. Your aunts going?'

She had told him yes, and he had grunted. 'Gave them a bit of a shock, I dare say.' He patted her kindly on the shoulder. 'Well, you deserve a bit of the good life, Fran; you'll make a fine wife. Litrik's a lucky man.'

Litrik telephoned the next day, pleasantly brisk and businesslike. The date of the wedding was fixed, not quite three weeks away, and he would drive over three days before that and fetch her. Her aunts, he observed, would be taken care of by Tuggs, who would fetch them the day previous to the wedding and drive them back home again on the day following that. 'A short stay, I'm afraid,' he told her with no trace of apology, 'but I have an important conference in Brussels and there will be no chance to entertain them.'

'Do I have to tell them?'

She heard his quick impatient breath. 'I'll write to them. You have left the hospital?'

'Yes. Litrik, we are being married in church, aren't we?'

'Certainly. There is a civil wedding first, of course. The *dominee* is a personal friend of mine and he understands the situation. We will go and see him together. Cold feet?'

'Certainly not. How is Lisa?'

'In seventh heaven, bless her.' His voice warmed. 'She is really happy.'

Which made the whole thing worthwhile, reflected Fran as she wished him a rather sober goodbye.

* * *

She was neither impetuous nor impulsive; she spent the first day or so making lists and then took herself off to Bath, where she bought ivory satin, white tulle and fine lace and bore them off to the little woman who had made clothes for half the town for most of her life. If she was surprised to find that Fran wanted her wedding dress to be an exact copy of the mouse in the picture book she forbore from comment, but cut and stitched and fitted until an exact replica lay spread out in her workroom. When Fran went for a final fitting she allowed herself the observation that she had never expected the dress to turn out quite so exquisite. 'You'll look a treat, Miss Fran,' she declared. 'Mind you let me have a photo.'

There were other clothes to buy, of course, but first she had to drive the aunts to Bath so that they might purchase suitable finery. They had taken the news that they were to be fetched by Tuggs without too much argument, possibly because of the letter the doctor had written to them. Aunt Kate had been tart about the shortness of their visit to Holland, but, as Fran had pointed out with her usual common sense, he was a busy man and a prominent one in his profession and his work was very important to him.

Aunt Kate had sniffed. 'I suppose that, now you are to be married, we can no longer expect any care and attention; we three old ladies will have to manage as best we can.'

Fran stilled a rebellious tongue and took a deep calming breath. 'You are none of you old—why Miss Hawkins at the hospital is only a couple of years younger than you, Aunt Polly, and she works full time and housekeeps for her brother as well. And you forget that you have Winnie.'

'And that's another thing,' moaned Aunt Kate. 'Litrik insists that she should come to the wedding with us. I cannot think why.'

'I've known Winnie for years, Aunt Kate, she is my friend and Litrik knows that.' She added, with a touch of asperity, 'I'm taking her into Bath tomorrow to buy herself a hat.'

'I do not know what has come over you, Francesca. We have all said that you are a changed young woman.'

'I expect it's because I'm going to be married. I thought you would be pleased about that, Aunt.'

Aunt Kate looked uncomfortable. 'Of course we are pleased, but we had rather expected that you would stay here and look after us.'

'Well now I'll have a husband and a little stepdaughter to look after instead,' observed Fran cheerfully. She dropped a kiss on her peevish aunt's cheek and went upstairs to try on three pairs of new shoes, a Jaeger suit, two crêpe de Chine dresses, a tweed skirt, a jersey dress with a wildly expensive belt and a handful of sweaters and blouses. She had spent a lot of money, but she had never felt the urge to buy many clothes before; there had been no reason to do so. She had always looked nice but unspectacular; now she had gathered together a wardrobe she hoped would be suitable for a doctor's wife. There was still money in the bank; right at the back of her mind was the dim thought that one day she might need it.

She wrote letters to Lisa, in English but interlarded with an occasional Dutch phrase. Litrik had been as good as his word. A rather formidable lady had telephoned to say that she had been requested to give Fran as many lessons in Dutch conversation as possible. She was a hard taskmaster, but, by the time Fran had packed her bags, said goodbye to her friends and organised her aunts' journey so that they would have no worries, she had learned a score of little sentences off by heart, and any number of everyday words. 'The grammar will have to be learned later,' her teacher had told her. 'At the moment you have none, but persevere with what you have learned and practise daily. Your accent is tolerable and you can make yourself understood basically. I trust that Dr van Rijgen will be satisfied.'

'Oh, I am sure that he will,' declared Fran warmly. 'I can't thank you enough—I mean, Dutch doesn't sound like nonsense any more, if you know what I mean.'

She beamed at the lady, who found herself smiling back, at the same time wondering what Litrik van Rijgen could possibly see in such an ordinary girl. Nice eyes, pretty figure, sweet smile and a charming voice, but hardly scintillating.

He arrived exactly when he had said he would and was received by the aunts, sitting as they always did in their chairs in the drawing room. Fran, trotting to and fro between the kitchen and the dining room, hadn't heard the car. She opened the drawing room door and poked her head round it. 'Aunt Kate, Winnie wants some sherry for the soup…' She caught sight of the doctor, who had got to his feet at the sight of her, and went a little pink. 'Oh, you're here—hallo, Litrik.'

He crossed the room and put his hands on her shoulders and kissed her. 'I wondered where you were,' he remarked blandly. 'I supposed you to be in your room doing last minute things to your hair or something. Are you cooking the supper?'

The faint edge to his voice made the aunts wince. 'Winnie's doing that,' Aunt Polly hastened to say. 'Francesca always helps.'

He had kept an arm round her shoulders. 'Can Winnie spare you for ten minutes? I'm sure your aunts will forgive us if we have a short time together, perhaps in the garden? There are several small points to settle and we must leave early in the morning.'

He smiled gently. 'We might take the sherry with us and go through the kitchen…'

Fran took the bottle from the sideboard cupboard, reflecting that there was more to Litrik than she had thought; the aunts hadn't a chance. She gave him a shy smile, assured her aunts that they would be ten minutes, no more than that, and led the way out of the room. She was rather warm from the kitchen and her hair had escaped its neat bun; she didn't feel at her best, but on the other hand, Litrik had smiled at her like an old friend.

Winnie took the sherry, ushered them out through the kitchen door and told them severely that they'd better be back in ten minutes otherwise the chicken would be overdone.

In the soft evening light, Fran turned to look at him. 'Don't you like the aunts?' she asked.

'Charming ladies; also, as I have already said, selfish to their fingertips. Do you spend all your time in the kitchen?'

'No—oh no, but you see Winnie is not as young as she was and there are little jobs I can do to help.'

'And can your aunts not help occasionally?'

'They are not used to doing anything like that.'

He took her arm and strolled across the stretch of grass behind the house.

'No last minute misgivings?' he wanted to know.

'Only that I might not fit into your kind of life.'

He let that pass. 'You will find Lisa not quite as well as she was. I think that perhaps we were a little optimistic…'

She looked at him appalled. 'You mean, less than six months?'

'I'm afraid so.'

'I'm so sorry. I can't bear to think of it.'

'Then don't. Let us think instead of securing her a happy life while she is with us.'

'Oh, I promise that I will do that—anything…'

'She is in transports over her new dress—did you manage to get a dress resembling her story book mouse?'

She answered him seriously. 'Yes, down to the last button. No whiskers or tail of course!'

He smiled down at her and put a hand out to tuck away a strand of hair.

'But mousy hair in abundance. You'll be ready to leave by eight o'clock in the morning?'

'Yes. I have two cases and my wedding dress in a box. Will breakfast at just after seven suit you?'

'Very nicely. We say goodbye to the aunts this evening.'

'Well, yes; they don't like to be disturbed too early.'

'Then let us go and join them. Did I tell you that Dr and Mrs Beecham will be driving over the day before the wedding? They'll be staying with us.'

'And the aunts?'

'Of course. The house is large enough. Nel is over the moon opening up the entire place.'

At the kitchen door, Fran paused. 'It'll work, won't it?' she asked him.

His voice was reassuringly warm. 'Oh, yes, Francesca, it will work.'

CHAPTER FOUR

It was already warm when they left in the morning with Winnie to wave them goodbye. The aunts had been ready to bid them goodbye on the previous evening, managing to convey that although they were happy for Fran's future happiness they were themselves about to enter a period of deprivation caused by her permanent absence. Fran, remembering that as they drove away, felt vaguely guilty. She sat silently, wondering how her aunts would manage until Litrik spoke. 'Stop worrying, Francesca.' His voice was briskly friendly. 'Your aunts will manage very well; they do not really need you—they enjoyed making use of you. I am convinced that within a month we shall hear that they have found a suitable companion to take your place.'

He gave her a quick sideways smile which somehow reassured her. 'Now let us go over our plans for the next few days...'

A quite lengthy business which kept them occupied until they stopped for coffee. The hovercraft was full, for it was the height of the holiday season. Fran drank the coffee and ate the sandwiches which were brought to her and then sat quietly, not bothering to think, while Litrik, his briefcase open on his knees, wrote busily. He must have a great deal to do, she thought idly, but didn't pursue the thought; each time she had seen him he had appeared calm and unworried. She closed her eyes and nodded off on that reassuring thought.

They didn't stop again once they were on dry land and they were at the house as the clock on the dashboard showed the hour of five.

Litrik got out and came round to open her door. 'I've an

hour,' he told her. 'We'll have tea, shall we, and then I'll have to leave you until about eight o'clock.'

He didn't wait for her answer for Tuggs was already coming down the steps to greet them and fetch the luggage. And, 'Welcome, Miss Manning,' he said warmly. 'We're all that glad to see you, and there's Lisa in such a state of excitement.'

'In the drawing room?' asked Litrik, and took Fran's arm as they went indoors.

The drawing room looked as lovely as she had remembered it, with the late afternoon sun pouring in and the soft colours of the furnishings glowing against its walls. And Lisa in her wheelchair, with faithful Nanny close by, her small face alight with excitement. The moment they went in she burst into talk and the doctor strode across the room and picked her up carefully and carried her to where Fran had hesitated.

'Mama,' shrieked Lisa and leaned from her father's arms to hug her. She broke into a babble of Dutch then and, obedient to a look from Litrik, Fran sat down and he put Lisa on her lap.

The child was thinner and paler although there was nothing in her manner to show that she wasn't as well as she had been. Fran glanced at Litrik in low-voiced talk with Nanny; he looked completely at ease and Nanny was smiling—perhaps he had become over-anxious… Fran settled down to one of the conversations she and Lisa so enjoyed, both understanding about half of what the other was saying and making up for the rest by a lot of giggling.

But soon Nel brought in the tea, smiling and nodding at Fran and shaking hands and presently Litrik came back and took Lisa on to his knees while Fran poured out.

'Nanny has gone to have her own tea; she'll be back presently so that you can unpack and rest if you want to. Dinner will be later than usual and Lisa will go to bed at her normal time. Tomorrow my family will arrive but not until lunchtime.

I'll be at the hospital till about noon. And in the evening you and I are going to see the *dominee.*'

She had expected a busy few days before the wedding although the idea of meeting his family rather daunted her. Supposing they disliked her? And what about her clothes? It was still full summer and she had brought some pretty dresses with her as well as her new outfits. Would it be long dresses in the evening? She sat there, tell-tale thoughts worrying their way across her face.

'One thing at a time, Francesca,' said Litrik gently. 'Pour the tea, will you? Lisa wants to watch you unpack. Would you mind?'

'Of course not; in fact I'd like that very much.' She busied herself with the silver pot and the delicate china and joined in the cheerful talk about the wedding.

Nanny came back presently and Litrik went away, promising to look in on his small daughter when he got back home. His, 'Nel and Tuggs will look after you, Francesca,' were kindly uttered and she found it amusing that halfway to the door he remembered to come back and kiss her cheek.

She had wondered how she would fill in the time before he came home again but she need not have worried. Nanny wheeled Lisa's chair into the lift behind the staircase and, at a smile and a nod from Fran, left her in the large room which was to be hers. It was in the front of the house with a wide balcony. There was a bathroom and dressing room leading from it and it was furnished with beautifully polished pieces in yew and applewood. The floor was thickly carpeted and the three french windows were draped in old rose brocade, matching the spread on the bed. The dogs had joined them, sitting quietly side by side, satisfied now that they had got over the excitement of their master being back home.

Her cases had been unlocked and opened, both of them on a long chest against one wall, but the box with her wedding gown was unopened on the *chaise-longue* at the foot of the bed. She opened that first because that was what Lisa wanted to see most. The little girl's gasps of delight as she spread the dress on the bed more than repaid her for the trouble she had taken over getting it just right. She wheeled the chair close to the bed so that Lisa might finger the material and examine every inch of it and then opened one of the cases and unwrapped the present she had brought. A mouse dressed in a miniature replica of her own wedding finery. It had been a fiddly business making the mouse and then dressing it, but, at the sight of Lisa's ecstatic face, she had no doubt that it had been worthwhile.

The unpacking was hilarious, for she had to describe each garment in English while Lisa strove to copy her and then insisted on teaching her the Dutch, and when Nanny came to fetch Lisa she was drawn into it, too. But presently Lisa was borne away for her supper and bed, which gave Fran the chance to have a leisurely bath and change into one of the thinner dresses, sitting to do her face with extra care and arrange her hair with her usual neatness. And by then it was time to go and say good night to Lisa, a protracted visit as it turned out for Lisa wished to be told a story.

'In English?' asked Fran, mentally surveying her small stock of Dutch phrases.

English it seemed would do very well; it had to be a long story, lasting for several nights and never mind if she couldn't understand any of it, and it had to concern one of Lisa's beloved mice.

Fran, who had a splendid imagination, began an involved tale, interlarded with the odd Dutch word and helped out by a wealth of hand waving and a variety of voices. She didn't hear or see Litrik come into the night nursery; she was sitting on the bed beside Lisa, quite carried away while Lisa sat enthralled. When he sat down on the bed beside her she came to a halt, feeling foolish, although Lisa broke at once into delighted chatter. He put an arm across Fran's back and took his daughter's hand in his and said something to quieten her, then, 'Do go on,' he begged, 'I always enjoyed a good fairy story.'

'Well, that's the end actually; it's in instalments you see.' She felt shy and a bit silly.

'Then I must be sure and hear the second part.' He said something to Lisa and made her laugh and Fran got up and bent to kiss the child good night. The doctor did the same and the child tugged at his arm.

'It seems you are to be kissed, too,' he murmured to Fran and brushed her cheek lightly.

Fran caught sight of the child's eager little face watching them: she leaned up and kissed him with considerable warmth and felt his quick surprised breath.

They ate dinner, a delicious meal, at an elegantly laid table, the doctor completely at ease and Fran, outwardly at least, her usual calm self. They talked of this and that, made no mention of the wedding and discussed the weather. No one, thought Fran, spooning the luscious sorbet Tuggs had put before her, would know, just seeing us here like this, that we are going to be married in three days time. She glanced up and found his eyes upon her and blushed guiltily as though she had spoken her thoughts aloud.

Tuggs had gone to fetch the coffee and take it to the drawing room when Litrik said blandly, 'We'll have to do better than this, won't we? Do you suppose we might forget our true feelings towards each other and pretend that we at least like one another? It will get easier once we start. Supposing we go to the drawing room and discuss the wedding like two old friends? In fact, could we not regard the whole exercise as an undertaking agreed upon between two people with one object in mind, to keep Lisa happy?'

Fran poured the coffee and handed him his cup. She said slowly, 'I've been selfish, I'm sorry—let's start again.'

'That's generous of you, Francesca, for the blame is mine;

I have rushed you along without giving you time to, er—get into the part.'

He smiled at her with a charm to put her instantly at ease.

'Your family?' she asked him. 'I'm scared of meeting them, you know. I mean, do they think that we're...well, that you wanted to marry me?'

'I have told them that I have found the girl I want as a wife. That's true enough, isn't it? I am not a man to show my feelings too often and they wouldn't expect it.'

'And me?' Fran ignored grammar in her anxiety to get the matter clear. 'And what about my feelings?'

'I am sure that you will act your part admirably, Francesca. Shall we consider ourselves partners? I give you my word that I will do all in my power to make life easy for you.'

'And your friends?'

'They will come to the reception after our wedding, possibly we shall be invited out to dinner or drinks from time to time, but that should present no difficulties for you. You realise that your days will be largely taken up with Lisa?' He added bleakly, 'I very much doubt if she will be with us for Christmas.'

Christmas, from the viewpoint of early August, seemed a long way off. All the same Fran gave a little shiver. 'There is always hope.'

He didn't answer that. 'I have arranged to see Ivo Meertens, the *dominee,* after tea tomorrow. He understands the situation perfectly; you can say anything you like to him, ask him any questions, voice any doubts. We will go to his house and you can be sure that anything you say to him will go no further.'

'He—he does approve of what we are doing?'

'Yes. You see, Francesca, we are not hurting anyone, neither of us is emotionally involved, neither of us is hurting the other. On the other hand, we are making Lisa's remaining months happy ones.'

'I accept that,' she told him seriously. 'I promise you I will do my best to make Lisa happy.' Suddenly it was all a bit too much. She mumbled, 'Do you mind if I say good night? I'm tired...'

He got to his feet at once. 'Of course, it's been a long day. I breakfast at eight o'clock if you like to join me, but if you would rather, your breakfast will be brought to you in bed.'

'In bed? I can't remember when I had breakfast in bed. I'd rather have it here with you, Litrik.'

'Splendid.' He walked with her to the door and opened it and as she went past him stopped her for a moment with a hand. 'Good night,' he said and kissed her gently.

She had meant to go over the day's happenings in the peace and quiet of her bed but she was asleep the moment her head touched the pillow. In the morning, sitting up in bed drinking the tea Nel had brought her, there seemed no reason to do so. Besides if she was to have breakfast with Litrik she would have to get up and dress.

The faint lingering doubt that his friendliness and warmth of manner of the previous evening might have reverted to his usual chilly politeness was dispelled when she got downstairs, and she gave a small relieved sigh as he got up from his place at the table, wished her good morning and begged her to help herself to whatever she wished.

Breakfast was in a small room behind the dining room, with a round table and pretty rosewood chairs, a sideboard upon which were several covered dishes, and a wide window overlooking the garden. The sun streamed in making everything warm and bright and normal. Fran settled down to a good breakfast, all her overnight fears banished.

'Lunch will be at one o'clock.' Litrik's voice broke into her thoughts. 'Mother and the family will arrive about half past twelve; I shall be home by then.' He got up ready to leave. 'Have a happy morning with Lisa.' And since Tuggs had come into the room he paused by her chair and kissed her.

The morning passed quickly, walking round the garden with

Lisa and Nanny; there was no lack of conversation even if it was a bit muddled. With Lisa borne away for her rest Fran hurried to her room and took an anxious look at her person in the pier-glass. She had put on a cotton dress in leaf green with a wide white collar and soft leather belt round her slim waist. There was nothing more she could do about her face and hair, she decided. She went back downstairs and wandered into the drawing room and found Litrik there.

Her, 'Oh, good, you are back,' was uttered with a warmth quite unlike her usual calm voice and he said, 'Nervous? You don't need to be. Have you had a pleasant morning?'

He was so casual that she bit back all the things she wanted to say. 'Very nice, thank you,' she told him.

He crossed the room and stood in front of her, picked up her left hand and slid a ring on to her finger. 'My grandmother's—I'm glad to see that it fits.'

She looked at the sparkling diamond surrounded by sapphires in an old fashioned gold setting, and then at him, a question in her eyes.

'No—Lisa's mother had no interest in the family jewellery, but I fancy that perhaps you will like it?'

'Oh, I do, it's so beautiful. Thank you very much, Litrik.' Rather awkwardly she lifted her face to his and kissed his cheek. She had wondered once or twice about a ring but now she was taken by surprise. She was bewildered by the sudden urge to burst into tears for no reason at all. Well, there was a reason; he had given it to her with a casualness which made a mockery of the giving. But what else was there to expect? She said quietly, 'I shall take great care of it while I am wearing it.' For, of course, she would return it within a few months...

There was the sound of a car driving up to the door and he said, 'Shall we go and meet my mother and father?'

She had no need to be nervous; his father was an elderly edition of himself, white haired, self-assured and with a warmth in his manner which Litrik lacked, and his mother was splendidly tall, beautifully dressed, with a face which had no pretentions to good looks and the kindest of smiles.

They greeted her with a pleasure she hadn't expected and his mother said at once, 'We are so happy to have you in the family, my dear, and I speak for everyone. There are rather a lot of us but don't let us overwhelm you.' She twinkled nicely at Fran. 'When we have a few minutes to ourselves we will go somewhere quiet and have a good gossip.'

Her English was faultless. Fran smiled rather shyly, 'I shall like that,' and found that Litrik had taken her hand while they were talking.

'Lisa is over the moon,' he told his mother. 'The two of them had an instant rapport.' He broke off at the sound of voices in the hall. 'The family,' he observed and flung an arm round Fran's shoulders. She needed it; her knees were wobbling with fright.

To Fran, who had no family other than her three aunts and Clare, the steady stream of aunts, uncles, cousins, nephews and nieces was quite bewildering. Litrik, standing at her elbow, meticulously introduced her to each and every one of them and she smiled and shook hands and kissed cheeks and forgot their names immediately. One or two of them stood out from the rest: Great Uncle Timon, a giant of an old man with a splendid head of white hair and a fierce moustache and a command of English which left her blinking. And the two aunts from Friesland, Tante Olda and Tante Nynke, formidable in elegant black dresses, gold chains draping their splendid bosoms, leaning over her from their superior height and, surprisingly, positively motherly towards her. There were children, too, well behaved and polite and palpably relieved when they were sent into the garden to play, taking Nanny and Lisa with them. There were perhaps twenty-five people there although it seemed at least twice that number. It was a mercy that they all spoke English with an ease she envied; there had been no need for her to have worked so hard at her Dutch lessons before she had left home for there would be no chance to air what little knowledge she had. Anyway, she would be terrified to try it out on these self-assured relations, even though they were behaving so kindly towards her.

She gave a little shiver; she was a fraud and it was all wrong that everyone should be so bent on making her feel that she was one of the family.

Litrik, chatting to a thick-set middle-aged man whom she vaguely identified as Uncle Hilwert, felt the shiver and drew her a little closer. He said lightly, 'Uncle Hilwert is anxious that we should have a large family. He was the eldest of ten children and he has six sons and daughters, all married.' He glanced down at her, smiling easily. 'We must do our best, mustn't we, Francesca?'

She managed a smile, trying to imagine Litrik surrounded by half a dozen children. Of course, he was marvellous with Lisa but then she was just one child and a very sick one to boot. Six all bursting with childish health presented rather a different picture. She had gone a little pink and given Litrik a quick look and found him still smiling.

Uncle Hilwert was joined by Litrik's sisters, Jebbeke and Wilma, who wanted to talk about the wedding. Fran liked them; they were friendly, anxious to put her at her ease and, at the same time, didn't fire questions at her. They teased Litrik gently and then carried her off to join a group of younger cousins.

'You can have Fran back presently,' declared Wilma cheerfully. 'After all you'll have her for the rest of your life and that's years and years...'

He let her go at once with some laughing remark and she wondered if he felt as bad about it as she did. She must stop thinking like that, she reminded herself as she crossed the room with Wilma and Jebbeke. She had promised that she would fulfil her side of their bargain and that was all that mattered. The circle of cousins opened out to absorb her and it wasn't until they had had their drinks and Tuggs had announced lunch that Litrik came looking for her.

They sat side by side with Lisa squeezed in between them. The little girl didn't say much; she ate her lunch carefully and, as Fran saw with some disquiet, with no appetite, but every now and then a small hand crept into hers and gave it a squeeze. Lisa at least was happy.

There was a general move into the gardens after they had had coffee, the grown ups strolling around, going from group to group, the children milling around happily, taking it in turns to sit with Lisa.

'Happy, darling?' asked Fran, sitting down beside her on the grass near to her chair. Lisa beamed at her. 'Happy,' she echoed. She had the mouse bride clutched under one arm and she was a little flushed. Fran sat quietly, for the child was tired; she took a small hand in hers and said, 'Go to sleep, darling,' and Lisa, understanding her, closed her eyes. Nanny, ever watchful, nodded and smiled at Fran, and wheeled the chair carefully into the house.

Litrik slid down on to the grass beside her. For such a large man he was remarkably light on his feet. If she had expected him to have made some soothing or encouraging remark, she was mistaken. All he said was, 'This isn't too good for Lisa, but she had set her heart on it, and she is happy. Do you like my family?'

'Very much.' If he could talk in that rather offhand way, so could she. 'They've all been very kind...'

He turned two suddenly cold eyes upon her. 'Naturally. You are to be my wife and I am the head of the family.'

She said tartly, 'Oh, I had hoped that they liked me for myself, not because I was marrying you.'

He smiled; the slow mocking smile she remembered so well from his lectures when some unfortunate nurse had given him a silly answer to his question.

'Do not allow such nonsense to cloud your common sense,

Francesca, but, if it will allay your fears, I assure you that, to a man, the family have taken you to their hearts.'

'I am glad to hear it. They must have been surprised; I don't think I'm at all what they expected...'

'What should they have expected?' he asked idly.

'Well, someone tall and willowy and fair, beautifully dressed and used to living in large houses.'

He said abruptly, 'They are two a penny, Francesca; you are unique.'

She wanted to ask him what he meant by that but his mother and the two aunts from Friesland bore down upon them and he whisked her to her feet and gave her a little push. 'Mother's dying to see your dress; you'd better satisfy her curiosity, my dear.'

She took the three ladies into the house and up to her bedroom and displayed her wedding gown and felt pleased at their admiration. 'You will be a pretty bride, my dear,' declared Mevrouw van Rijgen. 'You are so small and slender. You will not mind living in Holland?'

'Of course, she won't,' observed Tante Olda in a shocked voice. 'She will be happy wherever Litrik is. This is his home and now it will be hers.'

Mevrouw van Rijgen eased her feet out of her elegant pumps. 'Nevertheless, life will be different, I'm sure. Litrik has a great many friends and there will be entertaining. You will, I am sure, Francesca, be a delightful hostess and a splendid wife to Litrik—not the easiest of men,' she added with a twinkle. 'What is he like as a doctor? I have often wondered but how could I ask him?'

'He is a splendid doctor; the patients like him; they trust him, too, and that means a lot...'

'And the nurses, do they like him, too?'

Fran smiled. 'Oh, yes, but only from a distance, if you see what I mean; he is—well, he is a bit intimidating without knowing it.'

'He doesn't intimidate you?' queried Tante Nynke.

Fran shook her head. 'No, not in the least.'

'You are a calm girl,' stated her future mother-in-law, 'and an ideal wife for Litrik.' She got up and made her stately way in her stockinged feet to where Fran was sitting on the dressing-table stool. 'I am so very happy to have you for my third daughter, my dear.'

She kissed Fran's cheek and, for the second time that day, Fran wanted to cry. Here was someone she could learn to love, an ideal mother-in-law, and within a few months she would never see her again. Her pact with Litrik which had seemed so straightforward was getting out of hand.

They had tea scattered round the drawing room, with Lisa sitting on her father's knee. Probably the happiest person in the room, reflected Fran, listening politely to Great Uncle Timon booming the van Rijgen family history into her ear. She was rescued by Litrik.

'Time we paid our visit to Dominee Meertens,' he observed and whisked her out the room with the remark that they would be back in good time for dinner. Fran went to drop a kiss on Lisa's small cheek as they departed. *'Tot ziens,'* she whispered and Lisa giggled and answered with the 'bye, bye' Fran had taught her.

There were two cars at the door, the Daimler with Thor and Muff sitting patiently inside it, and a dark blue Bristol with Tugg's head inside its bonnet.

'Tugg's leaving in a few minutes to collect your aunts,' observed Litrik. 'He'll leave the car at Schiphol and fly over—there will be a car waiting for him at Heathrow. He'll drive down, spend the night at an inn and fetch your aunts in the morning. They'll be here by tea time tomorrow.'

They walked over to the Bristol and Tuggs withdrew his head to say, 'Just off, sir. Nel's got everything in hand. I should be back with the ladies by four or five o'clock tomorrow.'

'Good. Get a decent night's sleep, Tuggs. Wim will be in to

clean the cars and do any odd chores so take a couple of hours off when you get back here. Nel's got enough help in the kitchen and house?'

'Ample, sir. Never had so many willing helpers—there's nothing like a wedding...'

He beamed at them both and Litrik opened the Daimler's doors, urged Fran into the front seat, whistled to the dogs in the back and drove to the village.

The *dominee*'s house was by the church, an austere red brick edifice with square windows, a neat front garden and a half-open door. The *dominee* appeared at the door as they got out and as they reached it they heard a subdued confusion of sounds; someone was doing five finger exercises on a piano, children's voices were raised in fierce argument, a dog was barking, and someone, somewhere, was singing with more noise than talent. The *dominee,* probably inured to such domestic sounds, took no notice of them but merely raised his voice a little.

'Come in, Litrik.' He shook hands and turned to Fran. 'And this is Francesca.' He wrung her hand. 'Just as you described, too. The study will be the best place for our talk. My wife will bring coffee and then we can talk.'

His English was fluent but heavily accented and he had a booming voice which Fran considered might be of great advantage in church.

His study was a dark room, full of books, a massive desk taking up one corner. He waved them to chairs and when his wife came in with the coffee tray introduced her to Fran. She was a tall young woman with ash blonde hair and blue eyes. She shook hands with Fran, kissed Litrik and said in awkward English, 'Later when the wedding is over, we must become friends.'

'I'd like that,' said Fran, taking an instant liking to her. She saw her go with regret; the *dominee* was a bit overpowering and Litrik... She wished she knew him better.

She poured the coffee when she was asked to and sat drinking it while the two men discussed some knotty problem concerning the village hall. But presently they put their cups down and the *dominee* leaned back in his chair and addressed her.

'Litrik has told you that I am aware of your reasons for marrying. We discussed it at some length when he first decided to ask you to be his wife. His reasons, unusual though they are, are sound and compassionate and I have no doubt that you agreed to marry him for those reasons. You must dispel any doubts you may have, Francesca; you are hurting no one; you are bringing a great deal of happiness to Lisa for the last few months of her life. The fact that there is no emotional tie between the two of you ensures its success. You are, as it were, working together as you would to cure a ward full of patients, only in this case it is a small child.'

He had got up as he had been speaking and was pacing up and down the room. Now he stopped in front of her, frowning fiercely. 'Have I made myself clear? Your marriage will be as sincere as any other which I have performed; that it is undertaken for the reasons of which I have spoken is a secret between the three of us.'

Fran felt a bit overpowered; this, she felt, was only half-strength; she wondered what one of his sermons would be like when he could employ the full thunder of his voice. Yet she liked him; he was sincere and, she felt sure, fearless, and there was no denying that he had dispelled any doubts that might have been lurking. She looked at Litrik and saw that he was watching her intently.

'I don't think that I had any doubts, but I've not really had the time to think about that. I'm grateful and relieved that you agree with what we are doing and that we'll have your support. There is just one thing…' She cast the doctor an apologetic look. 'When we—when we no longer need to be married, will it be possible to annul our marriage quickly and quietly? Litrik has already told me that it shouldn't be a problem but I was thinking about his family.' She turned her shoulder to Litrik so that she couldn't see his face. 'They have been more than kind to me and accepted me...' She added fiercely, 'I'm not being saintly or anything like that, but I don't want them hurt or Litrik's career ruined.'

Litrik was staring at the back of her head from under lowered lids. 'What about your own career?'

'You said you'd see that I got a job,' she mumbled over her shoulder.

'So I did. I know that Dominee Meertens will reassure you about the annulment, just as I can reassure you that my career won't suffer in the least and we shall do the best we can, the pair of us, not to upset the family.' His voice was suddenly harsh. 'Marriages go on the rocks, you know. What has happened once can easily happen for a second time. Only we shall I hope part without rancour.'

'Remember Lisa,' said the *dominee* suddenly. 'Nothing is quite as important as her happiness.'

'No—no, of course not.' Fran studied the *dominee*'s face; he was a fierce man but a very good one. She smiled at him. 'While we are here, could you tell me if the service is very different to ours; my cousin who is married to a Dutchman wrote and described it to me, but it was all a bit vague.'

He beamed back at her. 'Ah, of course. This calls for more coffee and Siska.' He opened the door and raised his voice above the various noises coming from round the house, and when his wife appeared gave her the coffee tray. She was back within minutes and sat down by Fran and poured out and presently she and the *dominee* described the service between them.

'You know about the civil ceremony first?' asked the *dominee*.

'Oh, yes. Litrik explained.'

'Good. So you see that the ceremony is simple and short. The difference is that he will come with you to the church. You have bridesmaids?'

'No—you see Lisa can't be one...'

He nodded. 'Of course. It will be a happy occasion for her and for all of us.'

She and Litrik got up to go presently. They had nothing to say until he stopped the car in front of his own door but then Fran, unable to contain herself any longer, asked, 'Why didn't you say something? Why did you just sit there? You let Dominee Meertens do all the talking...'

'My dear Francesca, I had already stated my case. What was needed was a third party to give an unbiased opinion.'

'And just supposing he had opposed the whole thing? He might have changed his mind...'

'Which answers your question.' He got out and opened her door and took her arm as they went up the steps. Just in case someone was watching from the house, Fran thought peevishly.

They went together to say good night to Lisa and as they went down the staircase Fran paused halfway. 'Will everyone be dressed up?' she wanted to know.

'I imagine so. Eve of the wedding isn't it, more or less? Tomorrow there will be another dinner party but this evening is rather special—your welcome into the family.' He added kindly, 'Worried about what you will wear?'

'Well yes. I've only some summer dresses with me and some things I bought for later on. There is a skirt and top though...I don't want to let you down.'

'You would never do that. Supposing I got Wilma or Jebbeke to come along to your room presently?'

'Oh, thanks—they could tell me if I had the right things.'

The top and skirt were pronounced just the thing and indeed, surveying her person in the long wall mirror, she had to admit that they did something for her. Litrik, coming across the room to meet her when she got downstairs, bent to kiss her cheek and murmured, 'Charming, my dear. Did you show yourself to Lisa?'

She nodded, smiling shyly, feeling relief.

The evening was a thumping success; dinner, elaborate and beautifully served, took up the greater part of the evening and afterwards the younger members of the party rolled back the silken rugs in the drawing room and danced.

Fran, who loved dancing and did it well, took to the floor with Litrik and presently everyone was dancing.

Her sleepy head on the pillow, she reflected with surprise that she was happier than she had ever been in her life; she wasn't sure how that was possible when she remembered Lisa, excepting that the little girl was happy, too. She smiled at the memory of the child's excited little face and the small delicate hand tucked into hers. Fran closed her eyes, her last thought of Litrik's light kiss brushing her cheek as they had said good night. Most of the family had been there watching, which was why he had kissed her; all the same it had been nice.

The lovely weather held. Litrik was called away to an emergency at the hospital during the morning and Fran took Lisa for a walk in her chair while the older ladies went to supervise the flower arrangements in the church. Litrik was back for lunch and they all scattered into the grounds of the house afterwards to sit about and gossip. But as they left the table Litrik had taken her arm, saying, 'You haven't seen the house yet, have you? We'll go round now.'

It had taken most of the afternoon; the drawing room, the dining room, a dear little parlour at the back of the house, Litrik's study, a billiard room and several small rooms used for mending and sewing and doing the flowers. Upstairs there were seemingly endless bedrooms, all of them beautifully furnished with bathrooms cunningly fitted into corners and most of them with balconies. There was a floor above, too. 'The nurseries,' explained Litrik in a disinterested voice, 'and more guest rooms. There is another floor above this one. Tuggs and his wife live there, and the maids.'

Fran, following him obediently from room to room, could think of nothing to say.

The aunts arrived at tea time and she bore them away to their rooms to tidy themselves and listen to their account of the journey. A most rewarding experience, they told her, they had been taken the greatest care of by Tuggs. The car had been comfortable and, since no mishap had occurred during their flight to Schiphol, they were willing to concede that flying was a pleasant mode of travel.

She led them down to the drawing room for tea and was relieved when Litrik took charge, introducing them to each member of the family and settling them finally with the two aunts from Friesland and his mother.

Dinner that evening was as elaborate as on the previous evening but there was no dancing afterwards. The civil ceremony was at ten o'clock on the following morning and everyone would have to be up reasonably early.

The party broke up soon after eleven o'clock and Fran, having escorted her aunts to their rooms and wished them good night, went soft footed to take a last look at Lisa. The child was asleep and there was no denying the fact that her small face looked pinched and white. Fran went to her room, undressed and got into bed. At least, she reminded herself, Lisa was going to be happy for a few months.

She woke early in another glorious morning, too lovely to stay in bed. She nipped to the window and pulled back the curtains and opened the door on to the balcony. It was quiet except for the birds; she leaned her elbows on the railing and took stock of the garden below and then became aware that Litrik was standing under the copper beech beyond the lawn. He had the dogs with him and was wearing slacks and an open-necked shirt.

'Come on down,' he urged her. 'We can have a few minutes' peace and quiet before we're engulfed.'

Fran tossed her mane of mousy hair over her shoulders, suddenly aware of wearing nothing but her nightie. 'All right, I'll be five minutes.'

Slacks and a top would do; she thrust her feet into sandals, washed her face and tied back her hair and trod quietly through the sleeping house.

He was waiting by the open front door, the dogs pacing to and fro, anxious not to miss their walk.

Litrik said without preamble. 'This is your last chance, Francesca. You're still willing to go through with it?'

She fell into step beside him, the dogs bustling around the pair of them. She had never been so sure of anything in her whole life before, although she didn't quite know why.

'I'm quite sure,' she told him in a steady voice. 'I went to look at Lisa last night before I went to bed—she looked so pale and ill. I'll not let her look like that...'

He tucked her hand under his arm. 'I beg your pardon for asking you that, Francesca. You are not one to back out of a promise, are you? Between us both we'll keep her happy.'

They turned back towards the house and saw Tuggs coming towards them.

'There's your early morning tea,' he told them and then, accusingly, 'you didn't ought to be seeing each other before you are wed.' He sounded severe. 'Unlucky, some say.' He added hastily, 'Not that you'll be unlucky, sir and miss.'

Litrik laughed and clapped him on the shoulders. 'Indeed we won't, Tuggs. Let's have some of that tea, shall we? Is everything going well?'

'Bless you, yes, sir. Nel's got everyone organised.'

He left them to drink their tea then and presently Fran said in a matter-of-fact voice, 'Well, I'll see you later,' and sped away to take a bath and have a good breakfast in her room as time-honoured custom dictated.

CHAPTER FIVE

LISA came to watch her dress and various cousins and aunts and Litrik's mother paid admiring visits. 'Delightful,' pronounced Mevrouw van Rijgen. 'That is the prettiest dress—how proud Litrik must be, my dear.'

Fran murmured a nothing; she thought it very unlikely that he was even interested enough to notice what she was wearing, although presently, when everyone had left for the *raadhuis* and she went downstairs to the hall where Litrik was waiting for her, she felt a thrill of pleasure at his look of surprised admiration. He handed her her bouquet and they went together to where the Daimler, its windows wreathed with flowers, stood waiting with Tuggs, spruce and sporting a buttonhole.

'Now there's a sight for sore eyes,' he told them happily. 'I never saw a handsomer pair.'

Fran smiled at him. No one could call her handsome, although Litrik in morning suit and top hat fitted that description. Indeed, he looked to be every girl's dream of a husband; it seemed most unfair that he was, so to speak, to be wasted on her. But only for a few months, she reminded herself soberly.

There was a small crowd outside the *raadhuis* and the wedding chamber inside was packed. She saw Lisa, right in front with Nanny, and Dr and Mrs Beecham and her aunts and Litrik's parents; the rest was a blur of faces. The ceremony was short and when the ring was put on her finger she didn't feel in the least married. She signed her name obediently, received her marriage book and left the *raadhuis* on Litrik's arm, to get back into the car and be driven the short distance to the church.

Dominee Meertens was waiting for them there and this time things made sense; now she felt well and truly married. She glanced up at Litrik's face as they turned to go down the aisle and found him smiling; he would be happy now, she thought, because Lisa would be happy, too. The smile was really for her but that was to be expected. She must remember what Dominee Meertens had said: they were working together for the child's happiness.

They went down the aisle followed by the family and a great many people she supposed were friends of Litrik's. Almost at the door she saw Clare and Karel smiling and waving and she smiled back; they would be at the reception presently and she would be able to talk to them, perhaps invite them over for a day... There were more people outside the church now, as well as photographers and guests showering them with confetti and rose petals. Fran smiled and smiled and got into the car at last with Litrik beside her, her bouquet clutched in one hand, the other, with the gold wedding ring, on her silken lap.

She sought in vain for something to say; what did newly wed people say to each other? Or perhaps they just held hands, too happy to speak... It was a relief when Litrik said lightly, 'Well you should feel well and truly married, my dear, twice over.'

'Yes, well actually, I didn't feel awfully married at the civil ceremony. But I liked the church service. How pretty Lisa looked in that pink dress.'

It was easier after that; they talked about the reception and the number of guests who would be coming and the unfortunate manner in which Great Uncle Timon had blown his nose so violently during the prayers. By the time they reached the house, Fran had recovered almost all of her normal calm and when the first of the family arrived, she was standing in the drawing room by the open doors leading to the gardens, with Litrik beside her, looking composed and almost pretty in her wedding finery.

For the next few hours she lived in a kind of mosaic of voices and laughter, eye-catching hats, champagne and a seemingly never ending stream of people offering congratulations. Clare, radiant in yards of flowered chiffon, kissed her warmly.

'Darling, you look lovely. What a day—gosh, you must be over the moon!' She glanced around her. 'This gorgeous house, and I've never seen so much heavenly food. Is he very rich?'

Fran glanced at Litrik's broad back turned a little away from them while he talked to Dr Beecham. 'I expect so.' A reply which puzzled her cousin.

The aunts, determinedly British amongst so many foreigners, nonetheless assured her that they were reassured by the undoubted respectability of Litrik's family and friends, and confessed that they were enjoying themselves. 'It is a pity that our stay is to be so short,' commented Aunt Kate, 'but we do realise that Litrik is a busy man. We hope that you will pay us a visit before very long.'

Aunt Janet sighed. 'It is a pity about the little girl. She has a splendid Nanny, I am told.'

'Yes everyone loves her and she is always happy…'

'She seems to like you,' Aunt Kate sounded doubtful.

'We are both fond of each other. She is my little daughter now…'

Litrik had turned back to her; she felt his hand tighten on her arm, and when she looked at him he was smiling. 'Our Lisa is very precious to us isn't she, my dear?'

Aunt Kate, who prided herself on plain speaking, observed sharply, 'Such a pity that she is an invalid. Will she get better?'

Fran didn't wait for Litrik; she said impulsively, 'Of course she will. She has the very best of treatment.'

'Naturally,' declared Aunt Kate drily, 'with an eminent physician for her father.'

Only Litrik's hand on her arm stopped Fran from speaking her mind at that. He said smoothly, 'I am sure you would like to see round the gardens.' He had caught the eye of a youngish cousin, who made his way towards them. 'Lucas, Francesca's aunts haven't seen the rose garden. Would you like to take them there?'

It was Aunt Polly, who hadn't spoken at all, who lingered behind for a moment to whisper, 'I'm sorry, my dears,' before hurrying away to catch up.

They were surrounded by guests at once. There was no chance to say anything and after that there were the toasts, and since Fran was English a wedding cake to cut, and then more guests.

But presently, after the tea and cakes brought round by the waiters, everyone but the family took their leave. Mevrouw van Rijgen took off her hat and her shoes and settled on one of the sofas, the older ladies sank thankfully into comfortable chairs, the men went off to the billiard room and the young ones went out into the garden. There was to be a family dinner party and directly after that everyone would leave. Fran found it strange but when she mentioned it to Litrik he said blandly, 'But my dear, of course we are to be left alone; your aunts are to stay with my mother and father, Tuggs will go over and drive them home tomorrow.'

He took her arm. 'Let's go for a stroll and take Lisa with us?'

'Like this?' she said, looking down at her satin-clad person.

'Why not? You have to wear your wedding gown until the last guest has gone.'

'Oh, do I? Then let's go into the gardens—Lisa is looking

tired, bless her! perhaps we could sit somewhere quiet for a while and she might doze.'

They sat under the mulberry tree, the three of them, not talking, and no one bothered them until it was time for Lisa to go to bed. Fran wheeled her round while she said good night to everyone and then handed her over to Nanny and said, 'Yes, I will come and say good night,' to the girl, knowing that she understood that.

'Papa?' asked Lisa.

'And Papa.'

They went upstairs together presently, she and Litrik, and sat on the small bed talking quietly about the wedding until the child's eyes closed.

Outside in the corridor, Fran said, 'I'll go and tidy myself ready for dinner.'

He gave her a casual glance. 'You look all right,' he told her and her bosom swelled with indignation. Brides didn't look all right, they looked lovely or charming or even beautiful. She turned away to cross the gallery above the stairs but he stopped her. 'Just a minute. Lisa expects to have her morning tea with us—I'll tell Nel to see that it's taken to your room and—I'll join you there.' He grinned, looking years younger. 'If you remember in the picture book of hers, Mama and Papa Mouse take tea together with rows of small mice tucked in between them.'

She was still smarting from his casual acceptance of her appearance. She said haughtily, 'I have already told you that I will help you in any way to make Lisa happy.' She opened her door and whisked through it before she would let him see the tears in her eyes. The day had been a happy one until now, she had actually felt married to Litrik, sure that they would be able to live together as friends, even enjoy each other's company, but now she wasn't so sure. She was just a means to an end, to keep Lisa happy for a few months; he didn't think of her as a person at all; he was a cold-hearted, autocratic, hateful man, and he hadn't changed one iota from the sarcastic egotistical lecturer of her student days.

She did her face and rearranged her veil and then went on to the balcony. The August day was fading into a soft glow and the gardens were quiet now. She would have liked to have stayed there but they might think it strange if she didn't join them. She went down to the drawing room and Litrik crossed the room and took her hand. 'Here you are, my dear. A champagne cocktail before we go in to dinner?' And he stayed with her, going from group to group, suave and charming. He should have been an actor, reflected Fran, whose drink had gone straight to her head.

Dinner, served a little earlier than usual so that everyone could get home that night, was magnificent: oysters, smoked salmon, devilled crab or creamed kipper fillets, followed by fillets of sole bonne femme and then crown roast of lamb or wild duck with black cherry sauce and finally trifle and a pavlova cake with a pear and raspberry filling. Fran, who had eaten only a couple of the tempting morsels served at the reception, enjoyed every mouthful, the whole having been helped along nicely by the champagne. It was a merry meal with a great deal of talk and laughter, but at the end of it, when everyone had gone back to the drawing room for coffee, the goodbyes were begun. Litrik's parents were the first to leave, followed by the rest of the family. Some of them were driving back to Friesland and as the last of them disappeared down the drive Fran asked, 'Did they have to go? Surely they could have stayed the night and gone in the morning?'

Litrik had turned to her with the faintly mocking smile she disliked so much. 'My dear girl—on our wedding night? An unheard of thing!'

She had blushed and walked away from him, back into the drawing room, suddenly feeling lonely. Even the aunts would have been company but they had kissed her good night and wished her well with a faint air of self-pity; they would miss her, they said, and Litrik, overhearing Aunt Polly's comment that they would have to manage as best they could now, allowed himself a smile.

He had followed her into the drawing room. 'Breakfast at the usual time?' he asked her. 'With Lisa, of course. I've a full day's work tomorrow but I should be home by tea time. I'm sure you and Lisa will find plenty to do.'

She turned to face him. 'Oh, yes, we've so many plans... It was a very nice day.' She paused, it seemed rather a lukewarm way of describing one's wedding day but he, at least, hadn't even called it that. She would have to go to bed content with the fact that she had looked all right.

She said abruptly. 'Good night, Litrik,' and turned and flew up the stairs and into her splendid bedroom, where she undressed very fast and then spent far too long in a hot bath, having a good cry. He could have said something nice even if it wasn't true. After all it had been her wedding day. His family and friends had been sweet and admired her dress and said how pretty she had looked. She hadn't quite believed them but it had been nice to hear, all the same. She got into bed at last with a headache from too much champagne and crying, and then got out again to creep along the corridor to take a look at Lisa. There was a night light by her bed and she looked small and frail by its dim light. Fran turned and went back to her room, pausing to look over the gallery to the hall below. The house was quiet, although there were lights below. As she stood there she saw the study door open and Litrik came out and close the door behind him. She bolted back into her own room then and leapt into bed and turned out the lamps, which when she thought about it was silly and quite unnecessary.

She slept, although she hadn't thought she would, to be wakened by Nel with her early morning tea and a minute later a tap on the door and Nanny carrying Lisa, pink cheeked and eyes sparkling.

Nanny, settling her carefully beside Fran, said softly, 'Good morning, Mevrouw. There is fever this morning, will you tell the doctor?'

Fran nodded, 'Yes, of course, Nanny. He'll want to see you?'

'I think yes, Mevrouw.' Nanny slipped away and Fran lent an ear to Lisa's happy chatter, understanding most of it. When there was a knock on the door and Litrik came in in his dressing-gown she stared at him open-mouthed and then remembered that he was to have his tea each morning *en famille* because that was what Lisa expected. His good morning was cheerful and he bent to brush her cheek before sitting down on the bed beside his daughter, embarking on a long conversation with her while Fran poured the tea, but presently he asked in English, 'You slept well?'

'Yes, thank you.' She wondered why he looked at her so intently, unaware that her nose was pink as were her eyelids from crying. She handed him a biscuit and after a moment offered him more tea.

'I must say this is a pleasant way in which to begin the day. Very domestic.'

'Yes. Nanny wants to see you before you go.'

He nodded calmly. 'Yes, I can see why. A quiet day if you can manage it, Francesca. There are several pleasant walks round here if you feel like it. If you can manage the chair down to the lake you could sit there—she loves that and she may sleep.'

'I'll do that. It'll give Nanny some time to herself, too.'

He put down his cup, ruffled Lisa's hair and kissed her gently and got up. 'I'll leave you to dress, both of you, though you look very nice as you are.' He smiled slowly at her look. 'And I mustn't forget this, must I?' He bent and kissed her again, this time without haste, and Lisa laughed and clapped her hands and gabbled something to her father.

'We are agreed, Lisa and I,' he told Fran, 'that you are a perfect mama.'

'That is at least something,' said Fran tartly, and, at his sudden cold stare, instantly regretted the remark.

Despite her outward serenity, she had been nervous about her new life, but she need not have been. Nanny and Nel and Tuggs nudged her carefully through the day, always appearing just when she was in doubt about something, gently suggested coffee, a walk in the grounds with Lisa, lunch with the little girl and Nanny on the shady veranda at the back of the house, and perhaps a swim in the pool, tucked away in a corner of the gardens, while the little girl had her afternoon nap.

When Lisa awoke, she took the little girl down to the lake on the other side of the lane running past the house. By the time Litrik got home she was feeling her feet sufficiently to greet him in what she hoped was a properly wifely fashion under Lisa's sharp eyes. The three of them played cards until Lisa was borne off to bed and Litrik went to his study, saying that they would see each other at dinner. Which left Fran free to go to her room and put on one of her new dresses.

She was agreeably surprised how pleasant the evening was. True, as soon as dinner was over, Litrik excused himself once more, but they had talked easily enough over the meal and he had observed that they might expect a good many friends to call within the next few weeks and, as well as that, dinner invitations. 'And I shall be free on Saturday—we might take Lisa to the sea for the day; this weather can't last much longer and it may be our last chance.'

They had had their coffee at the table and presently Fran said, 'Well, don't let me keep you from your work,' and got to her feet, followed with unflattering briskness by Litrik. 'I'm quite tired,' she told him mendaciously, and, since Tuggs was in the room, 'don't be late, will you?'

'I'll be as quick as I can, darling.' Uttered in just the right kind of voice. She blushed and Tuggs looked sentimental.

It was too early to go to bed; she went through the hall and into the drawing room. There was a grand piano at one end with a wall sconce shining invitingly on to its keyboard. The room was only dimly lighted but there was a log fire burning in the great hearth. Fran closed the door after her, went to the piano and sat down before it. She was by no means a brilliant pianist but she had talent and feeling. Perhaps if she played for a little while she might be able to throw off the vague feeling of disquiet… Half an hour of Delius, Chopin, Debussy and as much as she could remember of the score of *Cats* soothed her, uplifting her spirits sufficiently for her to embark on *Me and My Girl* when something made her pause and look round. At the other end of the room, sitting in the great wing chair by the fire, was Litrik, stretched out comfortably in the fire's warmth.

'Don't stop,' he begged her, but she got up, closed the piano and stood very straight beside it. 'If I disturbed you, I'm sorry,' she began.

'Not in the least, you play delightfully. Did you know that Lisa loves music? You must play for her some time.'

He got up from his chair and walked towards her. 'You did not find the day too difficult?'

'No, everyone has been so kind, I—I felt quite at home.'

'Good. One day soon we must go to Utrecht and you can buy some clothes.'

'There's no need.' The idea of spending his money bothered her.

'You are mistaken. We shall be invited out; I have a number of friends who will ask us to dine and later we must give a dinner party ourselves. For these you must be suitably dressed. I am a wealthy man and well known.'

She thought of her carefully chosen wardrobe which had seemed so right when she had bought it. Evidently it hadn't been suitable at all; he might even be ashamed of her. She swallowed mounting rage.

She said in a high voice, 'Ah—fringe benefits, how delightful. May I spend as much as I like?'

'Within reason...'

'Well, since I have no idea of your income, nor do I wish to know, that's going to be difficult, isn't it?' Her eyes glittered with temper. 'But don't worry, I'll do you proud—I've always wanted to wear *haute couture*.'

She went past him towards the door. 'You can always mortgage the house,' she told him flippantly as she closed the door behind her.

She didn't hear his low laugh; she was shaking with rage as she went up to her bed. Presently, sitting up in bed, she made a list on the back of an envelope. It was a long list; every single garment she could think of was on it and even roughly priced. The total cost ran into four figures. She cast paper and pen from her and turned out the light. She had married him to make Lisa's short life happy and for no other reason. He had said nothing about dinner parties and social occasions; well, if he wanted a dressed-up puppet he should have one. Pure silk, she reflected sleepily, cashmere, Gucci shoes and handbags and wildly expensive leather belts, she would have them all.

He played his part very nicely in the morning, joking with Lisa while they had their tea and Fran, because she had a promise to keep, was everything that Lisa expected of her. They spent another leisurely day, culminating in Litrik's return, tea on the veranda and a boisterous game of Ludo. In the evening, as the two of them sat down to dinner, he had an urgent call to go to the hospital in Utrecht, so that Fran ate alone and, since he didn't return, went to bed.

The days were falling into a pattern. It seemed that, for the time being at least, no one expected her to take over the housekeeping, something she hadn't wanted to do anyway. She was kept busy enough with Lisa, arranging the flowers, talking with Litrik's family on the telephone and, when there was a spare half hour, inspecting the cupboards Nel opened for her to look through. But as Tuggs was careful to explain, Lisa came first, the running of the house could come later.

The fine weather held; with an excited little girl cocooned on the back seat, they set out for Noordwijk-aan-zee with the dogs and a picnic hamper and somehow, once they were there, with Litrik pushing the chair along the water's edge and Fran strolling along picking up shells and seaweed for Lisa to see, she dropped her guard, laughing and talking with a surprisingly friendly Litrik, a happy state of affairs which lasted all day. It wasn't until Lisa was safely tucked up in bed and they were sitting over their drinks before dinner that Litrik leaned across and tossed a cheque book into her lap.

'Lisa is due for a check up next week—on Monday morning. I suggest that you come in with us and go shopping while she is at the hospital.'

She stared down at the cheque book. 'Perhaps Lisa would like to come with me…'

'Far too tiring. Buy all you want and bring it home to show her.'

'All I want? You mean that, Litrik?'

'Did I not say so? Indulge yourself, Francesca. Presumably you like clothes as much as any other woman?'

She thought of her carefully made out list. 'Indeed I do. It will probably need more than one morning to buy all the things that I should like.'

'You can drive. There is a Mini in the garage—you can leave Lisa with Nanny.'

She said serenely. 'Thank you, I'll do that. And may I take Lisa for short drives around the country?'

'Why not?' He sounded faintly bored. 'The roads are quiet and you say you can drive.'

Tuggs came to tell them that dinner was ready and Fran was careful to keep their talk on safe grounds. The pleasant *bonhomie* they had enjoyed on the beach had gone; she supposed that it was all part and parcel of keeping Lisa happy—when she wasn't with them there was no need to pretend. Litrik was a reserved man and Tuggs and Nel wouldn't expect him to be otherwise, even though he was so recently married. She agreed pleasantly with him about the pleasure of their day; agreed, too, that they should accept the several invitations which they had received to dine with his friends. She accompanied him to the drawing room and poured their coffee, smilingly agreed, for Tuggs's benefit, that it was a pity that he had a lecture to prepare for his next teaching round, and picked up the knitting she had so fortunately packed, a soothing occupation, sorely needed. Her serene exterior masked a smouldering rage; Litrik had tossed the cheque book at her with the casual air of a man throwing his dog a biscuit. It had taken all her self-control not to throw it back at him, and now she was glad that she hadn't. She would go shopping and she would make sure that he wouldn't forget it in a hurry. Fran, usually so mild-tempered and kind, seethed with temper.

The knitting wasn't helping much. She went to the piano and lifted the lid and then went back to the big double door and made sure that it was closed before settling down on the piano stool. Litrik's study was on the other side of the hall and the house was large; if she kept her foot on the soft pedal, he wouldn't hear a note. She played Mendelssohn, Debussy and Grieg and at length closed the piano. She was crossing the room to pick up her knitting when a faint sound made her turn her head. Litrik was sitting in one of the big winged chairs in the bay window.

'Delightful,' he observed, 'but why the soft pedal?'

'How did you get in here?'

'Er—there is a small door from the back of the hall. I didn't want to disturb you. Even with the soft pedal down, it was obvious to me that you were taking your feelings out on the piano.'

Words—whole sentences of a vitriolic nature—were on her

tongue. She swallowed the lot, wished him an icy good night and went out of the room.

Since the next day was Sunday, they went to church, sitting in the family pew under the pulpit with Lisa in her chair between them. Fran, listening with half an ear to Dominee Meertens thundering what sounded like warnings of eternal damnation, allowed her thoughts to wander. Nothing could have been pleasanter than Litrik's manner that morning and she perforce, with Lisa's eyes upon them both, had to match his manner with her own. The strain of being a supposedly loving wife was beginning to tell on her. Being a mother to Lisa wasn't hard at all; the child responded to love like a flower to sunshine and Fran had not found it hard to love her. So unlike her father: no feelings at all, rude, arrogant and too much money for his own good. He needed taking down a peg; she would enjoy doing that. She frowned; she had entered into her pact with Litrik meaning to do all she could to help him make Lisa happy, but somehow it wasn't turning out like that at all. She was allowing her personal feelings to take over and it was Lisa who mattered. She glanced down at the little face beside hers and smiled and tucked a small hand in hers, promising herself silently that she would keep a guard on her tongue and try harder to like Litrik. She would, she reflected, like him very much if only he were different. She was prevented from pursuing this line of thought by Dominee Meerten's rolling periods coming to a stop and everyone getting to their feet for prayers.

Presently they made their way down the aisle to shake the *dominee*'s hand and then chat with acquaintances of Litrik. It was a splendid opportunity for Fran to air her sparse Dutch, which she did reluctantly but with an unconscious charm which earned her a good deal of praise, even if it was unmerited. What with that and her good resolutions during the sermon, the day proved to be pleasant enough. Litrik laid himself out to be an amusing companion and Lisa was at her happiest; it wasn't hard for Fran to play her part.

Indeed the day had gone so well that before she went to sleep she had almost decided to tear up her shopping list and make out another one of three or four basic outfits, reasonably priced. It was unfortunate that when she went down to breakfast, dressed for the day in one of the jersey outfits, Litrik should look up from his letters to remark, 'Ah, Mama Mouse, shortly to be turned into a swan, if I may mix my metaphors.' His cool gaze took in her unassuming appearance. 'And very much the mouse.'

Tuggs wasn't in the room and Lisa for some reason hadn't yet joined them. Fran sat down and poured herself some coffee with a hand which shook slightly and helped herself to a croissant.

'What—-nothing to say?' His voice was silky; he was needling her.

She buttered her croissant and took some black cherry jam. She had no idea why he was being so nasty but she didn't intend to let him see how much it could upset her. Mentally she added a few items unnecessary and expensive, to her shopping list. She had her rage nicely under control by now; she said serenely, 'I expect you've had a bad night, you'll feel better when you've had your breakfast. Sleeplessness always makes one scratchy...'

She gave him a clear look and a kindly smile as she spoke and was rewarded by his look of affront. And then disconcerted by his bellow of laughter. Nanny came in then with Lisa who wanted to know why he was laughing and he became gentle at once, giving her some joking explanation which made her laugh, too.

At the end of the meal Litrik said, 'You'll come to the hospital with us, Francesca; you can say goodbye to Lisa there—the shops are close by. The car will be in the hospital forecourt but if you want to leave parcels let the porter have them. We shan't be ready until noon at the earliest.'

She agreed calmly and with a smile, careful to preserve her image for Lisa's benefit, and the two of them went off to get ready for their trip to Utrecht, happily engrossed in the peculiar mixture of English and Dutch which they had made their own.

The hospital was vast and impressive; Fran would have liked to have seen more of it, but once they were inside Litrik had suggested, in the pleasant voice he used when Lisa was with them, that she should say goodbye for the present. So she said, *'Tot ziens,'* in a cheerful voice, hugged the little girl, smiled at Litrik and took herself off. It was barely nine o'clock. She had three hours and some of that time must be taken up with spying out the land. She nipped smartly into the centre of the city, only a few minutes' walk from the hospital, and did a rapid survey of the shops. There were plenty to choose from and at the end of half an hour she had earmarked the boutiques which had taken her fancy. By eleven o'clock she was able to heave a contented sigh and pause for coffee. Sitting at a pavement café outside a fashionable department store, she conned her list. She was, to date, the possessor of two of the new season's suits, one in a rich bronze tweed, the other in a soft blue wool, a beautifully cut and frightfully expensive winter coat, a couple of gaily patterned knitted outfits, a dark green suede skirt and waistcoat with silk—pure silk—blouses to wear with them, three after-six dresses in strikingly rich colours and several pairs of shoes, high-heeled and impractical; it seemed only sense to have bought a pair of soft leather boots as well. She found time to buy undies, too, and a quilted satin dressing-gown and matching slippers. It only remained to go then to the particular boutique she had earmarked and see if she could find suitable evening dresses. Never mind if she didn't have the chance to wear them; Litrik had told her to buy all she wanted: and she very much wanted the peach pink organza dress she had seen in the window.

She had less than an hour and she would have to collect several of the dress boxes she had arranged to pick up at the end of the morning. Much refreshed by the coffee she set off briskly.

The pink organza was even lovelier on than it was in the window. She hardly recognised herself when she tried it on for it fitted to perfection. Heaven send she would have an opportunity to wear it… The sales lady was middle-aged and clever and she spoke English.

'We have some charming dresses if Mevrouw would care to look at them?' She suggested, 'If Mevrouw leads a social life now is the time to choose a gown of the first fashion.'

'Something for dinner parties.' Fran already had her eye on a deep apricot crêpe dress with long sleeves and a pretty neckline. 'And I believe we have to go the *burgermeester*'s reception…'

'Mevrouw's husband is well known in Utrecht?'

'He is a doctor. Dr van Rijgen…'

The lady's eyes gleamed. 'Ah, yes, a distinguished man indeed. The wedding was reported in the paper recently. My felicitations, Mevrouw. And may I suggest the apricot crêpe and perhaps this Prussian blue silk with the pleated skirt—just the thing for a dinner party.'

Fran bought them all, paid their astronomical cost without batting an eyelid and, since she was assured that the dresses would be packed and sent immediately to the hospital, set off to collect the rest of her shopping.

She had to make two journeys and, slightly alarmed at the pile of dress boxes the porter obligingly stacked in his office, she waited. He had barely finished when she saw a nurse wheeling Lisa into the entrance hall and went to meet her.

Lisa hugged her as though she had been gone for days instead of hours, and Fran knelt down beside the chair and put her arms round the thin little body. 'You were a really good girl?' she asked, and repeated it in her fragmentary Dutch so that Lisa shrilled with giggles.

'You were missed,' said Litrik from behind her. 'Next time you must come, too.'

Fran got to her feet. 'I would have come this morning, but I wasn't asked.' She spoke lightly because probably the nurse could understand English and Lisa was watching them both.

'She's been a good girl she tells me.'

'Very good. We must think of a little treat for her. You have done your shopping?'

She looked so pleased with herself that he studied her face thoughtfully.

'Yes, thank you. My parcels are in the porter's lodge.'

The doctor watched everything being loaded into the car boot with an expressionless face. Fran, busy getting Lisa comfortable, glanced at him once and decided that he was furiously angry, but when he got into the car and turned to look at her she was surprised to see that he was smiling, his eyes gleaming with amusement.

'Paid in my own coin,' he murmured. 'For a mouse you pack a hefty punch, Francesca.'

And before she could reply he said something to Lisa which sent her off into peals of laughter. 'I can see that there will be no need to amuse Lisa for the rest of the day; she will want to see the lot and, from the look of things, that's going to take hours.'

Fran thought it prudent not to answer that but let Lisa chatter for the short drive back home. She had indeed paid him back in his own coin but strangely she didn't feel happy about it.

CHAPTER SIX

THEY had lunch as soon as they got in for Litrik had to go to his consulting rooms in the afternoon and then on to the hospital at Zeist.

The boxes and parcels had been borne upstairs and Fran, eyeing their number, went down to lunch feeling guilty. But Litrik made no mention of her morning, the talk was light-hearted while Fran coaxed the little girl, now very tired, to eat something, and presently when the meal was finished she said, 'I'll take her up to her bed—shall I keep her there for tea?'

'A very good idea. Why don't you take your shopping to the nursery when she wakes up and keep her amused while she rests? She can get up for her supper if she wants to; I'll leave that to you—I'll not be back until late this evening.'

Nanny was waiting; Fran told her what Litrik had advised and then went downstairs again. He was in the hall on the point of leaving.

'Before you go, how is she?'

He had his hand on the door and turned to look at her. 'Not good, I'm afraid.' His voice held no expression. 'We must make the best of September and October.'

'Litrik, I'm so very sorry.' Her heart was wrung with pity; without stopping to think she ran across the few yards between them and put her hand over his.

He didn't say anything but he looked down at her hand clasping his, his eyebrows lifted and she snatched away her hand as though his had been red hot. If he had slapped her face she couldn't have been more shocked.

He opened the door then and went out without a backward

glance, leaving her standing there, near to tears. When the sound of the car had died away she went into the drawing room and out into the garden through the doors at its end. The weather was still delightful but now there was a hint of early autumn in the air but her shiver had nothing to do with the cool wind. He was a monster, she told herself, and knew that that wasn't true. A monster couldn't love a child as he loved Lisa; go to such lengths to keep her happy. She went and sat under the mulberry tree until Tuggs came to find her. 'Mevrouw van Rijgen wishes to speak to you on the telephone, Mevrouw, if you would take the call in the drawing room?'

A dinner party, suggested Litrik's mother, quite an informal one, if they could manage the following Saturday evening. 'Just a few friends,' said Mevrouw van Rijgen kindly. 'I want to show you off, my dear!'

'It sounds delightful, but I'll have to ask Litrik. May I phone you back in the morning? He is not at home at present and I don't expect him back until later this evening.'

'Of course, my dear. How is Lisa?' And, when Fran hesitated, 'Things aren't so good, are they? I won't bother you with questions now. Ring me tomorrow, Francesca.'

Tuggs had put tea in the small sitting room, fussing gently around her, saying as he left her, 'We're all that upset to hear that Lisa isn't so well, Mevrouw. The doctor'll be cut to the heart and you, too—she loves you like you were her real mother.'

'Oh, Tuggs, I do hope so, but I've known her such a short time. You must all feel very bad about it. I—feel an interloper...'

He was quite shocked. 'Indeed no, Mevrouw. We're thankful that the doctor found you in time.'

'Thank you, Tuggs.' She remembered something. 'The doctor says that I may drive the Mini in the garage. I thought I'd take Lisa out sometimes—not far, but the country is so pretty and perhaps we can stop for tea or just to admire the view.'

'She'll like that. I'll see that the Mini is ready for you whenever you want it, Mevrouw.'

She smiled at his kind face. 'Thank you, Tuggs. You—all of you—have been so good to me.'

'A pleasure, Mevrouw. Will you be going to sit with Lisa this evening?'

'Yes. When I've had tea I'll spend the evening with her. The doctor will be back late this evening—you know that already?'

When he had gone she drank her tea and ate one or two of the little biscuits Nel had made and then presently went up to the nursery. Lisa was still sleeping but as Fran went in soft-footed, nodding to Nanny, knitting at the table, the little girl awoke.

'Tea,' she demanded, and to Fran, 'Mama stay.'

'Nanny, could you ask Nel to let us have a tray of tea? I've just had mine but Lisa might eat something if we have it together.'

And as Nanny got to her feet. 'I'm going to show the things I bought today to Lisa so we'll be all right until it's her bed time. Should we get her up for an hour or two do you think?'

'In her dressing-gown perhaps, Mevrouw. You will be all right?'

Fran nodded. 'Oh yes, Nanny. You go and have your tea in peace.'

Tea came and they shared the small meal together, and then Fran went to her room and fetched the pile of dress boxes.

She dressed in one outfit after the other with Lisa sitting in her chair clapping her hands and laughing with delight. The evening dresses were left until the last and by that time it was Lisa's time for supper and bed. Nanny, coming back, stopped in the doorway to exclaim, 'Mevrouw, what a beautiful dress—you look so pretty!'

Her warm admiration made Fran glow with pleasure; the pink was indeed beautiful and even in her over-critical eyes she looked less mousy in it. She said almost shyly, 'There's the *burgermeester*'s reception in a few weeks, would it do for that?'

The three of them spent a happy half hour examining everything and then Fran got out of the pink dress and into her sober jersey and, while Nanny saw to Lisa, took everything back to her room and hung each garment lovingly in the clothes closet. Tomorrow she would wear one of the knitted outfits, the saffron coloured skirt and patterned jerkin and one of those silk blouses. She sat down for a moment and took out her list. She had noted the prices of everything on it, now she added them up. The total made her gasp; even if Litrik were very rich, he would surely have something to say about the astronomical amount she had written down.

They played their part in the morning, with Lisa tucked up in Fran's bed with an affable Litrik sitting at its foot, drinking his tea. Fran scanned his face and marvelled that he was the same man as the coldly angry one of yesterday evening. Probably, she thought wryly, he'll look like that again when he sees how much I've spent.

She made an excuse to go down to breakfast before Lisa was dressed and found Litrik already there. He got up when she went into the room and she admired—for the hundredth time—his easy good manners.

She went straight to him and laid her neat list beside his plate.

'That's what I spent yesterday.' Try as she might her voice shook a little.

He waited until she was sitting down, pouring coffee with an unsteady hand, before he picked it up and read it. If she had expected anger or surprise she was to be disappointed. His face remained blandly calm and he showed no surprise. She said uncertainly, 'It's rather a lot of money...'

'I believe that I told you to buy what you wanted,' he observed, his voice as bland as his face. Without a trace of sarcasm he went on, 'Perhaps you didn't have sufficient time yesterday; if you need another few hours in Utrecht you can come in with me after lunch—I shall be home by noon—I'll be at my consulting rooms until four o'clock.'

She studied his face; it showed nothing but a disinterested politeness.

'I shan't need any more clothes for months,' she told him and saw the look of disbelief on his face. 'Besides, I've promised Lisa that we'll go for a short drive this afternoon—I'll be very careful.'

'Of course! We dine at Uncle Hilwert's on Friday, do we not? Not too many of us, I believe, and it won't be black ties.' He picked up the first of his letters. 'You'll forgive me if I read my post? There's not much chance once Lisa is here.'

So she drank some coffee and ate some toast, small and mouselike and unassuming despite the saffron skirt and the gaily coloured jerkin. For all the doctor cared, she might have been wearing an old sack; he hadn't even noticed... But Lisa did; she was examined, exclaimed over and admired by the little girl while Litrik smiled at her chatter and said nothing. Presently he got up to go, kissed his small daughter, and then paused by Fran's chair to brush her cheek lightly. 'I like the outfit—a great improvement,' he murmured.

He came home for lunch as he had promised but he had no time to linger over the meal. Nanny whisked Lisa away for her rest and Fran went in search of Tuggs to get a road map from him. The Veluwe would be too far, she had decided, but there was a good sweep of pleasantly wooded country and heath all around them. She pored over the country roads within a radius of twenty miles or so and planned their trip, avoiding the towns, criss-crossing the woods; the roads would be narrow but she was a good driver and there wouldn't be much traffic.

Under Tuggs's fatherly eye they set off presently, going eastwards from Ziest, taking a country road which would take her eventually in the direction of Doorn. She didn't intend to enter the small town, but by-pass it and drive on towards Maarn, turning north, making a rough circle. They had passed Maarn, gone under the motorway and taken a road between thick woods when they reached a crossroad. Fran had planned to go straight ahead, but Lisa had other ideas. The road to the left was nothing more than a narrow brick lane, overhung with trees, the signpost offering no more than four kilometres to Emminheide; not even marked on the map, when Fran looked for it. But nothing she could say would persuade Lisa to change her mind. She wanted to go to Emminheide and Fran gave in.

The road, being brick and rural, was uneven and only wide enough for one car. She drove slowly, since the road, unlike most Dutch roads, wound itself round a multitude of corners and the trees on either side prevented her from seeing any distance ahead. The woods on either side became, if anything, even thicker and she felt decided relief when they passed a small cottage, set back from the road. And presently they reached Emminheide: a cluster of small houses, a very large church and that was all. Fran drove on, wondering where the road led, for it must end somewhere, and after another half mile or so they saw another cottage, standing by itself in a small clearing; trees all around it, a well-tended little garden between it and the lane. There was an old woman in the garden and when she saw them she stopped picking the plums from a tree by the cottage and came down to the gate. Fran stopped and called good day and the old woman answered cheerfully.

'Tea?' asked Lisa.

There was no harm in asking. Fran drove the car carefully up to the gate and began a careful request for a drink for Lisa.

She added politely in her best Dutch, 'I will pay you, Mevrouw.'

The old woman came out of the gate and peered into the car, and she and Lisa carried out a brief conversation, at the end of which she turned to Fran. She spoke slowly now—Lisa must have told her that Fran's Dutch was fragmentary. Of course they could have tea. If Mevrouw would like to carry the poor little girl into the cottage they might sit in comfort and when they were rested, before they returned, they might like to see the lake behind the cottage. So beautiful, added the old woman, and very few people know of it.

There was plenty of time; Fran carried Lisa into the cottage and sat her down in the tiny parlour, seldom used except for important occasions such as weddings or funerals or family visits. It was overfull of tables and chairs and the walls were hung with old-fashioned pictures and photos, but there were some pieces of beautiful old china and a little cabinet housed silver spoons and dishes. They sat at the round table in the centre of the room and drank their tea and ate wafer thin biscuits, and when they had finished, Fran paid their modest bill and asked if they might see the lake. 'If it's not too far—I have to carry the little girl.'

The old woman nodded and smiled and led the way to the side of the garden and pointed to a path through the trees. Fran couldn't understand what she was saying but Lisa did and the child nodded and said, 'Two minutes, Mama.'

'You are learning English far quicker than I am learning Dutch,' said Fran, and laughed and at the same time sighed inwardly for Lisa's light weight seemed even lighter each time she picked her up.

The path was easy and well defined, leading through closely planted trees with no hint of what was to come. It ended abruptly at the edge of a fairytale pond, not large, but ringed with trees, fringed with rushes and reeds, its water a clear green dappled by sunshine. There were water coots among the reeds and the plop of fish. There was a willow tree drooping into the water and in season, Fran guessed, there would be kingcups, flags and meadowsweet. From where she stood she could see a water vole motionless on the bank. She heard Lisa's happy sigh and the skinny arms tightened round her neck. 'Pretty,' said Lisa. 'Stay.'

'All right, darling, just for a few minutes.' Fran walked carefully round the pond until she came to a fallen tree stump and then she sat down. 'Story,' demanded Lisa and, after a moment's thought, 'fairies.'

So Fran started off on one of her rather vague fairytales, made up as she went along, half Dutch and half English. But Lisa didn't seem to mind that, she listened avidly to every word, nodding her small head from time to time and, when Fran paused for breath, urging her on again.

'Look,' said Fran at last, 'I'll ask the old woman if we can come here some afternoons and have tea and sit here...'

She tried again in Dutch and Lisa understood. *'Geheim,'* she said, so seriously that Fran did her best to understand her, but in the end she said apologetically, 'Sorry, darling, I don't understand.'

Lisa pondered. *'Niemand,'* she ventured. Fran knew that. 'No one.'

'Weet,' said Lisa hopefully.

'Know?' cried Fran truly triumphantly. 'You clever girl! Secret, of course.'

They hugged each other for being so clever and then Fran carried her back down the path to the car and settled her in it before going to speak to the old woman who had come to the door to watch them. It took a little time to explain and in the end Lisa did it for her. The old woman nodded, pleased to have visitors and to earn a few *gulden* and after a deal of hand shaking, Fran turned the car and drove back the way they had come. They had stayed longer than she had meant to and even if Litrik wasn't home, Nel and Tuggs would worry.

They had time to tidy themselves up before he arrived and when he asked if they had had a pleasant drive Lisa burst into speech. He listened patiently and then said to Fran, 'I gather you've had an exciting afternoon, all very secret?'

'We had a lovely time,' said Fran, 'and yes, it's secret but quite harmless. I promised I wouldn't tell…' She hesitated. 'You don't mind?'

'Mind, my dear girl? Lisa has never been so happy. Far from minding I am deeply in your debt.'

He went over to little Lisa, sitting happy in her chair. 'What is it to be this evening?' he asked Fran over his shoulder. 'Snakes and Ladders or Ludo?'

He picked up the child and went to sit down in the big chair by the table and repeated everything in Dutch. It was to be Snakes and Ladders; Fran got the board and the counters and presently the three of them were deep in the game, cheating from time to time so that Lisa should win.

As Friday drew near, Fran found that she was nervous. She liked Oom Hilwert though he was a bit outspoken, but supposing there were people there she didn't know? Who couldn't speak English? Litrik would be ashamed of her… Common sense came to her rescue; everyone knew that her Dutch was of the kindergarten variety. She would wear one of her lovely new dresses and do her hair in the french pleat she had been experimenting with for the last day or two in the privacy of her bedroom. And if he didn't like it he could lump it, she told herself vigorously.

She took Lisa to the secret pool on Friday and they sat in the afternoon sunshine while she continued her fairytale, and then she carried Lisa to the cottage where the old woman gave them tea. And when they got home, since Litrik hadn't returned, Fran took the little girl up to her room and showed her the dress that she was going to wear that evening.

Litrik was late home; Lisa was already in bed by the time he got in and there was barely an hour before they had to leave for Oom Hilwert's house. They went together, as they always did, to say good night to her and after a whispered promise that she would come back, dressed for the evening, Fran left the two of them together.

The dress was beautiful. Fran, who had never had couture clothes and had always thought of them as being wildly expensive, suitable only for the models in *Vogue,* realised that she had been wrong. The dress transformed her; it clung where it should, fell free in graceful folds when she walked, and made her feel like royalty. She had managed the french pleat, too, and put on a pair of high-heeled satin slippers which added both to her height and her self-esteem. She picked up her little beaded bag, which she had been unable to resist, and the soft angora stole and went along to Lisa's nursery. The child was still awake and Fran sat down on the side of the bed and showed her the contents of her bag, allowed her to sniff the fine white hanky scented with *L'air du temps,* and then pirouetted slowly so that the full glories of the dress might be studied.

'Darling Mama,' said Lisa sleepily as Fran kissed her good night.

Downstairs Litrik was waiting, immaculate in a dark grey suit and a richly sober tie. She had expected, or at least hoped, that he would say something about her dress, even tell her that she looked nice, but although he studied her through half-closed lids for several seconds, all he said was, 'I should like you to wear these,' and handed her a long velvet box.

There was a double row of pearls inside with a diamond clasp. She took it out with delicate fingers and looked at him, and when he didn't speak said quietly, 'The family expect it, of course...'

He nodded. 'Yes, they've been in the family for a very long time—they're handed down.'

'Or lent,' said Fran matter-of-factly as she fastened the clasp and went to take a look in the great carved mirror over the fireplace. They were magnificent and she touched them lightly while a dim memory became sharp in her head. 'Pearls around the neck, stones upon the heart': a proverb dredged up from something she must have read a long time ago. And oh, so true. She turned away from the mirror. 'Must I wear them?'

'Of course.' He sounded a little impatient. 'You are my wife.'

She stood in front of him, her head a little on one side, looking at him. 'No, I'm not,' she corrected him. 'I'm Lisa's Mama. We mustn't let the whole thing get out of hand, must we?' There was faint rebuke in her quiet voice. She gave him a kindly smile. 'It's difficult, isn't it? It seemed simple enough. Besides, I hate deceiving people, don't you?'

He said very evenly, 'I believe I made it perfectly clear that I will do anything to make Lisa happy for the next few weeks—we can go into the rights and wrongs of the matter at the appropriate time.' He turned away. 'If you are ready, shall we go?'

They hardly spoke in the car and when they got to Oom Hilwert's house there was no need to for they were at once surrounded by the other guests. Fran had to admire Litrik's manner towards her, though: the considerate husband, steering her from one guest to the other, making sure that she had the drink she wanted, bringing her into the conversation, encouraging her to take part in it, so that before they went into dinner she was quite at her ease. She sat on Oom Hilwert's right, with a youngish man, a distant cousin of the family, on her other side, and between them they flattered her gently, admiring her dress, remarking on the pearls, and reiterating their pleasure in having her in the family. 'And I daresay Litrik's loaded you with jewellery,' observed Oom Hilwert, 'though you have the good sense not to wear anything but pearls with that dress.'

'Litrik wanted me to wear them,' said Fran serenely. It was a pity that he was sitting at the other end of the table and couldn't hear.

After dinner everyone gathered once more in the drawing room, a vast apartment heavily furnished and rather grand and gloomy. The talk was largely of the *burgermeester*'s reception on one evening the following week and led to the ladies gathering together to discuss what they intended wearing.

'And you, my dear?' enquired Litrik's mother. 'You have a pretty dress, no doubt. You look charming this evening.'

Fran thanked her nicely. 'Well I found a dress in Utrecht—it's pink…'

'Just the right colour for you, Francesca. You will be able to wear the earrings.'

Fran said warily, 'Oh, yes…' and was saved from saying more by Litrik strolling over to join them.

'Francesca, Oom Hilwert would like you to play for us.'

She smiled up at him while her eyes flashed indignant fire. There was no point in making a fuss and she wasn't going to give him the satisfaction of knowing that he had spoilt her evening. She crossed the room to the grand piano standing in one corner and sat herself down, outwardly composed.

'What would you like me to play?' she asked Oom Hilwert. 'I'm not used to playing in front of people and I'm only a tolerable player.'

The old gentleman beamed at her. 'Play what you wish, my dear, and we will enjoy it.'

She ran her capable little hands over the keys; it was a splendid instrument and she would try and do it justice. She began with Delius and then Schubert and wandered on through Frans Lehar and Strauss and Grieg and then back to Delius, stopping as quietly as she had begun, sitting with her hands in her lap.

They had sat quietly while she played, now they clapped and crowded round her, making much of her and someone said, 'Lucky Litrik, to come home to that in the evenings,' and everyone laughed and someone else said, 'I'll settle for Francesca, never mind the piano,' and they all laughed again. Fran laughed with them, taking care not to look at Litrik.

Driving home presently he said blandly, 'You were a great success, Francesca.' They were driving fast down the almost empty motorway. 'You didn't mind my making you play?'

She was astonished to discover that she wanted to cry. She said stonily. 'I minded very much, it was a rotten trick.' She added childishly, 'It would have served you right if I had sat down at the piano and played chopsticks.'

'Yes, it would, wouldn't it?' he agreed affably, 'only I knew that you wouldn't do that. Do you want me to apologise?' His voice was silky.

'Certainly not. It's of no consequence to me. After all you are behaving as I would expect you to behave.'

'Now why do you say that?' He sounded interested and amused, too.

'Anyone—any man who can reduce student nurses to a mass of shaking nerves before a lecture hall of people, is capable of any mean trick he chooses to think up.'

All he said was, 'For a mouse you have sharp teeth.'

She would have liked to have gone straight to her room when they got home but she stood in the hall, waiting for him while he took the car round to the garages at the side of the house. He looked at her and smiled as he came in and locked the door behind him. 'Friends again?' he wanted to know, and she heard the mocking note in his voice.

'No. Here are your pearls. Thank you for lending them to me.' She was of half a mind to tell him what his mother had said about the earrings. Let him find out for himself, she decided and uttered a rather gruff good night as she went up the staircase.

Litrik was free on the following day; they drove to the Veluwe and had a picnic under the trees, Lisa in a woolly jacket and Fran in the suede outfit, for there was a distinct nip in the air. Litrik was at his most urbane and Lisa was as merry as a cricket. Fran, watching her, couldn't believe that she was going to die. Watching Litrik, too, laughing and joking with her as though he hadn't a care in the world, she stifled a sudden deep sympathy for him. He had, after all, known of the situation for months and must have become reconciled to it. He looked up and caught her watching him and for a moment they stared at each other and then he turned away to tease Lisa gently and presently they were all engrossed in Lisa's favourite occupation—teaching Fran Dutch.

Almost a week went by, each day with its gentle routine and two more visits to the fairy pond where they sat, the two of them, while Fran laboriously wove her fairytale, almost as absorbed in it as her small listener. The old woman seemed to enjoy them coming, too; their tea was laid out for them in her little parlour and she liked a chat before they went home, sometimes leaving it to the last minute so that they were barely indoors and sitting in the drawing room before Litrik came back. For that was part of the secret; when he enquired as to their afternoon, Lisa would say that they had had a nice drive in the car and exchange a smile with Fran. 'Nice, Mama?' she would ask and Fran would answer, *'Geweldig,'* just to let Litrik see that she was learning Dutch fast.

They didn't go to the pond on the afternoon of the *burgermeester*'s reception; getting dressed for it would take up most of the evening and Lisa was to have a ringside seat from Fran's bed. As it turned out Litrik phoned to say that he would be home later than usual and they weren't to wait for him to have tea, so that the two of them, with Nanny for company, went up to Fran's room where she laid out the pink dress and, leaving Lisa in Nanny's company, went to take a bath. She had washed her hair the evening before and it hung very clean and shining around her shoulders—they wasted a good deal of time arranging it in various styles before she sat down in front of her dressing-table and did her face, applying the expensive new make-up she had bought. It didn't seem to make much difference and she turned her attention to her hair, putting it up in its usual french pleat, wishing the while that it was a dramatic black or dazzling blonde. It was time to put on the dress and she stood before the pier-glass studying her image while Lisa and Nanny uttered little cries of admiration. Well, the face and the hair might not be anything to shout about, but the dress certainly was. She danced a few steps round the room for Lisa's pleasure and stopped when there was a knock at the door and Litrik came in, dressed save for his tailcoat.

He dropped a kiss on Fran's cheek, hugged Lisa and wished Nanny a good evening and then sat down on the bed, his arm round the little girl, and studied Fran. Lisa babbled excitedly and he said, 'Very nice, very nice indeed, Mama—Lisa thinks you look like a princess.' He got up and fished the pearls out of a trouser pocket and, because Lisa and Nanny were watching, fastened them round her throat. 'Oh, and these,' he told her.

Pearl and diamond earrings, glittering and gleaming under the bright lights of the bedroom. She took them silently and went to put them on before the mirror and then, mindful as she was of their audience, turned to smile at him and thank him in her serene way.

'They look well enough,' he told her and went away to shrug himself into his tails, while she picked up the wide swansdown stole the saleslady had assured her was just the thing to wear with the gown. Litrik came back presently to say good night to Lisa and then stood patiently while she hugged and kissed Fran who bade Nanny good night and then rustled out of the room. She was scared stiff of the evening ahead of her. To anyone else she would have voiced her fright, but not to Litrik; instead she made rather vague small talk as he drove her into Utrecht.

She need not have worried. The *burgermeester* was a genial old man with white whiskers and twinkling blue eyes and his wife, small and round and grey-haired, was just as nice. Fran, with Litrik at her elbow, was introduced, chatted to and handed on to more dignitaries, all of whom appeared to be on the best of terms with Litrik and only too willing to get on the same terms with her. Presently there was dancing and they circled the floor rather sedately before Litrik relinquished her to one of the *wethouders,* who wanted to know if an English mayor and alderman were the same as the Dutch.

'All except for the names I think,' said Fran. 'This is a very handsome ballroom.'

She couldn't have picked a more suitable subject; she was treated to a long history of the *gemeentehuis* which lasted through the dance and a couple of encores before she was whisked away by one of Litrik's cousins, a young man, not much older than herself. 'You look beautiful,' he told her gaily and she laughed. 'It's the earrings,' she explained. 'I'm terrified of losing one, though.'

She danced without pause until supper was announced and Litrik very properly came to claim her. She thought that he looked a little severe and wondered guiltily if she should have sat out some of the dances with various of the elderly ladies. 'Shouldn't I have danced so much?' she asked anxiously, 'I rather forgot who I was…'

'I am delighted to see that you are enjoying yourself, Francesca. Certainly you may dance as much as you wish. I expect you would like to sit at a table with some of your partners.' He raised a hand to a half-filled table at the other end of the room and took her arm. There were half a dozen young men and girls there and she sat down happily while Litrik went to fetch her some food. He came back with an assortment of chicken patties, vol-au-vents and tiny sandwiches and sat down beside her. He wasn't severe any more. He seemed to be on such excellent terms with everyone there; indeed, she was vexed to see that he was deliberately charming the three girls, something he had never attempted to do with her. Deep inside her she felt sad and bewildered by it. She shook the feeling off and applied herself to the talk around her, laughing rather more than she usually did.

They danced together again after supper and for the last dance. She couldn't but help notice the sentimental glances the older ladies were casting upon them. Litrik had noticed, too; he said gravely to the top of her head, 'You do realise that I am considered to be a very lucky man?'

It was on the tip of her tongue to ask him if he considered himself lucky, too, but she refrained. Instead she said worriedly, 'Really, it would have been better if I weren't to meet so many people. I could have had a cold or something—I mean, it would be easier for later on.'

He said very quietly, 'Shall we cross that bridge when we come to it, Francesca?'

It was late when they got back home and the house was quiet. 'There will be coffee in the kitchen if you want it,' Litrik told her, but she shook her head. 'I'll go to bed. I'll take a peep at Lisa first.' She paused at the bottom of the staircase and asked in a forlorn voice, 'Did I look nice?'

She thought he wasn't going to answer her. 'Very nice,' he said at length in a dry as dust voice. He wasn't even looking at her, but brushing something off his coat sleeve. He looked very handsome standing there and quite remote. She took off the pearls and unhooked the earrings and retraced her steps and handed them to him. Her good night was uttered in her usual quiet voice although she didn't look at him. She went up the stairs carefully because her eyes were full of tears and she couldn't see very clearly.

She undressed slowly, hung up the pink dress and got into a nightie and then crept along to the nursery; Lisa was asleep and so was Nanny in her room leading off it. The little girl's face looked pale and thin in the dim light of the bedside lamp and Fran felt anxiety grip her; the child looked dreadfully ill... She gave a gasp of pure fright as a hand came down on her shoulder.

'Don't worry,' said Litrik quietly into her ear, 'she is no worse. It's just that when she's sleeping it's more obvious how ill she is.' He gave her a friendly pat. 'Go to bed, Francesca.'

She turned away. 'Yes, of course.' She gave him a brief glance and he said softly, 'Why, you've been crying.'

He bent and kissed her on her gentle mouth, not the usual peck she was offered for appearances' sake, but hard and urgent. 'Go to bed,' he said, suddenly harsh, and she went without a word.

Before she slept she decided that he had been sorry for her because she had been crying about Lisa. But she had been crying before then, although she wasn't at all sure why.

September slid slowly towards October, taking with it a round of dinner parties, family meetings and lunches, pleasant leisurely drives through the Veluwe, and the now regular afternoon visits to the fairy pool. But it was getting too chilly to stay long by the water now. Fran, with Lisa wrapped in a rug on her lap, would sit on their favourite tree stump and add another chapter to her interminable story and then hurry back to the cottage for tea and a biscuit. And the day came when she knew that Lisa wasn't well enough to go there any more; fortunately the weather changed and they were forced to stay indoors and she continued her tale telling sitting comfortably in a high-backed chair drawn up to the log fire in the great hearth, with Lisa cuddled on her lap. She didn't need the sight of Litrik's grave face to warn her that there wasn't much longer to go now, although when he was with Lisa he presented a carefree manner and laughed and joked with her as he had always done. He said nothing to Fran, for there was no need, but she and Nanny, when there was no one about, talked about it and wept a little, something Fran thought Litrik wouldn't tolerate.

And the day came when Lisa stayed in bed and from then on Fran and Nanny took it in turns to be with her, only leaving when Litrik came home, to sit by the bed and always talk cheerfully to Lisa about his day's work and his plans for Christmas; and Lisa, lying propped up against her pillows with her mouse bride beside her, listened happily.

It wasn't long before there came a day when Litrik, too, stayed at home, sitting by the child's bed, her hand in his, talking to her in a perfectly normal voice with Nanny sitting knitting at the table and Fran on the other side of the bed stitching dolls' clothes which would never be needed. Tuggs brought trays of coffee and sandwiches and during the afternoon Litrik told Fran and Nanny to go into the garden for half an hour, but nobody wanted meals and nobody made any attempt to undress that night. Lisa died, as they had prayed she would, in her sleep just as the sun was turning a chilly dawn into a bright morning.

CHAPTER SEVEN

THAT evening, sitting alone by the fire in the drawing room after sharing a dinner with Litrik which neither of them had eaten, Fran went back over the long sad day. She had seen very little of Litrik; he had gone to his study and telephoned the hospital and Professor van Tromp, who had been looking after Lisa, and then he had emerged to shower and shave and drink a cup of coffee before shutting himself up in his study again. His face had been a grey mask of tiredness and he had hardly spoken to her. Professor van Tromp had come shortly after breakfast and when he had left again, she had gone to the nursery to help Nanny, thankful that in that kindly young woman's company she could cry if she wanted to. Litrik hadn't come to lunch; Tuggs had taken a tray of coffee to the study and she had sat at the table, pushing the food round her plate. In the afternoon she had wandered round the garden, longing to help Litrik in some way, but when she had offered to do so that morning he had told her curtly that he would do everything necessary and would telephone the family.

Even a walk with the dogs had been denied her for in the early afternoon he had emerged, whistled to Muff and Thor and left the house with them. When he had returned she had offered tea and been curtly thanked and refused.

It would have been so much easier for them both if they could have talked about Lisa and comforted each other, but he didn't want her sympathy nor had he any to offer her. Dominee Meertens had come in the morning and spent a little time talking to her but she had been too unhappy to listen, although she had been grateful.

She looked up in surprise as the *stoelklok* chimed midnight and Tuggs came into the room. 'Shall I lock up, Mevrouw?' he wanted to know. 'The doctor is in his study and I don't like to disturb him. The dogs are with him or I'd have given them a run...'

'You lock up, Tuggs, and I'll go and see if the doctor will go to bed. He must be tired; there has been so much to do.' She smiled at him from a sad face and he smiled back.

'It's been a bad day for us all, Mevrouw. Shall Nel fetch you up a nice warm drink before you sleep?'

She shook her head. 'No, thank you, Tuggs; if Nel would leave the coffee on the hob I'll get the doctor a cup if he wants it. You and Nel go to bed. You had a wakeful night and a long day, too.'

The house was very quiet once he had made it secure for the night. Fran sat on by the dying fire, thinking about Lisa and the fun they had had together. At least the little girl had been happy and had loved her a little, just as she had loved Lisa. When next she looked at the clock it was almost an hour later and she got up and crossed the hall to the study and knocked on the door and, without waiting for an answer, went in.

Litrik was sitting at his desk sprawled in his chair, staring ahead of him, his face a calm mask. He glanced at her briefly. 'What do you want, Francesca?'

'Litrik, come to bed, it's gone one o'clock and you had no sleep last night.' And when he took no notice, she went up close to him and said gently, 'Lisa was so happy and content, can you not try and think of that? And she loved you and you loved her as you always will. I—I'm so sorry, Litrik...'

He said with a kind of cold politeness, 'What can you possibly know about it? You haven't had a child!'

She didn't answer that. 'Would you like some coffee? Nel left it ready.'

'No, thank you. Go away, Francesca. Just for a time you and I have nothing to say to each other.'

He was wrong, of course, but she saw that she wouldn't be able to make him see that. Feeling defeated, she left him there alone.

He was at the breakfast table in the morning and wished her good morning and expressed the hope that she had slept well. 'I shall be at home today,' he told her. 'Family and friends will be calling. I've arranged the funeral for Friday, here in the village. Just family will come back here for a little while. Perhaps you will discuss with Nel what arrangements are needed to be made. I thought that we might send Nanny on holiday for a few weeks...'

'You're not discharging her,' said Fran quickly. 'I'm so glad—she would break her heart.'

He said evenly, 'She's been with us since Lisa was a year old—she is part of the household.'

'And I'm not,' thought Fran miserably. As soon as he decently could he would arrange things so that she could go back to England.

She drank coffee and crumbled toast, mindful of his remark that they had nothing to say to each other.

Litrik's parents arrived during the morning, and then his sisters; they were warmly sympathetic and Mevrouw van Rijgen observed very positively that although Fran had been Lisa's stepmother for such a short time, she had brought the child a happiness she had hankered after. 'So you mustn't grieve too much, my dear,' she said kindly. 'It has been a sad blow to all of us, especially to Litrik, but happily you are here to comfort him.'

Fran was profoundly thankful that he wasn't there to hear his mother say that.

More people came, friends—old friends of Litrik's who, it seemed, had known him for years. Fran said all the right things, dispensed coffee and tea and longed for the day to be over. The visitors went at last and they dined together, carrying on a polite conversation, not a word of which did she remember later. She went to bed directly afterwards, pleading a headache, thankful that Litrik was going to the hospital in the morning and would be out all day.

She breakfasted alone and since he had already left the house she told Tuggs that she was going for a drive and presently got into the Mini and took the well-remembered road to the fairytale pond.

It was a sad autumn day, not raining but damp and grey, and the old woman wasn't in her garden. Fran got out of the car and knocked on the door and, bidden to enter, gave her sad news in her slowly improving Dutch.

The old woman nodded and smiled and patted her shoulder to show that she understood. She pushed a chair forward and urged Fran to sit down. *'Koffie,'* she said and trotted off to her tiny kitchen and came back presently with two cups and saucers on a tray, looking kindly into Fran's tired unhappy face. Presently she said, 'You can come here whenever you want to, Mevrouw.' And somehow that made Fran feel better; she didn't suppose that she would be in Holland much longer, but this funny little cottage was somewhere to come. She thanked the old woman and asked if she might walk to the pond.

There were damp leaves strewn all over the path now and the trees were looking woebegone, but the pond was still lovely even on such a sombre day. Fran sat down on the tree stump once more and looked at the still, grey water. She had never felt so lonely or so unhappy. She grieved for Lisa and she was saddened, too, because Litrik didn't want her or her sympathy. It was as though at the child's death, he had discarded her; she had fulfilled her part of their agreement and now he had no further interest in her... She sat up straight at her sudden astounding thought: he might not want any more to do with her, but the idea of never seeing him again struck her with sickening force. Without him life would never be the same any more. She was quite bewildered, for he behaved towards her at best as a casual friend and at worst as though he couldn't bear the sight of her. So how could she possibly love him? She reminded herself of his coldness, the faint mockery with which he looked at her, his total lack of interest in her as a person. That he had always behaved in exactly the right manner towards her when Lisa had been with them meant nothing; the happy picnics, the games of Ludo and Snakes and Ladders, the laughter and early morning teas, all of them had been to give Lisa happiness.

She watched the water coot weave in and out of the reeds and then disappear. In all fairness, she thought, when Litrik had made his astonishing proposal, he hadn't offered her friendship or even liking, only his promise that, when she returned to England, he would see that she would get a job again.

She shifted a bit more on the tree stump, feeling the chill creeping up her legs. But to be honest, she hadn't expected anything else from him, had she? And it had all seemed so simple and straightforward, hadn't it? But it wasn't any more. She had grown to love Lisa even in the short time that she had known her and as well as that she had grown to love Litrik's home; now there was nothing more she could ask of life than to stay there with him for the rest of her life and his. Only he didn't want her.

She got up and walked slowly back to where she had parked the car, waved goodbye to the old woman and drove back to the house. It was late afternoon by then; Tuggs brought her tea in the little sitting room and she sat with the dogs, thinking about Lisa and thinking of the future. She would have to stay for a little while after the funeral but there was nothing to stop her planning what she would do when she went back to England. Not to the aunts, of course; they would never understand in the first place. Sooner or later they would have to be told but not just yet. And she would try for a job in London and make a new life for herself.

Litrik came back for dinner. He asked her kindly enough if she had found the day trying, expressed relief that she had taken the car for a run and went on to talk about his work at the hospital. He didn't mention Lisa once, merely remarking as they crossed the hall to the drawing room for their coffee that he hoped that she and Nel had arranged things for Friday.

'Yes,' said Fran, 'everything is seen to.' And before she could add to that he went on, 'I've spoken to Nanny. She will take a few weeks' holiday starting on Saturday. Her home is in Friesland; Tuggs will drive her there.'

He was sitting in his chair by the fire and she thought with compassion that he looked every day of his age, his grief hidden under that bland mask of a face. She opened her mouth ready to pour out the sympathy she felt and then closed it again; they had nothing to say to each other—he had said that and she mustn't forget it. She had no idea that loving someone who wasn't even interested in you could hurt so much. They drank their coffee, not talking much, and presently he went away to his study.

It was raining when she got up in the morning and when she got downstairs Tuggs met her with the news that Litrik had gone in to the hospital at Zeist and she wasn't to expect him until the evening. 'A mercy that he is kept so busy, Mevrouw, if you'll pardon the liberty.' He gave her a worried look. 'Not a nice day for you to go out, Mevrouw.'

'No, I'll take the dogs for a walk and then I'll go over to Bloemendaal and see my cousin—I'll stay for lunch, Tuggs, but I'll be back round about tea time in case Nel wants any help. Everything is all right for tomorrow, isn't it?'

It was mid-morning by the time she got back with the dogs and had dried them and settled down in the small sitting room. Clare was in when she phoned and eager to see her; she got into her new Burberry and the smart little hat that went with it, put on some elegant shoes and drove off.

She hadn't told Clare about Lisa; that was something she

would have to do during her visit with as little emotion as possible. Clare's baby was due in two months or so and she was living in a happy world of her own which it would be cruel to disturb.

She hadn't seen her cousin since the wedding although they had talked on the phone; Clare and Karel had been away staying with his parents and they wouldn't have heard of Lisa's death.

She parked the car and rang the bell and ran up the stairs to the flat, stifling a strong urge to pour out the whole unhappy business to Clare—she realised she couldn't do that; Dominee Meertens had said that only the three of them knew the true facts of the marriage… It wasn't her secret.

Clare was waiting at the open door and they hugged each other delightedly. 'Gosh, you look marvellous!' declared Fran. 'It's not too long now, is it?'

She cast off her raincoat and hat and her cousin eyed the suede outfit with envy. 'Well, look at you,' she declared, 'and those shoes—Fran, I hardly recognise you.' She gave Fran another look. 'Come in and have coffee—it's all ready, and you can tell me why you've lost weight and look as though you haven't slept for nights on end.'

Which made it easy for Fran to tell her about Lisa. 'It has upset us all,' she finished, 'and Litrik is broken-hearted—he adored her.' She paused. 'So did I.'

'What a mercy he married you,' observed Clare. 'You've got each other and that's all that matters, isn't it?' She gave Fran a long thoughtful look. 'So that's why you look so unhappy—you had me worried…'

Fran passed her cup for more coffee. She didn't want it, but it was something to do. 'And I want to know all about you and the baby—when is he due? Not long, surely?'

Clare was only too ready to talk about it and presently Fran was shown the baby's outfits and the dear little room Karel had decorated and fitted out.

'And once he is here, we shall come over and see you,' declared Clare happily. 'Will you be here for Christmas or will Litrik take you over to England? Not that it would be much fun to be with the aunts.'

'Well,' said Fran calmly, 'he's not said anything but then I hadn't expected him to; and he is very busy at the hospital—there have been several cases of legionnaire's disease and he specialises in tropical diseases and fevers, you know.'

She steered the talk back to the baby and Clare chatted happily until Fran said reluctantly that she would have to go.

'Oh, of course, Litrik gets back about tea time, I suppose, and you like to be there. Come and see me again, Fran.' Clare kissed her warmly. 'And next time you'll be your old self.'

Fran managed a laugh. 'Oh, dear, have I been such a wet blanket?'

'No, love—just unhappy and hiding it very well.'

It was a nasty afternoon turning rapidly into evening, with a cold rain falling steadily and a lot of traffic on the roads, even the country roads she took. It suited her mood; depression sat heavily upon her; the sight of Clare so happy, bubbling over with excitement about the baby, had filled her with an envy she didn't realise she possessed. It was impossible not to dream a little—to be happily married to Litrik who loved her and to have his babies. Fran, lost in her dream world, put out her right-hand indicator and turned left and was subjected to an indignant fanfare of horns.

She was surprised to find Litrik at home when she got in. She said awkwardly as he came into the hall, 'I spent the day with Clare. I didn't know you would be back before dinner.'

He took her raincoat and threw it over a chair. 'She is well, I hope?' he enquired politely, and stood aside for her to go into the drawing room. He spoke pleasantly and she did her best to follow his lead. 'Oh, fine—the baby's due in about eight weeks.' She sat down near the fire. 'What a wretched afternoon. I came home through the side roads and everything was very gloomy.'

He had come to sit opposite to her. 'I'll explain tomorrow's arrangements, shall I? Very simple, but it helps to know something about them beforehand.'

And during the next day, which was sad and difficult, she had been grateful for the things he had told her. They had helped her to play her part without faltering, act hostess to his family and friends and hide her own grief under a calm exterior. Only when everyone had gone and they were standing in the hall as Tuggs closed the doors on the last of the family, did she say suddenly and incoherently, 'You don't mind—I'd like to go—a headache…'

He had been so kind and thoughtful, perhaps only because there were other people there, but she didn't think so—it was as though he had understood at last that she was grieving for Lisa, too. But now she couldn't bear another minute of it. She had to get away and pull herself together. She loved him so much that she was terrified of showing it in some way and her longing to comfort him was almost unbearable. He had gone through the day with a calm face, courteous to everyone who had come, but now she wondered what he would do.

He answered her incoherent excuses with impersonal kindness. 'Of course you must be tired. I'll get Nel to send up something on a tray for you later on.'

She said quickly, 'I'll come down for dinner—you'll be alone…'

'I've a good deal to do—letters to write; I'll be too busy to miss you.' He smiled as he spoke, dismissing her, and she went to her room. Even if he weren't busy he wouldn't miss her, she thought drearily.

She didn't expect to sleep but she did and in the morning she felt better. Moping and moaning weren't going to help; she would have to pick up the threads of life again and wait patiently until Litrik considered it the right moment to get the annulment. It was no use trying to alter things; she had known exactly what he had planned from the very beginning and she had agreed with him. She hadn't been in love with him then, of course, which complicated things, but that was something she must learn to get over as soon as possible.

She dressed and went down to breakfast, outwardly serene. He would be away all day, he told her in the pleasant impersonal manner which chilled her so, and he would be flying to Brussels on the following day—a deliberate arrangement to get him away from home, she felt sure. Having to keep up the pretence of their marriage now that Lisa wasn't with them any more must be irksome to him. After all, her reason for being there in the first place had gone; she had no place with him any more. She replied suitably to his news, expressed the wish that his visit would be successful and asked in her matter-of-fact way if there was anything she could do for him while he was away.

There wasn't and there wasn't any way of being sure when he would be back. An answer she had expected anyway.

They were alone in the room and he bade her goodbye in a manner which put her very much in mind of his leave taking on her wards, pausing just long enough to tell her that if necessary he could be reached at the phone number he had left on his desk in the study.

She sat at the table, listening to him talking to Tuggs in the hall and then to the sound of the receding car. Tuggs came in then to see if there was anything she wanted and she told him briskly that she would take the dogs for a walk and then drive into Zeist to buy some embroidery wools.

'And I'll stay out for lunch, Tuggs. Shall I come and see Nel now?'

She went to the kitchen for her daily talk with that lady. Until now it had been brief, for Lisa demanded all her attention, but now there was time to learn a few useful words and pick up a few hints about the housekeeping, a waste of time really since she wouldn't be there for long enough to need them, but it kept her occupied.

She walked the dogs for an hour and then drove to Zeist, to potter round the shops there, drink coffee and then fill in another hour choosing knitting patterns until she could go to the Hermitage Hotel and have lunch.

She didn't drive straight back but meandered around the country roads, losing her way several times so that the afternoon was fading when she got home. The drawing room looked inviting and the dogs were glad to see her; Tuggs brought tea and she sat down by the fire, just for the moment enjoying an illusion of content, broken by Tuggs with the afternoon post. There was a letter from her aunts—she wrote to them weekly but they wrote seldom and when they did their letters unsettled her. They had a companion housekeeper now who apparently did nothing right and expected free evenings and a weekend off once a month, during which time, if Aunt Kate was to be believed, the aunts starved, froze to death and suffered all the privations of being neglected. Fran sat with the letter on her lap when she had read it and wondered if she should go back and live there with them when she went back to England. Perhaps it was her duty; on the other hand, when she had lived with them they had found fault with her continuously and matters would not improve. Far better to go right away and start again. She began to think what she might do, resolutely refusing to dwell on a future without Litrik; her heart might be breaking but she must ignore that and no one need ever know. She was debating the advantages of a post in London in a teaching hospital against a job in Canada or New Zealand when Litrik walked in. She hadn't expected him to come home before dinner and she jerked up in her chair as the dogs went to meet him.

'I startled you. I'm sorry, Francesca.' His glance fell on the open letter in her lap. 'Letters from home?'

He had sat down on the other side of the fireplace with

Muff draped over his feet and Thor sitting beside him. 'You've had a pleasant day?' he wanted to know.

'Yes, thank you. Would you like tea?'

He shook his head. 'I had a cup at the hospital.' He glanced at his watch. 'I must go again in an hour—a private patient at my rooms. Don't wait dinner for me. Perhaps you would ask Nel to leave something for me—sandwiches will do.'

She asked, 'Are you going to the hospital before you leave tomorrow? Will you want an early lunch?'

'I must leave here soon after six o'clock—I've a lecture to give in the morning. I'm catching an early plane from Schiphol.'

She said quietly, 'I see,' and then, because it was something to say, 'do you know Brussels well?'

'I have been there on various occasions.' He got up and fetched the small pile of letters on one of the tables and then sat down again. 'You don't mind if I read my post?'

'No,' said Fran and wished that she had her knitting with her. They were like two strangers who, having met for the first time, didn't like each other but felt impelled to make polite conversation. A waste of time, she thought, suddenly pettish, when we could be talking about Lisa and helping each other through this ghastly time. I could even have gone to Brussels with him...

She sat composedly, the picture of serenity, and the doctor, glancing at her over his letters, looked a second time before going back to his reading and then almost reluctantly looked at her again. He asked abruptly, 'You'll be all right while I'm away?'

That surprised her. 'Oh, yes, there are the dogs and so much to do...'

He looked a little taken aback. 'Much to do? What?'

'Well, as I said—the dogs. They like a good long walk, don't they? And then I talk to Nel about the meals and so on, and there are always letters to write and knitting to do and I can take the car to Zeist or Utrecht.'

'Do you miss your work at the hospital?' he asked abruptly.

'I didn't; perhaps I do now. You see, I've always...that is, a nurse's life is busy.'

'You don't dislike the idea of going back to it?'

'Not in the least.' Her voice was quite steady. Perhaps he was going to tell her that he'd see about the annulment. She shrank from hearing about it but at least he was talking to her.

She was to be disappointed; he put his letters aside and got up to go. 'Well, I must be off—I'll phone from Brussels before I leave there. Good night, Francesca.'

She wished him good night in a bright voice and only when she heard the car start did she get up and go upstairs to her room. She could howl her eyes out there in peace.

She felt much better after that; indeed a small well of indignation spread quite rapidly from somewhere deep inside her. She had done her best to keep her side of the bargain and he could have shown some gratitude, at least. Lisa's death had hit him hard, but it had made her very unhappy, too, and he hadn't seen that—but then he hardly ever looked at her...

She walked down to the village the next morning, put fresh roses from the garden on Lisa's grave and then had coffee with Dominee Meertens and his wife. The house was quieter now for the children were in school and they sat comfortably in the rather untidy sitting room, talking in a pleasant desultory fashion until Mevrouw Meertens asked, 'Did you not want to go with Litrik? He would have been glad of your company.'

Before Fran could answer the *dominee* said, 'Well, he would have very full days. I imagine it would hardly be worth your going, Francesca?'

She agreed and threw him a grateful glance. Perhaps she

could have a real talk with him sometime and find out what Litrik proposed to do and when.

She spent the afternoon at the piano and after her solitary dinner went to bed early.

Litrik didn't telephone for three days; he would be back for dinner that evening, he told her over the phone and, after a polite enquiry as to her well being, rang off. It was unfortunate that his mother had been driven over for a brief afternoon visit and was sitting near enough for her to hear Fran's side of the conversation, businesslike yeses and noes and no endearments of any sort. When Fran had sat down again Mevrouw van Rijgen passed her cup for more tea and remarked, 'Is Litrik a difficult husband, my dear? Not that you are likely to tell me. His first marriage was so unhappy you know; he became so—so remote, and now losing Lisa has upset him badly. We had hoped that when he married you it would help him to accept the fact that she was dying and to regain his happiness.' She hesitated. 'A happy home life and children... He is very fond of children.'

Fran poured herself more tea. She said in a calm voice, 'I think it's early days for Litrik to feel better about Lisa—he loved her very much and even though he had known for months that there was no hope for her, it was still a dreadful shock. We all miss her, you know. I wish I had known her for longer.'

'Yes, well, my dear...I dare say a few weeks spent quietly here with you will help him. It has been hard to talk to him since his first marriage broke up; you are a sweet girl and gentle and I think you will succeed where the rest of us have failed.' She added abruptly, 'He can be unkind but I believe that he doesn't mean it.'

She put down her cup and got up. 'I must go home. I've enjoyed our little chat, Francesca. Give my love to Litrik when he gets back, and tell him we hope to see you both soon.'

She kissed Fran with warmth and went out to the waiting car, leaving her to ponder over their talk. Did Litrik's mother suspect that things weren't quite as they should be with a newly married couple? Not that it mattered now, very soon they would part and once she was back in England she would be forgotten in a few months' time. They would be very kind about it; an unfortunate mistake made by both of them and luckily dealt with in time before there were any children. Finally she fell to daydreaming over little Litriks and their sisters running round the house, rushing to meet a devoted Papa each evening while she stood, presently to be held close and kissed.

She dressed carefully for Litrik's return and went to sit in the drawing room with the tapestry work she had started. He came in quietly and she paused with her needle poised to say serenely, 'Hallo, Litrik. I hope you had a successful time in Brussels and a good journey back.'

It sounded very stilted in her eyes, but it was either that or jumping up and flinging herself into his arms and that wouldn't do at all.

He went to pour a drink and offered her sherry before he sat down opposite her. 'Have you been lonely?' he asked abruptly.

She answered him evasively. 'I've had a visit from your mother—she came to tea. And I went to Dominee Meertens and had coffee. The weather's been quite nice; that meant the dogs and I have been able to walk miles.'

'You haven't answered my questions.'

She took a couple of stitches very precisely. 'One doesn't have to be alone to be lonely,' she told him coolly.

'While I was away I had time to think. I've treated you badly, Francesca, and I'm sorry. You were sad and I did nothing to help you. It's been a difficult time and I made it worse for you. I'm grateful for what you have done and you did it splendidly.'

She glanced at him. 'I loved Lisa,' she said baldly.

'Yes, I know.' He bent to stroke Muff's ears and then throw an arm round Thor. 'Francesca, there is something you are entitled to know. I have told no one else and don't intend to. Lisa wasn't my daughter.' And, at Fran's sudden surprised gasp, 'No, don't say anything yet. My first wife had an affair before we married unknown to me. She was pregnant then. It wasn't until some weeks later that I found out quite by chance that she had done her best to get rid of the child without my knowledge. She failed but Lisa was born handicapped. Her mother would have nothing to do with her—rejected her completely and left us both. I swore then that Lisa would have every possible chance to live and be happy. She has been my first concern since then.'

'Why did she marry you?' whispered Fran. 'Couldn't she have married the father?'

'He had no money. I happen to be wealthy, I was also infatuated.'

'And her mother?' Fran's voice was still a shocked whisper.

'Has been dead for five years.'

'And you still love her?'

He looked at her with hard eyes. 'I never loved her—love and infatuation are two quite different things. Love to my mind, is something one reads about—a myth...'

'That's rubbish!' said Fran sharply. 'What about your parents and your sisters and Dominee Meertens and his wife and Clare and Karel? Of course it's not a myth and if you loved someone you wouldn't talk such nonsense.'

He smiled at her mockingly. 'Why, Francesca, one might almost think that you were speaking from experience.'

She saw that he considered it so ridiculous that there was no need to be serious about it. She said merely, 'I use my eyes,' and changed the subject abruptly. 'Your mother hopes to see you soon.'

'We'll go over this weekend. Was my father with her?'

Fran shook her head. 'No, he had to attend some meeting or other.'

'They like you...'

'I'm glad of that.' She chose some wool with care and threaded her needle. He went on deliberately, 'And I find that I like you, too, Francesca, though unwillingly.'

Her heart rocked against her ribs. 'Then when we part we shall be able to do so in a friendly fashion.' She gave him a considered look. 'When is that to be, Litrik?'

'I have thought about that, too—I think we must wait a little while longer.' He was staring at her so hard that she felt the colour creeping into her cheeks. She didn't look away. 'I'm quite ready to go when you want me to.' She folded her work and laid it on the table by her chair.

'There's the gong—I expect you are hungry?'

Dinner passed off well enough; Litrik when he chose could be an amusing companion. They went back to the drawing room for their coffee and Fran, not wishing to push her luck, went to bed shortly afterwards. Litrik had seemed to enjoy her company; he had confided in her, admitted that he liked her; it wasn't much, but it was better than the cold silences she had had to put up with. She would have to leave, of course, but at least not just yet. For that she was thankful. Every single minute of his company was something to treasure for the future.

CHAPTER EIGHT

A WEEK went by, during which Litrik came home for lunch each day and returned in the early evening and even, on two occasions, for tea. They had gone to lunch with his parents, sustained an unexpected afternoon visit from Tante Olda and Tante Nynke, on their stately way to visit friends in Valkenburg, and had Professor van Tromp, a large quiet man who said little, to dinner. He and Litrik wandered off after dinner to the latter's study. They returned full of apologies; they had had a most interesting discussion, he explained to her, and begged her forgiveness. 'But of course, being a doctor's wife you will understand,' he ended kindly and drank the coffee she had ready for them and took his leave, inviting her at the same time to visit the hospital if she should care to do so. 'Although I dare say Litrik has been badgering you to do so already.'

As they went back into the drawing room Fran asked thoughtfully, 'Why don't you? Invite me to see round your hospitals—and your consulting rooms? Wives are supposed to take an interest in their husband's work, aren't they?' And, when he didn't answer, 'I am a little tired of this pretence and surely you must be, too. When Lisa was alive there was a reason for it.'

She was standing in the centre of the room, looking at him. 'How long does it take—an annulment, I mean?'

His voice was very even. 'A little while—we must talk about it.'

She had been feeling off colour all the evening, now her head began to ache most vilely. Perhaps because of that she snapped, 'No, we mustn't. You said that we had nothing to say to each other.' She walked to the door murmuring a good night, longing for her bed. For some reason the staircase was unending; by the time she reached the gallery above she was worn out and icy cold. She undressed quickly, her head hammering so hard now that all she could think of was getting into bed. She was sliding into its comfort when she got out again, put on her dressing-gown and went back into the gallery, making for the stairs. She felt ill, but at the same time there was something that she simply had to say to Litrik. She reached the staircase and started down it. Her head was a ball of fire, some demon was pouring ice water down her spine, her legs had no bones. Halfway down she paused; the stairs spread away from her, curiously flattened so that she wasn't certain where the next tread was. She put out a cautious foot, missed a step and tumbled headlong.

Litrik, in his study, with a pile of notes before him, ignored them, seeing instead a pair of lovely eyes in a tired face, and listening to a regrettably snappy voice telling him strongly that they had nothing to say to each other. He frowned as his thoughts were interrupted by a series of soft gentle bumps and the slithering of Fran's small person. He got up and went into the hall; it was past midnight and the house had been silent for some time.

Fran lay in an untidy heap, almost at the bottom of the staircase. She had knocked herself out, which was a pity, otherwise she would have heard—even if she hadn't believed—Litrik's, 'Fran—my dear little Fran,' uttered in a voice quite unlike his usual cool tones.

There was a reddened bump already visible on her forehead which told its own tale. He lifted her eyelids and looked into her eyes, took her pulse, made sure that there were no broken bones, then scooped her up and carried her upstairs to her room, where he put her on the bed, took off her dressing-gown and tucked her up. Only then did he go to the bell-pull by the fireplace and give it a sharp tug. There wouldn't be anyone in the kitchen at that time of night, but the Tuggs had their sitting room only a short distance from it and the bell was loud. While he waited he went back to the bed and took another look at Fran. Her face was pale and the bump was getting bigger but that wouldn't account for her obvious high fever.

He began to examine her carefully and when Tuggs, cosily dressing-gowned, came into the room he said, 'Get my bag from the study will you, Tuggs, and then go to the kitchen and get some ice and some cloths to put in it. My wife has knocked herself out falling down the stairs, but I believe she has some kind of infection.'

Tuggs, beyond a worried 'Tut tut', wasted no time on words. He was back in no time at all with the bag and went away again without a word.

Fran's temperature was high enough to make Litrik raise his eyebrows. He studied her face carefully in an impersonal and professional manner, sure that the concussion was secondary to the sudden high fever. He got up and shaded the bedside light carefully, pulled a chair close to the bed and, when Tuggs came back, wrapped ice in the linen hand towels he had brought, and held it over her forehead. He didn't look up as Nel came quietly in to stand beside him. She spoke in a whisper and he listened patiently and shook his head, answering her softly, and presently, after an anxious peer at Fran, she went away to get the coffee he had asked for.

'And Tuggs, will you go to my study and bring up the papers on my desk—the pile in the centre in a folder.'

'You'll stay here, sir?' Tuggs hesitated. 'Me and Nel will gladly sit with Mevrouw.'

'Thank you, Tuggs, I know you would, but I'll stay just to make sure she is all right when she comes round. She will probably be sick and feel peculiar; perhaps it'll make things easier if I'm here. You both go back to bed—I'll get you on the house phone if I need you'. He glanced at the faithful

Tuggs. 'Don't worry—my wife's picked up a virus infection I believe—that's how she came to fall downstairs. A few days in bed will put her right again.'

It took more than a few days. Fran came round in the early hours of the morning to see Litrik sitting by her bed, writing busily. She still had a fearful headache; indeed, the whole of her ached but her head felt clearer. He had looked up and seen her eyes open and on him and got to his feet and come to take her pulse and feel her hot forehead. 'That's better,' he told her soothingly. 'I'm going to give you something for the headache I'm quite certain you've got, and you'll go to sleep again and feel better by morning.'

He had turned her pillow and it felt blessedly cool to her poor hot head and he asked her if she wanted a drink, and offered her something in a medicine glass, and then another drink, and she had slept again, to wake in the morning feeling almost sensible once more, but disinclined to so much as turn her head on the pillow. When she saw him still sitting in the chair she muttered, 'Have you been there all night? You must go to bed—I'm quite all right now, but if you don't mind I don't think I'll get up just yet.'

His low laugh made her frown. 'You won't get up until I tell you that you may, Francesca, and I warn you that if you do you will fall flat on your face. I shall go away presently and Nel or one of the maids will be here.'

He got up and went to the door. 'I shall be home for lunch. Tuggs will take any calls. Nel will give you something to bring down the fever; drink as much as you can manage.'

He might just have finished a ward round, thought Fran drowsily.

Incredibly, it was more than a week before she crept from her bed, sat in an easy chair, and crept thankfully back again. The concussion hadn't been severe; the bump had subsided, leaving a yellow and purple bruise, but the virus had taken longer to go, and it had taken a good deal of the energy she possessed with it. But despite her small size she was strong and healthy and within a few days of getting up again she was downstairs, rather pale and a good deal thinner.

Litrik had visited her daily morning and evening, sitting down by her bed to tell her any small items of family news and read her the many letters written by his family, as well as long screeds from Clare and the brief stiff letters from the aunts, flavoured with the faint suggestion that if she chose to marry a foreigner and live on the continent, she must expect to fall a prey to unpleasant illnesses. She had chuckled weakly at this and Litrik laughed with her.

His father and mother came to visit her, as did Jebbeke and Wilma, and, since the weather was fine even if cold, she was wrapped up warmly by Nel and taken for short drives by Litrik. It was three weeks before she felt herself again, and once more went walking with the dogs and going down to the village to visit Dominee Meertens and his wife. It was on one of these visits, while his wife was out of the room with the idea of fetching the coffee, that she asked diffidently if Litrik had said anything to him about the annulment.

'Yes, he has.' The *dominee*'s booming voice had sunk to a discreet level. 'And at a suitable moment I have no doubt he will speak to you, Francesca.'

She had to be content with that; she had the sense to know that Litrik wouldn't have said anything while she was ill and she had been thankful for that, shutting her mind to her inevitable departure.

But Litrik said nothing. They began to go out and about again to friends for dinner, to the theatre and even, to her surprise, to the hospital in Utrecht, where she had a guided tour of the hospital while Litrik delivered a lecture to a hall full of students, coming to collect her in Theatre Sister's office, where he sat drinking coffee and behaving in a manner which she imagined an attentive husband might. She had been bewildered for there was really no need for him to go to such lengths.

The next afternoon she drove the Mini to see the old woman. It was a blustery day with grey clouds scudding across a cold blue sky, but the old woman, muffled in an old coat, was working in her garden. She stuck her fork in the ground when she saw Fran getting out of the car and came down the path to meet her. It took Fran a moment or two to unravel the old woman's Dutch. Her knowledge of that language was getting better by the day and she could at least make herself understood. Her companion nodded sympathetically as Fran explained her long absence, invited her to drink a cup of coffee and suggested that while it was being prepared perhaps she would like to walk to the pond. Even on such a dreary day as this, said the old woman, it was beautiful. She spoke proudly as though she owned the pond, which, reflected Fran, perhaps she did. She nodded her acceptance of the coffee and went out of the garden and along the path between the bushes and trees, mostly bare now, until she came to the pond. The old woman was right, it was beautiful, its water reflecting the stormy sky, its banks littered with fallen leaves. And the tree stump was still there; Fran sat down on it. Perhaps Lisa's happy little ghost was beside her; certainly her memory was vivid. She sat for a few minutes, grateful for the peaceful quiet all around her and presently went back to the cottage where she drank her coffee and carried on a muddled but animated conversation with her hostess.

She couldn't stay long, Litrik would be back before six o'clock and she had made a point of being home when he got in. When Lisa had been alive he had come home in time for tea if he possibly could, but now he had taken to staying at his consulting rooms each afternoon. There was, after all, no need for him to hurry home any more.

She saw very little of him; breakfast was never a protracted meal and if he was in for lunch that, too, was by no means a leisurely meal. Only in the evenings would he sit with her before dinner, talking pleasantly about nothing that mattered, making small talk at the table and then, when they had had coffee, going to his study. She saw more of him if friends or family came to dinner or they went out, but although she longed to be with him, the effort of hiding her real feelings was getting a bit too much.

She bade the old woman goodbye, promised to return in two days' time and drove home.

It was the following week, her fourth visit since she had been ill, that she arrived at the cottage to find no sign of the old woman. Her two cats were sitting on the doorstep, looking anxious, and there was no smoke coming from the chimney. Fran walked up the little path, looking around her. The garden fork was stuck in the earth beside a row of carrots, half dug, and the cats, when she reached them, looked hungry. She knocked on the door and heard nothing in the silence all around her. She knocked again and this time she did hear something, a weary rending cough.

'Bronchitis,' said Fran to the cats, her nurse's instincts taking over, and she tried the door. It opened. The cats shot past her into the tiny lobby. The little sitting room was empty and cold; she went into the kitchen and at once saw the old woman huddled on a chair by the old-fashioned pot stove, now out. She looked ill and exhausted and when she tried to speak coughed instead so that Fran begged her to save her breath. It would take too long to ask her slowly thought out questions and then puzzle out the answers. She filled a kettle at the old-fashioned stone sink, lighted the Calor gas ring and found the coffee pot. She found milk, too, in an icy little pantry, put some on to heat, and then gave the cats each a saucerful.

Between bouts of coughing the old woman drank a cupful of coffee and Fran was relieved to see a little colour creeping back into her cheeks. She sought feverishly for the Dutch for blanket and dredged it up from the back of her head with great relief. The old woman pointed a feeble hand towards the ceiling and Fran climbed the ladderlike narrow stairs and found an attic above, one corner boarded off to make a bedroom of sorts. There were blankets here; she took two and made her precarious way back down the stairs and tucked them round her patient and then set about dealing with the stove. There was an empty bucket beside it. She picked it up and went outside and round the cottage to the back where there were some broken-down sheds. There was a small pile of egg coals there, some small logs and several broken wooden boxes. Firewood, said Fran happily, and found a lethal looking axe propped against the wall with which she attacked the boxes. She wasn't very expert but she was desperate to get the house warm. Armed with her bucket of coal and the wood she went back indoors, cleaned the stove as best she could and laid the fire, following her companion's muttered instructions very carefully. The stove obliged, roaring up the flue pipe in an alarming manner until, obedient to the old woman's urgent directions, she opened this and shut that and added more coal.

It was growing dark and she lit the oil lamp on the kitchen table, washed her grimy hands and found a basin. The old woman wasn't too keen on being washed, but she looked a little better by the time Fran had sponged her face and hands and presently dozed off, waking for coughing bouts and dropping off again. 'Food,' said Fran to the cats and remembered the hens the old woman kept—she and Lisa had seen them on one of their visits scratching contentedly in a wired-in enclosure behind the cottage. They would need to be fed and the eggs collected; she had no idea how long the old woman had been ill but she began to doubt if she had been able to cope with the hens. Fran went quietly out of the house again and explored the sheds. In one of them she found a sack of what she hoped was chicken feed. She filled a dipper and made her way to the hens, who rushed to the wire as soon as they saw her and fell to with a good deal of clucking. There was an egg box behind the chicken house; she opened it cautiously and found eggs. 'Egg and milk,' said Fran, and sped back to the cottage.

Her patient was still in uneasy sleep. She got the egg and milk ready, found some stale bread in an earthen crock, warmed more milk and gave it to the cats. The kitchen was warm now and, by the lamp's light, looked quite cosy. Dusk had slipped into darkness and she drew the curtains over the one window. The old-fashioned wall clock struck seven as she did so and she was shocked at the chimes. There was no way of letting anyone know where she was; the old woman couldn't be left even for the short time it would take her to drive back to the village and try to find a phone. She would have to spend the night and hope that someone would go past the cottage in the early morning. The old lady woke and Fran coaxed some of the egg and milk down her reluctant throat, and, when she could take no more, gave the rest to the cats and went to fetch more of the egg coals. The stove smelled vilely but the warmth had revived the old woman; if she could keep her going until the morning… Fran sat down on one of the hard wooden chairs at the table, thankful that for the moment, at least, her patient was asleep.

Presently she told herself she would warm up the coffee, it would keep her awake. The cats had curled up on the blankets, cocooning their mistress, and for the moment there was nothing for her to do except think how angry Litrik would be.

In this she was mistaken. He had arrived home at his usual hour to find Tuggs looking anxious. 'It's Mevrouw, sir—always home by now and no sign of her…'

'Where did she go?' Litrik sounded calm.

'Well, that's the worry—I don't know. When Lisa was alive they used to go off together, ever so happy, some afternoons, and they always got back before five o'clock. And for the last week or so Mevrouw has driven off at just the same time and come back here soon after four o'clock.'

'And you've no idea where they—she goes?'

Tuggs shook his head.

Litrik was putting on his car coat again. 'I remember that it was mentioned one day—a secret they told me, but that was all. Do you suppose that anyone in the house has any idea?'

Tuggs slid away through the baize door into the kitchen regions and the doctor stood motionless, staring at the wall before him. Presently Tuggs came back with Bep, the elder of the two young maids who did the housework. She was a sensible girl. 'Yes,' she said, in answer to Litrik's questions, 'once, when they got back a bit later than usual and it had been raining, I helped them with their wet things and they were talking. A fairy pool they were talking of, and an old woman in a cottage.'

The doctor thanked her gravely, told Tuggs to get the car out again and went to his study, where he spread a map on his desk and studied it carefully. He found what he sought presently, picked up his bag and went out to the car where Tuggs was waiting.

'It's a long shot, Tuggs, but worth a try. Stay here, I'll phone you if I need you.' He paused. 'And if there are any messages make a careful note of them.'

Tuggs voiced the doctor's thought. 'If there's been an accident, sir, we'd have heard by now.'

Litrik nodded, got into the car and drove away. He knew the surrounding country well, he reached the crossroads and turned down the narrow lane and went slowly through the village. Half a mile further his headlights picked out the Mini parked untidily on the side of the lane.

He parked behind the Mini, leaving his lights on, took his bag from the car and went up the garden path.

There was a faint glimmer of light coming from somewhere inside and then the sound of someone coughing. He knocked on the door and when no one came, knocked again, this time loudly and at length. He was rewarded by the glimmer of light becoming stronger and then Fran's voice calling in her slow Dutch, 'Who's there?'

'Litrik—open up, Francesca.'

The door was flung open and Fran with the lamp in her hand stood gazing up at him. She said breathlessly, 'Thank God you've come! How did you know? She's ill, the old woman who lives here, and I don't know what to do...'

He crowded into the tiny lobby, kissed her fiercely, took the lamp from her and went into the kitchen, where he set the lamp on the table, took off his coat and went to look at the old woman, awake now and looking bewildered.

He treated her very gently, asked her quiet questions while he took her pulse and temperature and, without disturbing the cats, contrived to go over her chest with his stethoscope. Then he wrapped her up again, gave her a reassuring pat and turned to Fran.

'So, tell me all you know and what you've done.'

So she told him and when she had finished he nodded. 'You did well. It's bronchitis and she tells me she refuses to leave here. I'm going back to the village to find someone to come out here and look after her. I'll phone Tuggs at the same time. Everyone at the house is beside themselves about you.'

But not you, thought Fran silently, though all she said was, 'I'm sorry to have worried them. What do you want me to do?'

He smiled a little. 'What a practical girl you are. What is upstairs?'

'An attic and a bedroom boarded off. There is a second bed in the attic.'

'See if you can find any sheets and blankets and make up the beds. I'm going to give her an antibiotic now. Provided she will stay in bed for a few days I think she will recover. Is there any food in the house?'

'The eggs I fetched, some milk and stale bread. There's not much coal—it's that pressed coal dust. Oh, and nothing for the cats.'

'I'll tell Tuggs. Now come and hold this arm for me.'

The house was very quiet when he had gone. She sped up the stairs once more and poked her nose by the light of a candle into a cupboard in the attic and found sheets and blankets and an old eiderdown. She took them all downstairs again and spread them round the stove and went back to look for the old woman's night clothes—a voluminous nightie, spotlessly clean, and a thick shawl. She found towels, too, and a jug and basin and an old-fashioned stone hot water bottle.

It took a little time to take all the bedclothes upstairs again and boil the water for the bottle but that done she set to to make up the beds, wrap the nightie round the bottle and bury it into the bedclothes. She went downstairs then and saw that Litrik had been gone for almost an hour. The old woman was awake again and coughing. Fran heated more milk and got her to take it, and was thankful to hear the car stopping in the lane.

Litrik had someone with him, a middle-aged woman with a long face and bright blue eyes, who shook her hand as he said, 'This is Juffrouw de Wit; she lives in the village on her own. I suppose one would call her a girl Friday in England. She is sensible and willing to stay until Mevrouw Honig is better. Tuggs is coming over with food and so on. Have you made up the beds?'

'Yes, but there is only one hot water bottle.'

'Tuggs is bringing one with him.' He went to bend over his patient while Juffrouw smiled widely at Fran and took off her coat and carefully removed a hard felt hat from her head. Fran thought she would have made an excellent nurse.

The two of them went upstairs then and Litrik followed with Mevrouw Honig in his arms, and left them to get their patient undressed and into her warm nightie and shawl and sitting comfortably against the pillows Fran had found. It wasn't so cold in the attic now; the chimney breast took up a good deal of the attic wall and was beginning to warm it. Mevrouw Honig coughed and sighed and dozed off, leaving Fran and Juffrouw de Wit to tidy up and go back to the kitchen. Litrik had fetched more coal and stoked up the stove. He was in his waistcoat and shirt sleeves, washing his hands at the sink, when there was a knock at the door. 'Tuggs,' he said over his shoulder. 'Let him in, please, Francesca.'

Tuggs beamed at her as he edged past, carrying a big box. 'We've all been in such a state, Mevrouw—what a relief to know you are safe and sound. Is this the kitchen?'

He put the box on the table and Fran and Juffrouw de Wit unpacked it. The contents were all that was most needed: milk and fresh bread, a simple dish of sliced meat, neatly covered, for Juffrouw de Wit, an egg custard, tea and coffee, sugar, tins of soup and a packet of scraps of things suitable for the cats. There were candles, too, and soap and a bottle of Dettol. Juffrouw looked her satisfaction and began to tidy everything away into the pantry, and Litrik put on his jacket and shrugged on his coat. He went upstairs then to take another look at his patient and when he came down gave Juffrouw de Wit the antibiotic pills which would have to be taken and his instructions as to the care of Mevrouw Honig. Fran, listening, made out that he would pay a visit on the next day.

They drove back then, Tuggs leading with Fran just behind him and Litrik last of all. They caused quite a stir going through the village.

It was nice to be fussed over as she went into the house. Nel with Bep and Corrie, the younger maid, had formed a kind of welcoming committee to take her outdoor things and exclaim over her, even though she didn't understand all they said. She went up to her room and took a look at herself in the looking-glass. Then she saw that she looked frightful; her face was grimy and her hair hung in wisps and her dress was smeared in coal dust. She washed and did her hair, changed her dress and went downstairs and found Litrik waiting for her. He handed her a glass of sherry, remarking that she looked as though she needed it, which remark, considering that she had just spent ten minutes improving her appearance, was unfortunate. She drank the sherry rather fast and it went straight to her head. She had had no tea and it was now late evening and she was famished. She blinked away a sudden vagueness in her surroundings and Litrik, watching her, observed blandly, 'I dare say you're hungry, but would you like another sherry first?'

The look she gave him was so unhappy that he put his glass down and took her hands in his.

'Francesca—what is it? Do you not feel well? What's wrong?'

Everything was wrong; she was tired, she was hungry and she was hopelessly in love with a man who didn't care a row of pins about her. But, of course, she couldn't tell him that. 'How did you know where I was?' she asked.

He didn't appear to have noticed that she hadn't answered his questions.

'Bep remembered hearing Lisa talking to you about a cottage and a fairy pond; I know the country round here and I had a map—it wasn't difficult.'

He didn't tell her that he had sweated with fear, imagining her overcome by disaster and him unable to find her. He had been beside himself under his calm.

He let her hands go. 'There's the gong. You must be as famished as I am.'

It was long past their normal dinner hour but Nel had succeeded in offering a delicious meal. Fran listened to Litrik's easy talk about nothing much and answered when she should. It wasn't until he told her that Nanny, who hadn't come back from her holiday because of her mother's illness, was coming back on the following day that she smiled.

'Oh, I'm glad and I'm sure that Nel and the girls must have missed her. What will she do now that...?' She stopped.

'Lisa isn't here,' finished Litrik. 'Nel has plenty for her to do, so Tuggs tells me. Nel wants to see you about it—pickling and jam making and so on.'

Fran said slowly, 'There's no need to see me. I mean, Nel has been housekeeper here for years, hasn't she? And since I'll be gone...'

'Ah yes, but perhaps you would like to stay until the New Year? Have you anything in mind?'

'Well, no.' She added a little desperately, 'But I'd like to go as soon as you can arrange everything.'

He made no attempt to persuade her to say that she would stay. They went back to the drawing room and he told her, rather unnecessarily she thought, about the splendid Christmas and New Year celebrations. 'Everyone comes here,' he told her smoothly, 'we have a great tree in this room and the whole house is decorated and Nel turns out the most delicious food. Friends call and we give a party at New Year, and if it's cold enough we skate. A pity you won't be here to enjoy it all.'

She couldn't bear any more of that; she went to bed but before she went she asked, 'Do you want me to go and see Mevrouw Honig tomorrow?'

'I'll be home to lunch and I've no appointments until after four o'clock. We'll both go.'

He opened the door for her and as she went through she paused, her tongue uttering the words she had no intention of saying. 'Why did you kiss me like that?'

He didn't smile. 'An unavoidable reaction,' he observed. 'Good night, Francesca.'

In bed, curled up between fine linen sheets, she thought of Mevrouw Honig and Juffrouw de Wit and wondered what would have happened if she hadn't gone to the cottage that afternoon. It would have been nice if Litrik had said something kind about her hard work there, for it had been hard work. If she had been a dainty blond with big blue eyes and a helpless manner he would have praised her to the skies; as it was he took her for granted. She went to sleep on a wave of self-pity.

The morning was taken up with settling Nanny in again and hearing her news and then going to the kitchen to agree to Nel's suggestions about pickles and jams, and after lunch she got into the Daimler beside Litrik and was driven to the cottage.

It was one of those days when approaching winter allowed a forgotten autumn day to take over. The sun shone and although it was chilly there was little wind. They went up the path together and Juffrouw de Wit opened the door, her long face wreathed in smiles.

They were ushered into the small front room, very clean and neat but cold since there was no fire in the stove. But fortunately Litrik said that he would see his patient at once and at the same time swept Fran into the kitchen where Juffrouw de Wit had hurried to make coffee. It was warm there and Fran sat down at the table and listened to her companion's account of the night. All was well, she was told, Mevrouw Honig had slept fairly well and the cough seemed less severe. The doctor would be pleased...

He came down the precipitous stairs presently, ducking his head to avoid knocking himself out in the doorway, and accepted coffee while he listened to Juffrouw de Wit repeating everything she had said to Fran.

He allowed himself to be cautiously optimistic, he told Fran; the old woman was better but would need several days in bed still. Then he turned his attention to Juffrouw de Wit once more, listening patiently to what she had to say, and then writing down fresh instructions.

'Is she all right for food?' asked Fran.

It seemed that someone had walked from the village that

morning and brought milk and groceries with them. There was enough and to spare, declared Juffrouw de Wit.

They sat for a little while before Fran went up to see Mevrouw Honig. The antibiotic was already doing good work, the old woman was a better colour and she smiled at Fran and muttered something and Fran mustered her Dutch and wished the old woman a speedy recovery.

She and Litrik went down the garden under Juffrouw de Wit's approving eyes and as she went through the gate Fran asked, 'Would you like to see the fairy pool? I think Lisa would like that.'

He cast her a quick tender look, which she didn't see. 'I should like that.'

She led the way along the path and when the pond came into view she stopped for him to catch up with her. It was very quiet and the only movement was from the water coots on the far side of the pond.

'We always sat on that tree stump,' said Fran and two tears ran down her cheeks. She put up a gloved hand and wiped them away and blinked hard to hold back the rest of them, sniffing like a child. Litrik took a snowy handkerchief from a pocket and turned her round and mopped her face and she took it from him and blew her nose in a resolute fashion and said steadily, 'I am sorry, I didn't mean to cry. We were always happy here.' She looked up at him. 'You're not angry because we didn't share it with you?'

He stared down at her for a long moment and then shook his head. 'When I asked you to marry me it was because I wanted Lisa to have all the happiness she could before she died. You gave her that happiness; how could I possibly be angry?'

She watched a coot slide into the reeds just below them, and said sadly, 'I was happy, too…'

He asked abruptly, 'But not any more. I had wondered?'

'Well, everything is a bit uncertain, isn't it? I feel a fraud now, that is why I'd like to go.' She added politely, 'When it's convenient.' She looked around her and then back at his quiet face. 'It's been like a dream, hasn't it? But dreams end and we have to go our separate ways again.'

'You want that Francesca?'

'Yes, oh yes, I do... You must see...'

He said very quietly, 'You want to go back to nursing—to your old life in England? If that is your wish, then I will do all I can to help you.' He turned to leave the pool. 'Dreams don't have to end,' he said.

She wasn't really listening, which was a pity; her mind was already busy with the ways and means of getting a job. Not London—something remote, preferably in the country where she could find her way back to her old life once more. When that was done she could go to London and get a good post and make nursing her career. She sighed at the very idea and Litrik turned to look at her.

'Don't worry, Francesca, you shall go just as soon as I can arrange it. You may have to come back briefly for the annulment but I'll do all I can to make things easy for you.'

She turned to take a final look at the pool. She could hardly see it through her tears.

CHAPTER NINE

LITRIK didn't come into the house with her, but drove off straight away to Utrecht, saying he would be home shortly before dinner, so she had a solitary tea by the fire and then went in search of Nanny who had elected to repair the tapestry on one of the massive armchairs in the drawing room. She was a clever needlewoman and, as she pointed out to Fran, only too glad to make herself useful. 'Until such time as I can be a nanny again,' she added and looked hopefully at Fran.

Fran bent over the chair, hiding her red face, murmuring vaguely. These were the awkward moments Litrik hadn't troubled to consider; they cropped up all the time and each time she felt like blurting out the truth. She began, a little feverishly, to talk to Nanny about Clare and the expected baby, a successful red herring which got her through the next five minutes and out of the room, with the excuse that she must walk the dogs.

She walked for miles, thinking about Litrik's promise that she could return to England as soon as he could arrange it. He hadn't sounded in the least put out about it; perhaps he was relieved that she had brought the subject up—it would have been an awkward subject for him to broach. All the same, he might have shown some regret. She turned for home, determined to start her packing as soon as possible so that she could go immediately he had arranged her journey.

To be thwarted within half an hour of his return home. Great Aunt Olda would be celebrating her eightieth birthday in four days time and the whole family would foregather to make it an occasion. Naturally, he pointed out, they would go. The great aunts lived to the north of Leeuwarden in the village of Rinsumaard, something over a hundred miles. He had arranged to be free on that day, they could drive up for lunch and return after dinner in the evening. And perhaps she would go into Utrecht with him and choose a suitable present.

She went with him the following morning since he wasn't due at the hospital until after lunch and spent an absorbing hour in a jeweller's shop choosing a diamond brooch for Tante Olda. Its price staggered Fran but, as Litrik pointed out, one wasn't eighty years old more than once and such an event called for something special. He took her to lunch after that, to Smits Hotel, and then drove her back home before returning to the hospital.

She suggested diffidently on their way back that she might get out the Mini and visit Mevrouw Honig and he agreed readily. 'I shall be going to see her tomorrow some time, but I'm sure she will be glad to see you. Could you find out if Juffrouw de Wit has all she wants? Anything she needs I can take with me tomorrow. And take a look at Mevrouw Honig, will you, and let me know how she is. Juffrouw de Wit is a worthy soul, but she isn't a trained nurse.'

So Fran got into the Mini and drove herself over to the cottage, to be met by Juffrouw de Wit with a most satisfactory report of her patient's progress. Certainly the old woman seemed better; beginning to eat again, said Juffrouw de Wit cheerfully, and taking her pills regularly. Fran checked her temperature and pulse and saw that her breathing was easier; the worst was over and she would be able to give Litrik a good report when he got home.

She supposed it was inevitable that she should be asked if she would accompany him the next morning to see his patient. He had private patients to see at midday and no rounds at the hospital until the afternoon. She got into the car beside him with the dogs nicely settled on the back seat, taking with her a few small luxuries Mevrouw Honig might enjoy, happy to be there beside him. He hadn't said any more about her leaving but it wouldn't be long now, she imagined. Once they had visited Tante Olda he would tell her.

Litrik was pleased with his patient's progress; another few days and she might get up. They drank coffee with Juffrouw de Wit, handed over the odds and ends Fran had brought with her, and drove back. This time there had been no suggestion of going to the pond.

Fran watched Litrik drive off from the house and went to pay her usual visit to the kitchen and then to Nanny, still industriously plying her needle, and after lunch she telephoned Mevrouw van Rijgen, doubtful about what she should wear to Aunt Olda's party.

'Bring a pretty dress with you, my dear,' counselled Mevrouw van Rijgen. 'It's only family but Tante Olda will expect us to do honour to the occasion. Something short. Litrik tells me you are driving back after the party—a pity you can't stay the night but I expect he had a full day of appointments ahead of him.' There was a faint query in her voice and Fran made haste to say that he was very busy and couldn't manage to get away for more than just the one day. She rang off and went upstairs to go through her wardrobe. She would wear the blue woollen suit and take one of her after-six dresses—the mulberry silk velvet with the long tight sleeves and the satin sash. There were high-heeled velvet slippers to match and perhaps the pearls would be lent to her again.

They left soon after breakfast on Tante Olda's birthday, taking the route through Amsterdam and Hoorn and over the Afsluitdijk so that Fran might see something of that part of Holland. 'For,' as Litrik pointed out blandly, 'you might not have another opportunity to see our famous sea dyke. We'll drive back down the other side of the Isselmeer, but it will be dark then, of course.'

He was at his most interesting pointing out various landmarks which he thought might interest her and never once mentioning the fact that she would be going away very soon.

She had hoped, when he had remarked upon her not seeing the Afsluitdijk again, that he would say something about her leaving, but it seemed that it was the last thing he was thinking of.

They stopped for coffee in Alkmaar; it had meant that he had gone into the town expressly for that purpose, but, as he pointed out, they had the time to do so and, like the Afsluitdijk, it was a place it would be a pity for her not to visit while she had the opportunity.

She drank her coffee rather silently, thinking that he seemed determined to remind her that any day now she would be gone, and at the same time he seemed equally determined not to tell her when that was to be.

They arrived at Rinsumaard just before midday, to find a big gathering already there. The aunts lived in a large, rather forbidding house on the edge of the village, it had a large garden around it and its furnishings were opulent and at the same time gloomy. Wilma, greeting Fran in the hall, whispered, 'Isn't it overpowering? All dark oak and family portraits—you ought to see the kitchens. How nice you look. Come and say hallo to the aunts. Tante Olda is having a lovely time…' She turned to Litrik who had been talking to his father. 'Have you bought something fabulous? I've never seen so many handsome presents.' She lifted her face for his kiss. 'Come on, then we can have a drink before lunch.'

Tante Olda received their congratulations and the brooch with dignity and the command that Fran should return to talk to her later on. 'I rest in the afternoon,' she observed, 'but we must have a little chat before you leave this evening. Such a pity that you have to return tonight; I only hope that Litrik is a careful driver.'

Fran assured her that he was. Very careful but fast, only she didn't say that; she wasn't a very fast driver herself but sitting beside Litrik she enjoyed the exhilarating speed.

She got separated from him after that and during luncheon,

since he was sitting at the other end of the vast oval table, she could only get a glimpse of him now and then around the vast floral centrepiece. And after lunch, when the aunts and the elderly had retired for their post-prandial naps, Jebbeke and Wilma carried her off to see the gardens and then explore the house.

'It's like a museum,' said Jebbeke. 'We all hate it, but it's been in the family for years and years and it'll go to Uncle Hilwert, who doesn't want it.'

Fran agreed that it wasn't her idea of a cosy home and thought with sudden longing of Litrik's house, just as big but somehow it was a home, its rooms comfortably furnished, with firelight and lamplight and the dogs lying around and Nel and Tuggs and Nanny. She was going to miss them all—and she was going to miss Litrik for the rest of her life.

'Don't look so sad,' said Wilma, and flung a friendly arm round her shoulders. 'You and Litrik won't have to live here, nor will your children. And aren't you lucky? We are all coming to you at New Year, you know that I expect. We have a lovely time—it's a kind of tradition. When Litrik can tear himself away from his patients you must come and spend a weekend with us.'

Fran wondered what they would think of her when Litrik told them that they had decided to part. He would allow no blame to attach to herself, she know him well enough for that, but all the same she felt guilty.

'You're looking sad again,' said Jebbeke, 'You need a cup of your English tea.' She glanced at her watch. 'It will be in the red salon.'

The red salon was exactly that: red carpet, curtains and upholstery, with a glittering chandelier overhead and stern faced ancestors staring coldly down from the red panelled walls. Several of the family were already there and Litrik crossed the room to join them as they went in.

He included all three of them in his smile, but he spoke to Fran.

'What do you think of the house, Francesca? A little overpowering isn't it? Come over to the fire and have some tea; the aunts aren't coming down until we meet for dinner.'

Tea was a pleasant interlude and presently they scattered again, the men to play billiards, the ladies to enjoy a discussion of the latest fashions, and presently they went upstairs to the various rooms allotted to them to change for the evening.

Fran found herself in a vast room, heavily furnished in the Beidermeyer style with a bathroom and dressing room leading from it. There was no sign of Litrik although his clothes had been laid out in the dressing room. She undressed and had a bath and then dressed quickly in the mulberry velvet. She was sitting at the dressing-table doing things to her face when she heard Litrik in the dressing room, and then presently in the bathroom.

She was quite ready, still sitting at the dressing-table when he tapped on the door and came in. He looked quite splendid in his black tie and her heart turned over at the sight of him and then thumped so loudly that when he came to stand beside her she was afraid that he would hear it.

'A dreadfully depressing room,' remarked Litrik, and added silkily, 'not conducive to connubial bliss.'

She was thinking up a suitable answer to this when he took the pearls out of a pocket and fastened them round her neck. His fingers were cool against her neck and businesslike. He had the earrings, too, and watched while she fastened them, staring at her reflection in the mirror so that she found it difficult to keep her composure.

'Shall we go?' he asked. 'Out of this door, I think—it will look better if we are together, will it not?'

He gave her a brief mocking smile as she went past him.

Everyone had gathered in the drawing room, with Tante Nynke arriving just a few minutes ahead of Tante Olda, who swept in with a fine sense of the dramatic, wearing black satin and a great many diamonds. There were drinks then and a slow procession into the dining room, and this time Fran was between Litrik's cousins, young and only too delighted to entertain her while they ate their way through iced melon, poached salmon, roast pheasant and a magnificent ice pudding, and all of these helped along with champagne. Fran laughed and talked and ate hardly anything, aware of Litrik's eyes upon her face from the other side of the table.

Everyone gathered in the drawing room after dinner, groups forming and dispersing and reforming while Tante Olda sat by the fire in state, talking to first one and then another of the family.

The evening was far gone when Jebbeke tapped Fran on the arm. 'Your turn,' she said lightly. 'Tante Olda wants a chat.'

Litrik had been standing nearby and he had heard his sister. He smiled and nodded at Fran as she crossed the room and sat down beside the old lady, to be looked over by a pair of very shrewd eyes.

'I'm getting tired,' observed Tante Olda, 'but I wanted to talk to you, Francesca; we have had so little opportunity to get to know each other. I do not intend to pry but there are two questions I wish to ask you, and since you are a sensible and honest girl I have no doubt that you will give me truthful answers.'

She was silent for so long that Fran decided that she had dozed off. But she hadn't.

'I am devoted to Litrik—we have always been close, he and I. As a small boy…' She fell silent again and went on in a quite different voice, 'After the disastrous fiasco of his first marriage he changed. Oh, outwardly still charming and an amusing companion, but beneath that, cold and detached, just as though he would never care for anything or anyone again—except for little Lisa, of course. For her, he was his true self.

But underneath that coldness there is still the real man, warm and passionate, and you, my dear, are the one to find that man again.' She gave Fran a searching look. 'You do love him, Francesca?'

Fran's heart answered before her sensible head could frame a reply. 'Yes, I love him—I love him so much.'

The old lady nodded in satisfaction. 'You want to have his children?'

'Yes, oh yes, more than anything in the world, but...'

She was interrupted by Litrik's voice behind her. 'Sorry to break up your gossip.' He sounded lazily tolerant. 'I've just noticed the time as I was talking to Father and we really must go—I have a round in the morning.'

Fran had gone pale. How long had he been there and what had he heard?

She glanced quickly at him; his face was calm, his voice casual and his father was standing at the other end of the long room. A stealthy glance told her that Litrik couldn't have had the time to cross the room and overhear what she had said. She heaved a sigh of relief, kissed the elderly proffered cheek, thanked Tante Olda prettily and then accompanied Litrik round the room, saying goodbyes.

It was really goodbye this time, she thought sadly.

Someone had packed their things and fetched the car to the door. She had put her winter coat into the car and now Litrik wrapped her into it and they drove off to a chorus of goodbyes.

It was a cold dark night with frost sparkling on the roof tops and the fields. Litrik drove fast and almost in silence and presently she slept.

The house was warm and welcoming; they drank the coffee Nel had left out before Fran wished Litrik good night. 'I enjoyed it', she ventured a little shyly. 'You do have a nice family, Litrik.'

He gave her a mocking smile. 'Such a pity that you will

never get to know them, Francesca. As you have pointed out to me, that is by your own wish.'

There was nothing for her to do but wish him good night for the second time and go up to bed.

She came down to breakfast very late the next morning and he had already gone. She spent an hour with Nel and Nanny, telling them about Tante Olda's party, and then took the dogs for a walk and, because she had slept badly, she dozed in front of the fire after lunch.

Litrik came back at tea time. She sat up as he came into the room and he said pleasantly, 'Catching up on last night's sleep?' He put an envelope on the table beside the chair. 'Your tickets, Francesca. I wasn't able to get you a flight—I've booked you on the night ferry to Harwich for the day after tomorrow.'

She had been expecting it for days and now it had come and she was too taken aback to speak. She picked up the envelope and peered inside. The tickets were there, sure enough, and she said faintly, 'Oh, thank you.'

Litrik sat down in his chair and stretched out his legs, the epitome of relaxed comfort. 'You'll get into London about mid-morning, that gives you plenty of time to go on down to your aunts if you wish, or find an hotel.' He picked up the first of the pile of letters waiting for him. 'I'll see that you have sufficient money and write you a reference—that's what you wanted, isn't it?'

It was a little more than Fran could stand. Illogically she was thunderstruck at the suddenness of it all—she had just one day in which to pack her things and say goodbye to Mevrouw Honig and Dominee Meertens. And what was she to say to the staff?

She said savagely, 'How absolutely beastly of you!'

He lifted his handsome head from the letter he was reading. 'Why, my dear Francesca, you have been badgering me to let you return home for days—I'm surprised at you.'

He lowered his eyes to his letters again and she said in a choked voice, 'Well, I'd better go and start packing.'

When she left the room, Litrik rang for Tuggs and, when that faithful friend came, 'Now listen, Tuggs, there are one or two things I want you to do.' Tuggs listened carefully and went back to the kitchen and when Nel asked him what the doctor had wanted, he told her to ask no questions and she would be told no lies!

Fran, in her room, took a wistful look at the lovely clothes she had bought with Litrik's money, and began to pack the things she had brought with her. She would have to travel in the Jaeger suit for she had no coat with her but she could wear a sweater with it and hope that it wouldn't be too cold a day. Having done this she did her face and hair and went downstairs for dinner, to hold a desultory conversation with Litrik and agree with every appearance of pleasure to his suggestion that, as he intended visiting Mevrouw de Wit in the morning, she might like to go with him.

The old woman was well on the way to recovery, sitting downstairs in a chair by the fire Juffrouw de Wit had kindled in the parlour. She accepted Fran's gift of fruit and biscuits, assured her that she would soon be on her feet once more and asked her if she wanted to go to the pond.

It was after they had all had coffee that Litrik said that he would like to examine his patient and if Fran wished to go for a stroll perhaps she would like to go now. 'Ten minutes,' he said. 'I must be in Zeist by eleven o'clock.'

So she trod the well-known path once more for the last time and went to sit on the log and watch the coots and listen to the few birds. It had been a happy place with Lisa, but now it was sad; she went back before the ten minutes were up, took a brief farewell of the two ladies and got into the car. Litrik talked cheerfully about his patient during the brief drive back and left at once for the hospital, and she went to the kitchen where she told Nel and Nanny that she would be going to England on the following day. They received her news calmly, hoped that she would have a good time and plunged into the question of whether she wanted all the guest-rooms opened and prepared for Christmas. Somehow she escaped answering that and took herself and the dogs for a long walk and directly after lunch went to say goodbye to the *dominee*. She was hurt and surprised at the matter-of-fact manner in which he received her news, and still more disappointed at his vague answers to her anxious questions about the annulment.

'You are anxious to leave us?' he boomed at her.

'Yes—no—that is—I can't explain…' And to her relief he said no more.

Feeling frustrated, she shook hands with him and his wife and as he went down the garden path with her she was perplexed to hear him say, 'Most satisfactory—this is something I had hoped and prayed for.'

She wanted very much to ask him what he meant—he must have been referring to Lisa. She didn't go straight back to the house, but walked on towards the lake, making and discarding plans for her future. She had a little money of her own but she would have to decide quickly where she wanted to go and then look for a job. Litrik had said that he would see that her career wouldn't suffer and she believed him; it would help a lot if she made up her mind before she left the next day, then there would be no need to write to him.

She wandered on, trying to envisage a future without him and filled with despair at the thought. But that was a waste of time and the sooner she stopped mooning after him, she told herself briskly, the better. She would tell him that she would like to work in Scotland; she wasn't fussy where but preferably in a large hospital where there was plenty of work. Her mind made up, she turned for home, pecked at her lunch and went to her room to finish her packing. That done, she spent half an hour fingering the lovely things still hanging in the closet, wondering what Litrik would do about them. They were too small for Nanny, and his sisters were big girls. Besides, they had more than enough money to buy anything they wanted. It was a pity she must leave the winter coat, it would have been a comfort on the journey.

Litrik didn't come home for tea and although he came in just before dinner, he went out again almost immediately they had finished. She sat in the drawing room knitting, her mind refusing to think any more.

He was at breakfast, wishing her good morning as usual and, before he went to the hospital, warning her to be ready to leave at eight o'clock that evening. 'I shall be back by six o'clock so will you arrange dinner for an hour earlier than usual—we can leave directly after that.'

'We?' asked Fran startled. She had expected Tuggs to drive her to Utrecht to catch the boat train.

'Naturally I shall drive you myself.'

He had gone, leaving her to spend her last day roaming round the house and the gardens. At least she would have the chance to talk to him about her plans, for the drive to the Hoek would take an hour, perhaps more. She had herself nicely in hand by the time he returned in the evening, made rather feverish small talk during dinner, said goodbye to everyone and got into the Daimler. It was a brilliant night, the wind still and with a silver moon giving sparkle to the frost, and there was not much traffic. She settled down beside Litrik and began to compose the various questions in her head. They had skirted Utrecht before she had them exactly as she wished and then she forgot every one of them as they passed a road sign.

'We're going the wrong way,' she said urgently. 'Emmeloord and Leeuwarden—the Hoek's the other way.'

'We are not going to the Hoek,' said Litrik calmly.

'I'm going to miss the boat… Why not?' She took a steadying breath. 'Where are we going?'

'To a cottage I have near Sneek.' He gave a great sigh. 'You see, my dear, I am in love with you and I cannot let you go.'

The road was straight and empty before them; he slowed the car and stopped. 'I believe that I have loved you for a long time now, perhaps since that first time when I made you cry during that lecture—afterwards I felt as though I had wounded some small creature and left it to die. Then I met you again and I knew that you were exactly the mother Lisa had wished for for so long—a mouse, she had said, and that is what you are, a small beautiful mouse with a soft voice and lovely eyes and a gentle mouth and I knew for certain then that I loved you. Only you had made it clear that for you our marriage was purely for Lisa's sake and I have tried very hard to keep to my side of our pact.'

Fran stirred in her seat. 'Could we get out?' she asked softly. 'Please?'

He went round the car and took something from the boot and opened her door and she saw that he had her coat over his arm.

'I went to look in your room—I guessed what you would do. You see how well I know you, my darling? I asked Nel to pack some of your things and put this into the car.'

He helped her into it and buttoned it up cosily under her chin and took her arm and began walking along the road. Fran looked into his face, very clear in the moonlight. 'I love you,' she said, 'but how did you know? Because you do know, don't you?' She frowned. 'You heard me and Tante Olda?'

'I eavesdropped quite shamelessly, my darling, reminding myself that all is fair in love and war. You see, I know Tante Olda very well indeed; she has this habit of asking searching questions. I know you, too, and I knew you would answer her honestly.'

'You could have told me on our way home.'

'You slept, my love. And I wanted to be sure—that's why

I gave you the tickets. And you seemed pleased so that I wanted to hurt you.'

'Well, you did,' declared Fran, 'and I really can't think why I love you so very much for sometimes you are so tiresome.'

He stopped and swung her round into his arms and let out a great bellow of laughter. 'Oh, I will try so hard not to be tiresome,' he promised her and kissed her gently and then very hard and indeed, and presently he took her arm again and began walking back to the car. And as they went he stopped to kiss her once in a while. 'Love in the moonlight,' he observed, 'there is nothing quite like it.'

'Tell me,' said Fran, 'this cottage—are we going to stay there?'

'For a week—Mama's retired cook lives there and looks after it for me; Tuggs will have phoned her and told her to expect us.'

'Supposing that I had insisted on going to the Hoek?'

'I should have kidnapped you,' said Litrik, and kissed her once again.

THE GIRL WITH GREEN EYES

by

Betty Neels

CHAPTER ONE

THE vast waiting-room, despite the cheerful yellow paint on its Victorian walls, its bright posters and even a picture or two, its small counter for tea and coffee and the playthings all scattered around, was still a depressing place. It was also a noisy one, its benches filled by mothers, babies and toddlers awaiting their turn to be seen by the consultant paediatrician. From time to time a name would be called by a plump middle-aged sister and another small patient with an evidently anxious mother would be borne away while those who were waiting rearranged themselves hopefully.

The dark, wet day of early February was already dwindling into dusk, although it was barely four o'clock. The waiting-room was damp and chilly despite the heating, and as the rows of patients gradually lessened it seemed to become even chillier.

Presently there was only one patient left, a small fair-haired toddler, asleep curled up in the arms of the girl who held her. A pretty girl with a tip-tilted nose, a gentle mouth and large green eyes. Her abundant pale brown hair was scraped back fiercely into a top knot and she looked tired. She watched the two registrars who had been dealing with the less urgent cases come from their offices and walk away, and thought longingly of her tea. If this specialist didn't get a move on, she reflected, the child she was holding would wake and demand hers.

A door opened and the sister came through. 'I'm sorry, dear, that you've had to wait for so long; Dr Thurloe got held up. He'll see you now.'

The girl got up and went past her into the room beyond, hesitating inside the door. The man sitting at the desk glanced up and got to his feet, a large man and tall, with fair hair heavily sprinkled with silver and the kind of good looks to make any woman look at him twice, with a commanding nose, a wide, firm mouth and heavily lidded eyes. He smiled at her now. 'Do sit down—' his voice was slow and deep '—I am so sorry that you've had to wait for such a long time.' He sat down again and picked up the notes and doctor's letter before him; halfway through he glanced up. 'You aren't this little girl's mother?'

She had been waiting and watching him, aware of a peculiar sensation in her insides.

'Me? Oh, no. I work at the orphanage. Miranda's not very easy, but I mostly look after her; she's a darling, but she does get—well, disturbed.'

He nodded and went on reading, and she stared at his down-bent head. She had frequently wondered what it would be like to fall in love, but she had never imagined that it would be quite like this—and could one fall in love with someone at first glance? Heroines in romantic novels often did, but a romantic novel was one thing, real life was something quite different, or so she had always thought. He looked up and smiled at her and her heart turned over—perhaps after all real life wasn't all that different from a romantic novel. She smiled with delight and his eyebrows rose and his glance became questioning, but since she said nothing—she was too short of breath to do that—he sat back in his chair. 'Well, now, shall we see what can be done for Miranda, Miss...?'

'Lockitt—Lucy Lockitt.'

His firm mouth quivered. '"Lost her pocket, Kitty Fisher found it..."'

'Everyone says that,' she told him seriously.

'Tiresome for you, but I suppose we all learnt nursery rhymes when we were small.' With an abrupt change of manner he went on, 'If you could put her on to the couch, I'll take a look.'

Lucy laid the still sleeping child down and the doctor came over to the couch and stood looking down at her. 'I wonder why nothing was done when hydrocephalus was first diagnosed. I see in her notes that her skull was abnormally enlarged at birth. You don't happen to know why her notes are so sparse?'

'They've been lost—that is, Matron thinks so. You see, she was abandoned when she was a few weeks old, no one knows who her parents are; they left her with the landlady of the rooms they were living in. They left some money too, so I suppose she didn't bother to see a doctor—perhaps she didn't know that Miranda wasn't quite normal. A week or two ago the landlady had to go to hospital and Miranda was taken in by neighbours who thought that there was something wrong, so they brought her to the orphanage and Dr Watts arranged for you to see her.'

Dr Thurloe bent over the toddler, who woke then and burst into tears. 'Perhaps you could undress her?' he suggested. 'Would you like Sister or one of the nurses to help you?'

'Strange faces frighten her,' said Lucy matter-of-factly, 'and I can manage, thank you.'

He was very gentle, and when he had made his general examination he said in a quiet voice, 'Take her on your lap, will you? I need to examine her head.'

It took a considerable time and he had to sit very close. A pity, thought Lucy, that for all he cares I could be one of the hospital chairs. It occurred to her then that he was probably married, with children of his own; he wasn't young, but he wasn't old either—just right, in fact. She began to puzzle out ways and means of getting to know something about him, so deeply engrossed that he had to ask her twice if she was a nurse.

'Me? Oh, no. I just go each day from nine in the morning until five o'clock in the afternoon. I do odd jobs, feeding the babies and changing them and making up cots—that sort of thing.'

He was running a gentle hand over the distended little skull. 'Was there no nurse to accompany Miranda here?'

'Well, no. You see, it's hard to get trained nurses in an orphanage—it's not very exciting, just routine. There's Matron and a deputy matron and three state enrolled nurses, and then four of us to help.'

The doctor already knew how many children there were; all the same, he asked that too.

'Between forty and fifty,' she replied, then added, 'I've been there for four years.'

He was measuring the small head with callipers, his large, well-tended hands feather-light. 'And you have never wished to train as a nurse?'

'Oh, yes, but it hasn't been possible.'

He said smoothly, 'The training does tie one down for several years. You understand what is wrong with Miranda?'

'Not precisely, only that there is too much fluid inside her skull.'

'It is a fairly rare condition—the several parts of the skull don't unite and the cerebrospinal fluid increases so that the child's head swells. There are sometimes mental symptoms, already apparent in Miranda. I should like her to be admitted here and insert a catheter in a ventricle which will drain off some of the surplus fluid.'

'Where to?'

'Possibly a pleural cavity via the jugular vein with a valve to prevent a flow-back.'

'It won't hurt her?' she asked urgently.

'No. It will need skilled attention when necessary, though.'

He straightened to his full height, towering over her. 'Will you set her to rights? I'll write to Dr Watts and arrange for her to be admitted as soon as possible.'

Lucy, arranging a nappy, just so, said thickly round the safety-pin between her teeth, 'You can cure her?'

'At least we can make life more comfortable for her. Take that pin out of your mouth, it could do a great deal of damage if you swallowed it. What transport do you have?' He glanced at the notes before him. 'Sparrow Street, isn't it? You came by ambulance?'

She shook her head, busy putting reluctant little arms into a woolly jacket. 'Taxi. I'm to get one to take us back.'

'My dear girl, it is now five o'clock and the rush hour, you might have to wait for some time. I'll arrange an ambulance,' he stretched out an arm to the telephone, 'or better still, I'll take you on my way home.'

'That's very kind of you,' said Lucy politely, 'but it wouldn't do at all, you know. For one thing the orphanage is in Willoughby Street and that's even more East End than here, and for another, I'm sure consultants don't make a habit of giving lifts to their patients—though perhaps you do if they're private...'

The doctor sat back in his chair and looked her over. 'I am aware of where the orphanage is and I give lifts to anyone I wish to. You have a poor opinion of consultants... We are, I should suppose, exactly like anyone else.'

'Oh, I'm sure you are,' said Lucy kindly, 'only much clev-erer, of course.'

His heavy eyelids lifted, revealing a pair of very blue eyes. 'A debatable point,' he observed. 'And now if you will go to the front entrance I will meet you there in a few minutes.'

He spoke quietly and she did as he asked, because she had to admit to herself that he had that kind of voice and she was tired. Miranda had gone to sleep again, but once she woke she would want her tea and her cot and would fly into a storm of tears; to be driven back to the orphanage would be a relief. She was already late and it would be another half-hour or more before she was home. She sat on a bench facing the door so that she would see the doctor when he came, but he came unnoticed from one of the corridors at the back of the entrance hall. He paused before he reached her and gave her a long look; she was pretty enough to warrant it, and seen in profile her nose had a most appealing tilt... He spoke as he reached her. 'The car's just outside. It will be better if you carry her, I think; it wouldn't do to wake her.'

They crossed the hall and he held the door for her and went ahead to open the door of the dark grey Rolls-Royce outside. She got in carefully and he fastened her safety-belt without disturbing the child, and then got in beside her, drove out of the forecourt and joined the stream of traffic in the street.

Lucy waited until they stopped in a traffic jam. 'You said Sparrow Street, and it is, of course, only the staff and children use the Willoughby Street entrance.'

'I see—and who uses the Sparrow Street door?' He edged the car forward a few yards and turned to look at her.

'Oh, the committee and visiting doctors and the governors—you know, important people.'

'I should have thought that in an orphanage the orphans were the important people.'

'They are. They're awfully well looked after.' She lapsed into silence as the big car slid smoothly ahead and presently stopped in Willoughby Street. The doctor got out and opened her door for her and she got out carefully. 'Thank you very much for the lift, it was kind of you.' She smiled up into his impassive face.

'I'm coming in with you, I want to see the matron. Where do you live?'

'Me? In Chelsea.'

'I pass it on my way home. I'll drop you off.'

'I'll be at least fifteen minutes...'

'So shall I.' They had gone inside and he indicated the row of chairs lined up against the wall of the small reception room. 'Wait here, will you?'

He nodded to the nurse who came to meet them and walked off, leaving Lucy to follow her to the back of the building where the toddlers had their cots and where the sister-in-charge was waiting. It was all of fifteen minutes by the time Lucy had explained everything, handed over the now wakeful Miranda, and said goodnight.

'Thanks for staying on over your time,' Sister said. 'I'll make it up to you some time.' She smiled nicely because Lucy was a good worker and didn't grumble at the unending task of keeping the toddlers clean and fed and happy. We could do with a few more like her, she thought, watching Lucy's slender shape disappearing down the corridor.

There was no sign of the doctor when Lucy got back to the reception-room. Perhaps she had been too long and he had gone without her, and she could hardly blame him for that—he had probably had a long and tiring day and was just as anxious to get home as she was. All the same, she sat down on one of the hard wooden chairs; there was no one else there, or she could have asked…

He came five minutes later, calm and unhurried, smiling genially, and accompanied by the matron. Lucy got to her feet and, rather to her surprise, was thanked for her afternoon's duties; it was by no means an uncommon thing for her to take children to hospital to be examined, and she was surprised that anyone had found it necessary to thank her. She muttered politely, added a goodnight and followed the doctor out to his car.

'Exactly where do you live?' he enquired of her as he settled himself beside her.

She mentioned a quiet road, one of those leading away from the Embankment, and added, 'It is very kind of you. I hope it's not taking you out of your way?'

'I live in Chiswick. Do you share a flat?' The question was casual.

'Me? No. I live with my parents…'

'Of course, now I remember—is your father an archaeologist, *the* Gregory Lockitt?' And when she murmured that he was, 'I met your parents some time ago at a dinner party. They were just back from the Andes.'

'That's right,' she agreed composedly, 'they travel a good deal.'

'But you prefer your orphanage?' His voice was kindly impersonal.

'Yes.' She didn't add to that, to explain that it was a job she had found for herself and taken on with the good humoured tolerance of her parents. She had been a disappointment to them, she knew that, although they had never actually said so; her elder sister, with a university degree and distinguished good looks, was personal assistant to the director of a City firm, and her younger sister, equally good-looking and chic with it, worked in one of the art galleries—moreover she was engaged to a young executive who was rising through his financial world with the ruthless intention of reaching the top before anyone else. Only Lucy, the middle sister and overshadowed by them both, had failed to be a success. There was no question but that they all loved her with an easygoing tolerance, but there was also no question that she had failed to live up to the family's high standards. She was capable, sensible and practical and not in the least clever, and despite her gentle prettiness she was a shy girl. At twenty-five, she knew that her mother was beginning to despair of her marrying.

Dr Thurloe stopped the car before her home and got out to open her door, and she thanked him again. Pauline and Imogen would have known exactly what to say to make him interested enough to suggest meeting again, but she had no idea; the only thought in her head was that she wasn't likely to see him again, and that almost broke her heart. She stared up into his face, learning it by heart, knowing that she would never forget it, still bemused by the surprise of loving him.

His quiet, 'A pleasure, enjoy your evening, Miss Lockitt,' brought her to her senses again, and she bade him a hasty goodnight and thumped the door knocker. He waited by his car until Alice, the housekeeper, opened the door, and then he got into the car and drove away. Perhaps I should have asked him in, reflected Lucy uneasily as she said hello to Alice.

'And who was that now?' asked Alice. 'Nice car too. Got yourself a young man, love?'

Lucy shook her head. 'Just a lift home. Is everyone in, Alice?'

'In the drawing-room and 'is nibs with them.' She gave Lucy a motherly pat. 'Best go and tidy yerself, love—they're having drinks...'

Lucy went slowly upstairs to her room, showered and got into a wool dress, brushed out her hair and did her face. She knew her mother disliked her wearing the clothes she had worn at the orphanage, even though they were covered by an overall and a plastic apron. She didn't hurry—there would just be time for a drink before dinner, and that meant that she wouldn't have to listen to Cyril, Pauline's fiancé, prosing about stocks and shares for too long. She went slowly downstairs, wondering if her sister really loved him or whether she was merely carried away at the prospect of being the wife of a successful businessman, with a flat in town, a nice little cottage in the country, two cars and enough money to allow her to dress well and entertain lavishly. In Lucy's opinion, none of these was a good reason for marrying him.

She found them all sitting round the fire in the drawing-room and her mother looked round to say, 'There you are, darling. Have the orphans been trying? You're so late...'

Lucy took the drink her father had handed her and she sat down beside him. 'I took one of them to be seen by a specialist at the City Royal; it took rather a long time.' She didn't say any more, for they weren't interested—although they always asked her about her day, they didn't listen to her reply. And indeed, she admitted to herself, it made dull listening compared with Pauline's witty accounts of the people who had called in to the art gallery, and Imogen's amusing little titbits of news about the important people she met so often. She sipped her sherry and listened to Cyril clearing his throat preparatory to addressing them. He never just talked, she thought; he either gave a potted lecture, or gave them his opinion about some matter with the air of a man who believed that no one else was clever enough to do so. She swallowed her sherry in a gulp and listened to his diatribe about the National Health Service. She didn't hear a word; she was thinking about Dr Thurloe.

Later, as Lucy said goodnight to her mother, that lady observed lightly, 'You were very quiet this evening, darling—quieter than usual. Is this little job of yours too much for you, do you suppose?'

Lucy wondered if her mother had any idea of what her little job entailed, but she didn't say so. 'Oh, no, Mother.' She spoke briskly. 'It's really easy…'

'Oh, good—it doesn't bore you?'

'Not in the least.' How could she ever explain to her mother that the orphans were never boring? Tiresome, infuriating, lovable and exhausting, but never boring. 'I only help around, you know.'

Her mother offered a cheek for a goodnight kiss. 'Well, as long as you're happy, darling. I do wish you could meet some nice man…'

But I have, thought Lucy, and a lot of good it's done me. She said 'Goodnight, Mother dear…'

'Goodnight, Lucy. Don't forget we are all going to the Walters' for dinner tomorrow evening, so don't be late home, and wear something pretty.'

Lucy went to bed and forgot all about the dinner party; she

was going over, syllable by syllable, every word which Dr Thurloe had uttered.

She got home in good time the next evening. The day had been busy and she felt the worse for wear, so it was a relief to find that her sisters were in their rooms dressing and her parents were still out. She drank the tea Alice had just made, gobbled a slice of toast and went to her room to get ready for the party.

The Walters were old friends of her parents, recently retired from the diplomatic service, and Lucy and her sisters had known them since they were small girls; the friendship was close enough for frequent invitations to their dinner parties. Lucy burrowed through her wardrobe, deciding what to wear. She had a nice taste in dress, although she wasn't a slavish follower of fashion, and the green dress she finally hauled out was simple in style with a long, full skirt, long, tight sleeves and a round, low neckline. She ran a bath and then lay in it, daydreaming about Dr Thurloe, quite forgetting the time, so that she had to dress in a tearing hurry, brush out her hair and dash on powder and lipstick without much thought to her appearance. Everyone was in the hall waiting for her as she ran downstairs and her mother said tolerantly, 'Darling, you're wearing that green dress again. Surely it's time you had something new?'

'You'd better come with me on your next free day,' said Imogen. 'I know just the shop for you—there was a gorgeous pink suit in the window, just right for you.'

Lucy forbore from saying that she didn't look nice in pink, only if it were very pale pink like almond blossom. 'Sorry if I've kept you all waiting. Pauline, you and Imogen look stunning enough for the lot of us.'

Pauline patted her on the shoulder. 'You could look stunning too,' she pointed out, 'if you took the trouble.'

It was pointless to remind her sister that the orphans didn't mind whether she looked stunning or not. She followed her father out to the car and squashed into the back with her sisters.

The Walters gave rather grand dinner parties; they had many friends and they enjoyed entertaining. The Lockitts found that there were half a dozen guests already there, and Mrs Walter, welcoming them warmly, observed that there were only two more expected. 'That charming Mrs Seymour,' she observed, 'so handsome, and I dare say very lonely now that she is widowed, and I don't know if you've met—' She broke off, smiling towards the door, 'Here he is, anyway. William, how delightful that you could come! I was just saying…perhaps you know Mrs Lockitt?'

Imogen and Pauline had gone to speak to Mr Walter; only Lucy was with her mother. She watched Dr Thurloe, the very epitome of the well-dressed man, walk towards his hostess, her gentle mouth slightly open, her cheeks pinkening with surprise and delight. Here he was again, fallen as it were into her lap, and on his own too, so perhaps he wasn't married or even engaged.

He greeted his hostess, shook hands with Lucy's mother, and when Mrs Walter would have introduced Lucy he forestalled her with a pleasant, 'Oh, but we have already met—during working hours…'

He smiled down at Lucy, who beamed back at him, regretting at the same time that she had worn the green, by no means her prettiest dress. She regretted it even more as the door was opened again and Mrs Seymour swept in. A splendid blonde, exquisitely dressed and possessed of a haughty manner and good looks, she greeted Mrs Walter with a kiss on one cheek, bade Mrs Lockitt a charming good evening, smiled perfunctorily at Lucy, and turned to the doctor. 'William!' she exclaimed. 'I had no idea that you would be here—I had to take a taxi. If I'd known you could have picked me up.' She smiled sweetly and Lucy ground silent teeth. 'But you shall drive me home—you will, won't you?'

'Delighted, Fiona.'

She put a hand on his sleeve and said brightly, 'Oh, there is Tim Wetherby, I must speak to him—you know him, of course...'

It seemed that Dr Thurloe did. The pair of them strolled away and, since Mrs Walter had turned aside to talk to one of the guests, Lucy was left standing by her mother.

Mrs Lockitt gave her an exasperated glance. 'I want to talk to Mr Walter before we go into dinner. Do exert yourself, darling, and go and chat with someone—it is such a pity that you're so shy...'

A remark which made Lucy even more so. But, obedient to her mother's suggestion, she joined a group of people she knew and made the kind of conversation expected of her while managing to keep an eye on the doctor. That he and Fiona Seymour knew each other well was obvious, but Lucy had already decided that Fiona was not at all the kind of girl he should marry—he needed a wife who would listen to him when he got back from his work each day, someone who liked children, someone who understood how tiresome they could be and how lovable and how ill... Lucy nodded her head gently, seeing herself as that wife. She wasn't sure how she was going to set about it, but she would find a way.

'You're not listening to a word I'm saying,' remarked the young man who had been talking for a few minutes. When she apologised, everyone laughed—nicely, because they liked her—and someone said, 'Lucy's thinking about her orphans.' Her job was a mild joke among those she knew and there was no malice in the remark. She smiled at the speaker as they went in to dinner.

She sat between the Walters' rather solemn elder son and a young man attached to one of the foreign embassies, now home on leave, and she dutifully lent an attentive ear first to Joe Walter's explaining rather prosily about computers, and then to her neighbour on the other side, who was anxious to tell her what a splendid time he was having in his far-flung post. With an effort she smiled and nodded and said all the right things, and the doctor, from the other side of the table, thought how restful she was and how very pretty. She looked different, of course, dressed in that green thing and with her hair curling almost to her shoulders. She was sensible too, when it came to handling small children. He bent a bland listening face towards his dinner companion while he allowed the nucleus of a plan to take shape in his sagacious mind.

People sat around talking after dinner, and beyond a few passing remarks Lucy saw nothing of the doctor. Since she left with her family before he did, she had no chance to see him and Fiona Seymour leave together. She told herself stoutly that it didn't matter one bit, one day she would marry him, only she couldn't leave it too long, for she was twenty-five already. She was immensely cheered by the thought that Mrs Seymour, however well made-up she was, couldn't disguise the fact that she wouldn't see thirty again.

Back home, all of them in the kitchen, drinking hot milk before bed, her mother remarked, 'What a nice man William Thurloe is, so good-looking and clever and not an ounce of conceit in him.'

'We had quite a long chat,' said Imogen complacently.

'But Fiona Seymour has got her talons into him,' said Pauline. She added, 'He must be all of thirty-five—she'd make him a very suitable wife.'

'Why?' asked Lucy quietly.

Both sisters turned to look at her. 'She's what is known as a handsome woman, intelligent and always well dressed,' they chorused kindly, 'and she would look just right sitting opposite him at the dinner table. A splendid hostess...'

'But she can't be a hostess all the time—I mean, what about looking after the children, and seeing that he gets a good meal when he comes home late, and gets enough sleep...?'

Her family stared at her. 'Why, Lucy,' said her mother, 'you sound,' she paused, seeking a word, 'concerned.'

Lucy finished her milk and put the mug in the sink. 'I just think that Fiona Seymour isn't the wife for him. He was the specialist I took Miranda to see yesterday; he likes children and somehow I don't think she does.' She kissed her mother and father, nodded goodnight to her sisters and went up to her room. She had said more than she had intended to say, which had been silly of her. The doctor's future was nothing to her; she would probably meet him from time to time at some mutual friend's house, and he would greet her politely and go and talk to someone else, forgetting her at once.

It was raining dismally when she left home the next morning. The orphanage looked bleaker than ever as she got off her bus, although once inside it became more cheerful with its bright painted walls and colourful curtains. All the same, the morning dragged with its unending round of chores. She was ministering to a vomiting four-year-old when Sister came to find her. 'Matron wants you in the office, Lucy. You'd better go at once.'

Lucy handed over the small child, took off her apron and made her way to the office on the first floor.

Matron was quite young and well liked. 'Sit down, Lucy,' she invited. 'I've a favour to ask of you. Miranda has to go off into hospital in two days' time. Dr Thurloe has asked if you would be allowed to go with her—it's important that she is not too disturbed, and she responds to you. You would have to live at the City Royal for a few days—she would be in a room off the children's ward and you would have a room next to hers. You would be relieved for meals and off-duty, but it might be necessary for you to get up at night if she is very disturbed.' She smiled. 'And we both know what that's like.'

'Yes, of course I'll go, Matron.' Lucy smiled too; she would see Dr Thurloe again after all, and perhaps she would be able to say something witty or clever and get his attention—not just polite attention, but real interest... 'When exactly are we to go?'

'Have a day off tomorrow and report here at eight o'clock on the day after. I believe Dr Thurloe means to insert the tube later in the day, and I must warn you that you may have a difficult night afterwards. It depends on her reactions as to how long she stays there. You'll be free?'

'Oh, yes, Matron—for as long as you want me to be with Miranda.'

'Good, that's settled, then. I won't keep you longer.'

The day had suddenly become perfect; the children were little angels, and the hours sped away in a flurry of tasks which were no longer boring or tiresome. Lucy changed nappies, cleaned up messes, fed protesting toddlers and dreamt of the days ahead, days in which she would become the object of admiration—Dr Thurloe's admiration—because of some skilful act on her part—saving Miranda's life by her quick thinking, rescuing a ward full of children by her bravery in case of fire...a bomb outrage...burst pipes...? It didn't really matter what it was as long as it caused him to notice her and then fall in love with her.

She finished at last and went off duty and home. It was still raining, and as she hurried from the bus-stop the steady downpour brought her to her usual senses. She laughed out loud so that an elderly couple passing looked at her with suspicion. 'No more useless daydreaming,' she told herself briskly. 'You're too old for that anyway, but that doesn't mean that you aren't going to marry him some day.'

It was nice to be home for a day. She pottered around, helping her mother with the flowers, sorting out the sheets of scrawled writing which flowed from her father's pen as he worked at the lengthy task of putting together notes for the book he intended to write. At the end of the day she packed the bag that she would need while she was in hospital, washed her hair, did her nails and inspected her pretty face for the first wrinkles and lines. She couldn't find any.

She and Miranda were fetched from the orphanage by ambulance the next morning, and to everyone's relief the child slept quietly in Lucy's arms. It wasn't until they were in the room where she was to stay that she woke and, sensing something out of the ordinary, began to cry.

Lucy sat down, still in her outdoor things, and set about the task of quieting Miranda. She had just succeeded when Dr Thurloe came in.

His 'Good morning, Lucy,' was quietly spoken and uttered with impersonal courtesy before he began giving the ward sister his instructions, and presently Miranda, still snivelling a bit, was given an injection and carried away to Theatre, leaving Lucy free to unpack her bag in the adjoining room and envelop her nicely curved person in the voluminous overall she had been told that she must wear. Her duties, as far as she could make out, were light enough—certainly no worse than they were at the orphanage. The only difference was that they would extend for a much longer period each day, and quite possibly each night too. A small price to pay for seeing the doctor from time to time, and on his own ground too.

She drank the coffee that one of the nurses brought her; the nurse was a nice girl, but faintly condescending. 'Why don't you train as a nurse?' she asked.

'I'm not clever,' observed Lucy, 'but I like children.' She might have added that she had no need to earn her living, and that her mother and father found it difficult to understand as well as faintly amusing that she should spend her days feeding babies and toddlers and everlastingly clearing up their mess, only it didn't enter her head to do so.

'How long will it take?' she wanted to know, and was treated to a lengthy description of exactly what Dr Thurloe was doing. She didn't understand half of it, but it was nice to talk about him. 'I thought he was a physician,' she ventured.

The nurse gave her an impatient look. 'Well, of course he is, but he does this kind of surgery too. He's a paediatrician—that's a children's doctor.'

Lucy, who had looked all that up in her father's study, already knew that, but she expressed suitable gratitude for being told, and when her companion said importantly that she must return to the ward and continue what sounded like a mountain of tasks, she thanked her for her company and settled herself down to wait. It wouldn't be too long.

Miranda returned ten minutes later, borne in the arms of Theatre Sister and already rousing from the anaesthetic. There was just time for her to be settled in Lucy's arms before she opened her eyes, and then her small mouth was ready to let out an enraged yell.

'Hello, love,' said Lucy in her gentle voice, and Miranda smiled instead.

'Lucy,' she mumbled contentedly, and closed her eyes and her mouth too.

Dr Thurloe, standing silently behind her, nodded his handsome head. He had been right to follow his instinctive wish to have Lucy there; it would make things a good deal easier on the ward, and besides, she looked nice sitting there in that oversized overall. He had a sudden jumble of ridiculous thoughts run through his clever head; nurseries, rice pudding, children shouting and laughing, and small figures pattering to and fro...

He frowned. Fiona had told him laughingly only the other day that he saw enough children without needing any of his own. 'What you need,' she had told him in her charming way, 'is a quiet house to come home to, pleasant evenings with friends, and someone to talk to at the end of the day without any interruptions.' She had made it sound very inviting and, because he had been very tired then, he had more or less agreed with her, but now he realised that that wasn't what he wanted. He wasn't sure what he did want, and anyway, it was hardly the time to worry about it now. He went to bend over his small patient, taking no notice of Lucy, then he gave more instructions to his ward sister and went away.

CHAPTER TWO

THE day seemed very long to Lucy. She was relieved for her meals, but Miranda, now fully awake, became restless towards the evening, and the only way to placate her was for Lucy to take her on her lap and murmur the moppet's favourite nursery rhymes over and over again in her gentle voice. But eventually Miranda slept, and Lucy was able to tuck her into her cot and, with a nurse in her place, go to the canteen for her supper. The nurses there were casually kind, showing her where to get her meal and where she might sit, but beyond a few smiles and hellos she was ignored while they discussed their work on the wards, their boyfriends and their lack of money. She ate her supper quickly and slipped away unnoticed, back to the austere little room where Miranda was. The ward sister was there conning the chart.

'Had your supper? Good. Night Sister will be along in about an hour. I think it might be a good idea if you had a bath and got ready for bed while I can spare a nurse to sit here—that will mean that if Miranda wakes up later and is difficult you'll be available. Go to bed once Sister's been—but you do know you may have to get up in the night? I don't think there will be a nurse to spare to attend the child; we're rather busy…'

She nodded and smiled and went away, and Lucy set about getting ready for bed in her own small room, leaving the door open in case Miranda woke and the nurse couldn't placate her.

But the child slept on and Lucy bathed in peace, brushed her hair, got into a dressing-gown and padded back to take the nurse's place.

The nurse yawned. 'She hasn't moved,' she told Lucy. 'She looks like a cherub, doesn't she? If it weren't for that outsized head...' She glanced at her watch. 'I'm off duty, thank heaven; it's been a long day. See you in the morning.'

Lucy sat down. Miranda was sleeping peacefully, and her pulse, which Lucy had been shown how to take and record, was exactly as it should be. Lucy studied the chart and started to read up the notes behind it. The small operation had been written up in red ink in an almost unreadable scrawl and initialled W.T., and she puzzled it out with patience. Dr Thurloe might be an excellent paediatrician, but his writing appeared to be appalling. She smiled, pleased that she knew something about him, and then she sat quietly thinking about him until Night Sister, a small brisk woman, came into the room. She checked the valve, looked at the chart and asked, 'You know what you're looking for, Miss Lockitt? Slow pulse, vomiting, headache—not that Miranda will be able to tell you that... But if you're worried, or even doubtful, ring the bell at once. I'll be back later on, and if I can't come then my junior night sister will. I should go to bed if I were you. Her pulse is steady and she's sleeping, but I depend on you to see to her during the night.'

She went away as quietly as she had come, and Lucy did as she had been told and got into the narrow, cold bed in the adjoining room. She got up again in a few minutes and put on her dressing-gown again, and then tucked her cold feet into its cosy folds and rolled into a tight ball, and dozed off.

It was only a little after an hour later when Miranda's first restless whimpers woke her. She was out of bed in a flash and bending over the cot. Miranda was awake and cross, but her pulse seemed all right. Lucy picked her up carefully and sat down with her on her lap, gave her a drink and began the one-sided conversation which the toddler seemed to enjoy. Miranda stopped grizzling and presently began a conversation of her own, although when Lucy stopped talking her small face creased into infantile rage again, so that Lucy hurried into the Three Bears, growling gently so that Miranda chuckled. 'And Father Bear blew on his porridge to cool it,' said Lucy, and blew, to stop and draw a quick breath because Dr Thurloe had come silently into the room and was watching her. He had someone with him, a pretty, dark girl in sister's uniform, and it was to her that he spoke. 'You see, Marian, how well my plan has worked? With Miss Lucy Lockitt's co-operation we shall have Miranda greatly improved in no time.'

He nodded, smiling faintly at Lucy. 'Has she been very restless?'

'No, only for the last twenty minutes or so. She began to cry, but I think she'll settle down again.' She went red at his look; she had no business telling a specialist something he must already know for himself.

'I'll take a look while I'm here. Can you sit her up a little on your knee?'

He bent over her to examine Miranda and Lucy studied the top of his head; he had a lot of hair, a pleasing mixture of fairness and silver cut short by a master hand.

He straightened up and spoke to the sister. 'I think something to settle her, don't you, Marian?' He glanced at the thin gold watch on his wrist. 'Let's see, it's getting on for eleven o'clock.' He glanced at Lucy. 'A few hours of sleep will do you both good...' He took the chart from the sister's hand and wrote. 'That should see to it.' He walked to the door. 'Go to bed, Miss Lockitt; Sister will see that someone wakes you before Miranda rouses. Goodnight.'

He had gone before she could reply. She waited until the sister came back with an injection and then sat soothing Miranda until she dozed off and she was able to tuck her up in her cot once more. She wasn't very happy about going back to bed, but she was sure that Dr Thurloe wouldn't have suggested it if he hadn't been quite convinced that Miranda would sleep quietly for a few hours. So she got back into bed again and presently fell asleep, to wake very early in the morning and go and take a look at Miranda, who was still sleeping peacefully. Lucy took her pulse and was relieved to find that it was just what it was supposed to be. She was dressed and tied into her ample overall long before a nurse poked her head round the door. 'Oh, good, you're up already. I'll bring you a cup of tea just as soon as I've got the time. If she wakes can you wash her and pot her?'

Lucy nodded. 'Oh, yes. I expect I'll need clean sheets and another nightie.'

'In that cupboard in the corner, and there's a plastic bag where you can put the stuff that needs washing...'

The nurse's head disappeared to be replaced almost at once by the bulk of Dr Thurloe, immaculate and looking as though he had had ten hours' sleep. He was alone this time and his 'good morning' was friendly, so that Lucy regretted that she hadn't bothered to powder her nose or put on lipstick.

'Had a good night? You're up early.'

'So are you,' observed Lucy, and wished she hadn't said it; she must remember that they weren't at a dinner party but in hospital, where he was someone important and she wasn't of any account, especially in the bunchy garment she was wearing. And she felt worse because he didn't answer her, only bent over the cot.

'We'll have a look,' he said with impersonal politeness, and waited expectantly.

Lucy took down the cot side. She said in her sensible way, 'She's wet—I didn't like to change her until I'd seen Sister. Do you mind?'

The look he gave her was amused and kind too. 'I dare say I've dealt with more wet infants than you've had hot dinners. No, I don't mind! I'm glad she's had a good night. I don't intend to give her anything today though, and you may have your work cut out keeping her happy.'

He was halfway through his examination when the junior

night sister came in. She said sharply, 'I'm sorry, sir, I didn't know you were here.' And then to Lucy. 'You should have rung the bell, Miss Lockitt.'

'My fault,' said the doctor smoothly, 'I told her not to bother.' Which was kind of him, reflected Lucy, listening to him giving the night sister his instructions. 'And I'll be in some time during the day. I think Miranda will be all right, but we must look out for mental disturbance—there may be a deficiency...'

Lucy couldn't understand everything he was saying, but she presumed it wasn't necessary; she was there to keep Miranda quiet and happy until she was deemed fit to return to the orphanage. She supposed that would be in a couple of days' time and that she would be told in due course. The doctor strolled to the door with the junior night sister beside him. As he went out of the room, he said over his shoulder, 'Thank you, Miss Lockitt. Be sure and let someone know if you're anxious about anything, never mind how trivial it may seem.'

Lucy watched him go, wishing with her whole heart that she were the junior night sister, not only on good terms with him, but able to understand what he was talking about and give the right answers. Not for the first time she wished fervently that she were clever and not just practical and sensible.

There was no point in dwelling upon that; Miranda was showing signs of waking up, and she fetched clean linen from the cupboard and ran warm water into the deep sink in one corner of the room. She was very grateful when the nurse brought her a cup of tea, for the next half-hour was busy and noisy: Miranda was fretful and screamed her annoyance at the top of her voice. It was nothing new, and Lucy did all that was necessary, talking in her quiet voice all the while. When the ward sister came on duty and poked her head round the door with a 'Can you cope alone?' Lucy said placidly that she was quite all right, thank you, and the head disappeared without another word. She had Miranda tucked up in bed by the time a nurse came with the toddler's breakfast. 'Ring when she's had it,' she advised, 'and someone will relieve you while you go to the canteen.' She grinned widely. 'I bet you're ready for breakfast. Did you get a cup of tea?'

'Yes, thanks. Are you very busy?'

The nurse cast her eyes to heaven. 'You can say that again.' She darted off leaving Lucy to feed Miranda, who, clean and smiling again, was more than pleased to eat her breakfast.

The same nurse came back when Lucy rang the bell. 'Half an hour,' she warned. 'We've got theatre cases this morning, so it's all go. Someone will bring you coffee, though, and you'll get time for your dinner. I don't know about off-duty, I expect that Sister will tell you.'

Lucy went thankfully to the canteen; she was hungry, and besides, it was nice to have a change of scene. She was fond of Miranda and she saw a lot of her at the orphanage, but all the same she could see that her patience and good temper were going to be tried for the next day or two.

There weren't many people in the canteen. She took her tray to a table by a window and ate with her eye on the clock, and then hurried back to find Miranda sobbing and refusing to be comforted. It took a little while to soothe her again, but presently the little girl fell asleep and Lucy was free to walk round the little room and look out of the window. The hospital forecourt was below. She watched Dr Thurloe's car come to a dignified halt in the consultants' car park, and then studied him as he got out and crossed to the hospital entrance. He walked fast, but halfway there he paused and looked up to the window where she stood. There wasn't time to draw back; she stood there while he looked and presently went on his way.

She was in the canteen having her dinner when he came to see Miranda again, and that evening it was his registrar who paid a visit. And in the morning when he came with the ward sister his good morning to Lucy was pleasant but cool, and anything he had to say was said to the sister.

Miranda was to go back to the orphanage the next day; everything was going well and the matron there would know how to deal with any emergency. Miranda was to come to his next out-patients' clinic in two weeks' time. He paused to thank Lucy as he went away. She was watching him go with regret; at the same time her wish to marry him had never been so strong.

She took Miranda back the next day without having seen him again. He was in the hospital; his car was parked in the forecourt. She glimpsed it as she got into the ambulance which was to take them to the orphanage. She consoled herself with the thought that she would be taking Miranda to his clinic in two weeks' time. In the meantime she might be able to think of something to attract his attention. A different hairstyle? Different make-up? A striking outfit? Better still, a few amusing, witty remarks... She occupied her brief ride trying to think of them.

It was early afternoon by the time she had handed over Miranda and reported to Matron, to be told that, since she had had almost no time off in the hospital, she was to go home at once and not return to the orphanage until the day following the next.

'You enjoyed your stay at the City Royal?'

'Yes, thank you. I didn't have anything much to do, just keep Miranda happy and see that she ate her food. She was very good.'

'She slept?'

'Oh, quite a bit. I got up once or twice during the night, but she soon settled.'

'Good. Dr Thurloe seemed to be pleased with the arrangement; it took a good deal of the work off the nurses' shoulders. Miranda seems to need a lot of attention, but he thinks that she will improve fairly rapidly.'

'That's good. What will happen to her, Matron? I mean when she's older and more—more normal?'

'Well, as to that, we must wait and see. But she will always have a home here, you know. Now do go home, you must be tired.'

It was still early afternoon and only Alice was at home when Lucy let herself in. 'A nice cup of tea and a sandwich or two,' said Alice comfortably. 'You look tired, love. Your mother and father are at the Victoria and Albert. Someone there wanted your pa to see some old rocks that someone had sent from Africa—or was it the Andes? One of those foreign places, anyway. They won't be back until after tea. Imogen's working late and Pauline's going out to dinner with her fiancé.' She sniffed. 'You go and change and I'll have a snack for you in ten minutes.'

So Lucy went to her room, unpacked her few things, had a shower, washed her hair and wandered downstairs with her head in a towel and wearing a dressing-gown. Her mother wouldn't have approved, but since the house was empty except for herself and Alice she couldn't see that it mattered. Alice had made a pot of tea and cut a plateful of sandwiches and Lucy sat down at the kitchen table to eat them. Somehow she had missed dinner at the hospital, what with feeding Miranda and getting her ready to go back to the orphanage, and the nurses on the ward being in short supply since they took it in turns to go to the canteen. She lifted the edge of a sandwich and saw with satisfaction that it was generously filled with chopped egg and cress. She wolfed it down delicately, poured tea and invited Alice to have a cup.

'Not me, love,' said Alice. ''Ad me lunch not an hour back. You eat that lot and have a nice rest before your mother and father come home.'

Lucy polished off the egg and cress and started on the ham. The kitchen was pleasantly warm and cheerful. It was a semi-basement room, for the house had been built at the turn of the century, a late Victorian gentleman's residence with ornate brickwork and large rooms. It had been Lucy's home for as long as she could remember, and although her mother often expressed a wish for a house in the country nothing ever came of it, for the Chelsea house was convenient for her father's headquarters; he still travelled widely, taking her mother with him, and when they were at home he worked for various museums and he lectured a good deal. Lucy, a sensible girl not given to wanting things she couldn't have, accepted her life cheerfully, aware that she didn't quite fit in with her family and that she was a source of mild disappointment, to her mother at least, even though she was loved. Until now she had been quite prepared to go on working at the orphanage with the hope at the back of her mind that one day she would meet a man who might want to marry her. So far she hadn't met anyone whom she would want to marry—that was, until she'd met Dr Thurloe. An event which incited her to do something about it. She took another sandwich and bit into it. Clothes, she thought, new clothes—she had plenty, but a few more might help—and then she might try and discover mutual friends—the Walters, of course, for a start, and there must be others. Her parents knew any number of people, it would be a process of elimination. But first the new clothes, so that if and when they met again she would be able to compete with Fiona Seymour.

The front door bell, one of a row of old-fashioned bells along the kitchen wall, jangled and Alice put down the plates that she was stacking.

'Postman?' asked Lucy. 'He's late…'

'I'd best go, I suppose,' grumbled Alice, and went out of the kitchen, shutting the door after her as she went up the short flight of stairs to the hall.

Lucy sat back, a second cup of tea in her hand. There was one sandwich left; it was a pity to leave it. She took it off the plate and bit into it. The door behind her opened and she said,

'Was it the postman?' and turned round as she took another bite.

Alice had returned, but not alone. Dr Thurloe was with her, looking completely at home, elegant as always and smiling faintly.

'Gracious heavens!' Lucy spoke rather thickly because of the sandwich. 'Whatever are you doing here?' She put an agitated hand up to the towel. 'I've just washed my hair...'

She frowned heavily, all her plans knocked edgeways; instead of sporting an elegant outfit and a tidy head of hair, here she was looking just about as awful as she possibly could. She turned the frown on Alice and the doctor spoke.

'Don't be annoyed with your housekeeper, I told her that you wouldn't mind. You don't, do you? After all, I've seen you in a dressing-gown at the hospital.' He sounded kind and friendly and the smile held charm.

Lucy smiled back. 'Is it something important? Would you like a cup of tea?'

'Indeed I would.'

Alice gave a small sound which might have been a chuckle and pulled out a chair. 'The kettle's on the boil,' she informed him, 'and I've as nice a bit of Madeira cake as you'll taste anywhere, though I says it that oughtn't, being me own baking.'

'I'm partial to Madeira cake, and what a pleasant kitchen you have.'

He sat down opposite Lucy and eyed the towel. 'Do you know, all the girls I know go to the hairdresser every few days; I can't remember when I last saw a young woman washing her own hair.' He studied Lucy thoughtfully. 'Will it take long to dry?'

'No. It's almost dry now.' She poured him a cup of tea from the fresh pot Alice had put on the table. 'Is it something to do with Miranda? She's not ill...?'

'No, she's doing nicely. I wondered if we might go somewhere this evening and have dinner; I'm sure you would like to know the details of her treatment, and there really was no time at the City Royal to say much.'

He ate some cake and watched her, amused at her hesitation.

'Well,' said Lucy, 'Mother and Father—' She was interrupted by the telephone's ringing, and Alice answered it. She listened for a moment, said, 'Yes, ma'am' twice and then hung up. 'Yer ma and pa,' she told Lucy. 'They're going on to Professor Schinkel's house for dinner.' She added, 'I expect your ma thought you weren't home today.'

The look on Lucy's face made the doctor say quickly, 'Now isn't that providential, you will be free to dine with me, then?' That settled, he took another piece of cake and passed his cup for more tea. 'Your sisters won't mind?'

'They're both out too.'

'Then may I call for you this evening? Half-past seven or thereabouts? Somewhere fairly quiet? Boulestin's, perhaps?'

'That sounds very nice,' said Lucy, 'but only if you can spare the time...'

He looked as though he was going to laugh, but said gravely, 'As far as I know there will be no calls upon me until tomorrow morning at nine o'clock.' He got to his feet. 'Until half-past seven. I look forward to it.'

Alice showed him out and came bustling back. 'There now, what a nice gentleman, to be sure. Take that towel off and I'll dry that hair. What will you wear?' She began to rub vigorously. 'That's a posh restaurant...'

'Those sandals I got from Rayne's and haven't worn—and I'll leave my hair loose...'

'All right as far as it goes, but what about a dress? Sandals and hair aren't enough.'

'That silver-grey satin, you know, the one with the calf-length skirt and the wide lace collar and cuffs.' Lucy's voice, muffled by the towel, sounded pleased. It was a very pretty dress, so simple that it stood out among other more striking dresses, and the colour, she hoped, would make her look the kind of girl a man might like to marry, elegant but demure.

She left a note for her mother on the hall table, collected an enormous cashmere shawl in which to wrap herself, and her little grey handbag, and eased her feet into her new sandals. They were a little tight, but they were exactly right with the dress, and what was a little discomfort compared with that?

The drawing-room looked charming with its soft lighting and the fire blazing. She arranged herself to the very best advantage on a small balloon-backed chair covered in old-rose velvet, and waited for the doorbell.

The doctor was punctual to the minute, and Alice ushered him into the drawing-room, opening the door wide so that he had a splendid view of Lucy, delightfully pretty and at great pains to appear cool.

She got up as he came in, and said in her best hostess voice, 'Oh, hello again. Would you like a drink before we go?'

'Hello, Lucy. How very elegant you look, and so punctual. Almost unheard of and quite refreshing.'

She should have stayed in her room until he had arrived and kept him waiting, she thought crossly.

She said haughtily, 'I have to be punctual at the orphanage, it's a habit.'

'Of course. I booked a table for half-past eight; I thought we might have a drink there first. Shall we go?'

She smiled at him, she couldn't help herself; he looked so large and handsome and so assured. She wondered fleetingly if he ever lost his temper.

Southampton Street wasn't all that far away, but the evening traffic was heavy and slow moving, so it was well past eight o'clock by the time Lucy found herself at a table opposite the doctor. It was a good table too, she noticed, and he was known at the restaurant. Perhaps he took Fiona Seymour there... She wasn't going to waste thought about that; here she was doing exactly what she had dreamed of doing, being alone with the doctor, nicely dressed, looking her best, and hopefully at her best when it came to conversation.

It was a pity that no witty remarks filled her head; indeed, it was regrettably empty. She sipped her sherry and thankfully bowed her head over the menu card. She was hungry and he said encouragingly, 'I dare say you had a very scanty lunch. I know I did. How about the terrine of leeks with prawns for a start, and if you like fish the red mullet is delicious—or roast pigeon?'

'I couldn't eat a pigeon,' said Lucy. 'I feed them on the way to work every morning.' She was reassured by his understanding smile. 'I'd like the red mullet.'

It wasn't until these delicacies had been eaten, followed by a dessert of puff pastry, piled with a hazelnut mousse and topped with caramel, that the doctor switched smoothly from the gentle conversation, calculated to put his companion at her ease, to the more serious subject of Miranda.

'Do you see a great deal of her at the orphanage?' he wanted to know.

'Well, yes—not all the time, of course, but always each morning, bathing her and getting her to walk and that kind of thing.'

He nodded. 'You do realise that she will probably be backward—mentally retarded—but this operation that I have just done should give her a better chance. One would wish to do everything possible for her—she is such a pretty child, and if only she had been brought to our attention while she was still a baby we could have done so much more.'

'But isn't there any special treatment? She talks a little, you know, and although she's a bit wobbly when she's walking she does try.'

'I'm going to ask you to do all you can to help her, and don't be discouraged when she makes almost no progress. I know you have a busy day and there are other children to look after, but Matron tells me that Miranda responds to you much more willingly than to anyone else there. Once the shunt gets into its stride we should take advantage of that and get her little brain stimulated. If all goes well, she will be able to have therapy in a few months.'

'Do you get many children like her?' Lucy poured their coffee and reflected sadly that the only reason he had asked her out was to make sure that she was going to stay at the orphanage and look after Miranda. Well, he need not have gone to so much trouble, wasting an evening with her when he might have been spending it with the glamorous Fiona. It was quite obvious that she had no effect upon him whatsoever, despite the fashionable grey dress and the new sandals. He probably hadn't even noticed them.

He guided their talk into more general channels, and when Lucy said that she should really go back home since she was on duty in the morning he made no objection, but signed the bill and followed her out of the restaurant without one word of persuasion to remain a little longer—or even go dancing. But that was a good thing, for the sandals were pinching horribly and walking in them, even the short distance across the pavement to the car, was crippling.

'Take them off,' suggested the doctor as he started the car.

'Oh, you don't mind? They're killing me. How did you know?'

'You have quite a fierce frown which, I hasten to add, I am quite sure no one noticed except me.' He gave her a sideways glance. 'They're quite delightful though; indeed, the rest of you looks delightful too, Lucy. Demure and malleable. Are you demure and malleable, I wonder?'

She curled her toes in blissful comfort. 'No, I don't think so; I don't think girls are demure nowadays, are they? Anyway, I'm too old...and I'm not sure what malleable means—I thought it meant squashy.'

He gave a growl of laughter. 'I meant it to mean tender and gentle, and I wasn't aware that age had anything to do with being demure. How old are you?'

'Twenty-five. You're thirty-five, aren't you?'

'We might say that we have reached the ages of discretion.'

They had reached her home and he stopped the car gently, and when she made to get out he put out a restraining hand. 'No, wait.'

He got out and opened her door. 'You'll never cram your feet back into those sandals.' He picked them up and put them into her hand, scooped her out of the seat and carried her to the front door, where he asked her to ring the doorbell.

Alice answered the door, flung it wide to allow him to get inside, and said urgently, 'You're not hurt, love? What's the matter? You've not 'ad too much to drink?'

The doctor set Lucy gently on her feet. 'Her feet,' he explained. 'Her sandals were pinching and, of course, once they were off they wouldn't go on again.'

Alice laughed. 'And there's me wondering what on earth had happened. Your mother and father are in the drawing-room—you go too, sir. I'll bring in a nice tray of coffee and you, Miss Lucy, go and fetch a pair of slippers this minute—what your ma will say I don't know.'

'It could happen to anyone,' remarked the doctor mildly, and gave Alice a nice smile so that she said,

'Oh, well, perhaps it won't be noticed,' and went ahead of them to open the drawing-room door.

Lucy's mother and father were sitting one on each side of the hearth, her father immersed in a sheaf of papers and her mother turning the pages of Harper's. They both looked up as she and the doctor went in and her father got to his feet. 'There you are, Lucy and Dr Thurloe, how delightful. Come and sit down for half an hour—Lucy, run and ask Alice to bring coffee—'

'She's making it now, Father!' Lucy bent to kiss her

mother's cheek and wished she knew how to raise a graceful hand to greet the doctor in the same manner as that lady. 'Delighted to see you, Dr Thurloe. Do sit down. How very kind of you to take Lucy out to dinner.'

'It was Lucy who was kind, Mrs Lockitt,' he replied, and paused, smiling, as Mrs Lockitt caught sight of Lucy's feet.

'Lucy, your shoes? You've never lost them? You aren't hurt?'

'They pinched, Mother, so I took them off.'

'Well, really!' She turned her attention to her guest. 'I have been hoping that we might meet again, you really must dine one evening before we go to Turkey.'

'Kayseri, the ancient Hittite city—there have been some interesting finds lately, and I've been asked to go out there and take a look,' Mr Lockitt joined in. 'We plan to fly out at the end of next week.'

The doctor, much to Lucy's surprise, expressed his delight at the invitation, and Mrs Lockitt said, 'Lucy, dear, run up to my room and get my engagement book, will you? And do get some slippers at the same time.'

Lucy went slowly upstairs. Her parents, whom she loved dearly, were spoiling everything for her; she showed up in a bad light in her own home with no chance to outshine their intellectual talk—she had hardly scintillated over dinner, and since she had entered the drawing-room she had uttered only a few words. She found the book, poked her feet into a pair of frivolous satin mules and went back downstairs. Alice had brought in the coffee and Lucy's father had fetched the brandy; the doctor looked as though he had settled for the rest of the evening, already making knowledgeable replies to her father's observations—apparently he knew all about the iron-smelting activities of the Hittites, and he knew too where they had lived in Asia Minor.

As she handed round the coffee-cups he asked pleasantly, 'And do you not wish to go too, Lucy?'

Her mother answered for her. 'Lucy's a home-bird, aren't you, darling? This nice little job at the orphanage gives her something to do while we're away.' Mrs Lockitt went on, not meaning to be unkind, 'She hasn't had a training for anything. Of course, Imogen is the clever one in the family—she has this super job in the City—and Pauline works in an art gallery, and will marry at the end of this year. They are all such capable girls, and of course we have an excellent housekeeper.'

The doctor murmured politely and presently got up to go, and Mr Lockitt went to the door with him, so that beyond a stiff little speech of thanks Lucy had no chance to speak. There was nothing to say anyway. Her fragile dream, never more than a fantasy, had been blown away; he would think of her, if he ever did, as a dull girl not worth a second thought.

She bade her parents goodnight and went to bed. Surprisingly, just before she slept, she decided that somehow or other she would get to know him better, and eventually, in the teeth of all hazards, marry him.

CHAPTER THREE

FOR several days Lucy had no chance to put her resolve into practice. There was no sign of Dr Thurloe at the orphanage and it had been silly of her to imagine that she might see him there. Very occasionally in an emergency he might be asked to go there, but there weren't any emergencies; Miranda was doing very nicely—she was even showing small signs of improvement.

Mr and Mrs Lockitt, their journey arranged, had decided to invite a few friends as well as the doctor for dinner. 'Rather short notice,' observed Mrs Lockitt, 'but they're all old friends and we don't stand on ceremony. I suppose I'll have to ask Mrs Seymour…'

'Why?' asked Lucy, making a list of guests.

'Well, dear, she and Dr Thurloe seem to be old friends. Indeed, people seem to think that he might marry her—heaven knows she's trying hard enough—but I don't think he will. Mind you're home in good time and wear something pretty—the grey, perhaps?'

'Definitely not the grey. There's that rust velvet I've hardly worn…'

'Ah, yes. I'd forgotten that.' Her mother eyed her a little anxiously. 'You'll be all right while we're away, darling? It is such a pity that Pauline will be in Edinburgh at that Art Exhibition for the next two weeks, and Imogen tells me that she has to accompany Sir George to Brussels—for a few weeks, she thought. But you'll have Alice.'

'We'll be quite all right, Mother, dear. How long will you and Father be away?'

'Well, we aren't sure, it rather depends on what they've

found. I must say Turkey is as good a place as anywhere to go at this time of year. Of course, we'll phone you, darling.' She smiled at Lucy. 'Now, how many have we got? I thought we might have soup first, so comforting in this weather, and then that nice fish salad and lamb chops with new potatoes and green peas—I'm sure I saw some in Harrods. They cost the earth, but they are so delicious. I'll get Alice to make some of those chocolate mousses, the ones with orange, and cheese of course.'

Lucy wrote it all down tidily and handed it to her mother.

'Thank you, dear; you're such a good daughter. I'm so glad you're not a career girl, Lucy. You must find a nice man and marry him, darling.'

Lucy said, 'Yes, Mother.' It wasn't much use telling her that she had found the nice man. The chances of marrying him, were, as far as she could see, negligible.

She dressed for the dinner party with extra care and viewed the result with some satisfaction. The rust velvet suited her—it made her eyes greener than they were, gave her hair a reflected glint, and showed off her pretty figure to its best advantage. She was even more satisfied when she joined her family in the drawing-room and her mother exclaimed, 'Why, Lucy, how delightfully that dress suits you! There's the doorbell—I've put you between Cyril and Mr Walter...'

So much for her painstaking dressing; Cyril didn't like her, she was beneath his notice, and Mr Walter was a dear, but hard of hearing. She joined in greeting the first of the guests, moving from one to the other, watching the door out of the corner of her eye. Dr Thurloe came in alone and she beamed at him across the room; at least he hadn't given Fiona Seymour a lift. He smiled back as he greeted his hostess and host, but made no effort to join Lucy—probably because she was trapped in a corner by old Mrs Winchell, who was eighty if she was a day and invited to everyone's table although no one really knew why. Lucy, listening with patience to that lady's opinion of the government, watched Fiona Seymour, the last to arrive, make her entrance. She really was good-looking and this evening she was wearing a starkly plain black dress, superbly cut, with her hair swept into an elaborate arrangement of curls on top of her head. She had half a dozen golden bangles on one arm and several gold chains hung around her slender neck. Old Mrs Winchell turned to look at her, using her old-fashioned *lorgnettes* to do so. 'She's wasting her time,' she muttered, and then in her usual rather loud voice, went on to reorganise the government.

The talk at dinner was largely concerned with the forthcoming trip to Turkey, so that Lucy was kept busy listening first to Cyril carrying on about the rate of exchange, and then repeating to Mr Walter what people were saying at the table that he hadn't quite heard. The doctor, to her disappointment, was at the other end of the rectangular table, with Imogen on one side and Fiona on the other.

It wasn't until Mrs Winchell got up to go, forming the spearhead of departure, that he came over to Lucy. His casual observation that Miranda was making splendid progress, and his equally casual hope that she wasn't working too hard, doused any hopes she had had of conversation of a more personal nature. She answered him woodenly and bade him a brisk goodnight.

'Goodnight, Lucy. Your eyes are very green; is that because you are bottling up bad temper? I wish I had the opportunity to find out.'

He smiled with charm and turned at the touch of Mrs Seymour's hand. She smiled too, a quite different smile from the doctor's. 'Such a nice evening, Lucy. William, will you take me home? It's only a little out of your way.'

A dismal failure, decided Lucy, reviewing her evening as she got into bed. Fiona Seymour outshone her in both looks and clothes. What was the use of just being pretty—there were hundreds of pretty girls around, but not many Fionas with their dramatic clothes and subtle make-up. Lucy sighed heavily and went to sleep to wake the next morning filled with resolve to outshine Mrs Seymour. She had no idea how to do it, but something would turn up.

Which it did, but hardly in a manner which she expected or welcomed.

Her parents left for their journey to Turkey two days later, followed first by Pauline, who flew to Edinburgh, and then, the following day, by Imogen, the picture of smart efficiency, on her way to Brussels with Sir George. They had both taken an affectionate farewell of Lucy, reiterating all the instructions she had had from her mother and leaving their telephone numbers prominently displayed. The house seemed empty after they had gone, even though Alice and the daily cleaner had seized the opportunity to clean the place from attic to cellar. Lucy was glad to go to bed early and got up betimes in the morning, remembering in delight that today she would take Miranda to the City Royal to have a check-up by Dr Thurloe. It would be all very professional, of course, but at least Fiona Seymour wouldn't be there. The clinic was in the early afternoon; the morning seemed endless, and she had a few bad moments when Matron couldn't make up her mind if Lucy should go with Miranda or stay and take care of the smallest orphans whose usual attendant had gone off sick.

Lucy, her face serene, her insides churning, waited for Matron to decide and heaved a sigh of relief when that lady's eye fell on Miranda working herself into a rage with the girl who was to take Lucy's place.

'Oh, well—you'd better take her; they'll want her as quiet as possible at the clinic and she's getting quite worked up. I'll take over the little ones while you're gone. Perhaps you won't be away too long.'

So Lucy and Miranda set off together in the ambulance which had been sent for them and arrived to find the waiting-room packed to the doors. Outpatients Sister saw her come in and hurried towards her. 'There's been a delay,' she explained. 'Dr Thurloe was called away urgently just as we were starting. Luckily you're in the first ten to be seen so it shouldn't be too long. He'll be here any minute now.'

She bustled away and Lucy sat down, Miranda on her lap, grizzling a little because she didn't much like her surroundings. Lucy wasn't too keen either; it was a chilly blustery day, but the waiting-room was warm and stuffy—moreover, the babies and toddlers were noisy. That was only to be expected, of course, but after a time it was wearing to the nerves.

It was an hour before it was Miranda's turn and by then she was cross and whining fretfully despite Lucy's efforts to keep her amused. Lucy carried the child into the consulting-room, sat her down on the couch and wished the doctor a good afternoon. He said in a detached manner, 'Ah, yes—Miranda. I'll need to look at that shunt.' He looked tired and she wasn't surprised—having to deal with dozens of babies and children, all ill, all in various stages of peevishness, he must be exhausted. He smiled down at her suddenly. 'Hello, Lucy,' and then, 'You look hot and a bit cross…'

'I'm not cross, but I am hot. Half London's sitting out there.'

He nodded. 'If you'll get Miranda's things off I'll take a look.'

It was at that moment that there was a loud bang and all the lights went out. And moments later a voice screamed, 'It's a bomb!'

Lucy, her arms around Miranda, stayed where she was. The doctor's voice, swearing richly, sounded reassuring, and a moment later he had turned on a torch from his desk. 'Don't move,' he commanded. That was something she wouldn't have dreamed of doing anyway. 'The auxiliary lighting will come on in a moment. I'm going into the waiting-room…'

The din was fearful, children screaming and frantic mothers calling and, from the sound of it, everyone rushing to and fro.

She could hear the doctor's voice, raised in a commanding bellow, urging everyone to stay where they were, but panic had taken over, for the lights hadn't gone on again and those people nearest the doors had rushed to open them, but, because of the press people behind them, had been unable to do so. The clinic was situated in the semi-basement of the hospital and depended entirely upon artificial light, and the dark was Stygian. The door to the waiting-room burst wide open suddenly, and in no time at all the consulting-room was crammed with people all talking at once while the children screamed and the babies cried. Lucy got a good grip of Miranda and took a deep breath.

'Be quiet and stand still!' she shouted urgently, and, although her lung power was nothing like as powerful as the doctor's, some of the women around her heard and there was a moment's lull broken only by infant wailing. 'Keep still,' she urged, 'you're safe enough as long as you don't rush around. Do think of the children. The doors will be opened as soon as possible and there's auxiliary lighting.'

There was a good deal of murmuring and shuffling, but at least the frantic pushing and shoving seemed to have stopped. She could hear the noise in the waiting-room and see the flash of torches here and there; she heard the outpatients sister's calm voice and then the doctor, his voice loud and calm, as he made his way towards the doors.

She didn't understand why there was such a long delay before the doors were at last opened and at the same time the lights came on again. And then she knew the reason. They had been blocked by the first to reach them who, unable to get the doors open, had been pushed or knocked down by those behind them, frantic to get out too.

The waiting-room was in a state of chaos. Sister and the two nurses who were with her were already shepherding some of the mothers and children towards the further end of the waiting-room and out through the door there, while the doctor, head and shoulders above everyone else, waded to and fro through the mass of people, carrying children and babies away from the doors. Sister came back and poked her head round the consulting-room door. 'Everyone all right here? Come with me to the casualty-room and we'll check all of you and the children.'

There were a great many people in the waiting-room now, moving the injured away, comforting frightened children and still shaken mothers. Lucy picked up Miranda and followed the trickle of women leaving the clinic. There was no reason to stay—obviously the doctor had his hands full with his helpers, handing back babies and children to their mothers, and checking that no one was seriously hurt. In Casualty a nurse was taking names, making sure that no one was hurt or badly shocked, and cups of tea were being offered. To Casualty Sister's enquiry as to whether she felt able to get back on her own she answered calmly that she felt fine, but it would be best if she got Miranda back to her familiar surroundings as quickly as possible.

'You look a sensible girl,' said Sister. 'As soon as we can, we'll let Matron at the Orphanage know when you can come back.' She glanced at a restless Miranda. 'Dr Thurloe did a shunt, didn't he? I expect he'll want to see her just as soon as we've cleared up the mess in his clinic.'

There were a great many women sitting about, drinking their tea and mulling over the excitement of the afternoon; quite a few were to be taken home by ambulance, declaring that they were shaken too badly to get on a bus. Lucy made her way to Casualty entrance and into the street. It had begun to rain, a gentle drizzle which seeped through her clothes as she waited for a taxi. Miranda was well wrapped up, but she hated the rain and began to wail; it was a relief when a taxi stopped and Lucy got thankfully inside. Miranda was heavy, and she had to be held carefully.

By the time they reached the orphanage, the toddler was

crying in earnest. Lucy paid off the cabby and hurried inside, to get Miranda's clothes off as quickly as possible and ask one of the girls to tell Matron that they were back.

That excellent woman took in the situation at a glance; she sent someone for a cup of tea for Lucy, milk and biscuits for Miranda and then got her into her cot, all the while listening to Lucy's succinct account of the mishap at the clinic.

'It would have been all right if someone hadn't shouted that it was a bomb,' she remarked, 'but of course it was very dark, and once everyone started rushing around it was impossible to stop them, although Dr Thurloe was roaring like a bull. He had a torch, and so, after a few minutes, did Sister, but the clinic is a big place and it was packed with people.'

'And where were you?'

'In the consulting-room. Dr Thurloe was just about to examine Miranda. Sister said she'd let you know when we could go back to the clinic. It was hopeless to go on this afternoon, I think there were several people hurt when they got knocked over by the doors.'

'A mercy it was no worse. You're wet, aren't you. Get that coat off and drink your tea. When you've fed Miranda, go home, Lucy; it's already almost five and you'll be here as usual in the morning?'

'Of course, Matron. I'm sorry that Miranda has to go again, she does so hate it there. I think the noise bothers her.'

'Poor scrap. But we can't ask someone as important as Dr Thurloe to visit here unless it is an emergency or something serious. I might ask one of his registrars to come and see her here.'

It was six o'clock by the time Lucy got home; Miranda hadn't wanted her tea and it had taken time and patience to coax her to eat it, and when Lucy had at last left the orphanage it was to find the bus queue stretching for yards along the pavement. When she finally got home Alice came into the hall at the sound of her key in the lock.

'I was getting worried!' she exclaimed. 'You not home at your usual time—what 'appened?' She bustled Lucy out of her coat. 'All wet you are, and looking as though you could do with a nice cuppa.'

'Oh, Alice, I could. Look, I'll have a shower and change and then come down to the kitchen and tell you all about it.'

'Righto, love. And put on something warm, you look fair chilled.'

Fifteen minutes later Lucy went back downstairs. She had left her hair loose and had got into a thick green sweater and a tweed skirt and she felt a good deal better; a pot of tea would be heaven. She hoped that Alice had been inspired to make a plate of toast too. She opened the kitchen door and danced in. 'Alice…'

Alice was standing there all right, but so was Dr Thurloe, standing at the window, watching the feet of passers-by. He turned round as she came to a surprised standstill. 'Forgive me for calling at this unreasonable hour, but I wanted to make sure that you were all right after this afternoon's incident. I've seen Miranda, she's none the worse luckily. But you? You were all right? You stayed where you were?'

She nodded, trying to think of something to say and failing.

'Good. It could have been much worse, but several women were injured in the rush to get away and I've had to admit four children.' He frowned and she saw that he was concerned as well as angry.

'Well, you did all you could,' she said. 'I could hear you telling everyone to stay in their seats. It must have been impossible to move out there.'

'Yes. Panic is a terrifying thing. I'll make sure that it never happens again. It just so happened that the auxiliary lighting was being checked when the electricity failed—some workman accidentally severed a cable.'

'Oh, was that the bang?' She had a strong wish to put her arms around him and tell him that it wasn't his fault, although she knew that he felt responsible. 'Alice has made a pot of tea; would you like to have a cup?'

She didn't wait for him to answer, but fetched the teapot and put it on the tray Alice had set on the table, collected another cup and saucer from the dresser and sat down at the table while Alice fetched the plate of buttered toast from the Aga.

'Now just you sit there and enjoy your tea,' she advised them, 'while I pop up to your ma and pa's room and get it straight now it's been cleaned.'

She took herself off, looking pleased because the doctor had held the kitchen door open for her. He closed it and came and sat down opposite Lucy.

'I'm sorry you had to find your own way back,' he told her. 'Sister told me that you were going to get a taxi. Did you have to wait?'

'Only for a few minutes.' She passed the toast. 'Do you like strawberry jam? Alice made a batch last summer...' She got up and fetched a pot from a cupboard, found a spoon and handed it across the table.

They sat munching their toast thickly layered with jam, and since there was nothing more to be said about the afternoon's happening their talk became rather more personal. At least, the questions the doctor put were gently probing—so gentle, in fact, that Lucy didn't realise how much she was telling him. For her part she would have dearly loved to have asked him any number of questions, but she wasn't quite sure how to begin. He wasn't married, that she did know, but what about Mrs Seymour? And did he have any family? A mother, a father, brothers and sisters? She wished very much that she had either of her sisters' self-assurance; she was sure that neither of them would have hesitated.

The doctor's quiet voice broke into her thoughts. 'How long will your mother and father be away?' he wanted to know.

'It depends—if it's something interesting I expect they'll be in Turkey for some time.'

'You are not lonely? Your mother told me that your sisters would be away too.'

'Only for a week or two and I've got Alice, and Mrs Simpkins.'

His raised eyebrows looked a question. 'Our cat. She's in the airing cupboard with her kittens. I suppose you wouldn't like a kitten? Not yet, of course, they're only a few weeks old.'

'Er—my housekeeper has an elderly cat, a matron christened, through some misunderstanding—Thomas—I dare say she might like to have a kitten to mother.'

Here was a crumb of information, better than nothing. 'Have you a dog?'

'Two—Robinson and Friday; they like cats.'

Lucy laughed. 'Did you rescue them off a desert island?'

'In a manner of speaking.'

She poured more tea for them both. 'What breed are they?'

'A little bit of everything, I should imagine. You like dogs?'

She nodded. 'Only we can't have one; Father and Mother are away so much, Imogen and Pauline wouldn't have the time and I'm away all day too.'

'You don't need to work,' he suggested gently.

'Oh, no, but you see I had to do something; I can't just be at home. I—I found this job, I wanted to do something useful; I'm not clever, you see, and it's difficult to have a career unless you're clever.'

'Would you not rather prefer to marry?' He spoke with a casual kindness which prompted her to reply.

'Oh, yes, only no one's asked me.'

'You surprise me, you must know that you're a pretty girl.'

It didn't enter her head to be coy about it. 'Yes, but I'm

hopelessly shy and I don't know how to talk to people,' and at his quizzical look, 'I can talk to you.'

He agreed gravely, although there was a gleam of amusement in his eyes. 'I have enjoyed our talk and my tea.' He glanced at his watch. 'I am only sorry that I have to go out this evening.' He watched Lucy's face assume a wooden politeness. Her eyes, he noted with interest, were quite blindingly green.

'Of course. It was kind of you to call. I hope no one was badly hurt this afternoon.'

'Fortunately not. I should like to get my hands on whoever it was who screamed that it was a bomb.' He smiled at her. 'Thank you for my tea, Lucy.'

She went to the door with him and ushered him out, and then closed and locked the door behind him. Well, she knew a little more about him now, but she doubted very much if she would learn much more; she wasn't likely to see anything of him other than at the clinic, and probably Miranda wouldn't need to go again for a long time. Still, there was today's visit to be repeated, although he wouldn't have anything to say to her other than instructions to convey to Matron.

She cleared away the tea things and Alice came back into the kitchen, 'Gorn, 'as 'e?' Mostly she was careful with her aitches, but if she was disturbed or excited she tended to overlook them. 'I could 'ave cooked him a bite of supper.'

'He's going out,' Lucy was putting away the jam, 'he told me so.'

'That Mrs Seymour—the cook at number eleven knows 'er maid, says she's after 'im, ringing 'im up at all hours and cross as two sticks when 'e's not there or got something better to do. The cook told me that this maid says 'e's wedded to his work.'

Which cheered Lucy up. One could always marry a man who was wedded to his work, but not one who was wedded to Mrs Seymour. But all she said was, 'Well, he's old enough to make up his own mind, I expect, don't you, Alice?' She said it in a bright voice and Alice took a look at her.

'Men,' said Alice, and clashed a saucepan. Lucy had always been her favourite and she had seen the look on her face.

Lucy took Miranda to the clinic two days later, and although Dr Thurloe was there there was no chance to speak to him other than to say good afternoon and goodbye. This time there was a staff nurse there who whisked Miranda away for X-ray and tests and Lucy was politely asked to wait in the waiting-room. Miranda bawled to high heaven and on their return from X-ray and Path Lab the staff nurse handed her over to Lucy with a sigh of relief. 'My goodness, she's a handful,' she observed. 'Dr Thurloe wants her back in the consulting-room for a minute or two. Will you take her?'

Miranda, scarlet with rage still, sniffed and snuffled into Lucy's shoulder, but she had stopped screaming and allowed the doctor to examine her head; she even, after a few doubtful glances, smiled at him. He smiled back. Lucy was the only one with an expressionless face, all at sea as to how to behave. One minute the man was eating toast and jam in her mother's kitchen and the next sitting there as remote and grave as a judge. She played safe and said nothing at all.

He finished at length and by then the staff nurse was back again.

'I'll write to her doctor and let your matron have a copy. Miranda's progress is very satisfactory—I'll see her again in a month.' His smile was pleasant and detached. 'Goodbye, Lucy.'

She bade him goodbye gravely, then took Miranda back to the orphanage and got on with the rest of her day's chores. She was disappointed, but she wasn't downcast; she wasn't sure how to beat Fiona Seymour at her own game, but she was certain that she would get a chance to try. She was quite sure that she would make the doctor a splendid wife, just as she was equally certain that Mrs Seymour would ruin his life for him. When she got home she got out the telephone directory and found his name and address—a house by the river in Chiswick, one of a row of charming old houses with a frontage on the Thames and as peaceful a spot as one could wish for in London. She put the directory away thoughtfully; he had two dogs who would have to be exercised. Richmond Park or Kew Gardens seemed the obvious places for their run; he could take the car easily enough to either—probably not every day, she decided, as there must be quiet streets near his home where he could walk them, but at the weekends…

Her sisters were still away, and Alice saw nothing strange in her announcement that she intended having a nice long walk on the following Sunday. 'And I'll not be back for lunch, Alice,' said Lucy. 'If it's a nice day I could do with some fresh air.'

'I'll cut you a sandwich or two,' said Alice. 'Where are you going?'

'Richmond Park or Kew, I haven't quite decided.'

'Well, be careful, love, don't go off down any lonely paths. I'm not sure that your ma…'

'I'll stay on the main walks, Alice, and I'll be back for tea. Do you want to go to church?'

'In the evening—I'll have something in the Aga for supper.'

Lucy considered it a good omen that Sunday morning should be all sunshine and blue sky even though it was cooled by a March wind. She wore a new mohair sweater in shades of green to match her eyes, and a pleated tweed skirt; she tucked a scarf into her shoulder-bag, and, after a splendid breakfast and five minutes' listening to Alice's warnings, caught a bus. The temptation to take a look at the doctor's house was great, but she prudently skirted it and started to walk in the direction of Richmond Park. It had been silly of her to get off the bus on an impulse; now she got on the bus once more and stayed on it until it reached the park. She had

had to chose between Richmond Park and Kew Gardens, she couldn't be in both at once, and really, she reflected as she began to walk along one of the main paths, she was being childish in the extreme. She had had no idea that falling in love with someone entailed so much planning and plotting which was more than likely to no avail.

There were quite a few people about, most of them with dogs and children, and presently she began to enjoy herself. It was lovely to get away from the streets and houses, and as she walked she allowed herself to daydream: a cottage in the country, just for weekends, where the children could play while she and William gardened and Robinson and Friday roamed at will. A large garden, she decided, full of old-fashioned flowers and roses and with a large lawn where they could all play croquet. She wandered off the path a little way and sat down on a fallen log. Four children, she decided, two of each; the boys would be doctors like their father, and the girls would be pretty and clever besides. And she and William would grow old gracefully together—he would make a handsome old man... She looked up and saw him coming towards her, still fortunately on the right side of forty and certainly handsome.

He had the dogs with him; a small, nondescript dog with a curly black coat and a whiskered face who pranced up to her and offered his head for a scratch, and a shaggy-coated dog with a mild face and a splendid tail. He was very large and lumbered up to Lucy and bent over her, breathing gently on her face, and she pulled at his ear, glad of something to do for the doctor was standing in front of her, looking down at her heightened colour with amused interest.

'You're a long way from home,' he said, and he sat down beside her.

Lucy tickled the little dog under his chin and didn't look at him. 'It is a lovely day, and it's nice to get away from the streets and just walk.'

He nodded gravely. 'I come here every Sunday when I'm free, and quite often after breakfast for half an hour, once the mornings get light. Until then we have to make do with a brisk walk round the houses.'

'They're nice dogs,' said Lucy, 'and quite different.' She ventured a look at her companion. 'Did you get them from Battersea Dogs' Home?'

'No—Robinson,' he patted the large dog on a massive shoulder, 'was thrown out of a car on a motorway, and I happened to be behind the car, and Friday was left in a cardboard box on the side of the road.'

'How utterly beastly,' said Lucy fiercely, 'to do a thing like that to an animal! I'm so glad you were there—they must love you…'

'They're great company and they make a nice change from babies and children.'

Lucy turned an alarmed face to his. 'Oh, don't you like babies and children?'

'Of course I do—I wouldn't be a paediatrician otherwise, would I?'

'Oh, sorry, that was a silly thing to say.'

They sat in silence for a minute or so while she searched wildly for something to talk about; if he didn't speak soon she would have to get up and go. He stayed silent and she sighed soundlessly with her disappointment and said cheerfully, 'Well, I must be on my way. It was nice meeting Robinson and Friday.' She started to get up and put on her scarf, and he put out a large gentle hand and pulled her down again.

'Do you have to be home for lunch? Or are you meeting someone?' he asked.

She shook her head.

'Good, then let us walk together for a while. I've got the car here, I'll drive you back when you want to go.' He glanced at his watch. 'It's still early—if we take the next path on the left there's a coffee kiosk there.'

She didn't have to worry about something to talk about, for the doctor embarked on a meandering conversation which needed few or no replies. By the time they had reached the kiosk she felt quite at ease, so much so that she only just stopped herself in time from telling him that she had come to the park in the hope of meeting him. She went bright red at the thought and the doctor eyed her thoughtfully, wondering why she looked quite guilty—it could be nothing he had said, he was sure of that; maybe something she had thought…?

He said easily, 'You'll have coffee? Why not sit down on that bench and I'll fetch it?'

He wandered off, and the dogs, having drunk noisily from the bowl of water by the kiosk, followed him. They all came back very shortly, and, while the dogs roamed round close by, they drank their coffee. It was strong and hot and Lucy remembered the sandwiches Alice had packed for her. She offered them shyly and the doctor took one. 'Your Alice must be a treasure. My housekeeper runs her pretty close, she's a marvellous cook too. Which reminds me that I have to be back for lunch. Sunday is the one day when I can have people in.'

The bright morning lost its brightness; Lucy brushed crumbs from her gentle mouth and stood up at once. 'I don't suppose you have a great deal of time to meet your friends,' she remarked politely. 'Do you go to the hospital every day?'

'No, twice a week for rounds and outpatients, and one theatre day; I have a private practice too, and I'm consultant to a couple of other hospitals.'

'My goodness, don't you ever get tired?'

'Oh, yes.' They were walking back to the main path once more, and presently they were at the gates and a few minutes later in the Rolls with the dogs sitting primly side by side in the back.

The journey back was far too short, but not so short that Lucy didn't have the leisure to reflect upon the abject failure of her plan. She had been most successful in meeting him, true enough, but it had got her nowhere.

CHAPTER FOUR

Dr Thurloe got out when they reached Lucy's home, went with her to the door and waited until she had gone inside, declining her invitation to come in for a drink, as she had known he would. She hadn't wanted to ask him, but the social niceties had to be observed. She remarked suitably on the pleasures of her morning walk with him and bade him a cheerful goodbye. In the hall, with the closed door between them, she allowed herself a long sigh. All the same she had got to know him just a little more. The dogs, his housekeeper, guests for Sunday lunch—Fiona, of course. Lucy ground her perfect teeth at the thought.

'Back already?' asked Alice, putting her head round the kitchen door. She added innocently, 'Thought I heard a car.'

'You did. I met Dr Thurloe walking his dogs and he drove me back.'

'Didn't he want to come in for coffee?' asked Alice sharply.

'Well, no. We had some in Richmond Park, he's got guests for lunch.'

Alice made a tutting sound. 'A day in the fresh air would do 'im more good, and 'im stuck in that 'ospital all day and every day.'

'He doesn't go every day, he goes to other hospitals too, and he's got a private practice.'

'That's as may be, 'e still 'as to treat patients, doesn't 'e? From morn till night, and know what 'e's talking about too, and stuck in a stuffy room with germs being breathed all over 'im.'

She sounded indignant and Lucy made haste to agree; put

like that the doctor merited sympathy, although he hadn't looked as though he needed it that morning.

'He needs a good wife,' declared Alice, and Lucy agreed in a suitably casual voice.

Pauline came back from Edinburgh the following week and was instantly plunged into a new exhibition at the art gallery. 'There's a preview on Saturday,' she told Lucy, and, 'You're coming, I've got a ticket for you.'

'I'm working on Saturday morning…'

'I know that, darling—the exhibition is in the afternoon. Three o'clock, you'll have plenty time to dress up and get a taxi. I'll be on the look-out for you. Have you bought any new clothes yet?'

'No. I've not had any time.'

'It'll be a dressy affair. Wear that brown velvet suit and the Liberty scarf I gave you for Christmas.'

'All right. What kind of pictures are they?'

'Abstract.'

'Lines and squiggles? I can't make head or tail of them.'

'You don't have to, Lucy—just look interested.' Pauline added fretfully, 'I thought you'd enjoy it.'

'Oh, but I shall,' said Lucy quickly, 'and it's sweet of you to ask me.'

And indeed it was nice to have something to look forward to. The orphans took up most of her days, but there was still too much time in which to brood over Dr Thurloe. An outing might take him off her mind for a time at least. There had been no sign of him, but then why should there be? Miranda was settling down nicely and her next appointment wasn't for more than two weeks, and since Lucy's parents were away there was no chance of meeting him at a dinner party or drinks, for no one had thought of inviting her without them.

Her mother telephoned when she could, but, as she pointed out, they were sometimes in remote regions and it wasn't always possible. Her father was full of enthusiasm, she had told Lucy; excavations had uncovered evidence of a high level of civilisation more than a thousand years B.C. There was no question of their coming home for several weeks at least. Each time she asked, 'You're well, darling?' and without waiting for an answer said, 'That's good. Have a lovely time—I'll ring again when I can.'

A letter would have been more satisfactory, but Lucy doubted if her mother would have much chance to sit down and write letters, and she had been told not to write to them since they were moving around so much.

Lucy had plenty of time to dress on Saturday. The exhibition opened at three o'clock, and if she took a taxi she didn't need to leave home until ten minutes or so before the hour; she didn't want to be the first to arrive. Pauline wasn't coming home for lunch—she would have it with Cyril, who would, of course, be at the exhibition too. Lucy got into the brown suit and draped the lovely scarf around her shoulders and, after due thought, got into her high-heeled brown kid shoes. She wasn't keen on very high heels, but they looked good with the suit.

There were a great many people already at the art gallery when she got there. She took the proffered brochure and edged her way through the first room looking for Pauline. It was Cyril whom she first met.

He greeted her pompously. 'Pauline is besieged by eager viewers,' he told her. 'As soon as she is free she will come to you. I would offer my services in accompanying you round the room, but I feel that I should be at Pauline's side.'

'Oh, of course you must,' said Lucy, and wondered how her sister could bear him—and for the rest of her life, too. 'I'll start in this room and work my way round. Do let Pauline know and tell her not to worry about me.'

Cyril allowed himself to be swept away by a surge of people and she was left to examine the exhibits.

She went slowly from one to the other, glad that she had

the brochure, for otherwise she wouldn't have had the least idea what they were. She had reached the end of one wall and was starting on the next, contemplating a large square upon which were a series of lines and a few dots, when Dr Thurloe's voice, low in her ear, murmured, 'Noughts and crosses? Enlighten me, Lucy.'

She chuckled. 'It's called *Maiden with a Bucket*...'

'You astound me, any one of your orphans could do better.'

'Why are you—that is, do you like modern art?'

'No.' He sounded quite certain about it. 'Your sister very kindly sent me a ticket and it seemed churlish not to come. Do people actually buy these—these scribbles?'

'Oh, yes. Pauline works here, you know; she says it's a most successful and lucrative aspect of the art world.'

'Do you like them?' He looked down at her and thought how pretty she looked in that brown thing and how ridiculous her high heels were.

'Me? No. I have tried to because of Pauline, but I do agree with you that the orphans are better at it. There's Pauline...'

He took her arm and edged through the crowd and Pauline saw them and came towards them. 'There you are—and Dr Thurloe. How nice! This is so successful. Lucy, I won't be home until late, you'll be all right? I'll go back with Cyril to his flat and have dinner with him.'

She smiled widely at them and turned away with a quick 'bye' as an Arab in flowing robes accosted her.

Lucy had gone very pink. It was tiresome that Pauline had said all that about coming home late and would she be all right with the doctor standing there. Now he might possibly feel that the least he could do was to see her back home. She said hurriedly, 'Well, I'll say goodbye. I came to please Pauline, and I must fly or I'll be late.' She offered a hand. 'It was nice meeting you again.'

He took her hand, but he didn't let it go. They stood, rather close together because of the squash of people around them, and looked at each other while Lucy's pink face went slowly red and the doctor's firm mouth widened into a smile.

He said quietly, 'Could we escape together, do you think? And will you believe me when I say that I intended asking you to come to tea with me as soon as I saw you here?'

'I'd love a cup of tea,' said Lucy, quite sure that he would never lie to her or anyone else unless it was absolutely necessary.

He took her arm again and they went out of the gallery into the quiet Saturday afternoon street. 'The car's just round the corner.'

When they were in the car she asked, 'Where are we going?'

'My home—Mrs Trump likes the idea of having a kitten, but you ought to have a word with her first, don't you think?'

Which sounded reasonable enough.

She gave a small sigh of pleasure as she got out of the car in front of his house. It was the end one of the row of old houses in Strand on the Green, facing the river, pristine in its black and white paintwork and shining brass door knocker. There was a tub filled with snowdrops at each side of the door, and staring at them from the window alongside the door was a very large, fat tabby cat.

'Thomas,' said Lucy happily, and when the doctor opened his door she went past him into the narrow, high-ceilinged hall. It smelled of beeswax polish and very faintly of lavender, and the console-table and the two chairs on either side of it gleamed with years of loving care. There was a fine silk rug on the floor, and the walls were panelled waist-high, and above that the paper was a soft dim crimson.

The doctor caught her by the arm and swept her through a half-open door into a room with windows facing the water, and the cat got down off the window-seat and came to meet them, taking no notice of the sudden rush and barking of Robinson and Friday. She offered an elderly head for a rub and then, with her tail high and ignoring the dogs, went out of the room, to return almost at once, walking sedately beside Mrs Trump, a short, stout lady with a round happy face, a great deal of grey hair held up by combs and skewered ruthlessly by hairpins, and faded blue eyes.

'There you are, sir. And you'd like a nice cup of tea, I've no doubt.' She beamed at Lucy. 'And the young lady too. Trump will have the tea-tray in five minutes. Would the young lady like to refresh herself?'

Lucy was conscious of the doctor's amused glance. She darted a smile at him and said sedately, 'If I might leave my jacket somewhere?'

'This is Miss Lockitt, Mrs Trump; will you see that she has all she wants?'

'Indeed, I will, sir. You come with me, miss, if you would be so kind.'

Lucy followed her into the hall and then into a cloakroom under the gracefully curving staircase at the back of the hall. As she took off her jacket and set the very pale pink blouse to rights, she reflected that her mother wasn't the only one who could boast about her faithful housekeeper—obviously Mrs Trump was a treasure, and presumably the Trump she had mentioned would be her husband and another treasure.

The cloakroom, though small, contained everything needed for the maintainance of cleanliness and beauty. She left it, as Mrs Trump had put it, feeling refreshed and ready to make the most of an hour's company with the doctor.

He got up as she went back into the drawing-room, and the dogs got up with him and fussed around while he settled her in a chair by the fire. She looked around the room, warm, charmingly furnished and softly lit, and then at him sitting opposite her. Dear, darling William, she reflected dreamily, she was getting to know him after all; the gods, or whoever arranged these things, were on her side.

She couldn't stop her delighted smile, and he said kindly, 'You like my home, Lucy?'

'Oh, my goodness, it's perfect—what I've seen of it. It's not like living in London here, is it?'

The door opened before he could answer and a middle-aged, rotund man carrying a tray came in. He bade the doctor a grave good afternoon and repeated his greeting to Lucy when he was introduced. 'Mr and Mrs Trump have been with me for more years than I care to remember. My life would fall apart without them, wouldn't it, Trump?'

'There is that possibility, sir; I trust the occasion may never arise.' He lifted the lid of a silver muffin dish. 'Mrs Trump thought that a muffin might be acceptable, sir—such a chilly afternoon.'

'Muffins will be specially good, Trump. Switch the phone through to this room, will you? And have your own tea in peace.'

'Thank you, sir.' Trump made his stately way out of the room and Lucy was begged to pour the tea.

An hour passed pleasantly. Lucy, comfortably full of muffins and Madeira cake, had lost all count of time; she was far too busy probing delicately for details of the doctor's way of life, an exercise which was affording him a good deal of secret amusement. It was in a brief pause in their conversation that the long case clock by the door chimed a musical six o'clock, and she jumped to her feet like a guilty child. 'Oh, the time—I'm so sorry, I do hope I haven't delayed you. I dare say you're doing something if you're free…'

He didn't deny it. 'Plenty of time and only a few friends coming to dinner. I'll run you home.' He smiled at her very kindly. 'I have enjoyed our afternoon, we must do it again some time.'

Lucy smiled and murmured and her green eyes belied the smile. Nothing, she vowed silently, nothing would induce her to accept any invitation from him again. It was so obvious to her now that he had taken pity on her and sat, probably bored stiff, for two hours listening to her uninspired remarks. She paused in the doorway to say, 'There's really no need to drive me back, there'll be a bus at the end of the street...'

A waste of breath, for he said nothing at all, but summoned Mrs Trump with Lucy's jacket, helped her into it and ushered her out of his front door and into the Rolls-Royce parked there. She was far too cross to listen to his easy flow of talk as he drove her back to Chelsea, and almost before he had stopped in front of her house she had started to open her door.

A large hand came down on hers. 'Stay where you are,' he advised her, and got out of the car to open her door and help her out. He took her key from her and opened the house door, at the same time giving the door knocker a thump so that Alice came from the kitchen.

'There you are,' said Alice. 'I was just wondering where you'd got to.' She beamed at the doctor. 'You'll come in, sir?'

'Thank you, no, Alice.' He glanced at Lucy, standing silent and still cross, feeling like a child brought home from a party and handed over to Nanny.

'Thank you for my tea,' she said frostily. 'Goodbye, Dr Thurloe.'

'Goodbye Lucy. Shall you be in Richmond Park tomorrow morning?'

'No, I'm going out with a friend.'

She slipped past Alice and she heard him wish the housekeeper goodnight before he got back into his car and drove away.

Alice shut the door. 'Had a nice time, did you, Miss Lucy?'

Lucy heaved a great sigh. 'No, I did not, it was absolutely beastly.' She burst into tears and raced up to her room, and didn't come down until Alice came to tell her that her supper was ready in the dining-room.

'What time will you be going out tomorrow, Miss Lucy?' Alice wanted to know. 'To see these friends of yours?'

'I only said that,' explained Lucy, 'because I was afraid the doctor might take pity on me again...'

'Take pity on you? Whatever do you mean, love? He's the last man to waste 'is time, or I'm a Dutchman. If he wanted to take you out 'e'd 'ave meant it.'

Lucy shook her head. 'Oh, no, Alice dear, he's a kind man, and Pauline asked me if I'd be all right on my own with you, and he was there and he asked me to have tea with him at his house.' She added a little wildly, 'Just as he'd give a stray dog a good meal or feed a lost kitten...' She paused. 'Oh, dear, and that's why I went, because he said his housekeeper would like one of Mrs Simpkins' kittens and I was supposed to talk to her about it.'

'Never mind,' said Alice comfortably. 'You'll be bound to see him again.'

'Not if I can help it,' said Lucy, so fiercely that Alice gave her a sharp look. 'You go and sit by the sitting-room fire,' was all she said, 'and I'll bring you your coffee.'

'I'll help you wash up...'

'That you will not, I've had all day to idle away, and all the other days as well now there's no one here but you. Miss Pauline'll be back tonight?'

'She's going to Cyril's place for dinner, and I think she intends to spend the weekend with his parents and come back tomorrow evening. I'm sure Imogen will be back in a few days—I had a letter.'

When Alice brought the coffee she made the good soul sit down. 'You just stay there,' she ordered nicely and fetched a cup and saucer from the dining-room sideboard. 'Look, Alice, I don't want to do anything tomorrow, only wash my hair and do my nails and loll around with the Sunday papers. Wouldn't you like to take the day off—which you can while you have the chance? You'll be busy enough when Imogen and Pauline and my parents are back.'

'Your lunch—?' began Alice.

'I can cook, you know I can, you taught me. There's food in the fridge?'

'Of course there is,' Alice declared indignantly, 'but it's my place to cook…'

'Oh, Alice, of course it is, you shall cook me a luscious supper when you get back. You know you're dying to see your sister. Go after breakfast and come back after tea. I know Mother would approve.'

'You'll be all right alone? I'm not sure…'

'Oh, go on, Alice,' wheedled Lucy. 'I'm twenty-five, you know, and able to look after myself.'

'Oh, well, it would be nice to go over to Golders Green for an hour or two. But you're to phone me if I'm needed.'

'I promise, Alice.'

The house was quiet once Alice had gone the next morning. Lucy roamed around, played with the kittens, washed her hair and did her nails and then curled up with the Sunday papers. But she didn't read them for long; she went over Saturday's events, almost word for word. 'The trouble is,' she told Mrs Simpkins, who was sitting in her basket with her kittens, 'that I behaved like a silly girl. I'm a grown woman of twenty-five, and that's getting on, but I simply have no idea how to sparkle, though I dare say William wouldn't want that kind of a wife. It's nice to take out someone that looks like that odious Fiona, all gush and black velvet, but she'd be no good at all at the breakfast table if he'd been up half the night slaving over some ill child. I'd do very nicely, you know.'

She wandered into the kitchen and switched on the coffee percolator and found the biscuit tin. The front door bell jangled and she frowned. It could be Pauline and Cyril, or Imogen returned several days early. It could be anyone. She went to the door and opened it, remembering just too late to put up the chain first; it could be a thief.

It was Dr Thurloe and she gaped at him, colour flooding her face. She said idiotically, 'Oh, it's you.'

'Indeed it is I. On my way back for lunch from the park I thought I'd give your housekeeper a message for you about the kitten.' He smiled slowly. 'You changed your mind about spending the day with your friends?'

She said breathlessly, 'Well, yes—no, actually I wasn't going anywhere.'

He said smoothly, 'In that case will you come back with me for lunch? There will be one or two friends—quite informal. Come as you are.'

She gave silent thanks that she had put on a rather nice jersey dress that morning. She said uncertainly, 'Yes, but you weren't expecting me…'

'Another one more or less won't upset Mrs Trump, and I should be delighted if you could come.'

Her resolve not to accept any invitations from him dissolved like jelly in hot water. 'Well, thank you, I'd like to come.'

'In that case may I come in and collect a kitten?'

'Oh, yes, of course, they're in the kitchen. Do you know which one Mrs Trump would like to have?'

'Thomas is a Tabby, so perhaps a contrast? Black and white or ginger.'

She led the way to the kitchen where Mrs Simpkins, bored with her kittens, was stretched out before the Aga. The kittens were charming. They were looked at in turn, and finally the doctor chose the ugliest, if a kitten could ever be called ugly, but she had a large nose and a flat head and very round eyes. Mrs Simpkins merely yawned when Lucy took her to say goodbye, and took no notice when the doctor tucked her under one arm.

'Would you like a cup of coffee?' asked Lucy.

'Why, yes, I would. It will give this little lady time to feel independent.' He sat down at the table and Lucy switched on the percolator and fetched two mugs. The kitten went to sleep in the curve of his arm and when they got up to go Mrs Simpkins took no notice at all. Lucy, a soft-hearted girl, heaved a sigh of relief. 'Do you suppose they'll miss each other?'

'Perhaps, but not with grief; in the wild once a young animal is able to fend for itself it becomes independent. Mrs Simpkins still has three kittens and this young lady will have Thomas and Mrs Trump to spoil her.'

They got into the car and he transferred the kitten to her lap while he drove. At his house he took her straight through the hall and into the kitchen where Mrs Trump was standing at the table beating something in a bowl while Trump sat in a chair by the Aga, reading the paper. Thomas sat at his feet and all three of them looked up as they went in.

Trump got to his feet and Mrs Trump paused in her beating.

'Your kitten, Mrs Trump,' said the doctor, and sat the little creature down beside Thomas, who stared in amazement while the kitten sniffed delicately at her fur and then curled up beside her.

'Well, I never did!' exclaimed Mrs Trump. 'Look at the little darling and my Thomas, taken an instant liking to each other.'

'Highly satisfactory,' said the doctor. 'She'll need feeding four times a day for a week or two, Mrs Trump...'

'You leave that to me, sir, I'll give her just what's needed, and no going outside either.' She smiled at Lucy. 'The young lady will be here for lunch?'

'Yes, Mrs Trump.' He glanced at the kitchen clock. 'We had better go and have a drink in the drawing-room.' He took Lucy's arm and turned her round, whistled to the dogs who had gone to look at the kitten, and walked her through the door into the hall. They were only just in the drawing-room when the front door bell pealed.

Lucy, ushered across the room towards the brightly burning fire, heard Trump's voice mingled with that of a woman. Fiona, she felt sure, and turned to face the door, in time to see that lady make an entry.

'William, darling... I thought I'd get here first so that we could have ten minutes together.' She stopped as her eyes lighted upon Lucy. 'Oh, I had no idea...' She recovered immediately, kissed the doctor's cheek and went on, 'Lucy Lockitt, isn't it? From the orphanage? Has William taken pity upon you? Your parents are away, aren't they?'

'Hello,' said Lucy. 'They're in Turkey. I don't know if Dr Thurloe has taken pity, but he has invited me to lunch.'

She smiled charmingly. Her eyes, decided the doctor, watching her, looked like emeralds.

He said easily, 'Of course, you two know each other.' The doorbell rang once more and he went on, 'You know the Walters, Lucy...' They came into the room and Lucy was thankfully enveloped in their kindly warmth. She was answering their questions about her parents' plans when the last guest arrived. A colleague of the doctor's, the senior consultant surgeon at City Royal. A man of the doctor's age, already going grey and with a long thin face and a ready smile.

'You know everyone here,' said the doctor, 'but not Lucy Lockitt—her parents—'

'I know of them.' The man shook Lucy's hand as the doctor introduced him as Charles Hyde. 'I'm sorry my wife couldn't make it—you're her stand-in, I expect, and a very charming one, I must say.'

Lucy smiled and murmured. So that was why she had been invited—to make up numbers round the table. It was a pity she loved William so very deeply, otherwise she would have disliked him very much. Men! she thought, and curled a pretty lip.

Lunch, if it hadn't been for Fiona, would have been a delightful meal. The food was superb—lobster tartlets followed by roundels of lamb and finished off with a caramel mousse served with a coulis of raspberries, washed down by a Puligny Montrachet, a wine which Lucy found very pleasant. She knew very little about wines, but Mr Hyde, taking an appreciative sip, pronounced it to be a vintage white burgundy. 'Trust William to keep a good cellar,' he observed. 'Have you known him for long?'

'No,' Lucy replied, then added obscurely, 'Mother and Father are friends of the Walters.'

Mr Hyde glanced sideways at her composed face. 'Oh, quite. I expect you get tired of people asking you how you like working at the orphanage, but I have occasion to go there sometimes. A well-run place, I have always thought.'

'Oh, it is. But sad too—no mothers or fathers, or, if there are any, they don't want to know.'

He nodded. 'Sad indeed. You like children—babies?'

She smiled widely. 'Well, yes, I do, but I can't imagine anyone who didn't being able to work there.'

'We have four children of our own—they seem like an entire orphanage at times! Tell me, did you not wish to go to Turkey with your parents?'

'Well, no. You see, I'd not be of any use. I don't know enough about my father's work.'

Mrs Walter took possession of her after lunch so that she got no opportunity to speak to William even if she had wished to, for Fiona had stayed beside him, not only at the table, but afterwards as they sat around gossiping in the drawing-room. Presently Mrs Walter got up to go and the rest followed her, and when she offered Lucy a lift she accepted at once. It was obvious that Fiona wasn't going to leave with the rest of them, and when the doctor came over to her and offered to drive her home she said cheerfully, 'There's no need for you to bother, but thank you all the same. Mrs Walter will drop me off. Thank you for a delightful lunch.' She smiled too brightly; she wasn't going to concede defeat to the horrible Mrs Seymour, only retreat in good order, more determined than ever to have her dear William. Somehow; she had no idea how.

She refused the Walters' invitation to go back with them and spend the rest of the day, saying, without a grain of truth, that she was expecting a phone call from her mother.

'Isn't that a very long way to phone?' asked Mrs Walter.

'Mother hates writing letters so she rings up once a week instead.'

Lucy said goodbye and let herself into the house. There was the rest of the afternoon to get through, and the evening. She fed Mrs Simpkins and the kittens, switched on the TV and switched it off again, and instead went into the drawing-room, where she sat down at the piano and played all the more sentimental music she could call to mind. She played well and it suited her mood; a mixture of rage, unhappiness and a firm determination to marry William.

She was quite glad to go back to work on the Monday morning. Imogen and Pauline were both back again, and, although they were out most evenings, they slept at home and Lucy saw them briefly at breakfast most mornings. But she didn't see the doctor at all.

It was at the end of the week, as she got off the bus and started the short walk to her home, that she came face to face with a girl of her own age. 'Francesca!' She gave a small shriek of surprise and delight echoed by the other girl.

'Lucy, how lovely seeing you! You never answered my letter at Christmas—I'm actually on my way to see you.'

'You're here in London, on holiday?'

'Litrik is over here for a seminar. Heavens, isn't this fun?'

Lucy took her arm. 'Come for a quick chat; how long are you here?'

'We're going back in three days' time.'

'The babies? Are they here too?'

'Of course, and Nanny is with us. We're at the Connaught.'

They had reached the house and Lucy let them in and called to Alice, who came hurrying in to see who it was.

'Miss Fran—my goodness, it's years since I've seen you!' She eyed Fran's fashionable outfit. 'A real smart young lady too.' She smiled widely. 'I'll bring you both some coffee...'

'Tea, please,' they chorused, and took themselves into the drawing-room, to curl up on chairs and exchange news. They hadn't seen each other for some time, although they had been at school together for years, and after that had stayed with each other from time to time, but Francesca had begun to train as a nurse and gone to live with her three aunts who had discouraged, in the nicest way possible, too many young visitors to their home, so Fran and Lucy had seen less and less of each other even though they kept up a regular correspondence.

Over cups of tea they made up for not having seen each other for so long and presently Lucy said, 'You're happy, aren't you, Fran?'

'Yes. I can't imagine ever being happier. Lucy, why aren't you married? You're pretty and you must meet any number of men.' She put down her cup. 'There must be someone?'

'Yes, but he's not—not available. At least, I'm pretty sure he's not.'

'You're still at that orphanage you wrote about? Can you get some time off? Will you come and stay with us for a week or so? We'd love to have you. You might find a Dutchman as I did.'

'I've got some holidays due. I think I'd love to come Fran. Mother and Father are away, and Imogen and Pauline are out a lot. I'd love to see the babies too. Some time in the early summer perhaps?'

'Oh, sooner than that. Look, I must go or Litrik will worry.

I'll ring you before we go back and fix a date. Do you work on Saturday?'

'Only in the mornings, I'm home by one o'clock.'

At the door Fran said gently, 'You look sad, Lucy. Do you love him very much?'

'Yes, however, I'll get over it. I'd love to come and see you, I might even find that Dutchman!'

They laughed together and Lucy stood at the open door and watched Fran walking away down the quiet street in search of a taxi. She looked so happy and content, and was beautifully dressed too—never a pretty girl, she had blossomed into a charming *jolie laide*.

'That's what love does to you,' said Lucy to the empty street.

The seminar was over and the learned gentlemen who had attended it were drifting away or stopping to talk to colleagues or friends. Dr Thurloe wandered unhurriedly towards the entrance, discussing a knotty problem with Litrik van Rijgen. They hadn't seen each other for some months, but ever since they had been at medical school at Edinburgh Royal Infirmary, and later at Cambridge and Leiden, they had kept in touch.

Litrik glanced at his watch. 'Fran's gone to see an old friend, she said she would be back at the hotel about six o'clock—we've time for a drink.'

The pub on the corner was shabby and awfully dark, but almost empty. They settled at a table in a corner and Dr Thurloe said, 'Well, that's over for another year. A pity you can't stay for a few days. Give my love to Fran, she looks marvellous and the babies are enchanting.'

His friend looked faintly smug. 'Fran's a wonderful wife and the children are delightful. Why not come back to the hotel, just for a half an hour, and say goodbye in person?'

Francesca was back by the time they arrived, lying on the

floor of their sitting-room playing with the toddler's bricks, but she jumped up as they went in, greeted her husband as though they had been parted for weeks, held up his small son for a kiss and then turned to William, offering a cheek with the simplicity of a child. 'The baby's asleep,' she told them. 'Have you finished your papers?' She smiled at her husband. 'I've had a lovely time with Lucy, it was great to see her again. She's prettier than ever. I've invited her to stay, Litrik, you won't mind? She was getting off the bus and I was just walking up the road to her home. She's still at the orphanage.'

Dr Thurloe had been studying the baby in her carrycot, but he turned round slowly as Fran spoke. 'Not by any chance Lucy Lockitt of nursery rhyme fame?'

'Yes—do you know her? She never said.' Francesca paused, a dozen likely and unlikely ideas in her head. 'We were at school together and we've kept in touch. I said I'd give her a ring before we go back home and settle a date. She said early summer; I'd like her to come before then.'

Dr Thurloe spoke casually. 'Give me a date, will you? I have the ear of the Matron at the orphanage.'

'Oh, splendid. Can you let me know before I phone Lucy, then she can ask—and get it,' she finished hopefully.

'I can't see why not. I'll give you a ring some time in the morning.' He smiled gently. 'I must be going—a dinner date.'

'Who with?' Fran blushed at his look and said, 'Sorry, it's none of my business.'

'A handsome lady of thirty-odd years, widowed, comfortably situated and well versed in the social graces.'

Francesca stretched up to kiss his cheek. 'Then don't let us keep you, she sounds just perfect.'

'What for?'

She gave him an innocent look. 'Why, a doctor's wife, of course. It's time you married, William.'

CHAPTER FIVE

LUCY went to the theatre with Pauline and Cyril on Saturday evening. It was something put on by an arts club in one of the smaller theatres and extremely highbrow. She gave up trying to understand what it was about halfway through the first act and allowed her thoughts to wander to William. He would be out, she guessed, dining and dancing probably. Her evening would have been much happier if she had known that he was miles away in the Cotswolds, spending his day with the old professor who had taught him so well in Edinburgh. She was taken to supper after the play ended, and listened to Cyril discussing the dialogue at length. The play had its merits, he informed them gravely, but he then went on to tear it to pieces.

'If you knew it was going to be so bad, why did we go?' asked Lucy.

'I was given tickets,' said Cyril huffily.

It was a pity they disliked each other, she thought, and agreed politely to being taken home before he and Pauline went back to his parents' house for the night.

She tactfully thanked him very nicely before she went indoors, where she kicked off her shoes, drank the cocoa Alice had ready for her, and went to bed. Pauline wouldn't be home until after office hours on Monday, but Imogen came in soon after she did and came along to her room to suggest that they might spend the next day in the country. 'Though I must be back soon after six o'clock—I've got a dinner date. We could drive to Epping—no, we'll go on to Ingatestone and have lunch at that nice place. We haven't had a chance to gossip for ages, have we?'

From which remark Lucy deduced that her sister had something she wanted to tell her. 'It sounds lovely. What time shall we go?'

'Oh, elevenish. Alice could have the day to herself after breakfast.'

It was a bright morning when Lucy got up; March, having come in rather noisily, had now become as quiet as a lamb. She put on a jersey three-piece, with sensible shoes, and went down to breakfast.

Traffic was thin as they drove east through London, and it stayed that way until they reached Epping, although there were cars enough going towards the coast. Imogen parked the car and led the way into the hotel restaurant. 'We might go for a walk after lunch,' she suggested. When she would be told whatever it was that Imogen wanted her to know, decided Lucy, and took care to keep the talk general as they ate lunch.

They had been walking for ten minutes or so, saying nothing much, when Imogen said abruptly, 'I'm going to be married, Lucy.'

It was a surprise: Imogen, at twenty-eight, had already made her mark in the business world, she had a big salary, she was thought much of by her boss, and her future as an executive was assured. She knew her own worth and had never hesitated to let her family know that, and somehow they had all thought of her as staying single.

'Imogen, what a lovely piece of news! Who is he? Do Mother and Father know?'

'I cabled them yesterday. Of course, we shall wait until they're back home before we marry. You don't know him—he's a Canadian businessman, George Irwell.'

'I hope you'll be very happy,' Lucy said, and meant it. 'You'll be married before Pauline and Cyril.'

'Yes. I'm the eldest anyway...and what about you Lucy? Haven't you met anyone you would like to marry?' She didn't give Lucy a chance to answer. 'I suppose not, buried at that orphanage of yours. Such a pity, for you're pretty enough, only you don't bother much, do you?' She laughed, and added without meaning to be unkind, 'Mother has always said that you're the home-bird, whatever that means.'

A prospect Lucy didn't care to contemplate. It was a sobering thought which remained with her for the rest of the day, and she was quite glad when Monday morning came round again.

She was halfway through the morning when Matron sent for her.

'I don't want to hassle you, but would you care to take a couple of weeks' holiday in a week or two's time? There will be no one else on holiday and we can cover for you. You have always been very accommodating about fitting in with the rest of us. Any time in March or April will suit me; at a pinch we could manage the first week in May. Will you think it over and let me know?'

Lucy went back to Miranda and set about giving her her midday dinner while she thought about holidays. Fran had asked her to stay, but she remembered that she herself had suggested the early summer, so Fran might not be prepared to have her earlier than that. It was a pity, for if she took two weeks' holiday within the next few weeks she could hardly expect to get more time off before the autumn, especially as the other girls had their plans already made. She finished her day undecided what to do, aware that she would have to make up her mind before she saw Matron again.

As it happened, her mind was made up for her that very evening.

Both her sisters were out, Imogen with her George, Pauline with Cyril. Lucy had eaten her supper in the kitchen with Alice for company, and then wandered away to wash her hair. Only before she could do that the phone rang. It was Francesca.

'Lucy, we're leaving this evening in about an hour. Look,

couldn't you manage to come and stay with us before the summer? Surely you could get a couple of weeks off soon?'

'As a matter of fact, Matron asked me this morning if I'd mind taking two weeks either at the end of this month or in April.'

'Oh, good. Then you'll come; when?'

Lucy suddenly felt excited. 'Wait while I get a calendar. How about the last week in March, that's only a week away? You're sure—?'

'Don't be silly, of course I'm sure. Let's see, that will be the twenty-fifth on a Saturday. Litrik'll meet you at Schiphol; let us know the time the flight arrives when you've got everything fixed up. It'll be such fun, Lucy, there are years of gossip to catch up on. I must fly—Litrik's got the car waiting. See you.'

Fran put down the phone and smiled at her husband. 'That's settled. How clever of William to get round that matron. I wonder why he did. Do you suppose he fancies Lucy?'

'My darling, William is a kind man; I dare say he thinks that Lucy needs a holiday and he was able to make things easy for her.'

He smiled at her slowly and crossed the room to kiss her. Fran kissed him back. 'Is that so? They would make a very nice pair.' She frowned in thought. 'Do you suppose William might like to take a week or so's holiday and come and stay with us as well?'

'Matchmaker,' observed Litrik lovingly, and kissed her again. 'We shall miss that hovercraft.'

Lucy gave her holiday dates to Matron the next day, and when she got home that evening she told her sisters. They smiled at her with affection, remarked that it would be nice for her to have a holiday, and fell to the much more important task of making wedding arrangements. Lucy hadn't expected them to take much interest in such an ordinary happening as a couple of weeks' holiday; she went along to the kitchen and told Alice, who responded with all the warmth her sisters lacked.

'Now that'll be nice,' said Alice, 'and you be sure and take some pretty clothes with you, Miss Lucy; you never know, Mr Right might be waiting for you in Holland. Not that I set much store by foreigners.'

'Francesca married one,' Lucy pointed out, and ate one of the cheese tartlets Alice had just taken from the oven. 'She thinks he's absolutely marvellous.'

'Quite right and proper too,' said Alice, 'since 'e's 'er 'usband.' She whisked the tray of tartlets out of reach. 'You'll have no supper if you eat them now,' she threatened. 'There's grilled sole and spinach and no potatoes—Miss Imogen says she must lose half a stone before the wedding.'

'In that case,' said Lucy, reaching for the tartlets, 'I'd better have another of these, dear Alice.'

She spent the rest of the evening listening to her sisters tossing ideas to and fro; receptions, bridesmaids, which church and the best places for honeymoons were discussed in depth. They paused presently and looked at her. 'You'll be a bridesmaid, Lucy,' said Imogen. 'Pink taffeta and flower wreaths, I think...'

Pauline had other ideas. 'I'll have four attendants, I think—you, of course, Lucy. I don't think Cyril can manage any free time before July. Sea-green, I think, with darker green sashes. The others will be Cyril's little nephew and his two nieces.'

Three tiresome children, reflected Lucy, who loved children, all excepting these three—spoilt, quarrelsome and tending to whine. When she had agreed pleasantly to everything that was suggested she took herself off to bed, to lie awake and think of William Thurloe and wonder where he was and what he was doing. She told herself crossly that she must try not to think about him quite so much; she was still determined to marry him, but when she did think about him it must be positively. Not useless longings which got her nowhere. She rearranged her pillows and began to plan her holiday wardrobe. She would buy some clothes… It was a pity William wouldn't be there to see them. Sleep overtook her before she could feel sad about it.

Her mother, apprised of the forthcoming holiday, said, 'How nice, darling,' and plunged into an enthusiastic account of her father's latest find, the remains of an iron pot—proof, if they had needed it, that the Hittites really had known about smelting. Only when she had passed on this interesting information did she comment happily upon Imogen's forthcoming marriage, adding the rider that Lucy must be looking forward to being a bridesmaid twice over. 'A nice change from those orphans,' she declared with a little laugh, 'and enjoy yourself with Francesca, dear. Such a nice, quiet girl, and not at all pretty. Yet she has made a splendid marriage from what you tell me. You must see what you can do while you're in Holland, darling.'

Lucy said, 'Yes, Mother.' She had no need to go to Holland; just down the road to Chiswick.

She booked her flight, found her passport, fetched travellers' cheques and embarked on a day's shopping. March so far had been warm and sunny with occasional bouts of pouring rain. Fran had told her to be sure and bring a raincoat with her and a woolly or two, 'And something pretty for the evenings—I've planned a party and we shall go out to dinner and perhaps a concert.' She had sounded quite excited over the phone, and Lucy, immensely cheered at the prospect of some social life, went off and bought two new party dresses as well as a thin woollen suit in which to travel.

Each day she had gone to the orphanage hoping to see Dr Thurloe, but she never did. Miranda was improving by leaps and bounds, but she wasn't due to go to the clinic for another two weeks, when Lucy would be in Holland, so she would miss a chance of seeing him then.

It was on her last day at the orphanage before she started

her holiday that she met Fiona Seymour. It had been a busy day and she had hurried home, showered and changed and taken herself for a walk along the Embankment, to meet Fiona coming towards her, strolling along in a stunning outfit.

She stopped and Lucy perforce stopped too. 'My dear, you are the very last person I would expect to see. I thought you spent your days in the orphanage with those dreary children.'

'I work until five o'clock, and they're not dreary.' Aware that she had sounded snappy, Lucy added, 'It's a gorgeous evening, isn't it?'

'I suppose so, though I'm having to waste some of it. William—Dr Thurloe—was to drive me to Henley, I've a dreary aunt living there, but he phoned to say he has some emergency or other and he won't be able to take me. Luckily I have a number of other friends and no lack of offers to take his place, although I'm having to hang around until I can be called for. I got bored indoors.' She gave Lucy a quick rather malicious glance. 'William's upset, of course; we spend as much time as we possibly can together.'

Lucy racked her brains to find a suitable reply to this. 'He's a busy man,' she observed mildly.

'Of course, I suppose you see him occasionally with those precious orphans. It must be dire working with them, but I suppose if you haven't any prospect of marrying it's better than nothing.' She drew a breath and put up her hand to her mouth. 'Oh, my dear, that sounded awful! Do forgive me, I was only repeating what William said…'

Lucy had gone rather pale, but her voice was quite clear and steady and very quiet. 'It's most interesting, and I like children. I should hate to live the kind of life you do, although I dare say it takes up quite a lot of time, make-up and hair and so on, and dieting…' Her green eyes were like deep green pools, her smile charming. 'I must fly, I've so much to do before I go away. Bye.'

She isn't likely to repeat that to William, decided Lucy,

walking home rather fast, and I know I was rude, but she was rude first. And if William really said that about me I'll never speak to him again. She bounced into the house with such vigour that Alice came from the kitchen to see what was the matter.

'There you are, Miss Lucy. A pity you were out, that nice Dr Thurloe phoned to wish you a happy holiday—heard you were going from your matron, he said. I asked him to ring back, but he said he was going out.'

'Oh, he is, is he?' uttered Lucy rather wildly. 'As though I care what he does.'

She pounded upstairs to her room and Alice went back to the kitchen. 'So that's the way the wind blows,' she observed to Mrs Simpkins. 'We'll just have to wait and see, won't we?'

Mrs Simpkins, cleaning her whiskers after her tea, merely stared and yawned.

Right at the back of Lucy's head had been the idea that Dr Thurloe might phone again before she left, but the telephone remained silent and she started on her journey to Heathrow, speeded on her way by Alice and determinedly taking care not to look round in case the doctor, at the very last minute, should appear. Of course, he didn't, and she took herself through the routine at the airport and in due course boarded her plane.

She had met Litrik van Rijgen only twice before, at his wedding to Fran and during a visit they had paid to London just before the first baby had been born. When she saw him waiting for her at Schiphol she thought that he hadn't changed at all. He was a big man with greying fair hair and a handsome face, which in repose looked severe, although, reflected Lucy as she went towards him, it was unlikely that he was, for Francesca adored him and, as far as Lucy could discover from her letters, he made her blissfully happy. He saw her then, and smiled as he strode towards her.

'How very nice to see you again, Lucy.' He bent and kissed

her cheek. 'Fran is so looking forward to your visit—so am I. Is this all your luggage?'

He led the way out of the airport and ushered her into the silver-grey Daimler parked close by. 'We shall be home in about half an hour—it is about thirty miles, just the other side of Utrecht. You had a comfortable flight?'

She found him a very likeable man, and they talked comfortably together as he drove until he turned off the motorway and joined a country road, which was very peaceful after the rush of traffic on the motorway. The village they reached was small and dominated by a large church, and a hundred yards further on Litrik swept the car between brick pillars and along a drive bordered by shrubs and trees, rounded a curve and drew up before his home.

It was a solid flat-faced house with orderly rows of windows, each with shutters. The house door was reached by way of circular steps and was solid enough to withstand a siege. It was opened now by a thin elderly man and Francesca flew past him and down the steps, to receive a quick embrace from her husband before she flung herself at Lucy.

'Oh, isn't this fun! Come in…' She flashed a smile at Litrik and took Lucy's arm. 'Are you tired? Did you have a good trip? We'll have lunch in half an hour or so.' She called over her shoulder, 'You won't be long, darling?'

Litrik smiled at her and Lucy, watching them, felt envious of such quiet happiness. 'Five minutes, love.'

'This is Trugg,' said Fran, and waited while Lucy shook hands with him. 'He's our right hand. Come up to your room and I'll leave you for a few minutes to tidy if you want to.'

She led the way up the wide staircase to the gallery above the hall and opened a door. 'Here you are, Lucy; the bathroom's through that door, and if you want anything just ask, won't you?'

She dropped a kiss on Lucy's cheek. 'This is fun, it really is. Come down when you're ready.'

Left to herself, Lucy explored the pretty room, admiring the mahogany furniture and the pretty sprigged chintz at the window and the thick matching bedspread. And the bathroom was quite perfect, pink and white and furnished with a pile of fluffy towels, bowls of soap and bath essences and a wide mirror, well lit. She went back into the bedroom and sat down before the triple mirror on the dressing table. She was a girl who almost always looked immaculate; she powdered her nose, put on more lipstick and brushed her hair, took a quick look at the garden from the window, and went down the staircase.

There were a number of doors in the hall and she paused uncertainly as Litrik flung a half-open door wide. 'We're in here having a drink,' he said and she went past him into the drawing-room.

It was a grand room, furnished most beautifully with antique pieces which gleamed with the patina of years of loving care, but there were great comfortable chairs too, and two enormous sofas, one on each side of the hooded fireplace. French windows opened on to a garden alive with spring flowers and a fire burned brightly. But its grandness was mitigated by all the signs of family living: a teddy bear leaning against a wall cabinet, a pile of knitting cast down on one of the lamp tables, a pile of magazines and newspapers on the sofa table, and before the fire two dogs, a mastiff and a much smaller dog, rather stout and with a long curly coat. They got up and came to sniff her and she put out a hand.

'Thor and Muff,' said Litrik. 'You like dogs?'

'Oh, yes, but we haven't one at home, only Mrs Simpkins the cat and her kittens.'

'Mrs Trugg has a cat—Moses—Litrik fished him out of the canal. There's a donkey too, in the paddock, and horses—Litrik has taught me to ride,' said Fran.

They sat around talking until Fran said, 'Shall we just peep at the children? Nanny will have fed them—baby has purée twice a day now, though I still feed her.'

The two of them went upstairs to the nursery where a miniature Litrik was perched in a high chair more or less feeding himself, while a young plump woman sat by him with the baby on her lap.

'This is Nanny,' said Fran. 'She was here before we married and I hope she'll never leave us.'

She sat down and took the baby on her lap while they watched little Litrik having the last of his dinner. 'They will rest now,' said Fran, 'and we have them until bathtime—Litrik isn't always home, of course, but he is marvellous with them. Wasn't it nice having a boy and then a girl? We want another pair—four makes a nice family.'

Lucy said wistfully, 'You must be so happy, Fran.' And then, in case she sounded self-pitying, 'They'll have a lovely home; it's so beautiful...'

'The garden's lovely in the summer, and the country around is pretty.' Fran got up and put the baby back in her cot and tucked her in carefully, dropped a kiss on her small son's head, said something to Nanny to make her smile, and suggested that they might go down to their own lunch.

'I say,' said Lucy, 'I suppose you speak Dutch?'

'Yes, but I make lots of mistakes still. Nanny understands some English, and of course Trugg is English, although Mrs Trugg, who cooks and housekeeps, only has a smattering.'

Lunch was a cheerful affair—there was so much to talk about and Litrik, Lucy decided, really was a very nice man. It was no wonder Fran was so happy. Almost as nice as William, Lucy admitted, a thought which made her ponder about him and, almost as though Fran knew it, she asked casually if Lucy went to the City Royal much and if she knew any of the staff there. She avoided her husband's amused eye as she did so, and appeared very nonchalant.

'Well, yes, I go sometimes to the clinics...' Lucy went a

delicate pink. 'Some of the children aren't quite normal and they have to see a—a consultant.'

Such a vivid mental picture of William was imprinted behind her eyelids that for a moment she couldn't go on, and Litrik, apparently unnoticing of that, asked, 'Have they still got that out-of-date Outpatients there? As dark as a cellar, and it always smelled of damp clothes.'

A remark which led the conversation safely back to generalities.

The rest of the day passed pleasantly, Lucy playing with the children, being shown over the house and exploring the garden. In the evening, after one of Mrs Trugg's delicious dinners, they talked again; there was so much to say and, as Fran said, several years to catch up on.

Lucy, getting ready for bed, reflected on her evening. She had enjoyed it very much. Fran hadn't changed; she had beautiful clothes and an elegant hairstyle, but she was still kind-hearted, gentle Fran and Litrik loved her… 'And that is how I wish William would love me,' Lucy said to herself as she jumped into her very comfortable bed.

She woke once in the night, at a time when everything appeared to be at its blackest, convinced that she had no chance at all against the practised charms of Fiona Seymour. Fortunately when she awoke in the morning such a gloomy thought had no chance against daylight's common sense. She had as much chance as any other girl, she told herself stoutly, and sat up in bed to drink the morning tea that a nice cheerful girl had brought.

She was taken to church in the morning after a breakfast of hot rolls, ham and cheese and delicious coffee, and a quick visit to the nursery to see the children. Fran had been up early to feed the baby, and Litrik had been out with the dogs, and there was a pleasant air of bustle about the house.

The family pew was at the front of the church, under the pulpit with its vast sounding-board, and Lucy sat between

Fran and Litrik, unable to understand a word, and yet following the service very well—some of the hymns even had tunes she knew. The sermon lasted a very long time, and the *dominee* thundered above her head so that she had the impression that he disliked his congregation, but as they left the church they stopped to speak to him and she discovered him to be a mild man with a splendid command of English and a soft, gentle voice.

He was very pleased to meet her, he said, and if she could spare the time he and his wife would be delighted to see her at his house. She thanked him nicely and Fran said, 'We'll walk down one day; I'm sure you'll have a lot to talk about. Have the children got over their measles?'

She was assured that they had, and they parted on the best of terms, to walk home and spend an hour in the nursery before having drinks and their own lunch. In the afternoon Litrik drove to the Veluwe, this time in a station-wagon with the dogs at the back and Lucy and Fran behind him each with a baby. It was a sunny day, but windy; he found a sheltered spot presently, and they all piled out, poking around the hedges for primroses, walking beside a narrow canal where a duck family was swimming. The hedges petered out very soon and the road ran, narrow and empty, towards the flat horizon, the country between dotted with farmhouses and villages, their church steeples dominating the field around them.

'Just where are we?' asked Lucy, no longer sure of the points of the compass.

'It all looks alike, doesn't it? We have driven through the Veluwe, and now we are on its very edge, back to the fields and flat country. The Veluwe is rather like your New Forest, only very much smaller. It's a great holiday area, and away from the road there are quite a few charming houses. Arnhem is to the south of us,' he waved a large arm, 'over there is Utrecht, and beyond but more to the north is Amsterdam. We'll take you there before you go back.'

They wandered back to the car and went home to tea round the fire, with Litrik's small son on his knee and the baby asleep in her Moses basket. Lucy sat, not talking much, soothed by the charming room and the gentle talk. She looked at the dogs and thought that, if she almost closed her eyes, she could fancy that they were Robinson and Friday and that Litrik was William.

The days flowed gently into a week; Lucy, getting ready for a bath and bed at the end of it, reviewed them. Each day there had been something different, and, even though Litrik had been away from home for a good deal of the day, Francesca had thought of something to do.

They had gone to Utrecht, inspected the great tower, poked around the shops, had coffee at the Café de Paris, decided against climbing the hundreds of steps of the Dom Tower, and returned home to take the children for a walk, accompanied by the dogs, until Litrik came home and friends came in for drinks. They had gone one evening to Litrik's parents' home and dined there with their other guests, and the next day Litrik had gone early to the hospital and come home again in time to drive them all up to Friesland to visit his great aunts, two formidable ladies who would never see eighty again, but who had lost none of their powers of command. Lucy had been taken on a tour of the house, which was old and furnished with heavy tables and chairs which looked as though they had taken root. They had ended up in the red salon, which had quite overpowered her.

'Frightful, isn't it?' Fran had said. 'I'd hate to live here, though I like Friesland. We visit from time to time. Litrik has a large family.' It had still been light when he'd left, and they had driven back across the Afsluitdijk, into Alkmaar, so that Lucy might see something of that town, to skirt Amsterdam and take the road through Hilversum and so home.

On another day they had driven along the narrow quiet road beside the River Vecht, admiring the lovely old houses with their grounds bordering the water, built by the rich merchants of the eighteenth century. And one evening there had been people to dinner, and all this interspersed with the gentle day's routine and hours spent with the children.

'You must go and see Keukenhof next week,' Fran had said. 'It's a glorious sight now, you couldn't have come at a better time.'

Lucy had been tired then, but, although her head was full of all the sights she had seen, there was still room to think of William.

'Out with Fiona, I suppose,' she mumbled as she dropped off.

Litrik had Sunday free, he had said on the previous evening, and, sitting up in bed, drinking her morning tea, Lucy wondered what pleasures were in store for her. The maid had pulled the curtains back and the sky was blue, the sun was shining and there didn't seem to be too much wind. Lucy hopped out of bed, flung up the window and hung out to enjoy the expanse of velvety lawn and the flower-beds filled with tulips and hyacinths. The birds were singing too, and the sun held warmth.

'Come gentle spring, ethereal Mildness, come,' carolled Lucy from her window, just as the peace of the garden was broken. Litrik was coming round the corner of his house, the dogs with him, and, strolling beside him, his hands in his pockets, looking very much at home, was William.

She stared down at him, unable to believe her eyes, her mouth open while happiness almost choked her. The two men looked up then, and Litrik said pleasantly, 'Oh, good morning, Lucy. I think you know William? He's an old friend, come to spend a few days with us. Come on down and meet him.'

Lucy went on staring with nothing to say, and then a wide smile curved her mouth. 'Good morning,' she said in a wispy voice. 'I'll be down—' It struck her suddenly that she was hardly suitably dressed for a chat, and she withdrew her person smartly, only to poke her head out again, her hair in a tangle round her shoulders. 'Is Fiona with you?' she asked.

If Dr Thurloe was surprised, nothing of it showed on his placid face as he looked up at her. 'No, I'm alone.'

She nodded, still smiling, and shut the window, to dance across the room to the bathroom. While she showered she thought about what she would wear. It was still cool, although the sun shone and it was April. It had better be the jersey dress. She dressed rapidly, brushed her hair to shining smoothness, applied lipstick and raced downstairs.

The two men were coming out of Litrik's study as she reached the hall, and she went to meet them, quite unaware of the delight on her face. Indeed, she might have uttered a good deal which she would have regretted later if it hadn't been for Fran running down the staircase after her, calling out as she came, 'William—how delightful! Of course, you'll stay? And it won't be just babies and us…' She gave a well-simulated start of surprise. 'Oh, do you two know each other?'

She leaned up to give William a kiss and he said gravely, 'We have met—at the clinic and various dinner parties.'

'Oh, isn't it a small world?' Fran declared and both men agreed with a blandness which belied the gleam in their eyes.

But Lucy hadn't noticed, and she said now, rather shyly, 'It does seem strange meeting here. Are you on holiday?' And, in case he should think that she was prying, 'I am, I've been here a week already. I knew Fran at school.'

'There's nothing like old friends,' observed Dr Thurloe easily. 'How are you liking Holland?'

They went in to breakfast and Lucy, the seething of her feelings settling down under his casual friendliness, joined in the light-hearted talk.

Fran, pouring coffee, asked half laughingly, 'And how is that handsome lady of thirty-odd years—the comfortably situated widow with the social graces? You were going to take her out…?'

The doctor's eyes were on Lucy's face. 'Fiona Seymour? As handsome as ever. You must meet her next time that you come over, and see for yourself.'

Lucy buttered a roll and didn't look up. She said evenly, 'She dresses beautifully, Fran, and always in the right clothes, if you know what I mean.'

She looked up then, straight at William, and smiled at him. It was the kind of smile Boadicea might have had on her face as she led the Iceni into battle. He stared back at her; she was in a temper despite the smile, and her eyes sparkled like emeralds.

He said mildly, 'I suppose that matters to women; I don't think men notice such things.' He smiled gently. 'At least, only upon occasion.'

Lucy went slowly a very pretty pink, remembering that there had been far too much of her hanging out of her bedroom window. Just for the moment she could think of nothing crushing to say; when she did, she would say it.

CHAPTER SIX

SINCE it was Sunday, they all went to church and Lucy, sitting with Fran on one side of her making sure she could follow the service, was very conscious of William's bulk on her other side. She stood up and sat down just as she should, but she didn't understand a word thundered at her from the pulpit and, although she opened her hymn book obediently at Fran's direction, she had no idea of what they were singing. She was wondering how it was that Fran had heard about Fiona; William must have said something, but when? She sat there frowning until she was gently prodded to her feet for the final hymn.

They stayed talking to the *dominee* for quite a while after the service and then Litrik and William walked on ahead, leaving her and Fran to follow. They had a lot to talk about, and William wasn't mentioned.

Nanny was in the garden playing ball with little Litrik while the baby slept in her pram.

'Go and have your coffee, Nanny,' said Fran, 'and will you ask someone to bring ours out here? We'll stay with the children.'

The two men began a gentle game of ball with the little boy staggering happily between them, and Fran and Lucy went to sit by the pram. The baby was charming, pink and white and fair-haired. Lucy bent over her and murmured, 'She's beautiful, Fran, and she has such a pretty name.'

'Lisa—I asked Litrik if I could tell you about that and he said that he'd like you to know. You see, when I first met him he had a ward, a little girl with spina bifida. Her father had died—he was a friend of Litrik's—and her mother left her. So he became her guardian until she died soon after we married. She was a darling and we still miss her.'

She smiled rather mistily at Lucy, who thought, looking at her friend's expressive face, that there was a lot more to the story than that, but all she said was, 'Thank you for telling me, Fran. Little Lisa will fill her place...'

Trugg had put the coffee-tray on the garden table and they sat around drinking and making vague plans for the week ahead.

'You two girls can do what you like tomorrow,' said Litrik. 'William will come with me to Utrecht; we shan't be back until the early evening. There's the party on Wednesday, isn't there, darling? And on Thursday I've arranged to be free and we might all go to Keukenhof.'

Sunday lunch was a leisurely affair, and afterwards—she wasn't quite sure how it happened—Lucy found herself walking briskly out of the gate beside William.

'A good walk, just what we need after that magnificent meal,' he observed.

'I don't remember saying that I wanted to come.'

'My dear girl, where is your tact? I'm sure that Litrik and Fran would like an hour or two on their own—he's a busy man, you know, and he doesn't see as much of her or the children as he would wish.'

'Oh, well—I hadn't thought of that...'

'He loves his work, you know.'

They were walking along a narrow lane leading, as far as Lucy could see, nowhere at all. 'Do you love your work too?'

'Yes, and even when I marry it will still be a large part of my life,' he looked down at her, 'however much I love my wife and children.'

'You have children round you every day for hours—in the clinics and the wards, and I suppose at your consulting rooms. And then you'll go home to them?' She frowned a little thinking that Fiona, if she had children, would keep them out of the way with a nanny—they'd be in bed by the time he got home. There would be guests for dinner and Fiona waiting for him in some exquisite outfit…

'Now what are you dreaming up?' asked William. 'I suspect you have far too much imagination. If you are worried as to my future, don't be—I have it all nicely planned.'

Lucy stopped to admire the view, a gentle rise and fall of endless fields with a farmhouse here and there and cows in abundance. There was a farm cart coming towards them too, drawn by a great horse, plodding patiently. They stood aside to allow it to pass and William exchanged unintelligible greetings with the driver. Only when it had gone did she speak.

'I am not in the least worried about your future,' she told him coldly. 'Why should I be? Nor do I need to draw on my imagination about it, for it is a foregone conclusion, isn't it?'

He looked interested. 'Oh, is it? May I know?'

She said, still coldly, 'Why should I tell you something you already know?'

He said blandly, 'I believe we are at cross purposes. Never mind, time enough for that… I saw in the *Daily Telegraph* that Imogen has become engaged. Does she plan to marry before Pauline? And when do your parents return?'

The rest of their walk was taken up with what Lucy considered to be pointless chat. She returned to the house in quite a nasty temper, although she was too well brought up to show it. But she couldn't conceal the vivid green of her eyes. The doctor was quick to see that and smiled to himself.

The men left early the next morning, and after an hour or more in the nursery Fran got into her car and, with Lucy beside her, drove to Arnhem, where they spent the rest of the morning wandering round the open air museum with its replicas of old cottages, windmills and farms from a bygone age. 'You see,' explained Fran, 'there's not time to take you all over Holland, and here you get an idea of the history of each province. I wish you could stay another week, Lucy.'

'So do I, but I have to be back because one of the other helpers is going on holiday. There are never enough of us anyway.'

They had their coffee at the Rijzenburg Restaurant, a few miles out of Arnhem and, since it was almost lunchtime, ordered omelettes and salads at the same time. 'Though I must be back by two o'clock to feed the baby,' said Fran. 'Do you think I should spend more time with the children? Of course, when there's no one visiting, I'm with them almost all day.'

'I think you're a marvellous mother,' declared Lucy, 'and I think you must be a jolly good wife too.'

'Oh, good. I'm very happy, you know—I hope you find the right man, Lucy; being married is such fun.' She looked across the table at her friend. 'But there is someone, isn't there?'

Lucy went pink. 'Yes. But he doesn't know and I don't suppose he ever will, for I won't tell him.'

Fran said gently, 'Think about it, often things have a way of turning out well. Don't ever give up hope, Lucy.' She glanced at her watch. 'Heavens, we'd better go.'

Later that afternoon they took the children for a walk, with Lisa in her pram and little Litrik on his reins, and after that it was nursery tea and the fun of bathtime. The men came home then, and Nanny went away to have her supper while the four of them saw the little ones into their cots. There was a good deal of laughter and squeals of delight from the little boy, but presently he sat on his father's knee while his evening quota of nursery rhymes were recited and baby Lisa went to sleep at once.

With Nanny back, they went to tidy themselves for the evening and presently met again in the drawing-room to discuss the day's events. The two men had been busy, although they only touched lightly on their work. Lucy had the impression that if she hadn't been there Litrik would have gone into details, for it was obvious that Fran knew exactly what he was talking about and was interested too. She allowed her thoughts to wander presently, trying to picture Fiona listening to William when he got home with just such a look of rapt attention on her face as Fran had. But the picture refused to take shape; Fiona wouldn't want to know, she would give him a drink and tell him who was coming to dinner.

She stole a quick look at him, sitting at his ease, a glass in his hand, content after his day. And that was how it should be every evening, she reflected, and how it would be if only she could marry him. It would be so helpful if Fiona could meet a very rich man who liked her lifestyle. She looked up and found the doctor's eyes on her, and just for a moment she couldn't look away, unaware that her dreams were in her face.

He smiled slowly. 'Will you come to Amsterdam with me tomorrow, Lucy?'

She nodded. 'I'd like that very much, thank you. I expect you've been there before?'

He nodded. 'But it's a place where you can go back time and again and each time find something new. We shan't be able to see everything, but we'll pack in as much as we can.' He looked across the room to Fran. 'Will it be all right if we go directly after breakfast, Fran?'

'Of course, and come back here when you like. If you decide to stay out to dinner, just give us a ring. Are you going to the hospital again before you go back?'

'Wednesday…'

'But don't forget the party. About a dozen for dinner, and hordes coming afterwards.' She got up and went to sit by Lucy. 'What are you going to wear?'

It was a doubtful kind of morning when Lucy woke, and her suit seemed the most suitable thing to wear; if it rained it would afford some protection, and if it turned fine it would be just right for the time of year. She dressed with care, pinned up her hair into a french pleat, got into low-heeled shoes—for there was no knowing where William might take it into his head to go—and went down to breakfast.

They left directly that meal was over, and since Amsterdam was a mere twenty-five or so miles away they were there in just over half an hour. The inner city appeared to be jammed with cars, parked on either side of the numerous canals and wherever there was an inch of room on the narrow streets. But William drove straight on and presently turned into the forecourt of a hospital. 'I know the *Directeur*,' he said casually. 'We can park here for as long as we like.'

Which he did with a minimum of fuss before taking Lucy's arm and walking her out into the busy street. 'Coffee first,' he suggested, and crossed the road and plunged down a narrow alleyway which brought them out into a tree-lined street, teeming with people and traffic and lined with cafés and smart boutiques. They sat at a table on the pavement and drank their coffee, watching the passers-by while the doctor explained the layout of the city. 'Think of a spider's web,' he observed. 'The circular threads are the canals intersected by streets and alleys. Shall we walk first before we go on the canals?'

He knew his way very well, and they wandered in and out of narrow streets, across small, arched bridges, alongside the canals, admiring the patrician houses with their great front doors reached by double steps, their high windows and their gables, each one slightly different from its neighbours.

'What are they like inside?' wondered Lucy aloud.

'Delightful. Amazingly well modernised without spoiling their original charm. I've been in several—Litrik is old friends with some of the professors at the hospitals in the city. Two of them are married to English girls, I believe there are more than that number. Fran could tell you; she visits them from time to time.'

He led her into a narrow cobbled street lined with little

antique shops and waited patiently while she peered into their windows. Before walking back to the Dam Square, they went along Damrak and so to where the canal tours started. The boat they took wasn't very full, and the guide's voice was easy to follow because everything was repeated in English and French. When it was over and they were back on dry land Lucy said, 'That was marvellous; I must try and remember it all...'

'Well, you can always refresh your memory—it is only a couple of hours from home, you know.'

He beckoned a taxi and popped her into it. 'Lunch,' he said.

He took her to Dikker and Thijs in which elegant restaurant they ate a delicious lunch; onion tarts, grilled sole with tiny new potatoes and green peas, and, for Lucy, an enormous ice-cream smothered in whipped cream and chocolate sauce, while the doctor enjoyed a selection from the cheese board, and since they had the afternoon before them they drank sparingly from the hock he had ordered. Over coffee he made his suggestions for the afternoon.

The Rijksmuseum for a start, because when she got home everyone would expect her to have been there. 'The Begijnhof,' he went on. 'It's just off Spui, not too far from here. A circle of charming little houses where nuns once lived; the church in the centre is used for English Services. Then Rembrandt's house, and that, I think, is about all we can manage this time.'

'Oh, yes—it's very kind of you to take me round. I should never have seen all this on my own, and even if I never come again...'

He opened his eyes wide and their blue stare sent her heart thudding. 'But of course you will come again.'

He sounded so sure of that she didn't like to argue about it.

The afternoon was a kaleidoscope of old houses, famous paintings and exquisite silver and porcelain, all delightfully jumbled in Lucy's head so that sorting them out was going to take her quite a time.

'What a heavenly day,' she sighed happily, pouring tea. He had taken her to the Amstel Hotel, a fitting end to the day, for it was overlooking the Amstel with the barges going to and fro and an everchanging scene. She found it a delightful place, old-fashioned and solid and very elegant.

They took a taxi back to the hospital, got into the car and drove away from the city through solid traffic which at times hardly moved. But once on the motorway, William allowed the car to rush ahead, and it was still not yet seven o'clock as he stopped in front of the house.

Trugg admitted them with the hope that they had had a nice day, and begged them to go up to the nursery as Mevrouw was putting the children to bed. They left their outdoor things in the hall and went upstairs, to find Fran and Nanny bathing the children, a leisurely business entailing a good deal of splashing and childish shouting. They were joined within minutes by Litrik, and it was another half-hour before the children were tucked up for the night. The four of them dispersed to make themselves presentable for the evening, and presently foregathered in the drawing-room for drinks and to exchange news of their days. After dinner the two men went off to Litrik's study and the two girls spent the next hour or so checking the plans for the party.

'Do you plan to do anything in the morning?' asked Fran.

'No, I'd like to help you, if you need help.'

'Oh, good. The flowers—this is such a big house it takes all day just to do the downstairs rooms. Old Jan will bring in the pot-plants from the greenhouse, so if you could dot them around... He'll leave them in the garden-room beside the kitchen. The men will be out all day, which means we will be able to get on with everything. All Litrik's family will be coming, and his friends from the hospital and from Leiden too—there'll be about fifty of us, but only a dozen for dinner.'

Lucy said thoughtfully, 'You know, Fran, you haven't changed a bit—not you, that is, but you've taken to all this—' she waved expressively with her arms '—like a duck to water. Was it very difficult?'

Fran shook her head. 'No, you see, Litrik helped me, and Trugg and all the people who work here are quite marvellous, and I've a wonderful mother-in-law.' She went on casually, 'Has William got a mother and father?'

'I haven't an idea. We—we have only met occasionally. I had lunch at his home once—one Sunday with some of his friends. In fact, I only know that he has two dogs and a devoted housekeeper.'

'Well, he'd certainly need that; Litrik says he works a great deal harder than he should.' Fran smiled to herself. 'Litrik works too hard as well, but I nag him before it gets too bad.'

The next day passed pleasantly. In the morning Lucy was busy arranging the flowers here and there, and making herself useful running to and fro with Nanny, giving a helping hand with the children, and in the afternoon she washed her hair, did her nails and experimented with make-up. The men came home soon after tea, and the next hour was spent in the nursery before they went downstairs for a drink before going to dress.

Lucy, studying her image in the pier-glass in her room, hoped that William would find her worth a second glance, and, indeed, she looked charming. She had put on a new dress, amber silk with a long, full skirt, long tight sleeves and a ruched chiffon bodice and, excepting a thick gold chain, she wore no jewellery. She had allowed her hair to curl around her neck and, on second thoughts, hadn't used more make-up than usual. Nothing out of the ordinary, she decided, surveying her person with an eagle eye, and if Fiona Seymour were to have been among the guests Lucy would have stood no chance at all. She went downstairs and found Fran, very stylish in blue velvet, and Litrik correct in his black tie, sitting in the drawing-room, holding hands.

Litrik got up as she went in and said cheerfully, 'Drinks all round, I think, to get us in the mood.'

A moment later William joined them, the epitome of the well-dressed man at a party. He admired Fran and went to stand in front of Lucy. 'Charming,' he said, then added wickedly, 'Did it take all day?'

'Certainly not!' she retorted. 'I've been busy doing the flowers and playing with the children and running errands.' She gave an indignant snort. 'A good deal busier than you, I dare say.'

He smiled. 'Probably.' If he had been about to say more, there was no chance, for the first of the guests were arriving.

Lucy, after hopping into bed at two o'clock in the morning, lay wide awake just long enough to go over the evening. It had been tremendous fun; dinner had been a formal affair, the table appointments splendid, the food superb, and there had been no lack of enlivening conversation. She had sat between two cousins of Litrik's, both of whom had flirted with her in the nicest possible way; she had responded, hoping that William had noticed, but if he had his face remained blandly friendly and nothing more.

Presently, when the rest of the guests had arrived and they had all gone into the drawing-room, which had been cleared for dancing and with its double doors opening on to the covered veranda, she had been swept away to dance without a break. It was just as Trugg had announced that a buffet supper was being served in the dining-room that the doctor had appeared beside her.

'You're enjoying yourself.' It wasn't a question but a statement of fact. 'Let me get you something to eat before you disappear on to the dance-floor again.'

Lucy had made some casual answer, discomfited by the thought that he hadn't made any effort to dance with her. Not that she could blame him—there had been any number of pretty girls there, and he had danced with almost all of them. And, to make matters worse, they had joined a party at one of the bigger tables and, although he sat next to her, he'd made no effort to talk to her other than in the general conversation all around them. It had pleased her enormously when one of her dance partners had got up finally and came to bend over her chair. 'Tear yourself away from that ice and come and dance, Lucy. It's a waltz and I'm feeling romantic.'

She had got to her feet at once, smiling at him, allowing William the tail-end of a smile before she had gone back to the drawing-room. And she had danced every dance after that, with the *burgermeester*, the *dominee*, a selection of young men whose names she couldn't remember, and Litrik. It wasn't until the band had been striking up for the last dance that William had appeared beside her once more, swept her into his arms and danced her away. It had been a waltz and he'd danced well, and just for a moment she'd forgotten that he had ignored her for most of the evening, that he would probably marry Fiona, that when they got back to England she might not see him again for several weeks; she had been happy, floating round the vast room, her cheek pressed to his shirt-front, his arm around her. She could have gone on forever, but of course she hadn't. The music had ended in a final flourish and the party had been over. Perhaps, she thought sleepily, she could change her style, tint her hair, buy clothes in the forefront of fashion and not just those which suited her, do something really clever so that he would notice her—even accompany her father on his next excavation. She just had time to reject this last plan before she fell asleep.

She was awake again by eight o'clock and out of bed to see what kind of a morning it was. They were to go to Keukenhof and if only it were a fine day she would be able to wear the deceptively simple Jaeger outfit she had been saving for just such an occasion.

The garden was bathed in early morning sunshine and looked beautiful, and as she looked she was aware of Litrik and William with the dogs. They were striding across the paddock beyond the grounds. She showered and dressed and went downstairs, just in time to see their broad backs disappearing through the front door, and Fran, her head peering round the door of the small room where they had breakfast, said, 'Aren't they gluttons for work? But they've promised faithfully to be back here by eleven o'clock to take us to Keukenhof.' She eyed Lucy. 'I say, you do look smart, and just right for this kind of a day.' She opened the door wider. 'Come and have breakfast, and then help me bath the children; it's Nanny's morning off.'

Over breakfast Lucy asked, 'If it's Nanny's off-duty how can we go to Keukenhof?'

'She's coming with us. Twice a week she is free from half-past eight until half-past ten, so she takes the small car into Utrecht, has her hair done or shops, and so on. She likes it that way and it suits us very well.'

So the first part of the morning was spent in the nursery until Nanny came back and presently the men came home.

The party set off in two cars, Litrik with Fran, Nanny and the children, and William with Lucy—an arrangement which pleased her very well. Not easily disheartened, she was well aware that each time she spent with him gave her another chance to get him interested in her; so far she hadn't had much success, but she was a strong believer in kindly fate, although whether fate was going to be strong enough to overcome Fiona Seymour was a moot point.

They took the main road, circumventing Utrecht and, as they neared Amsterdam, turning south to Lisse. The Keukenhof gardens were just outside the town and, since it was a fine day, there were plenty of people strolling up and down the paths. They parked the cars, fastened little Litrik into his pushchair, tucked Lisa into her folding pram and set off. The flowers were a magnificent sight; huge beds of tulips, daffodils, hyacinths and still more tulips stretched as far as the eye could see. They wandered along for an hour or more and presently went to the restaurant, which was elegantly set among the background of trees and more flowers. They drank coffee and ate *broodjes* and little Litrik sat on his father's knee, eating his roll and gabbling away in a mixture of Dutch and English. And as for Lisa, good baby that she was, she slept peacefully in her pram.

There was still a great deal to see, and since Fran had said that they must go round the giant greenhouses so that she could order some plants for later on in the year they made their way there. 'I'll be ages making up my mind,' said Fran. 'William, you take Lucy with you and go at your own pace. We'll meet here at the entrance in half an hour or so, shall we? And if you're not ready by then we'll see you at the cars.'

The doctor proved to be a knowledgeable gardener, and, what was more, he ordered several boxes of bulbs for his own garden and then did the same for Lucy when she admired a particularly fine hyacinth. 'They send them over later,' he told her, and when she thanked him, 'Something to remind you of your stay in Holland.'

They were standing admiring a display of hothouse lilac when he observed placidly, 'Of course, you'll come back with me. So much easier in the car. I'll see about your ticket. I have to be home on Sunday, unfortunately—a dinner engagement I can't miss.' He glanced down at her, smiling a little. 'An important one I don't want to miss.'

She said stiffly, 'It's very kind of you to offer me a lift, but I can just as easily go by plane. I have my ticket…'

'Don't be tiresome, Lucy,' he said blandly. 'If you travel back with me there will be no need for Litrik to take you to Schiphol, and if we leave after breakfast on Saturday we'll be home for tea. I came by hovercraft.'

There was no point in arguing further; he was offering her a lift home out of consideration to his friends, and not because he wanted her company.

She said snappily, 'Very well, since it is convenient. Shall we go and find the others?'

'Tired of my company?' he asked silkily. And, before she could think of a suitable answer, 'That is an unfair question. You will either tell the truth or tell a pack of lies.'

'I am not in the habit of lying,' said Lucy haughtily.

'The truth wouldn't do either, would it?' he answered cheerfully.

At the cars he suggested that he might drive back to the house another way. 'So that Lucy can see a little more of Holland…' he explained, and Litrik agreed with him. 'A good idea. Take the road through Alphen aan de Rijn and Bodegraven. You can get a side-road from there which will take you north of Utrecht—you know the one I mean?—it weaves past the lakes and you can get to Bilthoven and Zeist. A peaceful, pleasant little run. You can get tea at Breukelen—there's a good hotel by the river, but come back to us if you don't feel like stopping.'

He smiled kindly at Lucy. 'You'll be quite safe with William; he knows this part of Holland almost as well as I do.'

He stowed his family carefully into his car, waved nonchalantly, and drove off.

Lucy got into William's car and sat silently until it occurred to her that he might think that she was sulking. Conversation, polite conversation, that was, was imperative. 'You come to Holland quite often?' she wanted to know.

'Off and on. I'm an honorary consultant at Utrecht and Leiden, which means that I come over to lecture from time to time and also act as an examiner.' He gave her a quick sideways glance. 'Will you be sorry to go back home?'

'Yes, I think I shall. I've been happy here.' She could

hardly add that that was because he had been there too. 'Fran is such a dear, and the babies are delightful. I like Litrik too.'

'A sound man. Fran is exactly right for him. I envy him—a wife, children and a lovely house that Fran has turned into a home...'

'You have a lovely house...'

'Indeed, yes. I really must add a wife and children as soon as possible.'

Lucy looked out of the window at the serene countryside. There was a potential wife waiting for him, wasn't there? Someone who would grace his table and manage his home to perfection. The children were another matter, but perhaps Fiona might change her mind... She said in a wooden voice, 'I hope you'll be very happy.'

He said placidly, 'I'm thirty-five and I've waited a long time for the right girl to come along. I know I—we shall be very happy.'

There seemed to be no answer to that. Lucy pointed out the sails of a boat apparently in the middle of a meadow and remarked on how interesting that was. He agreed gravely, 'The lakes are there—we shall turn off presently and you will have a better view. I think we might take Litrik's advice and have tea, don't you?'

A cup of tea was a panacea for all ills, she reminded herself, and agreed politely.

They stopped presently at a small, picturesque hotel by the water and sat watching the yachts gliding by in the quite stiff breeze while they drank their tea. Lucy, who had discovered that, contrary to the general idea, unrequited love had made no difference to her appetite, ate a mountainous cream cake with unselfconscious pleasure, watched, if only she had looked, by the doctor with amused tenderness.

They arrived back in good time to change for the evening and join Fran and Litrik for drinks before dinner. But before they went across the hall to the dining-room Fran said that she would just make sure the children were all right and Lucy went with her. They were both asleep, the baby's pale hair shining in the light of the small lamp near her cot, the little boy upside-down in his cot, clutching a teddy bear.

'Oh, Fran, you are lucky,' said Lucy softly, and in such a sad little voice that Fran looked at her.

'You'll be lucky too,' she said gently. 'I wonder what's round the corner for you.'

'The orphanage,' said Lucy bleakly. Nanny came from the day nursery then, and Fran stopped to speak to her, which Lucy thought was a good thing or she might have wallowed in self-pity.

She was very bright and chatty for the rest of the evening, something which puzzled all three of her companions, for she wasn't either bright or chatty by nature.

If she had been harbouring a secret hope that William might have plans to take her out on her last day, she was doomed to disappointment; at breakfast the two men were engrossed in their plans for the day—hospital rounds, an afternoon clinic, a visit to a retired professor and a meeting of consultants. There wasn't a minute to spare for anything or anyone else. They went off presently with the air of men well content with their world, and Fran took another slice of toast and poured more coffee for herself and Lucy. 'I thought we might go to Utrecht for a last look round,' she suggested. 'The men will be back soon after tea, so if you pack this afternoon we'll have a nice long evening with nothing to do. I shall miss you, Lucy.'

'I've loved being here, Fran. I'll remember these two weeks forever. And if I don't write often it's because I'm really quite busy…'

'I know, I shall phone you. Do you plan to stay at the orphanage?'

'I think so. I'm too old to train for anything, and besides, I'm not clever at exams and things like that. I took the job because I wanted to prove to Mother and Father that I could do something, and I really like my work.'

'You must come again, and I mean that.'

The pair of them spent the morning shopping, buying last-minute presents to take home and sweets for the orphans, and in the afternoon Lucy packed and put everything ready for going away in the morning. If she felt sad, nothing of that showed when the men came home. They sat round talking after dinner until late, and when she at last got into her bed Lucy was too tired to do more than give a long sigh before she slept.

They left after breakfast the next morning, with everyone standing on the steps to see them off. Amid cries of, 'See you again very soon,' and 'Have a good journey,' William drove out of the drive and into the lane on their journey back to England.

CHAPTER SEVEN

THE journey back to London was accomplished without a hitch and in comfort. The doctor drew up before Lucy's home at mid-afternoon, got out to unload her luggage, opened her door and then rang the doorbell. Alice welcomed them warmly, ushered them inside, suggested tea, and offered the news that neither Imogen or Pauline would be home until Sunday evening.

Anxious that William shouldn't feel obliged to offer her entertainment, Lucy said hastily, 'Oh, good, I could do with a day to sort things out on my own.' She added, rather belatedly, her invitation to have some tea before he went on to his own house, and, when he refused smilingly, she thanked him for her lift back, saying politely, 'I hope you have a nice evening.'

He didn't answer that, only smiled a little. 'I dare say we shall see each other from time to time,' he observed in a non-committal manner. 'Miranda will still need to visit me and you will probably be with her.'

She nodded and managed a smile, engulfed in a bitter disappointment that he had no plans to see her again unless it was at the clinic. And when he wished her goodbye a few moments later she made some inane remark about their holiday which, upon reflection, made no sense at all, but at least bridged the awkward gap between his goodbyes and departure. She stood on the doorstep and waved gaily as he drove away, and then went indoors and burst into tears.

'Things are never as bad as they seem,' said Alice, and gave her a motherly hug. 'You sit down and drink your tea and have a good cry if you want to, and then tell me all about your holiday.'

So Lucy sat down at the kitchen table with Mrs Simpkins on her lap and presently mopped her eyes, drank her tea and launched into an account of her two weeks in Holland. If there was a singular lack of information about the doctor, Alice didn't comment upon it. Instead she said briskly, 'You've 'ad two lovely weeks, Miss Lucy, and just you remember that. And now go and wash your face and telephone that nice Miss Fran and let her know you're back 'ome. And there's a note for you in the drawing-room from your sisters.'

'Is there a letter from Mother?'

Alice shook her head. 'I dare say she'll phone now you're back home.'

Lucy went upstairs taking her sisters' note with her. It bore out Alice's message that they wouldn't be at home until the following evening, and, beyond a vague hope that she had enjoyed herself, it was entirely taken up with their own doings.

Lucy read it twice and then went to look at her blotched face in the looking-glass. 'I should dearly love to wallow in self-pity,' she told her reflection, 'but a lot of good that would do. I shall plan a campaign.'

Alice had made a chicken casserole and followed it with one of her apple tarts, and over their meal Lucy discussed the forthcoming weddings, speculated over the dresses she would be expected to wear as bridesmaid, and observed that she was quite looking forward to going back to the orphanage. When she had helped Alice with the washing up, she declared herself tired after her journey and said goodnight. 'And I'll phone Fran before I go upstairs,' she told her old friend.

'Did you have a good trip?' Fran wanted to know. 'I hope William gave you a meal, you left so early.'

'We stopped on the way—just before we went on the hovercraft—and had an early lunch. We were back here in good time for tea.'

'Did you go out to dinner?'

'Well, no—William had a dinner engagement and I'm really quite tired.'

They gossiped for a few minutes more before Lucy rang off with the promise of a phone call later in the week.

Fran put the receiver down at her end and went back to sit by Litrik. 'I thought that there was something between William and Lucy,' she told her husband. 'He took her home, but he had a dinner engagement—I mean, if he was keen he would have asked her out… Do you suppose I've made a mistake, darling?'

Litrik lowered his newspaper. 'No, my love, but these things can't be hurried, you know. Lucy has a bee in her bonnet about this woman Fiona, and William, unless I am much mistaken, is holding back for a number of reasons. Give them time.'

'But they never see each other,' almost wailed Fran.

'My dearest, if William wants to see Lucy, he'll contrive to do so, be assured of that.'

Lucy spent Sunday sorting out her clothes, washing her hair, doing her nails and then going for a brisk walk along the Embankment, and if she was lonely after the cheerful company she had been in, she didn't admit it.

Everyone was glad to see her back on Monday morning, not least Miranda, who was much improved but still given to bouts of peevishness and screaming fits. Lucy, plunging into the day's work, found the hours too short; two of the girls who came in part time were off sick, and the rest of them were hard put to it to get through the ever-recurring chores. She went home late to find her sisters waiting for her.

'You must give up that job,' declared Imogen. 'It's ridiculous to work yourself to the bone like this. There's no need—'

'But I like my work, and it's useful, even if it isn't important.'

Imogen went red. 'You know Mother would love to have you at home, especially now Pauline and I will be getting married.'

'Well, I am at home each evening, and Mother and Father are often out or away.' She smiled suddenly. 'Don't let's talk about me—tell me if there are any more plans for the weddings.'

Her mother telephoned that evening too; they had discovered more iron pots and tools and now her father intended to travel some miles into the desert to investigate local tales of more finds. 'So we shan't be home for another few weeks, darling. Did you have a good holiday?'

She didn't wait for Lucy to reply. 'Ask Imogen to come to the phone, will you, Lucy? I want to know the exact date of her wedding...'

Both weddings were going to be rather grand affairs, Imogen's first, in July, and Pauline's in September, but the girls were already making lists of guests and wedding presents, and weighing the merits of oyster satin against white crêpe. Lucy, as keen as any girl to wear white satin and orange blossom, began to alter her ideas. Just to slip into a small church and get married without guests or bridesmaids seemed preferable. Perhaps, she thought wistfully, if ever she should marry, she would change her mind. Other girls' weddings weren't the same as one's own.

It was almost the end of the week when she saw William, but not to speak to. She had just stepped off the bus on her way home when the Rolls slid past. Fiona was sitting beside him, and as her eye caught Lucy's she smiled; it wasn't a nice smile, and she made no effort to draw William's notice to Lucy standing there on the pavement. Lucy would have been very surprised if she had. Somehow the little episode made her resolve to marry William quite hopeless, so that when she got home and found Pauline waiting for her with an invitation to join a party of friends for dinner and dancing on the following evening she accepted at once. It was to be quite a grand affair, Pauline told her—a celebration of Cyril's promotion. His sister and brother-in-law would be there, a couple of old friends, and Cyril's unmarried brother. A daunting thought if he was anything like Cyril, reflected Lucy, but an evening out would distract her thoughts from William.

It was a pity that the orphans had been particularly trying all day, so that when she got home an evening out was the last thing she wanted. But a hot bath and a pot of Alice's tea improved her outlook; she dressed with care in the grey dress she had hoped William would have admired, did her hair in a top knot fastened with a glittering bow, eased her feet into her sandals and went downstairs to join Pauline.

'That's nice even if it isn't new,' said Pauline kindly. 'It's a pity Imogen couldn't make it. Cyril will be here in a moment.' She studied Lucy's quiet face. 'Are you working too hard? You're thinner, aren't you, and a bit pale? Never mind, you'll be all the better for an evening out.'

Cyril came then, more self-important than ever, taking Lucy's congratulations as his rightful due before driving them off to the Savoy. 'Bertram will meet us there with the others,' he told them. 'His days are very full now that he has taken silk—he should go far.'

'I'm sure you'll go further,' murmured Pauline dutifully. 'This promotion is marvellous.'

Lucy, sitting in the back seat, watched the smug little nod he gave in answer. She hoped that Bertram would prove to be a different kettle of fish.

He was the counterpart of Cyril—she saw that the moment the party gathered in the foyer, and her heart sank. There was no hope to be got from the old friends either, as they were middle-aged and devoid of conversation, and Cyril's sister was a disheartened doormat, hardly speaking and, when she did, looking around her apologetically as though requesting permission to speak. Lucy, sitting next to Bertram and with the old friend on the other side of her, listened to the one deploring the young people of today and the other giving her a blow by blow account of some dreary lawsuit in which he had apparently shone. She murmured at intervals and ate the food on her plate with pleasure. There hadn't been much time for lunch at the orphanage, and she was hungry, but that proved to be a problem too, for everyone else was pecking at his or her food in a polite way and the old friend began a stern lecture on the evils of rich food and drink. Lucy wondered why he had come since he felt so strongly about it, and would have had a second helping of the delicious chicken à la King only Bertram pushed back his chair and invited her to dance in what she imagined might be his barrister's voice. She got up obediently and everyone else at the table looked up from their discussion about Fine Art and smiled kindly at her. Cyril's smile was particularly benevolent; she was having a treat and he was the donor.

Bertram was an appalling dancer; her feet, already a little painful from the too-tight sandals, became a problem which emptied her head of every thought other than evading his clumsy steps. They lumbered round the dance floor while he described just how astute he had been in the case of Biggins versus Potts. Lucy, concentrating on her feet, consigned the pair of them to the bottom of the sea and Bertram with them while she nodded and smiled and said, 'Did you really? You must be clever—of course, I don't know a thing about law...' A mistake, for he began to explain it to her. She pinned a smile on her face and winced as he trod rather more heavily on her toes, and just at that moment Dr William Thurloe danced past, Fiona Seymour in his arms. He looked straight at Lucy, half smiling, and she widened her smile for Bertram's benefit and gave William a small, cool nod. A really tremendous urge to evade Bertram's clutches, push Fiona out of the way and dance off with the doctor filled her person with a fierce wave of rage at meeting the pair of them when she least expected to, and when her feet were killing her too. Mercifully the music stopped, and they went back to the table, where she accepted dessert with relief and slid her poor feet out of the sandals.

She had barely had a mouthful of the caramel mousse when there was a general uprising of the men in the party and she looked up to see Fiona and William standing by the table.

'Pauline,' gushed Mrs Seymour, 'I have not yet wished you happy, and I must congratulate Cyril. When is the wedding to be? And I see that Imogen is to marry too. How exciting.' She gave a trill of laughter and looked across at Lucy. 'Don't get left behind, Lucy.'

Lucy smiled sweetly, her eyes glittering greenly. 'There's a proverb about the hare and the tortoise,' she said gently. 'Better still, do you know a writing of John Burroughs? It's called "Waiting".' She recited clearly, '"Serene I fold my hands and wait, Nor care for wind or tide nor sea; I rave no more 'gainst time or fate, For lo! my own shall come to me."'

There was a small outburst of clapping and laughter, and Pauline said, 'Darling, how very apt, and fancy remembering it—you were always quoting poetry when we were at school. I just hope it comes true for you.'

Fiona had been looking uncertain; she had been quite out of her depth, as she had never bothered with poetry and thought it rather silly and a waste of time. She said charmingly, 'Oh, of course it will. I dare say Lucy will surprise us all.'

She smiled around the table and Bertram said quickly, 'I say, would you care to dance? The band is splendid...'

It was the signal for the general movement towards the dance floor, save for Lucy, searching feverishly under the table with her feet, hunting for her discarded sandals.

'I won't ask you to dance,' said William in her ear. 'Although nothing would give me greater pleasure, I suspect that you have taken your shoes off. Would it not be a better idea to buy sandals which fitted your feet? And stop poking around like that—I'll get them and we can sit here comfortably while you cram your feet back in.'

He's so nice and ordinary, reflected Lucy, watching him bend his great height to forage under the table and put her shoes where her feet could reach them. He had done it without fuss and quickly, waving away a waiter anxious to be of help, and then he pulled out the chair beside her and sat down.

'And are you settling down after your holiday?' he asked.

'Yes, no—I don't know. It's been busy at the orphanage.'

'All the more reason to enjoy this pleasant little evening party,' his voice was silky, 'but I suspect that you are not doing so.' He lifted a finger and spoke to a waiter, then turned to look at her. 'I like that dress—I liked it last time too...'

Lucy blushed. 'Oh, do you? I thought—' She stopped, and started again. 'That is, I thought...' She gave up and sat looking at him for a long moment, watching the slow smile etch his firm mouth. The arrival of the waiter with champagne in an ice-bucket broke the spell.

William said pleasantly, 'I feel that, since we have joined your party for the moment, the least we can do is to drink to our—er—further acquaintance.'

'How nice,' said Lucy inanely. She hoped the band would go on playing for a long time yet.

William crossed one long leg over the other. 'You read poetry? Do you enjoy John Donne?'

'Very much, though sometimes I'm not sure if I understand all his poems, but some lines—they stick in one's head.' She added almost humbly, 'I'm not clever.'

'If by that you mean you can't add up two columns of figures at the same time or use a computer or understand the Stock Market, then no, you're not clever in the accepted terms of the word. On the other hand, you have an understanding of babies and children and animals, and that is a gift beyond mere cleverness. Also you have the gift of holding your tongue when others might regrettably allow theirs to run away with them.'

She said with something of a snap, 'You make me sound like a saint!'

'Heaven forbid! You're a girl with green eyes.' He smiled at her with a certain touch of mockery and got up as the rest of the party returned to the table.

Fiona tucked her arm in his at once. 'William, why didn't you ask Lucy to dance? Have you just been sitting there talking?'

He didn't answer her, only smiled a little and beckoned the waiter to uncork the champagne, and a moment later everyone was talking at once and happily toasting Pauline and Cyril. Presently William and Fiona went back to their table, and Lucy, glancing round with what she hoped was a casual air, saw them dancing again.

Bertram saw her watching them and said enthusiastically, 'I say, what a splendid woman Fiona Seymour is, and a marvellous dancer. She was very interested in the law—a most intelligent woman and a good listener.'

From which remark Lucy deduced that she was neither.

The party broke up soon afterwards, Lucy said goodbye to Cyril's sister and her husband, the old friends and Bertram and got into the car with Cyril and Pauline. She had eased sore feet into her sandals but they still hurt, which made the evening seem even worse than she'd thought it had been. By the time they arrived at the house she was sunk in gloom, for Cyril and Pauline had been discussing Fiona and William, taking it for granted that their engagement would be announced any day now. Lucy retired to bed in a dark mood and cried herself to sleep.

Pauline spent the day with Cyril on Sunday, and Lucy spent the day in the quite nice garden at the back of the house, weeding and digging and hoeing, and in the evening she had a long talk with Fran on the phone. Fran didn't mention William, which was a good thing, for Lucy was not in the mood to unburden herself to anyone who would listen. Indeed, when Alice questioned her about the dinner party she told her that it had been quite nice, but that Cyril's brother was just as prosey as he was. She described the food, the other guests and the splendours of the Savoy Hotel, but she didn't breathe a word about Dr Thurloe, although she longed to do so, and Alice was wise enough not to mention him either.

Lucy went to work on Monday morning cheered by the thought of a hard day's work ahead of her. One of the nurses was on holiday and Sister had days off. While Lucy had been in Holland a few of the older children had been taken to Madame Tussaud's and the trip seemed to have unsettled them, so that Sister had had her hands full for the rest of the week and had put off her free time. Before she had gone off duty on Saturday she had confided in Lucy that she thought she had a heavy cold coming on. 'I must have caught it during that outing, although that was ten days ago now, but it's since then that I've been feeling a bit under the weather. I feel a bit mean taking days off as we're short-staffed, but I really do need a break,' she'd said.

Lucy had assured her that they would manage, and reminded her that the nurse on holiday would be back in a few days' time and everything would be normal again. 'And until then,' she said cheerfully, 'I'm sure we'll cope. You have a good rest.'

Sister, knowing Lucy to be a sensible girl and not given to panicking in an emergency, presently went home.

The orphanage was already well into its day when Lucy got into her white overall, reported to the senior nurse and went to see Miranda. The child was making progress, slow but steady. Lucy fed, bathed and dressed her, gave her some toys to play with and started on the next toddler. There were only six children between one and two years at that time—there were a great many babies, and the vast majority were five- and six-year-olds, who went to the infant school close by. One or two of the toddlers appeared to have colds, Lucy noted, and at lunchtime one of the older ones was brought home from the school feeling poorly.

'Just when we're short-staffed,' said Matron worriedly. 'Thank heaven Sister will be back tomorrow.'

But Sister wasn't back in the morning. When Lucy got to the orphanage the next morning it was to find a harassed Matron; several of the older children were feeling poorly and the nurse who was due back from her holiday that day was still in Greece because of an airline strike. Matron was a level-headed woman, not easily put out. 'If it's flu,' she observed, 'we shall have our hands full.'

'If it would help, I could sleep here until Nurse Swift gets back,' suggested Lucy diffidently. 'And I don't mind working different hours…'

'Bless you, it would be such a help. I'll make up your hours when we are fully staffed again and all the children are better. Sister hopes to be back within a few days—some kind of cold, she thought, or flu.'

'Then if I may I'll go home at lunchtime and fetch a few things,' said Lucy, 'and let our housekeeper know.'

Alice didn't approve when she was told. 'I don't know what your ma would say, Miss Lucy—that nasty flu—you don't want to catch it.'

'Well, I dare say I shan't, Alice. You know I never catch anything. Dr Watts is coming this afternoon to take a look at the children. Will you tell Pauline and Imogen, and if Mother phones tell her I'm quite all right? I dare say I'll be home in a couple of days—it's only until this nurse can get back from Greece and Sister is better. There's a part-time nurse off sick too, and when she's back we shall be back to normal.' With that little bit of information Alice had to be content.

Dr Watts came late that afternoon, examined the sick children and then spent half an hour closeted with Matron and came out of her office looking serious. Lucy, passing the open door, heard him say, 'I'll be in first thing in the morning. We shall have to check every single child and baby, and all the staff. You must warn your staff—you say there's Nurse Swift on holiday? She mustn't come here. And get hold of Sister at once. I may be wrong—I shall be able to tell you if I'm right in the morning.'

Lucy had paused and unashamedly listened. Something serious, she guessed. Measles? Mumps? Just flu? Whatever it was, Dr Watts, the most phlegmatic of men, sounded concerned. She went on her way with a load of small garments for the washing machine, and when she got back to the nursery where the babies were she said nothing to the nurse who was there. Matron would tell them, and until then there was plenty of work to keep her busy. More than enough.

Normally one nurse did night duty, knowing that she could call upon Sister or Matron should things get too much for her. Normally the children slept well, and once the babies had been fed and tucked down for the night they slept too until their early morning feed. The nurses who lived in worked in shifts so that there was one on duty at six o'clock each morning to help the nurse on night duty, but it was obvious as evening approached that more than one nurse would be needed for the night.

'Do you suppose,' suggested Matron to Lucy, 'that you could stay up just for tonight? You should be able to get some sleep, only I don't want to leave Nurse on her own. I'll get up if necessary, but with so many children poorly she won't have much time to see to the babies. And there's Miranda...'

Miranda was being difficult; Lucy hadn't been able to spend as much time as usual with her, and she was working herself into a state.

Lucy was tired and her feet ached; she had been padding

to and fro all day, but then so had everyone else and she had just come back from holiday.

'Of course I'll stay up, Matron. If I can get Miranda to go to sleep I'll be free for the rest of the night to help out.'

'Good girl. I must confess I shall be glad when Dr Watts comes in the morning. I shall be in the office until midnight and be up to help with the feeds in the morning. As soon as the children are seen to for the day you must go off duty..'

Miranda took a long while to settle and the rest of the children were unusually restless and wakeful. Only the babies, once they were fed, slept peacefully. Lucy went in search of Nurse Stokes and found her taking a six-year-old boy's temperature. 'It's very high,' she whispered. She looked at the chart Matron had hung up at the end of his bed. 'It's gone up, too.' And by the morning, several of the other children were feverish too. Matron, up and about by six o'clock, studied each ill child in turn and then telephoned Dr Watts.

He came so quickly that Lucy wondered if he had been expecting Matron to call him, and after examining the most poorly of the children he went to the telephone. Twenty minutes later Lucy looked up from trying to get one of the small girls to drink and saw Dr Thurloe, in thin sweater and corduroys, standing in the doorway talking to Dr Watts. His eyes swept over her without any sign of seeing her; he needed a shave and his face was lined with fatigue. She wanted very much to go to him and put her arms around him and tell him not to worry. That was about the silliest thing she could do, she told herself, and applied herself once more to coaxing the little girl on her lap to drink.

Dr Thurloe was there for a long time, meticulously examining each child in turn and then going into Matron's office to talk to Dr Watts and Matron. On his way out he met Lucy, her arms full of clean baby clothes. He stopped and gave her a tired smile. 'Matron will be talking to you all presently,' he told her. 'I'm afraid we have an outbreak of legionnaires' disease on our hands. Some of the children must have picked it up when they had their outing while we were in Holland. They'll have to be sent to hospital and there are quite a few suspects. Matron tells me you're living in for the moment.'

Lucy nodded. 'Have you been up all night?'

He rubbed a hand over his unshaven chin. 'Yes. Why do you ask?'

'Well—I just thought it would be nice if you could go home and have a good sleep—'

He gave a shout of laughter. 'Don't waste your pity on me, Lucy!' He stopped abruptly when he saw the look in her face. 'I'm sorry, my dear, but sleep is the last thing I'm thinking of at the moment.' His eyes searched hers. 'You're going to be busy, do you know that? If you would rather go home, say so now. You aren't trained; you are under no professional obligation to stay.' He added, 'I believe that your parents might not like you to remain.'

'Pooh!' said Lucy forcefully. 'They're not here anyway, and I'm quite able to decide these things for myself, thank you. Of course I'm staying. I may not be trained, but I'm another pair of hands.'

He ran a hand through his hair. 'I'm sorry, I've said it all wrong, haven't I? And you must be asleep on your feet.' He bent suddenly and kissed her gently. 'Off you go, and do whatever it was you were doing, and then for heaven's sake go to bed. You look like a small dozy doormouse.'

She was sent to bed presently after a meal and awakened again at teatime, much refreshed, to plunge back into the never-ending round of feeding and cleaning up and bed making. Soon after five o'clock Dr Thurloe came again, this time the image of an eminent specialist in his sober grey suit and snow-white shirt, and he stayed for some time, checking the progress of several suspect cases and then examining the well ones as well. All the suspected cases were together now, and the babies had been moved to the floor above. That evening an agency nurse was to come to look after them during the night, and a second nurse would take her place in the morning, which left everyone else free to look after the toddlers and the older children—no easy task since so many of them were isolated.

Lucy was to go on night duty with another nurse, and, since her nursing skills were basic, she was given the well children to look after with strict instructions to warn someone at once if any of them showed any signs of the illness. The night shouldn't be too busy, a tired Matron had told her. 'Eight children are in hospital,' she'd added. 'Two of them are very ill, and there are another nine suspected cases here. Hopefully they are only suspected, but we shan't know that for a day or two. Nurse Swift will be back tomorrow afternoon, she refuses to stay away, and there is another agency nurse coming part time.'

The toddlers and older children slept in dormitories of six or eight beds, and they normally slept through the night, but their day had been disrupted and they were inclined to be querulous. Miranda, aware that something was wrong, was indulging in screaming fits. It was almost midnight by the time Lucy had the children quiet and settled and was able to sit down under the shaded lamp and con the instructions she had been given. She was interrupted by the soft-footed entry of Dr Thurloe. He looked fresh and well fed and immaculate, which only served to remind her that she was hardly looking her best. She was still tired, and it had seemed a waste of time to do more than brush her hair severely into a french pleat and leave her face unmade-up. All the same, she looked very pretty in the dim light of the shaded lamp.

He said, 'Hello,' softly and went on to ask a string of questions. 'Any trouble with Miranda?' he wanted to know finally.

'Well, she took ages to drop off—things have been a bit different, moving cots and children and so on, and she didn't like that.'

'You slept?'

'Yes, thank you. How are the children who went to hospital?'

'Holding their own, although there are two very ill little girls. Litrik phoned today—he and Fran send you their love.'

'Oh, that's nice. It seems such a long time ago...'

'But still very much alive in my thoughts. Yours too?' He stood looking down at her, smiling a little.

'Well, yes. Do you want to look at the children?'

'A quick round if I may, although I'm pretty sure this lot you've got here are going to be all right.'

'Are there any more cases—outside the orphanage?'

'Several. Don't get up, I'll just stroll round and cast an eye.'

He wandered off, in and out of the dormitories, and then back to where she was sitting. 'Everything quiet. Are you on permanent night duty?'

'I don't know. Nurse Swift will be back tomorrow and there's another agency nurse coming.'

He nodded. 'Matron is a most capable woman. Good-night, Lucy.'

He had gone as silently as he had come, leaving her to dream. But not for long—a small demanding voice wanting a drink of water brought her back to reality.

As for Dr Thurloe, he left the orphanage, got into his car and drove to Lucy's home. Late though it was, there were lights shining from several downstairs windows. He rang the bell and Imogen opened the door.

She gave him a look of smiling surprise. 'Oh, hello—do come in. Is this a social call? Would you like some coffee? Alice is getting ready for bed, but Pauline and I have been out and are only just back.'

He followed her into the drawing-room and Pauline looked up with a smile. There were fashion magazines all over the floor and a number of pattern books on the table. 'Hello, how nice to see you. As you see, we're busy planning our weddings. Do sit down—have some coffee?'

'Thank you, no. I can't stop. I thought you might like to know that I've seen Lucy at the orphanage. She's doing night duty and coping very well.'

'She's such a sensible girl,' said Imogen. 'Pig-headed about this job of hers, but she really likes it. Alice said there's flu there.'

'Legionnaires' disease, which is a rather more serious matter.'

'It's not catching?' Pauline looked up sharply. 'Lucy isn't ill?'

'No. It isn't transmitted from person to person, only through the air.'

'Oh, good. Seemingly she left a message to say she would stay at the orphanage for a few days. I dare say she'll phone when she wants to come home.'

The doctor said in an expressionless voice, 'Oh, I'm sure she will. It was kind of you to see me at this late hour. Goodnight, I'll see myself out.'

They chorused a goodnight and added vague wishes that they might meet at some future date. Alice was waiting by the door when he reached it.

'Miss Lucy—she's all right, Doctor? She's not working too hard? She won't catch anything?'

He smiled kindly at her. 'She's fine, Alice, working hard, but perfectly all right. I'll keep an eye on her.'

'She's such a dear girl, Doctor.'

'Yes, she is, Alice. Don't worry about her. Has her mother phoned?'

Alice shook her head. 'No. What shall I say?'

'Why, that she is living at the orphanage for a few days because some of the children are ill and they are short-staffed. Mrs Lockitt has no cause to worry.'

Alice stared up at him. 'She never worries about Miss Lucy—only that she doesn't get married.'

'Well, we shall have to do something about that. Good-night, Alice.'

Alice went back to the kitchen and began to lock up for the night. 'Well, I never did,' she muttered to Mrs Simpkins. 'I wonder if 'e meant what I think 'e did! And 'er sweet on 'im too. And would 'e know that?'

Mrs Simpkins blinked yellow eyes and curled herself into a tidy ball preparatory to a good night's sleep, so that Alice was obliged to answer her own question. 'Course 'e knows,' she told herself, and nodded her head in a satisfied manner.

Lucy, happily unaware of the interest being taken in her future, had no time to speculate about it during the next few days. Even with Nurse Swift and the part-time helpers there was an endless round of chores, and the news that Sister was laid low with legionnaires' disease had cast a gloom over everybody. Dr Thurloe came and went, sometimes with Dr Watts, sometimes alone; one of the suspected cases had turned out to be positive and had been taken to the hospital, and there were still several suspected cases among the older children.

Lucy worked through the nights and sometimes for part of the day too, and she didn't sleep well and began to look rather pale and wan. She had formed the habit of getting up long before she needed to and taking herself for a brisk walk through the dreary streets around the orphanage. It was on her return from one of these unsatisfactory outings that she came face to face with the doctor.

He took her by the shoulders and studied her face. 'Not sleeping? Feel all right? Suffering from a surfeit of orphans?' He didn't wait for her answer. 'Time that you had a day off.'

She said stiffly, 'Thank you, but I don't want one. None of us is having one and we can manage very well.'

He nodded. 'I am sure you can. Fiona asked me to invite you to her birthday party on Saturday…'

A little colour crept into her cheeks. 'How kind. Especially as she doesn't know me very well, but I can't accept. Please thank her from me when you see her. I hope that she has a happy birthday.' She added waspishly, 'They're fun, even when you're getting on a bit…' She gasped. 'Oh, I'm sorry I said that. I—I didn't mean it, she's quite lovely and striking even if she is—' She stopped herself just in time. 'What I mean is you must be very proud of her.'

She fled then, darting past him and down the passage, leaving him smiling and presently laughing.

CHAPTER EIGHT

THE days slipped by, and two more children were taken to hospital, but the other suspected cases remained well and the first little patients who had been in hospital for a week or more were responding well to erythromycin. All the same, everyone on the staff went round on the alert for shivering fits, coughs and high temperatures. Dr Thurloe came and went, and on one occasion Lucy was summoned to hold Miranda while he checked her shunt, during which he had little to say other than to ask a few questions and give some simple instructions.

'Miranda's doing well,' he told Lucy. 'What is needed shortly is a loving foster parent.' He spoke with pleasant aloofness, so that Lucy felt very aware of her humble status and burned with what was misplaced resentment. She didn't answer him and he looked at her briefly. 'Largely due to you, Lucy,' he added kindly. 'Now, I wonder if I might talk to Matron for a few minutes.'

The signal for her to carry Miranda back to her cot and tuck her up for her usual afternoon nap. The moppet had no wish to do anything of the sort. Kindly, Lucy sat with Miranda on her lap, carrying on the quiet gossipy talk which she liked and which soothed her, while Lucy allowed a small part of her mind to dwell on William. That she loved him she had no doubt; that she didn't understand him was very clear to her. One moment he was a friend, almost more than that, the next he was a kind, rather distant consultant who spoke to her with great civility and not a trace of friendliness.

She soothed Miranda to sleep at last and went away to feed the smallest of the babies.

The doctor found her ten minutes later. 'Alice asked me to give you these letters,' he observed.

'Alice?' She forgot she was annoyed with him in her surprise.

'I called to let her know how you were. She worries about you.' He smiled faintly. 'So do I.'

'Well, there's no need,' said Lucy tartly. 'I'm not a young girl, you know…'

He put the letters on the cot beside her. 'No, you're not,' he agreed, quite unruffled. 'You're a very pretty young woman, and at the moment, I suspect, a cross one.'

He went away before she could do more than goggle at him.

Two days later, just as things were beginning to quieten down, Miranda began to shiver and cough and run a high temperature.

'But she didn't go with the other children,' cried Lucy, cuddling the unhappy toddler on her lap.

'No, but while you were in Holland—the day you came back, in fact—she was taken out in her pushchair and, as far as I can make out, it was to the same area,' Matron sighed. 'There's no end to it. Dr Thurloe is on his way—she will have to be X-rayed, as she's chesty.'

The doctor, presenting an unshakeable air of confidence, confirmed Matron's fears. 'I'll have her in—she will need an X-ray and careful nursing.' His thoughtful eye studied Lucy, holding the child. 'If you can spare her, Lucy had better come too; Miranda must be kept content and as quiet as possible.' He turned away. 'Fix up an ambulance, will you, Matron? I'll just check those two suspects while I'm here.'

He went away, and so did Matron, leaving Lucy soothing Miranda. She could have done with some soothing herself. No one had asked her if she minded going to the hospital—not that she had the slightest objection, but it would have been nice to have been asked. 'I might just as well have been a chair,' she said indignantly to the moppet grizzling on her lap.

'Nothing—absolutely nothing would convince me that you look like a chair,' said William from the door. 'And if I have taken advantage of your good nature it is because I have a good deal to worry about just at this moment.'

Lucy twisted her head round to look at him. 'Oh, William, I'm sorry, I truly am. And you're tired too. Do you get enough sleep?'

His mouth twitched. 'Why, thank you, Lucy, just about enough. The worst seems to be over—they've traced the source to the water-cooling plant on one of the stores and it's being dealt with. There haven't been any fresh cases for three days. It is unfortunate that our Miranda should fall sick—you'll come to the hospital with her?'

'Yes, of course. Is she very bad?'

'No worse than several others, but we have the added complication of the shunt. Provided we can keep her happy and as comfortable as possible, she should do. I'll start the antibiotic course at once.' He turned to go. 'I'll see you at the City Royal.'

He might be a busy man, but he had found time to arrange for Miranda's admission. At the hospital, Lucy tucked her up in her cot in a glass-walled cubicle in one of the children's wards, and was led away to be shown where she was to sleep. It was a small room adjoining the ward, one of several set apart for mothers of ill children. 'And you can be free from one o'clock until teatime each day,' said the ward sister, a fierce, elderly dragon with a beaky nose and old-fashioned spectacles. 'I shall expect you to look after Miranda during the rest of the day and, if necessary, until she settles for the night. Have you an overall?'

Lucy said yes meekly, and presently unpacked her overnight bag and put away the few essentials she had stuffed it with, then went back to Miranda, who was lying back in her cot. She looked very ill and she was in a furious childish rage. Lucy took down the cot sides and sat her on her lap and talked to her.

She was still murmuring the tale of the Three Bears when Dr Thurloe and Sister came in. 'The child should be in bed,' Sister spoke sharply and Miranda let out an outraged yell.

'You are quite right, Sister,' said William suavely, 'but perhaps in this case it might be best if Miranda were pandered to; you know her case history, do you not? I am anxious that she is kept as quiet as possible until her chest clears. I'd like her X-rayed as soon as you can arrange it.'

He held out a hand and the house doctor, who had slipped in behind him, handed him a form. He filled it in and handed it to Sister. 'There is some consolidation in the lungs.' He spoke to the young doctor. 'Keep a sharp eye open, Charles, and let me know if you are worried. Miss Lockitt understands how the shunt works, but check it if you please.'

He smiled at the young man and turned to Sister. 'I know Miranda is in your very good hands, Sister.' He smiled again with great charm and that lady bridled and allowed her severe features to relax.

He turned to go. 'Take a look at the X-rays and let me know, Charles. I'll be at my rooms until six o'clock. Good day to you, Lucy.'

She was tempted to say, 'Good day to you, William,' but instead she allowed a respectful murmur to escape her lips, which caused Sister to cast her a look of limited approval. At least the young woman knew her place.

Miranda gave Lucy no peace for the rest of the day, and twice in the night she was called because Miranda's screams of rage were keeping the other children awake, so that by one o'clock the next day Lucy was more than ready for a few hours' freedom. A quick lunch, she thought, and then bed. Sister had told her sharply that she should take some exercise during the afternoon, but to curl up on her bed and sleep was all she wanted.

She went down the corridor to the lifts. The dining-room was in the basement, three floors down; she would have a hurried snack, she decided, her finger on the button. The lift door opened and William stepped out.

'There you are,' he remarked pleasantly. 'Get that overall off, I'll be outside in five minutes.'

'Why? I'm going to bed...'

'No, you're not. Just get out of that thing, never mind how you look. You're coming back with me for lunch and then you can lie in the garden and sleep.'

Her mind fastened on the one important thing in this speech. He didn't care how she looked, which was even further proof of his indifference to her. She said pettishly, 'I don't want to.'

There was no one to see them, and William started to unbutton the nylon garment she was wearing. She had a strong feeling that even if the corridor had been knee-deep in people he would have done the same. He finished the buttons and said, 'Well, take it off, dear, we shall be here all day and I'm hungry.'

The pettishness was giving way to a pleasantly vague feeling that she need not bother about a thing because William would see to everything. She took off the garment, folded it carefully and hung it over her arm. 'My hair,' she said. 'And I want to wash and do my face.'

'And so you shall.' His voice was soothing. He pressed the button, and, when the lift opened its door, pushed her gently into it. The lifts were in a row at the back of the entrance hall, and he walked across to the door, nodding affably to the hall porter as they went, and outside, stowed her tidily into the Rolls, got in beside her and drove away.

'I'm on duty at five o'clock,' said Lucy making a last attempt to be sensible.

'Yes, I know. I'll get you back in good time.' He didn't say any more and she sat back, her head pleasantly empty. If their journey had been any longer she would undoubtedly have gone to sleep, but even with the midday traffic it was brief enough. Urged to alight, she sat up as he got out and opened her door, scooped her out and marched her briskly up to the front door where Trump was already standing.

He greeted her with subdued pleasure, listening gravely while the doctor asked him to fetch Mrs Trump, and returned with that lady with commendable speed.

'One of the bedrooms, I think, Mrs Trump,' advised the doctor. 'You'll see that Miss Lockitt has all she needs?'

'Indeed I will, sir. You come with me, miss, there's ten minutes before lunch and you can take all the time you want.' With which contradictory remark Mrs Trump trotted up the stairs with Lucy behind her, swept open a door in a long, narrow passage facing the stairhead and bustled into the room beyond, where she pointed out soap, towels, powders, creams and hairbrushes in the adjoining bathroom, and then bustled away again, murmuring that she had just the meal for them both. 'Tired to your deaths,' she declared. 'Our dear doctor on the go all the time, and you too, I dare say, miss. Now you just put yourself to rights and then come downstairs.'

It was surprising what a wash, followed by the making up of her face and a fierce brushing of her hair, did to ward off Lucy's tiredness. She gave an appreciative sniff at the several bottles of toilet water standing on the dressing-table, cast a quick eye round the charming room, and went downstairs, wondering as she went if Fiona used that room. Not to stay in, she told herself hastily; the doctor, she felt sure, was a man to guard his reputation sternly. He behaved in a high-handed fashion, it was true, but she fancied that he had strict ideas...

He came into the hall as she reached it. 'Just time for a drink, in here.'

The room welcomed her, as did Friday and Robinson, Thomas and the ginger kitten, curled up in a bright patch of sunlight by the open french doors. She sat in one of the comfortable chairs and the sherry went straight to her head, so that she wished that she could sit there forever. Not that she was given the chance; ten minutes later, during which time William had carried on a mild conversation about nothing at all, she was invited to have her lunch and crossed the hall to the dining-room. Last time she had been there had been with the other guests sitting round the oval mahogany table; now there were just two places laid, side by side at one end. The table was covered by a damask cloth and there was a vase of lilies of the valley and forget-me-nots at its centre. The heavy silver gleamed and the crystal glasses shone and she wondered if William, even when alone, ate his meals in such splendour.

They had potato soup, its humble name concealing a flavour out of this world, followed by fillets of sole, mangetout peas and little new potatoes, and they finished their lunch with a magnificent apple pie with accompanying clotted cream. 'We'll have coffee here,' said William, 'then you can go into the garden and doze. I've a pile of work to do.'

A remark which brought her down to earth with a rush.

She slept, curled up on a soft mattressed lounger, and would have gone on sleeping for untold hours if the doctor hadn't wakened her a couple of hours later. 'Tea?' he wanted to know. 'There's half an hour or so before you need to go back.'

They had tea in the garden too, at a white-painted table under the copper beech in one corner. It was amazing, she thought, how such a small garden had been made to appear spacious with its small velvet lawn, its flower-beds, full of colour, and the high screen of trees. She accepted another of Mrs Trump's feather-light scones and observed that she could stay just where she was forever. A remark she wished to recall the moment she had uttered it, but since that was impossible she mumbled, 'Well, you know what I mean—it's so very pleasant after the City Royal.'

William agreed lazily and watched the quick colour fade again from her cheeks. 'You will have to stay there for some days,' he pointed out, 'and while you are there I just hope you will come here each afternoon. There's nowhere to go around the hospital, and it would take you too long to go home to Chelsea by bus. I'm free for a couple of hours on most afternoons. The car will be outside at one o'clock and I shall expect you.'

Lucy sat up straight. 'Really? How extremely kind of you, but won't it be inconvenient for you? I mean, don't you want to do things when you're free?'

He said carelessly, 'It will make no difference to me, Lucy. Either I dictate letters or catch up on reports and so on, and you are more than welcome to spend an hour or two in the garden.'

His reply chilled her and she thought about refusing his offer. But he had been quite right, there was nowhere to go around the hospital, and to get home and back by bus would take too long. She said meekly, 'Well, thank you, William, if you're quite sure I'm not being a nuisance.'

He took her back presently, leaving her at the entrance with a brief nod and a laconic, 'One o'clock, tomorrow.'

So each afternoon, she was driven to his home, given lunch and installed in a lounger and told to sleep, to be wakened by the pleasant clatter of teacups, with the doctor sitting nearby, reading a newspaper. She began to depend on these quiet hours; Miranda, while not desperately ill, was proving to be a bad patient, not wanting Lucy out of her sight and waking at night, screaming for her. There was little actual work for Lucy, but the days dragged while she did her best to keep the child happy and quiet.

It was almost a week later, after a splendid lunch at the doctor's house, that she was wakened by a tinkling laugh and, before she opened her eyes, she knew whose laugh it was. There was no sign of the doctor, although Trump was arranging the teatray just so, but a moment later, as she sat up, he came out of the house with Fiona.

Lucy got up and went and sat in a chair, aware that she was untidy and crumpled from her nap, a fact which Fiona turned to her advantage at once. She came across the grass, cool and beautifully turned out and oozing charm. 'Lucy—William has been telling me what a Trojan you have been, you must be exhausted. How I do admire you strong young women, I'm hopeless at illness—too sensitive.' She ran an eye over Lucy's flushed face. 'You poor dear, let us hope that they let you have a holiday when you're free of this child—you certainly need it.'

The doctor stood beside her, listening with an impassive face. He observed quietly, 'It's because Lucy is sensitive that she is so successful at caring for Miranda.' He smiled at Lucy, who didn't smile back; she had no reason to.

He hid a smile. 'Will you stay for tea, Fiona? I shall be taking Lucy back very shortly.'

'In that case I'll wait here for you, William; we can have a nice quiet hour or so here—it is such glorious weather.'

'I'm not coming back,' he told her blandly. 'I shall be at the hospital for the rest of the day, and then at a consultants' meeting.'

Fiona frowned. To sit and gobble her tea with William's eye on his watch was pointless. 'I might as well go.' She sighed wistfully. 'I see so little of you, William…' She frowned again, because that sounded as though they were little more than casual acquaintances, not at all the impression she wanted the silly, untidy girl sitting there to have. She gave one of her tinkling laughs. 'Oh, well, perhaps one evening.' She gave him a smiling, questioning look which wasn't noticed, so that her abrupt, 'Well, goodbye, Lucy. I hope you'll be looking better when we next meet,' was uttered in a snappy voice.

She went back into the house; Lucy could hear her voice, high and plaintive, gradually fading away, and presently William came back and sat down, and she poured their tea and embarked on a pointless conversation until he interrupted her without warning. 'You and Fiona don't like each other.'

She answered carefully, anxious not to upset him, since she thought he was so enamoured of the woman, while her loving heart longed to tell him what a frightful mistake he was making. 'Well, we haven't much in common. She's very attractive, and I should think she would be a most amusing companion and a splendid hostess. She dresses beautifully too.' She stopped then because he was looking at her so strangely. He wasn't smiling, and yet she had the impression that he was amused.

'That's very generous of you, Lucy.'

He smiled with such charm and gentleness that she spoke before she had time to stop herself. 'I'd like you to be happy, William.'

'And you think that Fiona Seymour will give me that happiness?' He got up, took her cup and saucer and pulled her gently to her feet. 'Listen to me carefully. She means nothing to me, never has—just someone to take out to dinner or invite to lunch. As you say, amusing and well dressed,' he paused, 'and empty of all feeling. She never asks me about my work either. It satisfies her that I am successful with sufficient money to live in comfort, and know all the right people. If I were to die tomorrow she would feel regret only because she would be forced to find another man to provide her with the kind of life she considers necessary for her happiness.'

'So why do you take her out?' asked Lucy tartly.

He sighed. 'I have been lonely. I love my work, I have friends enough, but that isn't all. I want a wife and children to come home to.' He bent his head and kissed her gently. 'You, Lucy.'

She stared up at him speechless. 'Me?' A great wave of delight swept over her, so that her breath caught in her throat. 'But would I do? I'm not at all clever, I told you that.'

'You are so anxious to be clever, my dear. You cannot see that a string of letters after your name and a highly paid job are of no consequence at all compared with kindness and patience and being able to listen—so many people have lost the art of listening... So would you consider marrying me, Lucy?'

She wished to throw her arms round his neck, but she forbore from that; he had asked her to be his wife, but he hadn't said that he loved her. Even making allowances for his reserved nature, she reflected, that was something that she thought he could have mentioned.

'I should like to think about it,' she told him in a cool little voice which disguised her bubbling excitement. She added, 'If you don't mind.' Anxious to make things clear, she added, 'You see, I thought you were in love with Fiona.' She frowned. 'Won't she mind?'

He looked all at once remote. 'I cannot see why she should mind—I have never at any time even hinted that I wish to marry her.'

'Oh, well, that's all right, then. All the same, I'd like to think about it.'

Of course she would marry him; her heart had told her that, but she had no intention of allowing him to think she would fall into his lap like an overripe apple. Besides, a little voice at the back of her head reiterated, he hadn't said that he loved her.

'I think I should go back,' she said, and without a word the doctor got up.

'We mustn't allow Sister to wait for you,' he said pleasantly, and swept her back into the house and thence into the car, and drove her back to the City Royal.

There was a message for her on the following day. He had gone to Northern Ireland for a consultation and would be away for two days. And when he came back he pronounced Miranda was out of danger and able to return to the orphanage, so that Lucy didn't see him to speak to. She left the hospital with mixed feelings; had William had a change of heart while he was away, or was he annoyed because she had asked him to wait for an answer? And at least, she told herself indignantly, he could have smiled at her.

She settled Miranda back in her own cot and was summoned to Matron's office. Almost all the children were back at the orphanage, although two of the older ones were still in hospital. Sister was back too, and two new assistants had joined the staff.

'You've earned a few days off,' said Matron kindly. 'Let me see, it is Tuesday—supposing you report for duty next Monday morning? I'm sure you must be anxious to go home for a few days.' She added a few words of thanks and Lucy, immensely cheered at the prospect of the best part of a week at home, stuffed her few odds and ends into her overnight bag and caught a bus for home.

Alice was delighted to see her, and over a pot of tea she told Lucy the news. 'Your ma and pa are on their way 'ome,' she declared. 'I 'ad a phone call from someone saying they were expected back very shortly, though 'e couldn't say when exactly. I've got in extra groceries and told the butcher... Miss Imogen and Miss Pauline will be 'ome for supper, they'll be ever so pleased.' She eyed Lucy narrowly. 'You look peaky, love. What you need is a nice quiet day at 'ome! Just you go and put your things away and I'll get you a nice bite of tea.'

It was nice to be fussed over by the kindly Alice. Lucy ate a splendid tea and then went away to wash her hair and do her nails and attend to her neglected make-up. 'Oh, Alice,' she said, 'it's so nice to be home again.' She smiled at her old friend and then surprised the pair of them by bursting into tears. 'I'm just tired,' said Lucy, between great heaving sobs.

'Course you are, ducks. You'll be right as rain in a couple of days. Worked you too 'ard, they 'ave, at that 'ospital. You just go and 'ave that bath and I'll find a nice drop of sherry for you when you come down.'

The dear soul gave Lucy an encouraging push towards the stairs and went in search of Mr Lockitt's best sherry.

As for Lucy, she lay in a blissfully hot and foamy bath and tried to sort out the niggling thoughts whirling around inside her head; none of them amounted to much, but she knew that she wasn't happy and she should have been. William had asked her to marry him, hadn't he? But without any of the romantic trimmings such an occasion surely warranted. She frowned heavily and got out of the too-hot bath, and presently wandered down to the kitchen to drink the sherry Alice had poured for her. She would have to wait until she saw William again, she decided; there was no use getting worked up about it. Fortified by the sherry, she went back to her room, dressed and did her hair and face, and presented her normal self to her sisters when they came home.

They were pleased to see her, enquiring with vague kindness as to whether she had had a boring time in the hospital and not waiting for an answer. But they were glad that she would be free for a few days.

'I had a cable from Father,' Imogen told her. 'It was sent to the office. He and Mother will be home the day after tomorrow. They want me to get a drinks party together so that they can say hello to everyone at one go. It was all very successful, and they'll probably be going back later in the year. So lucky you're here, Lucy. Will you get drinks and food organised for Saturday? I'll phone everyone—it's short notice, but I'm sure they will all come.'

The evening was spent in making plans for the party, and then, inevitably, more plans, this time for the weddings.

Lucy, who had been looking forward to doing nothing for a few days, found herself immersed in preparing for Saturday evening so that she really had no time to think about William. Of course, he was always at the back of her mind; she thought of him with love and longing and a good deal of doubt. Surely if he loved her enough to want to marry her he would have found the time to phone or scribble a note? But he hadn't said that he loved her, had he? The thought recurred at intervals during the next couple of days, and was never wholly absent even during the bustle and excitement of her parents' return.

Professor and Mrs Lockitt, although glad to be home again, were full of their expedition. It had been a tremendous success and every aspect of it had to be discussed and commented on. It fell to Lucy's lot to help with the unpacking, take loads of clothes to the cleaners, make appointments and make sure that everything was in train for the Saturday evening. Not that she minded—she was glad to be kept busy, and, as her mother pointed out, it made a nice change for her after her little job at the orphanage. Lucy agreed, placidly; no one in the family had understood about her work there, and she had long ago given up talking about it. Alice was the only one she confided in and the only one who really understood. But now there was too much to do to think about the orphanage. Caterers were supplying the food—tiny vol-au-vents filled with salmon mousse, creamed chicken, shrimps chopped with scrambled egg, minute sandwiches and *petit-fours*—but glass and china had to be got from the cupboards, flowers had to be arranged and furniture moved.

On Saturday evening Lucy went to her room to dress, satisfied that everything that needed to be done had been attended to. Two of Alice's nieces were coming in to wait, and Alice would be stationed in the kitchen, dealing with the refilling of plates and making sure that there was plenty of coffee should anyone want it, although that wasn't likely. Lucy showered, and, for no other reason than the fact that William had liked the grey dress, got into it.

Her mother frowned when she saw her in it. 'Darling, surely you've got something else than that grey dress? It's quite pretty, but haven't you worn it rather a lot?' She didn't wait for Lucy to answer, but hurried away to greet the first of the guests.

The big drawing-room and the conservatory beyond were soon full. The Lockitts had a great many friends and several distinguished members of the Archaeological Society had turned up, bent on hearing about the professor's finds. Imogen and Pauline had formed their own circle, leaving Lucy to circulate on her own. She was good at that, even though she was shy with people she didn't know very well, but she put people at their ease, moving from one group to the next, making sure that no one was left on their own. She knew everyone there and stopped to chat from time to time, and it was as she was turning away from old Mrs Winchell that she found Fiona Seymour at her elbow. She had known that she was to be invited, but had been at pains to avoid her. It was silly to feel guilty; William had said that he had no interest in Fiona other than that of an occasional companion for an evening out, and she had believed him, but Fiona didn't know that...

She said, 'Hello, Fiona. I'm glad you could come. It's lovely for Mother and Father to have all their friends here.'

'Well,' drawled Fiona, 'they aren't quite my age-group, but I've always enjoyed a party. A pity William couldn't make it.' She watched the colour creep into Lucy's cheeks. She went on smoothly, 'He's always so busy, bless him—he's been away for a couple of days. Northern Ireland again, you know. Of course, he hates to talk about it.' She watched the look of hurt puzzlement on Lucy's face and at once decided to risk passing on some news of her own invention. 'He's at my place now, but don't tell anyone.' She gave Lucy a conspiratorial smile. 'I'm going back and we'll have a cosy little supper together. The weekend together will do him good. He needs peace and quiet and someone who understands him.'

She watched the effect of her words and was satisfied. For good measure, she added, 'He always comes back to me.' She took a glass of wine from a waitress's tray. 'Will you be a darling and make my excuses to your parents? It's been lovely seeing you again. Still at the orphanage?' And when Lucy nodded dumbly, added lightly, 'William says you're one of the Marthas of this world, and I'm sure you are.'

She patted Lucy's arm and smiled her sweet smile and slid away.

'I can't stand that woman,' declared old Mrs Winchell, tapping Lucy sharply on the shoulder. 'What was she saying to you? You look as though you've just been stabbed in the back.'

Lucy looked at the elderly face staring at her with such shrewd eyes. 'Oh, nothing, Mrs Winchell, nothing that matters at all. Let me get you something to eat…'

Everyone went home presently, and Lucy, with the excuse that she should make sure that everything was cleared away ready for the massive washing up which would have to be done soon, kept herself busy until they sat down to a belated dinner. And, since the talk was all of the expedition and its success, and various discussions about their guests and, once again, the weddings, no one noticed that she was rather quiet.

'Tired, dear?' asked her father eventually. 'You look as though you could do with another holiday. Back to work on Monday?'

He smiled broadly; after four years he still regarded her job as something of a joke.

Lucy wasn't tired, she was numb, and a good thing too for she was unable to think. She replied suitably to her father's gentle teasing and listened to everyone's plans for Sunday. Her sisters would be with their fiancés, and her parents were lunching with friends who lived at Henley.

'I dare say you could come too, darling,' said her mother. 'They would never mind an extra guest.'

If William was back, Lucy's tired brain reminded her, there was just the unlikely chance that he might come to see her, even if it were only to explain... 'I promised I'd have lunch with Joe Walter.'

Her mother looked pleased. 'Oh, good, dear. He's such a nice boy, too and the only young man you know well, really, as I was saying to that elegant Mrs Seymour earlier. We shall be back quite late, I expect; they're sure to ask us to stay for the evening.' She looked at Imogen and Pauline. 'And you two? Will you be back for supper—I must tell Alice...' They told her no and she went on comfortably, 'Oh, well, Alice will give you a meal when you get back, Lucy. You'll be all right, dear?'

Lucy said that yes, of course she would, and when presently she lay in bed she planned her day. Joe was invention, of course. She cast around in her muddled head as to where she might go; there were various aunts and uncles and cousins, but they all lived too far away, and besides, if she went out there was a chance that she might meet William and possibly Fiona with him—something to be avoided at all costs. She decided to stay at home. She could garden and lie in the sun, and Alice could go off to her sister's for the afternoon—no one would know and Alice would never tell. She closed her eyes resolutely, determined not to think about William, but it was almost morning before she slept.

The family dispersed by mid-morning and Lucy went to the kitchen to explain to Alice. 'And, darling Alice, if—just if Dr Thurloe arrives before you leave—but he won't—tell him that I'm having lunch with Joe Walter.'

'If you say so, Miss Lucy, though why you have to tell a parcel of lies to such a nice gentleman is more than I can understand.'

'Thank you, Alice. There's—there's a good reason; perhaps

one day I'll tell you. I'm going to stay in the garden, it will be super in the sun with nothing to do. I'll get my lunch, so do go to your sister's as soon as you like. Don't come back until after tea—no one but I shall be here.'

Alice agreed reluctantly and presently the house was quiet. Lucy, in an old cotton dress, made coffee and took it out into the garden with the Sunday papers. There was a lot of day ahead of her, but if she read all of the papers properly it would take her until it was time for her to get her lunch. She had been reading for half an hour when the front door knocker was thumped. She shot out of her chair and went quietly into the house, and even more quietly upstairs, to peep out of a bedroom window which faced the street. William's car was outside. He didn't go away for several minutes, and she watched him with longing eyes as he got into the car. He drove away without looking about him, and she went back into the garden. The phone rang twice after that, but she let it ring, sitting with her hands clenched together and her feet boring into the ground to stop her from going to answer it.

The day dragged. She made a sandwich for her lunch, and welcomed four o'clock when she could have a pot of tea. And soon after that Alice came back, fussing because Lucy hadn't had a proper meal. She set about getting one as soon as she had taken off her hat and coat, and Lucy, tired of her own unhappy company, sat at the kitchen table with Mrs Simpkins on her knee and listened to Alice's soothing voice telling of her day. The thump of the knocker took them both by surprise. Lucy got up and went to the door. 'I'm going upstairs. Alice, if it's him tell him I went to lunch with young Mr Walter and I'm not back yet. Quick, Alice, and then perhaps he'll go away.'

She whisked herself upstairs, and Alice went to the door to confront a grim-faced doctor. He heard her out in silence. 'Thank you, Alice,' was all he said, and he went back to his car and drove away.

'What did he say?' asked Lucy, back in the kitchen.

'Just, thank you, Alice. He looked as though he was in a fine temper.'

Which he was. He had returned home very early that morning intent on seeing Lucy. Even Fiona, phoning to see if he was back and with some story about Lucy and young Walter tripping off her tongue, hadn't stopped him. He had been puzzled and then angry when he'd found no one at home, and when at last Alice had answered the door his rage, seldom in evidence, had threatened to choke him. Fiona would have been delighted if she had known the havoc her tissue of lies had wrought.

CHAPTER NINE

MONDAY morning began badly. Lucy overslept because she had lain awake for a good part of the night, unhappy thoughts running round her woolly head and none of them making sense. She missed her usual bus, too, so that she arrived late at the orphanage, with almost no breakfast inside her and a headache. Worse was to follow. As she sat with Miranda on her knee, patiently spooning porridge into the small, unwilling mouth, Matron joined her. Lucy wished her good morning and wondered why that lady looked ill at ease. Because she herself had been ten minutes late? It seemed unlikely, especially as she had explained to Sister about missing the bus. Matron sat down on the only other chair. 'We must have a talk,' she began briskly. 'The Board of Governors have been looking into the administration of the orphanage and have decided to make one or two changes. In short, one full-time member of the staff or two part-time members must be made redundant. I'm more than sorry that it must be you, Lucy—you have been such a good worker here and done so much, but, you see, the two part-time both need the money and, if you will forgive me for saying so, you don't. One has an invalid mother and the other is quite on her own and lives on her wages.'

She paused. Lucy inserted another spoonful of porridge with a gentle cluck of encouragement. 'I quite understand, Matron. I shall be awfully sorry to go, as I've loved working here, but it's quite true, I don't need the money.' She kept her voice quiet and steady with an effort. 'I would be glad to work here as a voluntary worker…'

'Yes, I'm sure you would, and I would have been so glad

to agree to that, but the board emphasised that only a certain number may work here, paid or unpaid.' Matron frowned, 'I can't see why—something to do with reorganisation, I believe. I can promise you that if this can be altered I will let you know at once.'

She got up, looking relieved. 'If you would just work this week out? And I promise you a splendid reference. Believe me, I did my best to persuade the governors, but they were adamant.'

On her way to the door she stopped and came back again. 'I almost forgot to tell you a splendid piece of news. Miranda is to be adopted, by a charming young couple—he's a curate here in London, and they are unable to have children of their own. They have had Miranda for odd days—while you were in Holland—and now she is well again they will come each day so that she gets used to them. She's very happy with them, and she will be with them as much as possible until she actually goes to live with them.'

'Oh, I'm so glad. She'll be happy to have a mum and dad, and she's so much better.' Lucy meant every word of it.

'Largely thanks to you, Lucy.'

It was fortunate that there was precious little time to sit around and mope; it wasn't until she got home that evening that Lucy allowed her thoughts to turn to the future. And even then she was thwarted, since both Imogen and Pauline were at home for the evening and, as was to be expected, they and her mother plunged into talk of the weddings, her father having prudently retired to his study. Lucy, agreeing with her usual calm to everything which was asked of her, consigned her future and William to the back of her head and shut the door on them. Time enough to think things over calmly when the shock of it had died down.

But it didn't; if anything, it got worse. She carried the hurt of it around with her and no one knew except Alice, who, quick to see that Lucy was worrying about something, winkled it out of her one evening when there was no one else at home. Even to her Lucy couldn't bring herself to talk about William, and at the moment she had no idea what she was going to do about him. She supposed that he had been feeling lonely without Fiona and got carried away, and she had hardly discouraged him, and, after all, there was nothing definite, for Lucy hadn't said that she would marry him. All the same, it seemed strange to her that he hadn't written or asked to see her and explain. True, he had called on the Sunday, but even from the glimpse she had had of him from the window he had looked to be in a towering rage. He probably felt a fool. The one thought that consoled her was that she had never even hinted that she loved him. And as for him, well, everyone, she told herself, could have a change of heart. He might, just for a moment, have thought she would make a good wife for him, and for all she knew he might have been unhappy about Fiona…

The week dragged to a close and she went to the orphanage for the last time, and at the end of the day bade Miranda and her small companions goodbye in a cheerful way, and in the same cheerful fashion took her farewell of the rest of the staff there, and, last of all, Matron. Not once did she complain at leaving, but assured everyone who asked that she intended taking a holiday and then looking for a similar job. 'But this time I think I'll go further afield,' she told them. 'I rather like the idea of Scotland.'

Matron looked at her with relief because she hadn't made a fuss. 'Well, remember that I will give you a splendid reference, Lucy.' They clustered round the entrance and she turned and waved when she got to the corner of the street.

It was a Friday evening and the bus queues were long, so she got home later than usual. Since everyone was in the drawing-room, it seemed as good a time as any to tell them. She hadn't expected sympathy, for none of them had ever taken her job seriously, and they offered none.

'Hard luck, darling!' her mother exclaimed. 'But how providential, now you will be at home to help me with the wedding arrangements.'

Pauline chimed in, 'It wasn't worth much, anyway, Lucy—one of those dead-end jobs that get you nowhere.

Imogen added, 'You'll be far more useful at home.'

Lucy bit back an answer to that; to stay home and do the flowers and write her mother's letters inviting friends and accepting their invitations seemed unimportant compared to caring for the daily needs of small orphans, but there was no point in arguing the matter. With a heavy heart and a docile manner she set herself to the trivial tasks her mother handed over to her. That she became a little pale and quiet over the next week or two went unnoticed, except by the faithful Alice, who went around her kitchen muttering to herself and breathing down fire upon the heads of those who had made Lucy unhappy. She even remarked upon Lucy's quietness to Mrs Lockitt, who looked surprised.

'Oh, I hadn't noticed, Alice. She's always been the quiet one, you know that. Anyway, she will be going to the reception in honour of her father next week; that should cheer her up.'

The reception was at Claridge's Hotel, a rather grand affair, and Mrs Lockitt had spent a good deal of time and thought on her dress. So had Imogen and Pauline, and they in their turn persuaded Lucy to get herself a new dress for the occasion. 'Something really striking,' they begged her, and sighed loudly when she showed them the soft grey chiffon dress she intended to wear. It was, in fact, quite charming and suited her, but it had no pretensions to high fashion, and they pointed out that no one was going to look twice at her if she wore it. Lucy forbore from telling them that she had no wish for anyone to look even once at her, and only filial duty was the reason for her going to the reception anyway.

All the same, they had to admit that when she joined them,

ready to leave the house, she looked charming in a gentle sort of way.

An opinion echoed by Dr Thurloe, catching sight of her standing with a group of acquaintances before the speeches began. He excused himself from the friends he was talking to and edged his way towards her. Despite his size and bulk, he was a quiet man; she had no notion that he was there beside her until he spoke quietly into her ear.

'You and I have to talk, Lucy.' His voice was pleasant, but there was a hint of steel in it which she was quick to hear.

'Why?' she asked baldly.

'Don't waste time being silly.' He smiled down at her and her heart turned over. 'How very nice you look, like a very beautiful grey mouse.'

'I don't think we have anything to say to each other.' She smiled brilliantly at an acquaintance and waved to him. A third party might be a good idea. William was being charming and it was going to her head. The acquaintance waved back and started to inch towards them, then caught William's eye and inched away again.

'Now, before we have to listen to the speeches—where have you been? On holiday? Ill?'

She said quite fiercely, 'You know quite well that I've been given the sack. They call it being made redundant, and, since you're on the Board of Governors and agreed to it, it's silly to pretend you know nothing about it.'

He said calmly, 'Well, I don't. I wasn't at the last meeting, I gave my vote to someone else to deal with. How did you know I was a governor?'

'I had a letter saying how sorry they were.' Lucy smouldered. 'Bah—they couldn't care less…and there was your name with all the other VIPs who run the orphanage.' She added thoughtfully, 'You do have an awful lot of letters after your name.'

'Yes, well, that's beside the point. We have to talk—can't we leave here and go somewhere quiet?'

She had become dangerously close to forgetting Fiona. 'There's nothing to talk about,' she said in a cold voice.

He stared at her downbent head. 'Perhaps not now.' He took her hand in his and looked at it. 'No ring?' he asked blandly.

Her green eyes flashed. 'I'm not getting married yet,' she told him sweetly, and turned tail and lost herself in the fashionable crowd around them.

She had made the remark for no reason at all other than to annoy him; it was a pity that it did nothing to clear up their misunderstanding. For the rest of that evening William made no attempt to seek her out again, although he took care to know just where she was and who she was with. It puzzled him that young Joe Walter wasn't there at her elbow, and, for her part, Lucy, chatting with her parents' friends and some younger ones of her own, was puzzled too. Where, she wondered, was Fiona? She cast any number of casual glances around the elegant reception, but there was no sign of her. It seemed strange that she was absent, for she was to be met at almost all the local social gatherings. Perhaps she was ill...

She had in fact, not been invited, and had done her best to persuade William not to go without her, but since she had been unable to see him her arguments on the telephone had fallen very flat. As she had put down the phone she had reflected that he had sounded both cool and casual. Perhaps it was time she gave up her efforts to attract him and looked around for someone else. There had been that American she had met a couple of weeks ago—a poor second to William when it came to looks, but certainly wealthier. William, she had to admit, had been singularly hard to captivate.

It was a pity that Lucy knew none of that, circulating in a very proper fashion, listening to what was said to her and not really hearing a word, although she looked deeply interested and said 'Really?' and 'Oh?' and 'How interesting!' just when she should, so that people told each other afterwards that she was by far the nicest of the Lockitt girls, even if the other two were outstandingly clever.

William, watching her without appearing to do so, found her enchanting, and was quite unable to believe that she and Joe Walter were intending to marry. He was prepared to wager every penny he possessed that she was the last girl in the world to behave as she was behaving now. It was a pity that he was engaged to give a series of lectures in Leiden at the medical school and would be going there early the next day, but he was a patient man and he could wait for someone he wanted more at the moment than anything else in the world. That there was something wrong somewhere was obvious, and possibly ten minutes' talk would have put it right, only Lucy, usually so malleable and gentle, was in no mood to talk, and matters would only be made worse. He waited until Professor Lockitt, as the guest of honour, had made his farewells and left with his family before he went home himself.

He didn't go to bed at once, but went to his study and wrote a note to Lucy, addressed the envelope and sealed it, and on his way to bed asked Trump to post it in the morning.

He left the house early the next morning, driving himself down to Dover to take the hovercraft.

Fiona Seymour rang his doorbell several hours later. She thought it unlikely that he would be at home, but she would have one more try before she gave him up for the American, and, being a determined woman, she intended tracking him down and giving him a last chance to fall for her. Being also a conceited woman, it didn't enter her head that his interest in her had been both passing and very superficial. She intended to weep a little to arouse his pity… Trump opened the door and bade her a polite but guarded good morning. He didn't like her, but no feelings showed upon his face. He listened gravely to her request to see the doctor and informed her with inward glee that he was away from home.

'Where?' she asked, and added, 'I dare say he told me, but I must have forgotten.'

'Abroad, madam, but I have no forwarding address. He will be travelling.'

She pushed past him. 'Then I'll leave a note.' She waited while he shut the door, her eyes taking in with regret the delightful furnishings in the hall which could have been hers… The envelope on the console-table caught her eye and she edged nearer so that she could see the address. And what, she wondered, would he have to say to Lucy Lockitt? She had been sure that he had believed her when she had told him that the wretched girl and Joe Walter were on the point of getting engaged. She went past Trump into the drawing-room, where he provided her with paper and pen and drew up a chair to the davenport in one corner of the room, and she composed a letter she had no intention of leaving for William and pondered the best way to take the envelope as she left the house.

It was easy enough as it turned out; telling Trump that she would take her letter with her in the hope of hearing of the doctor's whereabouts from one of his friends, she went back into the hall and, as he turned to open the door, slipped the envelope down the front of her dress. Once outside, she hurried away as fast as she dared just in case he should notice that it had gone. Providentially a bus drew up at a stop a few yards from the end of Strand on the Green and, although she did dislike public transport, Fiona jumped on and was borne rapidly away. Fortunately for her, because Trump, closing the door behind her, had swept a sharp eye round the hall just to make sure that everything was as it should be, and had seen at once that the letter had gone. There was no one in sight when he opened the door, so he closed it without haste and went thoughtfully to the kitchen where he conferred with Mrs Trump.

Fiona got off the bus within a few minutes, walked the short distance to her flat and, once there, opened William's letter. Fury at its contents turned her face ugly, but when she had read it a second time a look of cunning triumph took its place. Even if she had lost all hope of charming William into marriage, she could make sure that Lucy Lockitt didn't get him. But she had to have an excuse... She thought for a moment, and then put the letter in her handbag and went out on to the street and took a taxi to the end of the road where Lucy lived. She knew exactly what she was going to say and rang the bell with confidence.

Alice answered the door.

'Oh, good morning—Alice, isn't it? Is Miss Lucy in? Could I see her for a few minutes—just something I have to return.'

Alice admitted her. Lucy was at home, although no one else was, and the good soul, even though she disliked Mrs Seymour, had no reason not to let her in. She showed her into the drawing-room and went in search of Lucy, who was turning out an attic cupboard.

'Oh, bother,' said Lucy, well aware that she was dusty and a bit untidy. All the same, she went downstairs and into the drawing-room to bid Fiona good morning and ask her to sit down. 'Perhaps you would like coffee?' she asked politely.

Fiona shook her head. 'Sweet of you, but I'm on my way to my dressmaker—I shall need lots of new clothes...' She looked arch and Lucy wondered why. She opened her bag and took out something wrapped in tissue paper. 'William found this at the reception yesterday; he felt sure it was yours and he asked me to let you have it. He's gone abroad for a few days.'

Lucy took the packet and unwrapped it slowly. There was a brooch inside, but it wasn't hers. 'He's mistaken, it isn't mine. Perhaps you should take it to the police.'

'Oh, my dear—I'm so sorry to bother you, I wonder why he thought it was yours?' She gave her tinkling laugh. 'We had so much to talk about that it never entered my head to make sure he was right. And now actually I'm so happy and thrilled that I'm scarcely able to hold a sensible thought in my head. You would never know that he was such a romantic man, would you? But this morning I found such a charming letter when I opened my post.' She gave an angelic smile. 'I'm so excited that I must tell someone...' She opened her handbag and took out the letter. 'Poetry, my dear, can you beat that? He writes, "My dear, darling, do you know your Wordsworth? The bit that goes, 'The past unsighed for, and the future sure'? That's how I feel about you, and I believe you feel it too. When I return we will talk"'

'I don't think you should be telling me this,' said Lucy in a steady, expressionless voice, 'and I'd rather not hear it. I hope you will both be very happy.'

'What a sweet creature you are,' said Fiona gushingly. 'So understanding, especially as you were growing rather fond of him yourself.'

'William is a very nice person; I think there are a great many people who are fond of him.' Lucy got up. 'Do find the owner of that brooch, she must be so worried.' She went to the door and stood by it, smiling although it was an effort to do so. 'I hope you won't be late for your dressmaker.'

She shut the street door on Mrs Seymour and stood leaning against it, the tears pouring down her cheeks. Things had gone wrong between her and William, but she had still nurtured the hope that they would be put right. Now there was no hope of that. She had been a fool—she should have said yes when he had first suggested marrying her, but since she hadn't, and it didn't seem to have worried him overmuch, she had to conclude that it had been the spur of the moment—just an impulse. Perhaps Fiona had quarrelled with him and he'd wanted to annoy her.

Alice came from the kitchen, offered a large handkerchief and led her back to sit by the kitchen table. 'Now, you just tell me all about it, Miss Lucy. That woman—making mischief, I'll be bound...'

So Lucy told her, and it was a great relief to talk to someone about it, for she felt Alice was the only person who would understand—William would have understood, but telling him, even if she were able, would have made no sense at all.

She drank two cups of tea, listening to kind Alice's comforting clucks and wondering what she should do. Pack a bag and go away on a long visit to one or other of her aunts and uncles living in a variety of rural retreats around the country? Stay and pretend nothing had happened? Do something really drastic like joining the ATS? A notion nipped in the bud by an urgent peal on the door bell.

'Who's that?' she asked. 'Don't let them in, Alice; say there's no one here.'

Alice opened the door to a dignified but agitated Mr Trump. 'I've some urgent news for Miss Lucy, Alice. It's most important.'

'She said not to let anyone in.'

'Tell her it concerns herself and Dr Thurloe.'

Alice opened the door wide. 'Never mind me asking, you come on in.'

He followed her into the kitchen and Lucy, seeing who it was, frowned and then said, 'Trump, good morning. Is something the matter? Can we help?'

'Well, yes and no, miss. There's something I must tell you...'

He related the morning's happenings, not leaving out a single detail. 'So you see, miss, Mrs Seymour has the letter which was addressed to you, though I'm sure I don't know why she took it.'

Lucy's face, puffy and red with weeping, had taken on an instant prettiness. 'For me? That letter? She pretended it was for her—she read me some of it.' She smiled at the memory of it. 'Oh, Trump, I can never thank you enough for being so prompt. I know exactly what I must do.' She beamed at him. 'Do sit down and have a glass of beer and tell me where the doctor is.'

He accepted a chair and the beer with a grave inclination of his head. 'As to that, miss, I cannot say exactly. But I was told that he would be in Leiden in Holland for the rest of this week. I believe he is to give a series of lectures there. Presumably the authorities there would know.'

Lucy nodded slowly. 'Better still, those friends I stayed with; they know him well. I'll go there first and then I'll go to Leiden.'

'All that way, Miss Lucy, and supposing you don't find him?'

Lucy smiled radiantly at them both. 'Oh, but I shall,' she assured them. 'Thank you very much for coming, Trump. You have no idea what this means.'

Trump, who had a very good idea, smiled at her in a fatherly fashion. 'I'll be off, then, miss.' He paused. 'How will you go to Holland?'

'Catch a plane.' She glanced at the clock. 'I'll try and get a flight this afternoon.'

'In which case, miss, I'm sure the doctor would wish me to drive you to the airport. If you would be good enough to telephone me when you have made your arrangements I will return here with the car.'

'Not the Rolls?'

'We have a second car, miss, a small Daimler.'

'Well, thank you, Trump, that would be lovely. I'll ring you as soon as I know when I can go.'

On the afternoon flight to Schiphol, crammed between a stout lady who couldn't keep still and a gentleman who coughed a great deal and swallowed pills every ten minutes or so, Lucy took time to reflect upon her extraordinary behaviour. She had booked a seat on the plane, packed an overnight bag, changed into a thin jersey dress and jacket, primed Alice and left a note for her parents. They would possibly be quite bewildered, but not unduly worried; they travelled so extensively themselves that her unexpected trip to Holland would leave them only mildly surprised. Schiphol lay beneath her and she still had no idea what she would do. It had seemed vital to see William at once, but now she was actually in Holland she wasn't quite sure how to set about it. Fran might be able to help. She took the airport bus into Amsterdam and then a taxi to the station and caught a train to Utrecht. There she found a taxi to drive her out to Litrik's home. It was early evening by then, and the house, tranquil in the midst of its lovely gardens, seemed to welcome her. She rang the bell, suddenly feeling foolish.

Trugg opened the door and, to her everlasting relief, welcomed her with a smile and a total lack of surprise. 'A pleasure to see you again, Miss Lockitt. I'll fetch mevrouw...'

Fran was already running down the staircase. 'Lucy, how lovely! You've come to stay? I do hope so.' She tucked her arm in Lucy's. 'Come into the drawing-room, and, Trugg, please ask Mrs Trugg to make sure that the room Miss Lockitt had when she was here is quite ready for her.'

She opened the drawing-room door and urged Lucy into the room. 'Litrik, look who is here. Isn't it great?'

Litrik was on the floor, building a brick castle for his first-born. He got to his feet, and Lucy, looking anxiously at his face, could see nothing but pleasure at the sight of her.

'I feel awful coming like this,' she began, 'but I—I must see William, and Trump doesn't know where he is. At least, he said he was in Leiden, but he doesn't know just where.'

'Then you've come to the right place, and very sensible of you,' said Litrik kindly. 'William is staying with us, only unfortunately he went to Groningen this morning and won't be back until tomorrow afternoon or evening.'

'That's in the north, isn't it? I could catch a train...'

'Not this evening, my dear. It's quite a long journey—a hundred and thirty miles, two and a half hours' run—and what would you do when you got there?' He caught Fran's eye and smiled faintly. 'Fran has a Mini; I'm sure she won't mind if you borrow it and drive up in the morning.'

'Oh, that would be simply marvellous. You wouldn't mind really?'

'Not in the least, but upon reflection I think it might be a better idea if Trugg were to drive you, then he can bring the Mini back. You will, of course, come back with William.'

Lucy's eyes glowed like emeralds. 'Oh, will I? You won't tell him I'm here? He might not want—'

'Not a word shall be said. Darling, take Lucy up to her room and then we'll have a drink and hear all her news.'

They didn't ask her to explain why she had come. They talked about her parents and her sisters and the children, and listened with sympathy when she told them that she had left the orphanage, never betraying the fact that they had heard it all already from William. Presently they had dinner and, after another hour or so of undemanding talk, Lucy went to bed. She had had every intention of rehearsing exactly what she would say to William when she saw him, but she went to sleep instead.

Driven by a dignified Trugg, she left very soon after breakfast. 'Trugg will bring the Mini back,' said Fran, 'because of course, William will bring you back with him. I'm not sure, but I think he said that he had a lecture in the morning and then intended coming back here. Trugg will take you to the university buildings and see you safely inside. William is lecturing there in the big hall.' She embraced her friend with the remark that she would expect them back for dinner that evening, but earlier if they could manage it. Her matter-of-fact acceptance of Lucy's sudden appearance did much to steady the latter's nerves, which by now were jangling. The drive up to Groningen with the staid but friendly Trugg did much to steady her, and when they reached the university buildings she bade him goodbye and got out of the car without hesitation, although the sight of him driving away considerably lessened her resolution. All the same, she walked boldly through the great doors into the entrance hall, a dark, forbidding expanse of marble floor and dim walls, hung with portraits which looked even darker, and ringed around by busts of long-dead and learned men, each atop his pedestal. A little daunted, she looked around her and saw William at the bottom of the great stone staircase, talking to two elderly men. He looked stern and remote and, as always, faultlessly dressed, but she had no intention of letting any of these intimidate her and started across the marble space between them. She was a third of the way when he saw her, said something to his companions and came to meet her. If he was surprised or pleased there was nothing on his face to show it, but she was past caring about that. She fetched up in front of him and all her well rehearsed speeches flew out of her head. 'I had to come,' she told him breathlessly. 'It was that bit from Wordsworth, you know—"The past unsighed for, and the future sure," When she read it, I knew I'd have to tell you.'

William took her two hands in his; he saw that his long-held patience would have to be held for a little longer.

'Tell me about it, my darling,' he said, in the quiet soothing voice in which he spoke to his small, scared patients.

Lucy lifted her face, glowing with love and trust, to his. 'She came to see me yesterday morning—she said you asked her to, that you had found a brooch at the reception and that it was mine and you had asked her to return it. It wasn't until later that I knew that that was an excuse.' She frowned. 'I never wear brooches…'

She paused long enough for the doctor to ask gently, 'Fiona?'

She nodded. 'She saw your letter to me at your house—the

one with the Wordsworth in it.' She smiled radiantly for a moment. 'She took it while Trump wasn't looking and then came to see me. She said it was from you to her…' She stared up at his calm face and a tear trickled down her cheek. 'I wanted to die.'

The doctor took a very white handkerchief from his pocket and wiped away the tear, and she went on, 'Then Trump came and told me, so I knew.' She drew a long gulping breath and said uncertainly, 'I came as quickly as I could.'

The hall had filled quite a lot as they had been standing there; students in their variety of coloured caps, learned professors with bald heads, a sprinkling of ordinary looking people, looking rather out of place, all milling around the pair of them just as though they weren't there.

Lucy hadn't even seen them, and the doctor ignored them. 'One small point, my darling—this nonsense about you and Joe Walter…'

She remembered his remark about her ringless hand. 'Oh, did she tell you…? She wanted you to think that Joe and I…so, she could marry you.'

'Er—perhaps I might point out that I have never at any time wished to marry her.' He was still holding her hands tightly. 'The only person I want to marry is you, my dear heart, and I knew that the moment I saw you at the clinic.'

'So did I, only I didn't know it till later on,' said Lucy obscurely.

He let go of her hands, put his hand under her arm and started making his way through the throng.

'Where are we going?'

He didn't answer her, but turned into a narrow dark passage and opened a door. The room was even darker than the entrance hall, a gloomy mixture of dark green curtains and heavy leather furniture.

He pushed her in in front of him and closed the door. 'The

consultants' room,' he told her, 'but, as you can imagine, no one comes here unless there's a meeting.'

He grinned suddenly, and she saw with satisfaction that he was going to be fun to live with; under that sombre grey suit was a man who would be a delightful husband. She asked, knowing the answer, 'Why have we come here?'

He took her in his arms and drew her close. 'Because I want to tell you that I love you more than anything or anyone in this world, and, when I've made that quite clear, I'm going to kiss you, both of which I prefer to do in privacy.'

She held him off for a mere moment. 'William, do you think we could be married before Pauline and Imogen? Would you mind?'

He kissed her thoroughly before he answered. 'My dearest love, not only do I not mind, but I insist upon it. A special licence and a quiet wedding within the next week or two.'

An entirely satisfactory answer, reflected Lucy. She said meekly, 'Just as you say, William,' and lifted her face to his.

0702/73/MB45

Betty Neels Ultimate Collection Official Prize Draw Rules

NO PURCHASE NECESSARY

Each book in the Betty Neels Ultimate Collection will contain details for entry into the following prize draw: 4 prizes of a signed Betty Neels book and a weekend break to Amsterdam and 10 prizes of a signed Betty Neels book. No purchase necessary.

To enter the draw, hand print the words "Betty Neels Ultimate Collection Prize Draw", plus your name and address on a postcard. For UK residents please send your postcard entries to: Betty Neels Ultimate Collection Prize Draw, PO Box 236, Croydon, CR9 3RU. For ROI residents please send your postcard to Betty Neels Ultimate Collection Prize Draw, PO Box 4546, Kilcock, County Kildare.

To be eligible all entries must be received by **July 31st 2003**. No responsibility can be accepted for entries that are lost, delayed or damaged in the post. Proof of postage cannot be accepted as proof of delivery. No correspondence can be entered into and no entry returned. Winners will be determined in a random draw from all eligible entries received. Judges decision is final. One mailed entry per person, per household.

Amsterdam break includes return flights for two, 2 nights accommodation at a 4 star hotel, airport/hotel transfers, insurance and £150 spending money. Holiday must be taken between 1/8/03 and 1/08/04 excluding Bank holidays, Easter and Christmas periods. (Winner has the option of accepting £500 cash in lieu of holiday option.)

All travellers must sign and return a Release of Liability prior to travel and must have a valid 10 year passport. Accommodation and flights are subject to schedule and availability. The Prize Draw is open to residents of the UK and ROI, 18 years of age or older. Employees and immediate family members of Harlequin Mills & Boon Ltd., its affiliates, subsidiaries and all other agencies, entities and persons connected with the use, marketing or conduct of this Prize Draw are not eligible.

Prize winner notification will be made by letter no later than 14 days after the deadline for entry. Limit: one prize per an individual, family or organisation. All applicable laws and regulations apply. If any prize or prize notification is returned as undeliverable, an alternative winner will be drawn from eligible entries. By acceptance of a prize, winner consents to use of his/her name, photograph or other likeness for purpose of advertising, trade and promotion on behalf of Harlequin Mills & Boon Ltd., without further compensation, unless prohibited by law.

For the names of prize winners (available after 31/08/03), send a self-addressed stamped envelope to: For UK residents, Betty Neels Ultimate Collection Prize Draw Winners List, PO Box 236, Croydon, CR9 3RU. For ROI residents, Betty Neels Ultimate Collection Prize Draw Winners List, PO Box 4546, Kilcock, County Kildare.

MILLS & BOON
The Elizabethan Collection
Two historic tales of love, treason and betrayal...
Hot-blooded desire...cold-blooded treason...
Two dramatic tales set in the passionate times of Elizabeth I
Paula Marshall & Marie-Louise Hall